Retroshock

D.W. Murray

Sword of the Spirit Publishing

All contents Copyright © 2011 David W. Murray. All rights reserved worldwide. Duplication or reprints only with express permission or approved credits (see above). All trademarks are the property of their respective owners.

ISBN 13: 978-0-9838836-3-0

Published by Sword of the Spirit Publishing

www.swordofspirit.net

CHAPTER 1

The view of lower Manhattan was crystal clear from the restaurant atop the Regency Grand Hotel. City lights lit the night sky as an endless string of traffic flowed down Seventh Avenue, coursing through the canyon of skyscrapers.

Karen Danners sipped her wine as she gazed at the New York skyline. The fine vintage Bordeaux was far better company than the man who was presently rattling on in front of her. As a senior executive officer at the prestigious Colter Corporation, she was good at tuning out unnecessary chatter. Danners eased her foot out of her shoe, as the man's voice blended in with the ambient noise of the restaurant, and she thought back on a very long day.

There was a time when a hop across the pond was a matter of course. New York to Paris by day, the clubs at night, four hours sleep, her short cropped red hair slicked back, a splash of coffee, and she was good to go. But that was then. At thirty-seven, the daily challenges of an executive assistant to one of the world's wealthiest men were finally taking its toll.

The contract signing at the Stuttgart plant had nearly been snagged on a technicality, but with some clever thinking and a few well placed promises, she had gotten things back on track and landed the necessary signatures.

Then there was the red tape with the customs officer over sealed documents in her briefcase. The man was particularly difficult, and even though her German was rusty, she had managed to handle the situation calmly. By the time airport security realized she was a bonded courier boarding her own private jet, her schedule had been pushed back a full hour. Still she had to admit, she was grateful for the moment's rest that came with the delay. When Danners arrived in Paris, she had been whisked away to the French embassy.

"Rub elbows with the American diplomat. Be good to our French representatives, smile and guile."

Those were her orders. The tour of the embassy was as slow and boring as she had imagined, but when all was said and done, it was back aboard the plane for her return trip to the states. Five hours later she landed in JFK and was still moving fast. She handed off the sealed documents to a courier, hopped into the company limo, and in less than an hour was shuttled to mid-town Manhattan for her last assignment, dinner and wine at the posh Top of the Nines Restaurant.

Her "last assignment" was a simple matter really, the delivery of a note she had been given first thing that morning. No complicated contracts to sign, no wrangling or debates with shareholders. Just hand over the note and make sure the gentleman got it precisely at nine o'clock. That was the only directive. It was a little curious, especially since the note was in a plain, unmarked envelope.

However, since the person who had given it to her was himself a very curious individual, and the man to whom she was to give it to was someone whom she wanted nothing to do with, she had simply dropped the note in her purse and thought very little of it. Danners glanced down at her watch then looked at her "last assignment", who happened to be seated across from her. The man had been talking non-stop for nearly half an hour, yammering on as though his mouth were a machine fueled by the alcohol he had been consuming ever since she had arrived. Carl Grasso was not only her dinner partner and business associate, he was also, by far, the most consistently obnoxious, and self centered man she had ever met. He was the kind of man who enjoyed the sound of his own voice, a voice that had obviously spent quite a bit of time in the Bronx.

Danners smiled. The only amusing thing about the man was that no matter how rudely disinterested she appeared, he never seemed to notice. She wondered if that kind of insensitivity came naturally or was something he had to work at. Grasso clearly found himself clever and amusing, and his bombastic verbal assault was nothing she could ever truly prepare for.

She recoiled a little as he let go a laugh, as fake as the rug on his head. It was a big boisterous laugh that said, "I'm forty-five, filthy rich, and I want the whole world to know it, or at least everyone in my section of the restaurant."

There were a few side long glances, some raised eyebrows which Grasso pretended not to notice as he enjoyed the momentary spotlight. Danners forced a smile, which was more of a wince, then welcomed the interruption when the waiter arrived and set her piping hot steak dinner before her. The man was courteous, and the food looked more like a work of art than a meal.

"Thank you," she said, as the waiter dismissed himself. Danners savored the aroma of the sear broiled steak and was thankful for something else to focus on beside Grasso.

"You know what I'm sayin'?" he asked.

Danners glanced up, surprised by the question then watched as he just kept going, rambling on like she was just a speed bump in the conversation. *The conversation.* The thought reminded her of something her assistant KC had said when she first met Grasso and he had hit on her.

"With Grasso, you don't actually have to be in the conversation, just in the vicinity."

"You're a real charmer," Danners muttered as Grasso found another gear and the alcohol really took effect.

The topic was the same as usual, "money." Grasso's gray linen Armani suit jacket hung open like a bathrobe, and the thirty extra pounds he carried spoke of an extravagant lifestyle, rich with overindulgence.

Danners smiled enough to amuse the man then glanced at her watch.

"Eight fifty, ten more minutes," she told herself and took a bite of her steak. *Just get through it.*

Suddenly the voice across the table paused long enough to ask a question. "So, what do you think?"

For a moment Danners thought he was actually talking to her then decided to wait a few seconds longer to see if it was a question he actually wanted her to answer, or the kind he preferred to answer himself. Grasso just stared at her with his typical arched eyebrow and half smirk. He had obviously made some sort of point that he was proud of, but since she had ignored everything he said the moment was completely lost on her. Still she knew it was safe to respond.

"I was enjoying myself until you started getting philosophical," she said.

"Aw c'mon! Talk to me, or would you care for a recess, counselor?" Grasso paused long enough to swill his glass of wine, then stared at Danners like she was part of the meal.

"Well?... The question stands."

Danners smiled with a confident stare and simply bluffed her way into the conversation. "Everyone's entitled to their opinion, including you," Danners hated it when Grasso tried to match wits with her. As far as she was concerned, he was a chimp in a suit with barely enough brains to zip his pants.

"Look, it's a straightforward question," Grasso said. "Is money for power or pleasure? Honestly. Take this place for instance. It provides the best in food and entertainment. These people here are enjoying themselves at a price few can afford.

Sure it's expensive, but you pay for quality and you get it. That's the price of pleasure. At the same time this establishment is looking for the right clientele, those who can appreciate their kind of service, and we appreciate their selectivity... That's the power of price, all driven by money."

Danners looked into the face of the serpent and smiled. "Now you're just bragging."

"I'm not drunk enough yet," he said not missing a beat. "Don't miss my point. Look around you. These people experiencing all of this pleasure are people of affluence, power. So which is it?"

With her napkin in her lap, Danners put down her knife then used her fork to stab another slice of steak and paused to consider Grasso.

"Carl, money is a tool, nothing more," she said and popped the piece of meat in her mouth. Grasso nodded to give the illusion that he actually cared about what she had said.

"That's an interesting viewpoint, naive but interesting. The answer is power, and that's my point. If we have enough money, we can handle him."

Suddenly Danners knew exactly who and what Grasso was talking about. She set her fork down and wiped her mouth.

"Well you sound pretty sure of yourself as usual... So, do you even know what he's working on?"

Grasso poured another glass of his vintage Cardinale Red Meritage, and gulped it down like a hillbilly. He wiped his lips with the linen napkin, wadded it up in his fist, and shook his head.

"He won't tell me."

Danners smiled at his irrational logic. "You just finished telling me you can handle him."

"Handling him and getting him to talk are two different things." Grasso grabbed the wine bottle and emptied the rest into her glass.

"I thought you said he trusted you."

"I said I was workin' on it."

"Well perhaps you should work a little harder," Danners said, hating the smirk on Grasso's face. "They call you 'the facilitator,' don't they? The man who gets things done? That *is* what Mr. Colter is paying you for, isn't it? Results?"

"Yeah well, Lewis Colter doesn't know him like I do. This kid is no fool. He only lets me get so close. He's smart. Yeah, I know he's some kinda genius, but I mean the kid's street smart. He's always got an angle. But I'm startin' to read him better. He's tippin' his hand... Whatever it is, it's big."

"How big?" Danners said, then took another bite of her steak. Grasso leaned in to speak confidentially.

"I know for a fact, the Camden Foundation offered him two point six million just for a look, and he turned 'em down flat!"

Danners put down her fork. "Really? Are we paying him that much?"

"I don't know, but I'm bettin' Colter Corporation owns a piece of it."

Grasso sat back and opened his arms wide, like he had just laid down the winning hand at a poker table.

"We're on the top of the world, Karen. Life is good and you and me, babe, we got a ticket to ride." Grasso grinned with a wicked gleam in his eye.

Danners pretended to ignore the sexist remark, determined to keep the conversation on a professional level. "I've got my own ride, thank you. And I wouldn't be too confident. These kinds of people are known to be unstable. Anti-social behavior, unable to fit into their environment."

Grasso shook his head, and then took another sip of wine.

"He'll deliver. He's got till Friday to ante up, show and tell. If he doesn't, the company plays hard ball. And if the kid's smart, as smart as they say he is, we're golden."

Danners looked down at her plate and tried to focus on her meal. "I can't help but feel like you've got the bull by the horns and you're wearing red."

Grasso grinned and leaned back with his thumbs hooked in his lapels. "This ain't red. It's Armani, and it's payday, baby!" Grasso said with his usual vigor, which again drew stares as well as scowls from the people at the next table. Grasso raised his glass as if to offer a toast. Danners shook her head and glanced down at her watch.

"Nine o'clock... finally."

With that, she reached into her purse and pulled out the small envelope. It was a little crumpled and Danners made a show of straightening it out, to make it look more presentable. When she was done, she reached out stiffly and handed it to Grasso as though it was a summons.

"What's this?"

"He asked me to wait until nine o'clock to give you this."

Grasso looked at her guardedly as he reached out to take the envelope. He flipped it over front to back. The thing had no address or name and was as blank as could be. Grasso glanced up at her again with growing suspicion as he tore open the envelope and unfolded the note inside.

Danners watched his eyes scan the piece of paper. Grasso scoffed and smiled as though whatever he was reading was a joke, too childish for him to be bothered with. Suddenly, he stopped and his expression changed. His eyes darted back as though he had missed something important. Grasso held the paper closer and read more slowly now. His eyes widened and flooded with shock, then fear and anger, as he continued to read in sudden and growing desperation.

Danners gave a curious smile, and wondered what on earth could make the man go into such mental gymnastics. Whatever it was had not only managed to silence Grasso, but turned the braggart into a whining pup, a response that was well worth the wait. Then without any warning, Grasso screamed, or issued a sound as close to a scream as a man his size could muster.

"WHAAAT?"

He was still looking at the note when he shoved himself back from the table and leaped to his feet, knocking over his chair. Grasso crumpled the paper then tossed it aside and turned to rush for the door with the look of a madman. Unfortunately, Grasso was moving too fast for his expensive Italian shoes which were poorly suited for running on polished wood floors, as was Grasso's bulky frame. But by the time he realized his feet were no longer beneath him, he was already on his way down, clawing for anything to break his fall. Grasso grabbed the corner of the table next to them with a swipe of his hand, flailed his other arm wildly in the air, made an awkward half twist, wrenching himself around in an attempt to save himself, and only managed to look like he had just been shot.

The old gray haired couple at their table pushed back trying to get out of the way as their tablecloth, dinner, and everything else went over the side. Grasso hit hard and made a horrible racket with plates and silverware crashing all around him. A second later the man scrambled to his feet, and looked like a drunken bear, slipping and sliding, gripping people by their arms and pushing waiters as he struggled to gain momentum. Those nearby did their best to get out of his way as the crazed man defied the laws of gravity and battled to stay upright all the way across the restaurant then lunged out the door. The truth is, had he stood calmly and simply placed one foot in front of the other he would have made it to the door without incident, and hardly been noticed. "But where's the fun in that?" Danners thought.

The entire restaurant seemed to hold its breath as people looked around and rumors circulated. Although most admitted they hadn't actually seen what had happened, they did marvel at how the man could get up so quickly after being shot. Many claimed to hear the gun go off which was merely the sound of Grasso hitting the floor. Still, none of these people seemed particularly concerned with the whereabouts of the assailant or the gun itself. Everyone simply assumed that since the man was gone, so was the danger, and everything quickly went back to normal.

When the air of cool sophistication had returned, the couple next to her looked to Danners as though she might offer some explanation. Danners only smiled cordially then signaled to a waiter who quickly rushed over and picked up Grasso's chair. The young man apologized to the older couple, whose mouths had finally closed. With their dinner on the floor, the two sat quietly surrounded by all of the devastation Grasso had caused. The manager rushed over and showed expert calm. He made all the necessary promises and gestures then turned to Danners with some surprise since she was utterly untouched by any turmoil or strife.

"Is everything all right," the manager asked as he made a show of straightening the tablecloth and tried not to look flustered. Danners smiled politely as she raised her empty glass.

"It is now," she said. "More wine, please."

CHAPTER 2

The forty-foot marquee of Madison Square Garden was all aglow, and the main event was sold out. The capacity crowd roared as the New York Rangers rallied against the Canadian All-Stars in a preseason game. Air horns blared against the cacophony of chants of a jeering crowd. The Rangers had held off the favored All-Stars and after no score well into the second period, the crowd was whipped into a frenzy, in eager anticipation of the first goal.

The skaters sliced up and down the ice with the intensity of a play off game. Slap shots were a blur, and players hit the boards hard, hard enough to shake the shatter proof glass and send the spectators reeling backward. After two quarters, it was clear that reputations were on the line and there were no holds barred.

High in the skybox, two NHL sportscasters gripped their microphones, thrilled by the action and excitement. Jim Galano, the white haired veteran with his gravel voice, trained his eyes on the ice below while his younger partner sipped his beer.

Galano barked into his microphone, "Who could have guessed this kind of slugfest? What a game!"

Teddy Bartel, the younger talent, took his cue and dove right in with his trademark rapid-fire delivery. "What a game, indeed! I don't know about you, Jim, but this exhibition game looks more to me like the finals of the Stanley Cup Playoff."

"Absolutely!" Galano rasped. "These guys came to play. No doubt about it."

Bartel went into his shtick and picked up the action on the ice. Like an auctioneer rattling off bids with verbal dexterity, he managed to keep pace with the lightning fast play, without taking a breath.

"With thirty seconds left in the power play for the All-Stars, Linkov brings the puck across mid ice, looking for the open man. Chako picks him up at center as Linkov dumps it off to Medereth. Medereth catches the pass on his skate, drops back to gain control of the puck, and Katchek strips it away! He blows by him and Linkov tries to pick him up, but it's two on one! Mara and Katchek, Mara and Katchek, cat and mouse as Drulay comes out of the goal to cut him off and OHHHH! What a shot and what a save by Drulay!"

Galano chimed in with his gravel tone while Bartel reached for his beer. "Ladies and gentlemen, you're getting your money's worth tonight. The Rangers are sending the Canadians a message. Despite the talent and depth of this All-Star team they have not been able to take control and, "The Aggressor has been shut down."

Bartel wiped his mouth anxious to get back to the microphone.

"That's right, Jim. Labec's got no excuse. Normally he's a one-man freight train. But tonight these Rangers are picking him apart. Labec has not been able to get off a clean shot. Everything else aside though, with no score this late in the game, it's now a question of pride!"

"Absolutely. Who's gonna score the first goal? That's what it's all about. Hey, just listen to this crowd. You think they're into it?"

Just when it seemed the noise couldn't get any louder, New York substitutions brought more cheers as other Ranger players stepped onto the ice. At the same time a lone skater appeared behind the Ranger's penalty box. He held his head down and kept moving, only peering out occasionally from under his helmet to make sure he was going the right way. The blue and white Ranger's uniform was seriously oversized. The number thirty-two with the name Anderson was emblazoned on the back. The young man moved a little quicker as he approached the skater's bench and found the familiar face he was looking for. The team manager was right where he said he would be and held the door open to the player's bench. As the skater approached, he took off his glove and handed the coach two thick rolls of five hundred dollar bills. The manager shoved the money into his coat pocket then placed a firm hand on the young man's shoulder.

"One minute, that's it," he said firmly to restate the terms of the deal, a deal he now wished to god he had never made.

"One minute," the skater said and stepped into the player's box to join the team on the bench.

Josh Kensington sat down and pulled off his Ranger's helmet to run his fingers through his hair, which was already drenched with sweat. The twenty-five year old genius inventor tried to calm himself and act casual, so as not to be noticed. The fact that every player on the bench was already glaring at him seemed to make the wrong impression. Josh suddenly smiled broadly, as though he were more than welcome and then turned his attention to the action on the ice.

Like every spectator in attendance, Josh Kensington was a fan of the sport, but unlike anyone else, he was about to get the chance of a lifetime, the chance to skate with the Rangers, pros of the NHL. It was a golden opportunity, which had just cost him one hundred thousand dollars cash. Just sitting on the player's bench among the row of living legends by itself was worth the price.

He remembered only a week ago when he had met the team in a Philadelphia hotel and conned the manager. All he had said was, "College tournament play is faster." Then it was only a matter of rubbing salt into the wound. "College players are tougher and play for nothing." And that was all it took. Once the players got into it, the dares started flying left and right and the deal was made. It was an easy con, and he hated taking advantage of dumb jocks, especially when they were dumb jocks he so passionately admired.

Josh kept a lookout for stadium police milling around and shrank down in his seat, trying to look as small as possible which was no problem since everyone on the New York bench outweighed him by forty or fifty pounds. Indeed trying to fit in would be a challenge, especially since everyone down to the water boy was still looking at him like a den of angry bears with the scent of raw meat.

"Hey guys, what's the score?" Josh looked around and adjusted his helmet which barely fit any better than his jersey.

The real Jack Anderson, left wing for the Rangers, was suited up as well and snarled, "You let them score, in my jersey, you're a dead man.

Josh nodded as though they had been over it a hundred times. "If they score while I'm on the ice, you get a hundred grand a piece."

Gill Foster, the back up goalie, took off his helmet on his way by and shoved it into Josh's chest, nearly knocking him off the bench.

"Hey! Keep your money. You let 'em score, I'll kill you."

Josh gathered himself then called after him.

"Foster! You're a machine. You were great in game seven!"

Josh adjusted his pads and smiled. "That's motivation," he mumbled to himself.

The cold air at rink side made his senses tingle and reminded him of his varsity days in college. It was only three years ago, and he even thought about playing pro, but skill only counted for so much. He was too small for the game and smart enough to know that military defense contractors lasted a heck of a lot longer than pro hockey players. Still, he loved a challenge, and skating with the pros was just the thing to make his pulse race.

As for the "Grass-man," which was a nickname Carl Grasso hated but could do nothing about, Josh suspected the man may have gone into cardiac arrest after reading the note. Still, he was only following orders. Grasso had said to contact him before he did anything stupid. Even though this was "cool," if not just a little suicidal, he was sure it fell into Grasso's "Stupid" category and was something he would want to know about, even if it did send him into cardiac arrest.

The action flashed past the Ranger box and took the puck down the ice to the Canadian goal. The horn sounded marking the end of a two minute penalty and the Ranger assistant coach yelled, "Thirty two, left wing!"

Josh hesitated for a split second then jumped to his feet, adrenaline pumping and headed for the ice. He slid his mouth piece between his teeth and heard himself mutter, "What the hell am I doing?"

Josh stepped onto the ice of Madison Square Garden in front of a packed arena, looked across the rink, and locked eyes with the massive Scott Labec who happened to be stepping out of the Canadian penalty box at the same time.

At six' four" and two hundred and seventy-five pounds, Labec looked like a seven foot giant on skates. The Canadian launched himself onto the ice like a freight train on rails, full of power and determination. While at five eleven, a hundred and seventy five pounds, Josh scurried out of the box like an eager whippet.

The refs' attention was focused on the puck as the action wheeled around the Canadian goal. Josh started up the ice glancing around to check his position when the puck suddenly came hurtling back toward him.

Bartel called the play. "Anderson takes the pass and bobbles it. Looks a little shaky." The younger announcer focused in on number thirty two, and then covered up his mike and turned to Galano.

"Looks a little tiny," he said, but with a live broadcast, there was nothing they could do except go with the action.

The pass hit Josh's stick like a shot and snapped him out of his daze. He moved down the ice as Mara and Katchek crisscrossed in front of the goal, looking for the pass. They were only open for an instant. By the time Josh could think, the opportunity was gone and he was racing along the boards, looking at the two open men who were now covered. Josh did his best to keep his head up and not watch the puck like an amateur. Suddenly Labec appeared on the right, closing the gap to cut off the angle. The big man came at collision speed.

"Keep comin'...keep comin'!" Josh muffled through his mouthpiece.

There was clearly no shot on goal, but Josh suddenly darted toward Labec like he would cut around him then moved the puck to the right, right before Labec drove his shoulder into his face and leveled him. The Canadian checked him into the boards with an elbow that lifted Josh off the ice with enough jarring force to make the audience wince as Josh slammed into the glass, went limp and crumpled to the ice like a rag doll.

"OH! What a shot!" came the raspy voice of Galano. The wily sportscaster let the words reverberate in his headphones for a while before he finally covered up his microphone and had to ask, "Okay, I give up. Who is that?"

Bartel chuckled. "You mean, who was that?"

Josh laid there for a few seconds with his face on the ice then struggled to draw his knees up under him. By the time he looked up, Labec was off with the puck and gave a smirk over his shoulder as if to say, "That's what I think of your stupid move."

In that instant, it became personal. Josh jumped to his feet, shook off the cobwebs and hockey gloves then pumped his arms and dropped his stick looking for more speed. With only the sound of his skates carving the ice, adrenalin driving, heart pounding, Josh began to make up ground, determined to close the gap. Then with only a few feet left, he launched himself at the big man.

The Canadian never saw it coming. Josh's helmet hit Labec in the small of the back and laid the Canadian giant out on the ice, spread eagle. Both men went down hard as whistles sounded and the penalty flags flew. Josh climbed to his feet and the roar of the crowd. He had taken down "The Intimidator" on national TV at Madison Square Garden and couldn't have been more thrilled until he saw Labec who had broken the fall with his face and split open the bridge of his nose.

The sheer size of the man was enough to frighten any mere mortal, but with glaring eyes and blood spattered face, he was a nightmare. Labec wiped his nose with his sleeve, took one look at his own blood, ripped off his gloves and charged Josh like a mad bull.

Josh backpedaled and then turned and skated for his life. Normally other players would have rushed to help restrain the attacker, but the Canadians recognized it was a cheap shot and since Josh wasn't even a member of the team, the Rangers were content to watch the kid get pummeled.

Josh skittered around the ice, ducking and dodging behind New York players and Canadians alike, when another elbow was thrown, this one accidental, which started some pushing and shoving and in less than ten seconds several full blown fights had broken out between the Rangers and Canadians.

Up in the sports booth Bartel and Galano were slack jawed and speechless in front of their microphones as pandemonium broke out and "Anderson" ran around the ice like a crazed pinball bouncing from one brawl to another trying to escape Labec. The stunned announcers sat back and could only wonder aloud as whistles blew and garbage began to fly onto the ice.

"Who is that guy?"

Soon fists were flying among the fans down near the ice. They traded blows, shoving each other against the shatterproof glass and in the midst of a near riot, Carl Grasso appeared rink side escorted by two reluctant security guards. He had claimed there was an emergency with a friend and he needed to get to rink side, but once they entered the stadium, the guards were more than convinced about the emergency and forgot about Grasso. Once they reached rink side someone cried, "Look out!"

Grasso turned just as a wooden chair careened through the air and slammed into the glass wall next to him. Grasso shielded his face from the splintered wood when a second later one of the players raced off the ice and nearly knocked him off his feet. Grasso caught hold of the man, more for balance, tussling back and forth, until he realized who it was.

"JOSH?"

Josh looked up and grinned. "HEY! You made it!" he said, gasping for air.

"What the hell are you doing? Are you trying to get yourself killed?"

Josh glanced behind him. "I'm tryin' to stay alive!" he said just as Grasso looked up to see Labec barreling straight at them. Then with a rain of beer, a few enthusiastic fans toppled into the players' box. By the time Labec reached the edge of the rink, there was a full fledged bare fisted brawl and the police converged on the Ranger's bench.

As the crowd pressed in, Grasso shoved Josh toward the exit, amidst the fists and fighting, but before they could get clear, a guard cried out, "That's him!"

The man dabbed his nose with a bloody handkerchief then took a fist to the side of his head and disappeared from view with. With no time to waste and skates clicking on the
stadium floor, Josh scooped up his duffel bag, still dressed in full hockey gear, with Grasso right on his heels and moving fast, already sweating through his expensive beer stained Italian suit.

Moments later, a pair of double doors flew open in the alley at the back of the arena, and the two men crashed into the side of a black limousine with its engine running. Grasso fumbled for the door handle then dove inside with Josh and his bag right behind. The automatic locks slid down a split second later, just as a security guard rushed the limo. Grasso's driver casually checked his mirror, then gently applied the gas and pulled away, leaving the stadium guards and all the commotion behind.

Josh finally pulled his headgear off, his hair matted and glistening with sweat. Grasso clutched his chest and continued to gasp for air, while the twenty-five year old millionaire genius inventor looked out the back window, adrenaline still pumping. Josh turned around and pumped his fist, punching the roof of the car.

"YEAH! Oh, man! What a rush! YEAH! Hey, Jimmy! What's goin' on, man?"

The chauffeur, a black man in his fifties, peered up from under his chauffeur's cap. "Good evening, Mr. Kensington. How was the game?"

Josh grinned from ear to ear and sat up, with renewed energy.

"I went head to head with Scott Labec, man! All the way! LIVE! I hit him. You believe that? I hit him! Carl, did you see it? Oh man! I gotta see if I can get some network footage of the game. Don't tell me that wasn't fun!" Suddenly Josh took a breath and looked at Grasso who was still leaning back, trying to loosen his tie to get more air. His words came slowly, but steadily.

"I have never in my life been this close to such a raving LUNATIC!"

Josh looked at him with some concern.

"You okay, Carl? ... Hey Grass-man, you gonna make it?"

Grasso's mouth worked like a fish out of water. "Is it a death wish? Is that it? What did you think you were doing?"

Josh stared with wide-eyed anticipation.

"Living, man! What do you think? C'mon that was great... When he gave me the signal to go in, it was like a dream. Next thing I know, I'm out there, skating with the pros; everywhere I looked a superstar, Linkov, Katchek, Medereth, Labec, Drulay."

Josh looked away and seemed lost in his thoughts for a moment.

"I've always wanted to do that."

Grasso glared at the young man, unable to hold back.

"What? Do what? WHAT ARE YOU DOING?"

Josh just looked at Grasso and for the first time looked more like a little kid sitting there in the over sized jersey. Grasso attempted to calm himself.

"Look, I get it. You don't think like normal people do. I get it. But for Pete's sake, are you even aware of the kinda risk you're takin'?"

Josh happened to glance down and lifted up his foot. The front portion of the blade on his right skate was gone, snapped off at the base of the boot.

"Aw look, I busted a skate."

"FORGET THE SKATE!" Grasso wailed then tried to continue calmly.

"You have a net worth of eight hundred million dollars! If I could sell you on the open market I could easily get ten times that amount from any foreign government. Do you understand what that means?"

Josh hardly moved, trying not to upset the man any further as Grasso leaned in closer and pointed intently.

"Look, you are not going to have a melt down on me before you deliver the goods. This is too big. You got that? You hear me?"

"Hey, I'm just letting you talk. Sounds to me, like you need to let off a little steam. "

Grasso watched in frustration as Josh pulled off the Ranger jersey and took his street clothes out of the duffel bag. With a series of deep breaths, Grasso tried to find the strength to continue as Josh changed.

"You said phase one would be near completion. I need to know when that's going to happen. Even though I don't even know what phase one is or what it's even a part of, I still
need to be able to tell Mr. Colter you're on schedule."

Josh threw on his shirt, nodding all the while to acknowledge that he was still listening then shoved the hockey uniform into the half empty duffel bag at his feet. Grasso waited as long as he could then watched a while longer as Josh ran his fingers through his hair.

"Well? What do I tell him?"

Josh nodded and seemed a little more in touch.

"So, the natives are getting restless, huh? Starting to wonder if they're gettin' stiffed, right? Frankly, I don't blame 'em," he said, and shoved his feet into a pair of high top sneakers that looked like they were made to walk on the moon. "I mean think about it. Put yourself in their position. Look what happened when the Wright brothers started talking about flying."

"Josh," Grasso said, and held up his hands to avoid going down another rabbit hole.

"They could have thrown a net over those boys and nobody would have blamed them. But you know what it is? It's not the bizarre stuff that upsets people. I mean, an idea is just an idea, right? It's the concept of change. That's what scares 'em."

"Josh, why are you doing this?" Grasso rubbed his head, nursing a migraine as Josh proceeded to poke him in the shoulder to make the point.

"We're creatures of habit, routine. The only thing worse than change is big change. That's what this is. Flight to them was bad, but this is worse. Just the thought of it, the notion of
time travel. It messes with your mind on a whole bunch of different levels. It's like infinity. Just when you start to get the tiniest grasp on it, it gets big on you. The more you think, the bigger it gets. Pretty soon you're running off at the mouth and sound like you've been smokin' dope."

The words caught Grasso's ears and the man sat up a little straighter.

"Time travel? Whoa, wha-what do you mean, time travel. Is that some sort of slang, jargon? You don't mean real time travel."

Grasso looked at Josh like he was suddenly trying to see him through a fog.

"Come on, what? You're not actually talking about a,.I mean you didn't really make a"

Josh finished tucking his shirt into his jeans and smiled.

"Naaaw! You didn't, did you?" Grasso said, with a doubtful smile.

Josh called to the limo driver.

"Jimmy! 1412 West 39th," he said, and then took a breath and nodded at Grasso. "It's about time I showed you the lab."

The elegant stretch limo pulled up to a rundown tenement building on the lower west side of Manhattan, number 1412. Next door a condemned warehouse loomed in the shadows, a dark and ominous four story structure with boarded-up windows.

Grasso followed Josh out of the car, looking around cautiously as the young man slung the duffel bag over his shoulder and approached the dilapidated warehouse. Grasso watched reluctantly, looking back and forth at the dark warehouse and the old apartment building, wanting to stay closer to the well lit building.

Grasso took a few steps forward as Josh fished in his pants pockets for keys. Being a stickler for details, Grasso noticed that the buildings on either side of the warehouse had numbers, 1408 and 1412. The warehouse however, just sat there, a dark frightening structure, mysterious and seemingly uncounted.

"You've got to be kidding me. This is it? This is where you work?"

"It's secure," Josh said, reassuringly.

Grasso gave a weak smile.

"Oh yeah, if you're trafficking drugs or trying to hide a dead body."

Josh pulled a silver card out of his pocket and moved to the hinge side of the rusty old door where he slid the card into a tiny crack in the weathered frame. Grasso watched as three small cylindrical buttons rose out of the surface of the wood. Josh tapped the three points in rhythmic succession, initiating the code sequence. The cylinders receded with the sound of a huge air lock releasing pressure. When it was quiet, the card ejected and the door opened with a gentle "click." One casual push and. Josh stepped inside the darkened interior and then looked back at Grasso, still standing on the sidewalk.

"Coming, Alice?"

Grasso glanced back at the limo driver who shook his head with regret as though it might be the last time he would see the man. With that Grasso summoned his courage and entered the dark interior.

Josh walked in nonchalantly and dropped his duffel bag. The sound echoed just a bit and gave the impression of a large interior. Josh disappeared in the darkness ahead, and Grasso stopped at the duffel bag.

"I'll get the lights," Josh called from the shadows.

Slowly the lights faded up in gold sconces against the walls. Grasso looked in utter disbelief. This was not the dark, dank, cold environment he expected. He gazed up at the high ceilings then down the stucco and red brick walls to polished hard wood floors. Sculpted archways with Edwardian columns, interior stained glass and fine art paintings added to the expensive decor.

The first floor was open and comprised the living room, kitchen, and dining area. Grasso marveled at the elegant furnishings which were an eclectic blend of Modern and Mediterranean with genuine antiques mixed in for accents. One of those antiques stood next to Grasso, a seven foot cigar store Indian. Grasso jumped back and held his heart. The huge wooden figure wore a Fedora and held an umbrella draped over its arm and seemed more suited for a frat house than this posh environment. Josh called to Grasso. "Hang up your coat."

Grasso looked the wooden Indian up and down and decided to hold onto his coat, as he made his way across the floor to a waiting elevator. The wrought iron lift was early art deco, with inlaid mahogany walls, etched brass trim and gold railings. Josh stood just inside the elevator door as Grasso entered.

"No wonder you never want to eat over at my place."

"Actually, I heard you were a lousy cook."

Grasso nodded and conceded the point as Josh slid the gate closed.

"But at least you could have invited me over here."

"Truth is, I don't like you that much," Josh said with a straight face and pulled the brass control lever to activate the lift motor which hummed to life somewhere below them. Grasso frowned at the comment as the lift rose up the shaft.

The first floor disappeared below and with a gust of air they rose through the ceiling to the dimly lit second floor.

"Second floor, power tools, hardware, women's lingerie," Josh said as the elevator continued to climb. In the shadows Grasso could see what looked like the glow of a laptop on a mahogany desk, whirlpool lights of a shimmering spa, and the soft light of a reading lamp next to a quilted king size bed. Again the interior was beyond Grasso's wildest imagination. The lift continued to rise and Grasso stooped down to get a longer look at the hidden luxuries shrouded in shadows.

"Chicks must really dig this place."

With another gust of wind through the gates of the old elevator, they rose to the third floor. Grasso looked with eager anticipation, squinting into the darkness. The entire area was a network of girders, reaching from ceiling to floor, with air ducts, insulation and a hundred miles of thick insulated cable, a stark contrast to the posh environment below. The lift climbed steadily to the fourth floor and arrived with a gentle "ping," a modest introduction to the warehouse sized laboratory. Josh opened the gate and left Grasso staring in disbelief.

Thirty computer monitors and modular consoles arranged in a circular configuration glowed brightly in the darkness. Grasso staggered forward, gazing dumbly at the scene. In the midst of all the gadgetry, at the center of the room was a large dome shaped structure, which at first glance looked like something out of a Jules Vern novel. Its thick brass plated walls and steel rivets made it appear more suited for aquatic travel, than time travel.

Grasso fixed his eyes on the time chamber as the elevator door slid closed behind him and descended silently back down the shaft. Josh entered the lab as casually as a storekeeper opening up his shop and approached one of the instrumentation panels where he activated the main lights by voice command.

"Good morning, Hal."

"Good morning, Josh." The monotone voice of the computer was hauntingly similar to the killer computer of the sci-fi classic, *2001, A Space Odyssey*, but Grasso was too engrossed to notice the joke. He moved slowly as he came forward, trying to take it all in.

"This is incredible. How'd you keep this all a secret?"

Josh speed typed several initial command codes.

"I bought this place with a government grant that conveniently got buried in red tape. The city thinks the government owns it and the government couldn't care less. The utilities are hooked up to the property which I own next door. So for all intents and purposes, this place doesn't exist. That is until you stepped through the door."

"Uh-huh," Grasso nodded, oblivious to everything and walked toward the golden chamber, as though in a trance.

With a few more taps on the keypad, lights came on inside the time machine.

"And this is my baby."

A sea of cables and thick black hoses surrounded the time chamber and piped liquid nitrogen into the machine's metal hull. Grasso crept forward, still marveling at the sight before him and stepped across a yellow line, which happened to mark a perimeter around the entire time chamber. When both feet had crossed, the cuffs of his pants suddenly stirred, fluttering gently as residual kinetic energy radiated from the machine. Grasso jumped back.

"What's that?" he shouted, and stomped his feet vigorously, like a mouse had scampered up his pant leg.

Josh continued to work at the control panel without even a glance at Grasso.

"Pretty interesting, isn't it? It's some sort of energy wave that builds up around the machine whenever I power up. Don't worry. There's no radiation. It's completely inert. It just sits there."

"Oh yeah? You sure about that?" Grasso said, still looking for the mouse.

"Pretty sure. At these power levels it's harmless," Josh said, and moved to another control panel where he continued to bang out activation codes. "As far as I can tell, it's like a scab."

"A what?" Grasso said with a reluctant scowl on his face, as the generators hummed to life and powered up in earnest.

"You know, a scab, like scar tissue on a cut? Basically, the machine cuts a hole in the continuum of time, and the quantum energy tries to mend it, protect the hole, seal it back up. It's just a theory, but that's what it looks like to me."

Grasso watched his pant legs begin to flutter once more as the energy field made its way just beyond the line of the marker. "What happens if you're wrong?" he said.

"Total disintegration!"

There was a long pause, and Josh finally looked up from behind the console to see Grasso's eyes, bugging out of his head.

"Easy, Grass-man. I'm only kidding," he said.

Grasso exhaled then gave Josh a stern hard look. "Look, this isn't funny."

"Relax, you came to see the show, didn't you? Phase one? The energy field is only the beginning. When I power up all the way, the field actually becomes visible. I've only gone full power once, just a burst. But you can see it pretty good. I also had to construct hydraulic shocks, which act like landing gear for the chamber. They're retracted now, but the first time I throttled up was only at thirty percent and people in the neighborhood thought it was an earthquake an earthquake in New York."

Josh chuckled to himself as he checked the computer read outs. It was a joke that failed to amuse Grasso, who managed to stand his ground in spite of growing apprehension.

"Yeah, I can only imagine. So, how does it all work?"

Josh paused to look up.

"You're kidding right?"

Grasso just stared.

"You know anything about Quantum Mechanics?"

The stare was the same and Josh nodded.

"Okay, let's just say, time is essentially a mechanism subject to the laws of physics. That mechanism is altered when light particles are accelerated and refracted at a high enough frequency. Time captured within the chamber begins to separate into paradoxical transmogrifiers, its basic components.

Grasso kept the same blank expression while Josh humored him with a full explanation.

"Once I was able to slow time down enough to examine it, everything else was easy. That's when I discovered the GMS, Guidance Memory System, a way in which to measure units of physical time, to chart and map out specific locations and time destinations. I mean, without that, the whole thing is useless, right?"

Grasso seemed to snap out of it and smiled politely. "Right, so have you tested it?"

Josh moved closer to the warning markers then stooped down to check a few of the hose couplings.

"Not fully. I haven't actually stepped into another time. I've only gotten glimpses. Like I saw the crash of the Hindenburg." Josh shook his head and chuckled to himself. "Can you believe it? I was looking the wrong way and almost missed it. I saw the signing of the Declaration of Independence. Well I didn't actually see it because I think it was Ben Franklin who was moving all over the place and blocking my view." Josh jumped to his feet and pointed excitedly. "I did see Babe Ruth hit his last home run. That was sweet! He was even in color."

Grasso was incredulous and stared with his mouth hung open.

"You're serious. This, this is incredible!" He turned to the time machine. "I can't believe what I'm hearing."

Grasso fumbled to think of what to say next. "How, how about the future?"

When Grasso looked, Josh was pulling a customized pressure suit up over his shoulders as he talked.

"It hasn't happened yet. We're riding the crest of time, moment by moment. We can only experience the future in real time, as it happens. But there is a future relative to the past. Like, to the people of 1912 we are living in their future. So when we go to their time, our past, it's their present. When we return to our time we jump into their future, our present."

Grasso nodded and almost seemed to grasp the concept. Josh zipped up the suit and tightened the Velcro wrist straps on his sleeves.

"Welcome to time travel one-o-one," Josh said as he picked up a clipboard resting on the table next to him then drew a pen from the top of the clipboard and started going down the pre-launch checklist.

Grasso stared at the time chamber, with the white mist of liquid nitrogen wafting into the air, and only one word came to mind. "Incredible! Absolutely incredible!"

"That's what I said when I first realized this thing could actually work. Then it got crazy," Josh said as he finished his checklist and put the clipboard aside.

Grasso looked at the time machine with a little more apprehension.

"What do you mean, 'crazy'?"

The suit restricted his motion as Josh made his way closer, grinning with excitement as he leaned in like he was about to tell a secret.

"You ready for this? Here's where it gets big. 'The Clarence effect.'"

"What's that?" Grasso said with a shrug.

Suddenly Josh was calmer and spoke more slowly, with a sense of wonder.

"Remember that old Jimmy Stewart movie, *It's A Wonderful Life*?"

Grasso thought for a moment then nodded. "Yeah." he said and shrugged.

"Remember Clarence, the angel? He meets George Bailey on the bridge and makes it so George never existed."

"Yeah?" Grasso said, listening more intently.

"And everything changes, his wife, his mom, his friends, everyone he meets, all change. At the end, the moral is that every person's life effects the life of every other person; no matter how small, no matter how insignificant."

"Yeah okay, so?"

Josh looked at Grasso cautiously as though the man might actually be an idiot.

"So, don't you see? To look in on another time and watch reality unfold is one thing; a history lesson like you've never seen. But you're only looking. Fine. No harm. But to actually go there and interact as an alien presence in another time."

Josh backed away and opened his arms wide. "It's a literal time bomb. The slightest contact with the past could begin a catastrophic chain reaction that would effect people, places, things. Entire generations could instantly cease to exist as a result."

Grasso stared wide-eyed as the significance of what he was saying struck home. Josh sat down on a bench and slid his feet into a pair of bulky moon boots. Once they were secured and fit snugly around the legs of his pressure suit, Josh picked up his helmet and stood ready for time travel.

Grasso looked him up and down, confused.

"Well, hey! If that's true, then what's all this for?" he said pointing at Josh's outfit. "What are you doing?"

Josh slipped the helmet over his head, secured the air tight coupling around his neck and flipped the tinted face shield up. His lips curled into a mischievous grin.

"I'm going for a ride," he said.

With that, Josh turned and started toward the metal hatch of the time machine, his oversized boots clunking on the floor as he marched forward.

"Hey, wait a minute!" Grasso reached out for Josh and took a few steps to follow him when he felt the flow of energy, near the floor, pushing against his ankles once more. Like a child wading into water he decided he had gone far enough and backed away again.

"Josh! What about the time bomb? You just said –"

Grasso fell silent as Josh adjusted his pressure suit gloves and grasped the valve hatch on the chamber door. He turned it slowly until the locking bolts slid away and pressurized air hissed loudly as the time chamber door opened. Josh paused with one foot on the threshold and turned to look at Grasso once more before he stepped inside.

"Don't worry, I'm going somewhere safe, someplace where there's no possible interaction with any living soul."

Josh prepared to flip the face shield down. Grasso's mouth began to work feverishly, as he searched for something to say.

"I...I...I don't know about this," Grasso said and tried not to look totally flustered.

Josh smiled. "Hey, I'm coming right back," he said before taking one last look around and pointing to the floor. "Make sure you stay back behind the safety markers, okay?"

Grasso found the safety markers on the floor, took a few more steps back then looked up to hear the rest of the instructions.

"The landing gear will activate when I start her up. It makes a lot of noise, but that's nothing. All right. This is it. Wish me luck."

Grasso stepped forward once more then stepped back again when he remembered the safety markers.

"Wait a minute. You've never done this before. How do you know this won't kill you?"

Josh reached for his visor and took a moment to think before he lowered it.

"Good point. If it does, there's another suit in the closet. Take it and go back to the past and tell me not to do this."

With that, Josh closed the visor then climbed into the time chamber and locked the hatch door behind him. Grasso watched helplessly. "You're kidding, right?"

Inside the time chamber, Josh climbed into the seat of the pod cockpit, a cup shaped vehicle suspended by cables at the center of the chamber. The highly reflective skin of the underside of the vehicle shimmered dimly as Josh nestled in among the complex array of controls and instrumentation. The cockpit swayed gently as Josh strapped himself in and made sure the buckles were secure and then began the launch sequence.

Outside the chamber, there was a heavy vibration and Grasso stepped back as the time machine began to rise. Three monstrous hydraulic legs brought the base of the chamber to a height of six feet above the floor and held it aloft.

Grasso staggered further back and bumped into a computer monitor. He turned to see the screen and stared blankly at the image of Josh strapped into the cockpit of the pod. Suddenly Josh's voice came over the speakers.

"Carl, you there?" Josh said, flipping switches on the control console inside the cockpit.

Grasso looked across the myriad of instrumentation panels, keyboards, switches, and readouts, but not knowing where to look or what to do, he just spoke to the computer monitor.

"Yeah, I'm here," he said, which seemed to work.

Josh gave him the thumbs up sign from inside the chamber, then flipped a series of switches and paused for a few last minute instructions.

"Listen, there's a camera to your right. Can you check to see if the red light is on?"

"Grasso turned stiffly to see the camera. "Ah, yeah, it's on."

Josh spoke louder as the noise of the main generators grew and the time machine powered up to launch capacity.

"Great! That means all five cameras are recording. Keep your eyes open. I'll be interested to know what you see. I'm plotting time and location. The chamber only has enough juice for a ten minute time jump. So whatever happens, I'm stuck out there for ten minutes."

"Okay," Grasso said and felt silly responding, since he was little more than a spectator.

Seconds later the floor trembled as the time machine's hydraulic legs worked like giant shock absorbers, and the chamber was buffeted by the invisible forces of the time field. Two jet engine power plants grew louder as power increased. Josh's voice came over the TV monitor and Grasso leaned in to the speaker to hear what he was saying, afraid to miss a word and afraid to move a muscle.

"All systems nominal. Here we go. I'll reach a point of singularity in six seconds. The hole will open five seconds later and the time field will cover the chamber... I've got singularity! This is it! Three! Two! One!"

Carl Grasso's eyes widened as the force field fully materialized and covered the time chamber like a wall of living water. Suddenly, the lab was filled with static electricity and a pen flew off of a table. The object twirled through the air, straight toward Grasso and stuck to his arm. Grasso frantically brushed at his coat sleeve, like the pen was some kind of hideous bug. He tried to shake it off, then grabbed hold of it and peel it off. Once he was free, Grasso tossed it aside, only to have the pen do a U-turn in midair and stick to his chest.

Grasso resumed his struggle in earnest then paused when his hair began to rise and stand on end until each individual hair was taut as a wire and stood tall around his hairpiece, which also seemed to acquire a life all its own. Grasso clamped his hand down on it just as several sheets of paper flew across the room to join the pen and adhered to his chest. Soon ambient static electricity flickered and popped throughout the lab and Grasso's jacket stuck to him like shrink wrap while the energy field grew and his pant cuffs fluttered like sails in the wind.

A few more objects, a note pad, clip board and papers, stuck to his back. Grasso reached around twisting this way and that then gave up and stared ahead blankly with a head of clown hair; a picture of absurdity standing in the flickering light of the phantom energy field being generated from the time machine.

He watched the time chamber, wondering what would happen next, when he felt something move behind him. Grasso summoned the nerve and turned around slowly to witness the miniature time rift within the laboratory.

Grasso stared over his shoulder, and his eyes widened at the sight of himself standing there with his back turned, looking back in horror. He held perfectly still at the sight of the living mirror image, But strangely, every time he blinked, the time reflection blinked a second or two later. The bizarre image was just as unnerved as he was and shuddered just after he did Grasso did his best to hold it together and observed the mirror image of the time chamber in the background. Then, when everything began to synchronize, both Grasso's smiled at the same time and turned away, too afraid to say a word or look back again.

Inside the time chamber, the entire floor disappeared with a burst of light and the cable supports released the time pod, which dropped through the floor and accelerated like a missile. Josh held on as the nose of the pod dipped forward and he shot through the time corridor. With increased velocity and no point of reference, it was impossible to tell if he was going up or down or straight forward. The time pod shook violently as the time field plowed ahead, manufacturing the corridor mere inches before the nose of the time pod. The force of acceleration, and what seemed like air speed, pushed Josh back into his seat as he throttled back, putting distance between himself and the corridor, which forged ahead in time and space.

The young scientist glanced in the rear view mirror mounted next to his head and smiled at the amazing paradox. Ahead of the pod everything was a blur of unimaginable speed, while behind him there was no movement away from the lab at all. The cables which held the time pod floated in space, frozen in time, as the view of the lab merely grew dimmer, and he departed from the present. Soon everything went black, except for the time corridor ahead. A few more seconds and there was less buffeting and the ride was smoother. Josh reached for the control panel, and began the final countdown sequence while gripping the control handle.

"Three! Two! One! Mah-meeeeeeeee!"

Josh throttled up all the way, and the time pod rocketed forward punching a hole through the corridor and plunging into the abyss beyond.

Grasso watched the pulsating shell of energy that surrounded the time chamber as it crackled and sparked, alive and threatening. When it occurred to him that he might want to run for his life, the pen and papers dropped from his suit. His hair returned to normal, and he summoned the courage to look back. The frightened image of himself faded as the force field around the time chamber became increasingly transparent as the power diminished.

Grasso turned to the brilliant light of the video monitor that showed the inside of the time chamber. Within moments the light dimmed, the time chamber returned to normal, and the time pod became visible again. Grasso noticed the launch clock near the monitor, which was stopped at forty-seven seconds, and then looked at the monitor next to him in which he could see Josh still strapped in his seat.

"Thank God!" Grasso said, rushing forward and in his haste hitting the residual force field that still surrounded the time machine. Grasso literally struck the force field and was instantly trapped by the negative inertia of his own momentum. The effect was that he moved in slow motion. Grasso looked around in horror, trying to make sense of what was happening, when the energy finally thinned out and he fell forward.

Grasso took a moment to compose himself while the robotic legs of the time chamber retracted and the machine touched down. He looked around anxiously waiting, when the hatch lever turned and the door finally swung open. Grasso took a step and stared in amazement as Josh emerged, covered in snow and frost. Icicles fell from his pressure suit and cracked off of his oversized boots as he staggered out of the time chamber, completely unaware of Carl Grasso's presence.

"Josh?" Grasso said as he watched him limp past.

Josh pounded the frozen joints of his visor until he was able to crack the ice and raise the protective face shield. He shuddered and gasped for air. Grasso stayed close behind as the young man made his way toward the bathroom. Josh fumbled with the door knob, but his fingers were too numb and the gloves too clumsy. Grasso quickly reached around and swung the door open and then watched as Josh staggered in and turned the corner. A moment later there was the sound of running water.

"You...you all right in there?" Grasso called after him. But there was no answer.

Grasso entered cautiously and, to his dismay, saw Josh standing in the shower with the cold water steaming as it poured over the icy pressure suit.

"Wuh...wuh...we did it," Josh said, trembling uncontrollably, barely able to talk.

Grasso looked him up and down as chunks of ice fell from the suit and hit the shower floor.

"What happened to you?"

Josh gained a little more strength and tried to answer.

"No... interaction... had to pick... a place... a, a time... when there were no p-p-people."

Josh raised his gloved hands and made a feeble attempt to take off his helmet. Grasso reached into the shower and got his own sleeves wet as he unfastened the collar and removed it.

"Where did you go?" Grasso asked and laid the helmet aside.

Josh let the water stream down his face and run inside the suit as he turned to face Grasso.

"P-Polar ice cap. Ice age."

Grasso looked down at the trail of prehistoric snow and ice on the bathroom floor and smiled incredulously, and then looked up at Josh, thawing off in the shower.

Josh managed a weak smile, still trembling as the water poured over him.

"I was there. It works," Josh said, as the ice melted and steam rose off his frosted pressure suit.

"It works."

CHAPTER 3

Light flooded into the second floor bedroom. The king size bed was a tangle of sheets with Josh in the middle, face up and barechested, dressed only in plaid pajama pants. A bell tone sounded and stirred the young man as his own voice came over the answering machine. The recording was illogical and sounded like an American tourist reading from a Spanish-English phrase book.

"*Donde está la casa de Pay-Pay... Casa de Pay-Pay está aqui.*"

There was the obligatory "Beep!" which had no effect on the sleeping figure in the bed.

"Good morning, Josh, don't get up. I trust all is well."

The voice on the other end was liquid smooth and spoke with just enough feeling to sound sincere, a million dollar deal of a voice that Josh recognized but was not prepared to answer. He rolled over and muttered into his pillow as he pulled the covers over his head. It wasn't unusual for Lewis Colter to call personally, but whenever the multibillionaire defense contractor called his prized research scientist, it usually meant he wanted something.

"Good news, Josh. We've completed work on the new facility. Everything is to specifications and ready for your walk through."

Josh's face slowly emerged from under the covers, eyelids pressed shut, determined not to open, even though there was no chance he would go back to sleep.

"Karen Danners will send the limo over to get you and take you to the lab," Colter said, as though it was all agreed upon. Josh grumbled and reached out with eyes half closed, fumbling for the phone module on the night table. After several clumsy attempts, he hit the conference call mode, and called out to the phone.

"Morning, Lew. What can I do for you?"

"I believe I was just outlining that," Colter said, trying to sound both pleasant and generous at the same time. Josh shrank back under the covers, he voice slightly muffled.

"Look, I already said I have everything I need right here. I'm completely self-sufficient.

The silky voice persisted. "Just take a look at the facility. That's all I'm asking."

There was a brief pause during which Josh hardly moved. "Let me sleep on it."

"I see," Colter said. "Late night, last night? You are a busy young man, Josh. You might say, that's why we need to talk. It's about time."

Josh pulled the covers off of his face, his eyes staring wide at the ceiling.

"News travels fast," Josh said, and could see Colter smiling.

"Indeed it does. And I've found, you can pay to make it go even faster." Now that he had made his point, Colter slipped a little more patience into his voice to put Josh as ease.

"Look, go back to sleep. I'll meet you in my boardroom at one. As I said, Karen will send the car around to get you."

A second later, there was a quiet click and the conversation was over. Josh stared at the ceiling and then pulled the covers over his head in defeat.

At twelve thirty sharp, the sleek black limo pulled up outside the run down three-story brownstone. It was one of a fleet of Colter limos. There were twelve in all, each one armor plated, equipped with bullet proof glass and self sealing bulletproof tires. The limo was essentially a tank on wheels. Colter spared no expense on security or personnel.

The chauffeur was part of the security package. The man behind the wheel was the same driver who had made the getaway in the alley behind Madison Square Garden. Jimmy was laid back and cool, an ex-navy seal who never went anywhere without his Walther PPK semiautomatic pistol tucked in its holster under his jacket. The man put the car in park, and then settled back with his newspaper and waited for his passenger to arrive as usual.

"SOP," Jimmy thought and smiled at the routine, standard operational procedure.

Before he could get comfortable, he spotted another car in his rear view mirror, and then lowered his paper just as a gray gunmetal BMW roadster pulled up beside him. Josh Kensington sat behind the wheel of the sports car, smiling at the limo driver. It was a devilish grin that said, "You wanna go?" Josh revved his engine once then twice, then pulled away just fast enough to make an impression without squealing the tires. The vanity license plate on the back of the BMW, read E-MC2 a tribute to Einstein's theory of relativity. The limo driver just shook his head.

A few minutes later the roadster stopped at a red light, amidst the noise and bustle of lunch hour traffic. Josh waited, nestled inside the black leather interior of his car with one hand on the wheel, a foot on the clutch and a hand on the stick. His radio was tuned to a local rock station with a fast talking disc jockey hawking the usual group of products, from mattresses to tires and computer equipment.

Josh was grateful for any distraction that would take his mind off his meeting, and frankly was in no rush for the light to turn green. When the jockey had finished his obligations to the sponsors, a familiar heavy drum beat thump, thump, thumped over the speakers. Josh looked down at the radio and started bobbing his head up and down with the soulful rhythm just as the electric guitar kicked in, accompanied by a heavy base. When the unmistakable voice of Stevie Wonder started, Josh was right there with him.

"There is superstitious...writing's on the wall."

Josh tapped out the rhythm on the steering wheel and slid down, an inch or two, to accommodate the groove. With his head bopping and fingers drumming, the light could have taken forever now that Stevie was "workin' it" on the radio.

He was well into the song and feeling good when he noticed the college girls in the red Honda next to him, pointing and laughing. By the looks of it, they had been watching him for a while. It was an embarrassing moment, but now that he was busted, there was only one thing to do. Josh rolled down the driver side power window and with a few taps of the volume control on his steering wheel pumped up the volume and got on a serious groove. It was a free performance that involved a lot of lip-syncing and gyrations with his head and neck that would have put an older man in traction.

When the three girls started to sing back, Josh laughed aloud, knowing he was a hit. He looked to his right and saw a black Caddie and its driver, a sour puss, blue-haired old lady. She scowled at the shameful display of childish behavior, but since Josh now had three backup singers, he just turned up the music and belted out the lyrics with as much gusto as he could muster.

"When you believe in things that you don't understand, then you suffer. Superstition is the way."

The woman's expression only soured more, but mercifully the light turned green and with a last look of disgust, she pulled away. By the time Josh looked back, the three girls were gone and Josh put the car in gear. After the bit of fun, the momentary distraction was over, and he looked ahead to the Colter Industrial Bank Building looming above all the other towers on Park Avenue. The sixty-story scraper was an architectural wonder made of concrete, steel and bronze, entirely owned by Lewis Colter as were a dozen other towers on the strip. As traffic slowed again, a white Sikorsky helicopter streaked overhead, with the Colter logo emblazoned on the side. The private chopper slowed upon approach as it descended to the heliport atop the Colter building.

Josh checked his watch, "12:50. Right on time."

Ten minutes later, Josh pulled up outside the huge office building and parked squarely in the middle of a restricted zone. As soon as he stopped, two security guards appeared out of nowhere and approached the car. When they noticed the gold V.I.P. sticker in Josh's window both men quickly backed off and waved all clear.

Josh hopped out in his old worn bomber jacket, blue jeans, a cotton tee shirt and hiking boots, which was as formal as Josh cared to dress, even for board meetings. He locked the BMW by remote control, nodded to the guards once again, and had to admit working for Lewis Colter did have its perks. But now it was time to deal with the liabilities. With that realization, Josh put on his game face and joined the steady stream of people entering the office building.

The interior of the Colter building was as much a work of art as the outside. An indoor fountain and white Italian marble adorned the lobby. Shafts of light shone down through the glass atrium, illuminating modern sculptures of gold and bronze. People streamed up and down escalators. High above, a diagram of Copernicus's star chart etched in gold leaf, shimmered against the ceiling. Josh smiled, since it was his recommendation to include the masterful design when the interior was being built. He gazed up at the wonder and artistry which, as usual, escaped the people around him as they stepped off the escalator and headed for the elevators.

"The revolution of heavenly spheres," Josh said. He never ceased to marvel at the genius of the man behind the theory, a theory that had become scientific fact. It was all there, carefully diagramed, the life's work of one man. Again he welcomed the distraction.

"What an achievement. To unlock the mystery of the stars," Josh marveled. The sheer genius of the man could hardly be comprehended yet it was inescapable, as inescapable as the collision with the woman who was talking on her cell phone and looking down at her watch. The woman rocked back from the impact and dropped her briefcase as Josh grabbed her by the shoulders.

"I'm sorry!" Josh said, but one look at the woman told him he was lying. The blonde was a cosmopolitan knock out, dressed in a tan designer suit, that hugged her body in all the right places. She was young with an air of sophistication and professionalism that made her appear older and more mature.

She stepped back, which forced Josh to let her go, and then closed her cell phone with an expectant look that said, "Well?" Josh quickly bent down to pick up the leather briefcase and then came up slowly, trying not to stare at her legs on the way up, which he failed at miserably. He handed over the briefcase.

"Here you are. I'm terribly sorry. That was my fault," he said, hoping for a little conversation.

The woman merely regarded Josh with an annoyed glance, took the briefcase and continued on her way.

"I'm fine; thank you," Josh called after her as though she cared. He smiled nonetheless, enjoying the view as she walked away. A quick glance at his watch told him he had time. "What the heck!"

A crowd formed in front of one of the elevators and Josh made his way through until he was standing right next to the woman again. Now that she had made her lack of interest clear, Josh decided to have some fun. He stared at her and was so obvious the woman finally had no choice but to confront him.

"Is there a problem?"

Josh smiled at the sound of her voice and considered it a small victory. He also considered the question for a moment and tried to sound thoughtful.

"Disenfranchisement of the working class, a de-stabilized economy due to unfair trade agreements, economic imbalance among third world nations, world hunger? Can you be a little more specific?"

The woman gave Josh a weak smile, dripping with sarcasm, as if to say, "Nice try."

Josh smiled with childlike fascination. When the elevator arrived, everyone piled in until the lift was full and then stood quietly when the doors closed. Josh continued to beam his smile while the woman stared straight ahead and pretended he wasn't there. She felt safe since the elevator was an awkward place to talk and knew the man would be getting off before her.

"So you from around here?" Josh said as though he fully expected an answer, drawing the attention of everyone except the woman.

The tall, blonde held a determined gaze on the indicator lights above them, while Josh continued to stare and smile. Everyone else watched and waited. People filed out at their respective floors until eventually it was only the two of them left. Only the executive penthouse level, which required a security card to access the floor, remained. The woman finally turned to Josh, who was still smiling pleasantly.

"Last stop," she said flatly, and nodded to the open door.

Josh stepped forward and slid his key into the slot, which closed the doors again.

"Going up?" Josh asked and enjoyed the hint of surprise on the woman's beautiful face.

Josh put the card back in his pocket and the woman watched him with a look of sudden suspicion, as if to say, "Where did you get that?"

Josh folded his arms in front of him and smiled contentedly, as if to answer, "Wouldn't you like to know?"

Then as if to announce that the truce was over, she turned away again and gave Josh the coldest shoulder possible. A few moments later, the elevator doors opened onto the executive level. The silver letters of Colter Corporation were mounted on the wall and shone brightly. Josh got off the elevator, right behind the woman, who took several steps toward the giant logo, watching the man's reflection the whole time. Just as she was about to round on him, Carl Grasso appeared from around a corner and was moving fast. The moment the woman saw him, she became the picture of politeness and was full of apologies.

"I'm sorry Mr. Grasso. There's been a problem with the satellite link up from Tokyo. It looks like we won't have the eastern board members for your two o'clock via CLI, but they're still working on it."

Josh watched the woman in silent fascination as she continued in earnest, trying her best to be as helpful as possible while Grasso stood there, looking back and forth at Josh, anxiously waiting for her to finish. Josh simply stood by patiently as the woman continued and pretended to take an interest in whatever she was saying, even if Grasso wouldn't.

"They said it could be restored within the hour, but they wouldn't promise us anything. Something about a weak signal on their end due to repairs to the antenna array that..."

The woman paused when Grasso looked past her to Josh, aware that no man had looked past her since she was twelve.

"It's okay Grass-man. I know, you couldn't help yourself. All those dollar signs floatin' around your head. I know," Josh said and turned to the blonde. "A weak signal? Bad link? No problem. Carl here can just open his big mouth and the information should get to them in no time. Right Carl? Especially if it's high-level stuff, so sensitive a greedy, empty headed, bureaucratic lap dog like you can spill your guts."

Grasso shook off the insult.

"Just doin' my job. This is bigger than all of us, even you, Josh."

The woman was already flabbergasted by his absolute rudeness and her expression only changed slightly when she suddenly realized who he was.

"There's your problem," Josh said, then turned to the woman and added coldly, "Nice meeting you." Josh walked away down the hall, leaving the woman and Grasso behind.

KC Maltese, Karen Danner's beautiful assistant, watched Josh go and waited uncomfortably while Grasso tried to recover from the verbal attack and recall what she was saying.

"It's okay, KC. Tell their people to keep working on it. We'll go ahead without the board members and Colter will have Karen give them an updated transcript."

Before the woman could say a thing, Grasso chased after Josh. Once he was gone KC slumped her shoulders and could have kicked herself for not recognizing the corporation's top scientific researcher.

"That's it. I'm fired," KC said, with a sarcastic smile then turned and walked away.

The executive level of the Colter building was even more impressive and elaborate than the lobby. Bay windows and skylights illuminated the hall, with tapestries and artwork mounted on the walls between the twelve boardrooms. Josh ignored it all as he marched down the corridor. Grasso caught up to him and tried to keep pace as they approached Colter's executive boardroom.

"Will you wait a minute," Grasso said, breathing heavy.

"What did you tell him?" Josh shot back, refusing to look at him.

"What was I supposed to do? You can't keep this kind of a thing a secret."

"Yeah, I noticed" Josh said, with Grasso hustling beside him.

"Anyway, what's the problem? You stand to make a lot of money. This is the find of the century, the millennium. Hell, the whole history of the world. It's a sweet deal. Don't mess it up."

Josh glanced over at Grasso. "Wrong. This is no day at the office. You work for them. I work for myself."

Grasso grabbed Josh by the arm and spun him around, to stop him in his tracks.

"Is that so? Wake up, kid. All your little toys, your expensive lifestyle, it's all paid for by the Colter Corporation, that's Lewis Colter. So a word to the wise, don't bite the hand that feeds you."

Josh glared back and went nose to nose with the big Italian.

"This project is off the table. I never told them it was for sale, and it's not," Josh said.

Grasso reached out and Josh looked down at the card in his hand. It was glossy black plastic with the Colter logo "CC" embossed in white letters.

"What's that?" Josh said.

"A security pass. Just take it," Grasso said, more soberly as Josh held the card and examined it.. "Colter decides what's off the table, kid. Face it. If Colter wants it, he gets it!"

Josh shook his head. "It's not for sale," he said, then continued to the cherry wood doors of the executive boardroom. Grasso adjusted his tie, straightened his jacket and called to him.

"You signed a contract, Josh. That means they own you...You're meat."

Josh shrugged it off and smiled.

"Then let's go feed the wolves."

The moment Josh entered the board room, things got quiet and he immediately scanned the room to see who was in attendance. There were eight men and three women seated at the oak conference table. Josh recognized three of the men and was sure he had never seen the others. Still, in an instant he knew that this was much more than a meeting of show and tell.

One of the women was undeniably French. She was very fashionable, angular with short-cropped black hair, and an affected air of superiority. Josh took an instant dislike to her the moment he saw her. The older gentleman, seated next to her, with the well cropped beard and short turban was obviously Indian, perhaps Pakistani. The pendant on his white tunic and the rings on his fingers were large enough to be costume jewelry, but in this crowd, Josh knew they had to be the genuine article. There was a black man, an African diplomat, who wore a pleasant smile and a colorful tribal sash draped over the shoulder of a very conservative business suit. He sported a gold Rolex watch and what looked like a large sapphire pendant, which held the sash together. The rest of the board members were an assortment of equally rich and prominent fat cats who had obviously been called together from different corners of the world to meet the brainchild.

Once Josh scanned the room, he quickly realized that the board of eleven constituted a super corporate conglomerate. These were representatives of other nations and industry that had holdings in Colter Corp. And now that they had been banded together at the behest of Lewis Colter, they were a secret society of unimaginable wealth and power. One might speculate that this august gathering quite possibly fancied themselves as the self appointed guardians of humanity and the meeting was of an extraordinary nature, perhaps even sinister. Normally he would have scoffed at such an idea, calling it conspiratorial even paranoid, but now that Colter was aware of the invention, the notion was all too plausible.

In front of each person was a black binder, presumably a dossier on Josh, who according to all the best data available, was the most prolific mind to grace the planet since Albert Einstein, and he for the moment was the focus of their attention. Only one man on the planet came close to his level of genius, and Colter had bought him as well. Simon Pelitier sat near the center of the panel, a slight man of average height and conservatively dressed. With thinning, sandy brown hair and gold rimmed glasses, the renowned scientist wasn't much to look at. But his quick wit, prodigious intellect, and over inflated ego more than made up for it. Pelitier was fiercely competitive and at twenty years Josh's senior, he was in every sense of the word, a jealous rival.

Seated just to his left, at the center of the row, was the master of ceremonies himself, Lewis Colter. At forty-seven, Lewis Colter knew how to make an impression without even trying. The man was magnetic. At 6' 3" dark brown hair, blue eyes, and a lantern jaw, Colter was bigger than life. As the head of a modern empire, and a financial giant, Lewis Colter managed to remain understated, which added to his mystique. He was a private man of impeccable taste and keen perception. When it came to protocol and public relations, Grasso often said, "The man could read your pulse from across the room."

Josh tried to keep his pulse to himself as Colter glanced over and smiled, quickly going to work on the crowd, which was eager for a word or a glance. Josh had to admit, even in his quiet moments, Colter was a lion among lambs, powerful and always in control.

Just as the door began to swing closed behind Josh, Karen Danners entered and hurried past, on her way to her seat. With a stroke of her hand she slicked back her short red hair. The executive assistant took her place just to the left of Colter, opened her laptop, and flashed a brief smile to the other members of the board. Before the door could close completely, Grasso slipped into the room behind Josh and took a seat.

"Good afternoon, Josh." Colter gestured to the chair across from him, which would conveniently put him on display directly in front of the entire board and all its members.

"No thanks," Josh said. "I'll stand."

Colter simply kept going.

"I trust you had no problem getting here. How was traffic?"

Josh disregarded the chit chat and looked the panel up and down. He was being fattened up for the kill, and knew he had to keep moving if only to throw them off guard. Josh slipped his hands into his pockets, and the panel of onlookers shifted in their seats to watch as Josh meandered around to their side of the room. He moved behind them and pretended to admire the decor. Josh took a special interest in the row of exquisite original oil paintings hanging on the walls. He paused at a Renoir then continued to look at the other masterpieces as he completed his trip around the room.

"Nice copy," Josh said, with a nod toward the Renoir.

Colter smiled, impressed by the young man's powers of observation.

"Mea culpa, very good. The Renoir is a copy," Colter said, conceding the point.

"It's a good one," Josh added as he returned to his side of the table and took off the old leather jacket. Josh tossed it on the chair next to him and finally plopped down in front of the panel. He rubbed the arms of the oversized chair, took another look around the opulent boardroom and then grinned.

"This sure beats the heck out of selling insurance, don't it?"

Josh looked the panel up and down again and could tell they were taken aback by his boldness and perhaps even his lack of good diction, anything to keep them guessing and off balance. The statement was a reference to Colter's distant past, a dig that caused Colter's smile to fade somewhat.

Josh scanned the panel. "How's everybody doing?" Josh said, trying to stay on the offensive. No one answered, and since it was clear that Josh would be hard to handle, the panel remained silent for the moment and was perfectly content to let Colter rein him in.

Colonel Raymond Maxfield was the only other person Josh recognized. Maxfield was a heavy set, barrel chested, white haired gentleman with a crew cut sharp enough to shave the bark off a tree. He was seated at the end of the table to Josh's far right. Maxfield watched Josh with steely eyes and jaw set, ill amused by the young pup. The boy's intelligence meant nothing to Maxfield. He was a man of action, a hardcore, jar-headed ex-Marine from Texas, now military consultant for Colter Corporation. In truth, as far as he was concerned, the boy was a liability, a problem waiting to happen, and Josh knew it. He ignored the colonel's stony gaze for the moment and focused on the people he didn't know in order to keep the smoke screen going and have a little fun.

"Wow, looks like we've got half of the U.N. delegation right here."

Again, no one seemed amused.

Colter ignored the statement and tried to get the meeting moving forward.

"Josh, the board members expressed an interest in meeting you, and I–"

Josh smacked the table with an open palm, making a few board members jump.

"You know it's just a guess, but I bet that if a bomb went off in this room right now, the whole dang stock market would crash in a day," Josh said with a nice broad smile. "I'd probably even lose money. But, hey I'd be dead too, right? So there you go."

The board members looked at each other, a little unsure. Josh could see it on their faces, each one questioning whether this was really the individual responsible for all the scientific innovations that had made them billions. Josh smiled in earnest. One well placed incoherent statement was usually enough to bog down any well planned meeting and the foolish comment had served its purpose well.

Colter pretended to be amused but saw through Josh's thinly veiled attempt to disrupt the proceedings.

"I told you he was colorful," Colter said, and never took his eyes off of his prey. The panel of board members smiled, while others laughed heartily. And just like that, they were back on track and Colter had even established an advantage. He was aloof, and Josh was a clown. Colter's smile faded. "Personality and antics aside, you have been a tremendous asset and resource to each of us."

Josh nodded graciously, and folded his hands in front of him like an obedient schoolboy, ready for the day's lesson.

"Congratulations on your monumental success. Once again you've exceeded expectations," Colter said warmly, trying to ply Josh with compliments. The board members smiled and nodded their approval. A few applauded and eagerly awaited anything the young man might have to say.

"Thank you," Josh said. It was a cordial response, one that left everyone flat. When it was clear that the young man could not be coaxed or baited into giving any further information beyond what they had in their dossier, the board members stared in silent frustration. Colter's eyes turned cold as he tired of the charade.

"Name your price," he said, which was more of a command than an offer. Now that the issue of money was on the table, the panel seemed more focused and in control.

"You don't waste any time, do you? It's not for sale," Josh said, and managed to maintain his smile in defiance to Colter and everyone else in attendance.

Colter looked down at the dossier in front of him and closed the folder. He slid it away gently then drew his arms back, and placed his palms flat on the table. It was a gesture that said, "Let's get serious."

"As I said, you've worked very hard, and that kind of dedication should be rewarded." Colter paused to let the other board members lend their support, at which time they began to nod again, some board members more vigorously than others. Colter graciously allowed the idea to linger and gain support, after which he continued in a more warm and friendly tone.

"This is your opportunity, Josh, the opportunity to reap the benefits of your labor."

Again the others smiled their encouragement.

"No thanks," came the response and again their hopes were dashed.

Josh half expected someone to explode, but instead a quiet laughter came from the end of the table. Colonel Maxfield looked up from his folder, smiling wryly. The old military man spoke with his slow Texas drawl, "I thought you were supposed to be smart," he said, hating the young man's insubordination.

"Mr. Colter is trying to be tactful, son. So don't be stupid. He's not askin' ya, he's tellin' ya. Take the money." Maxfield smiled, like he always did after a good hearty threat. Josh nodded at the old soldier.

"Colonel Raymond Maxfield, a pleasure as always. It's been a while. By the way, I took your advice and read your book, the one on Tactical Engagement in Open Warfare. Insightful, I especially liked the chapter on aggression and superiority through domination. Speaking of domination, how's Mrs. Maxfield?"

Maxfield winced at the comment while Karen Danners and the other women on the board tried to suppress their laughter. Josh turned back to Colter, after poking the old bull with a stick.

"Hey look, you don't need me. You've got the smartest man in the whole world sitting right next to you. Anything I can do he can do better."

Josh gave Simon Pelitier a casual glance and the man hardly flinched at Josh's false humility. With that, the door opened and the beautiful blonde quietly entered the room and made her way quickly to Karen Danners. Josh's eyes followed her, as did every eye in the room, except Colter who had suddenly found his advantage and prepared to set the hook.

"All right Josh, but there is still the matter of the facility we've provided for you. You won't find a better laboratory in the world. Simon here has designed it. At least take a look and see what you think. We would appreciate any suggestions you might have to offer."

Josh hardly listened as the woman delivered her message to Danners and headed for the door. Josh turned his head and followed her like a tracking device and just as she reached for the door knob...

"Uh, Ms. Maltese…"

The woman stopped and turned stiffly, surprised to hear her name.

"Yes, Mr. Colter?"

Josh enjoyed the opportunity to stare a little longer, and took in everything about her as she stood there, her face, her smile and awkward mannerism when she was taken off guard.

"Josh, this is Katherine Maltese, Ms. Danner's assistant. Around here we call her KC."

KC offered a polite smile. "We met in the elevator."

"How do you do?" Josh said beaming once more. "The pleasure was all mine," he added with a flourish. The woman obviously agreed with her polite smile and refused to look at Josh again.

Colter laughed like the master manipulator and made his move. "Well, if you're not busy, Ms Maltese here could take you out to see the research lab at our new facility."

KC froze, while Josh's face lit up with mock surprise and he suddenly became the company man who was more than ready to cooperate.

"A new research lab? You know that does sound interesting. I guess I could find the time." Josh turned his chair to look at KC. "What do you say?" he asked, beaming like a school boy. The act was so transparent that it was hardly amusing, least of all to the beautiful blonde who did her best to hold onto her plastic smile.

"I'd be delighted, Mr. Colter," she said.

Colter waved them on. "Good," he said. "Take the rest of the day off. Give Josh the full tour."

Josh jumped up from the table like an eager pup, grabbed his jacket, and stood next to the woman.

"I'm all yours," he said, and proceeded where he had left off at the elevator. Embarrassed in front of the whole panel, KC stood there, unable to move, with her corporate smile frozen, and tried to think of how she had been roped into the assignment. Although she hadn't recognized Josh Kensington at first, he had still made an impression on her, one she could have done without. Aside from his chiseled good looks and boyish demeanor, there was something about the young man she found instantly annoying, and the idea that this so called "genius" was somehow responsible for the enormous interruption in her day only made matters worse. But since the order had come directly from her boss and there was absolutely nothing she could do about it, she cocked her head at a jaunty angle and with a perky smile she chirped, "Great!"

Josh wore a silly smirk on his face that was far too cheerful, and bordering on the obnoxious as he held the conference room door and KC held her temper. With her feet firmly planted she glanced toward Karen Danners, as if to apologize for the situation which was completely out of her control then eventually had to surrender and marched out the door.

CHAPTER 4

KC exited the office building moving with the long sultry stride of a runway model and didn't look back. People on the sidewalk watched the blonde approach the glistening stretch limo and the chauffeur who opened the passenger side door, when someone whistled. Like all attractive women KC had grown accustomed to whistles, however this was a different kind of whistle. It was loud and piercing, the kind that summons cabs across three lanes of traffic and brings them screeching to a halt at the curb.

When she looked, a set of car keys were sailing over the hood of the limo, straight toward her face. KC caught them in front of her, tossed her hair and watched Josh head around to his BMW parked behind the limo.

"Let's take my car; you drive," he said, and waved to the limo driver. "Hey, Jimmy."

Once again Jimmy just shook his head at the young man who had refused him earlier and was now about to steal his pretty passenger. KC stood next to the limo driver with the keys in her hand and glared at Josh, who appeared puzzled as he waited beside his car.

"You can drive a stick, can't you?"

KC glanced at the gunmetal roadster, and her expression quickly changed to one of determination.

"Thank you, Jimmy. I'll call you if I need you," KC said, and moved past the limo driver.

Jimmy watched her leave then lowered his head and mumbled, "Good luck."

KC rounded the BMW. With a press of a button, she deactivated the alarm with the keyless entry, opened the door and slid into the driver's seat. Josh's silly smile returned as he climbed in on the passenger side.

The inside of the roadster was spotless and well kept. Josh watched the young woman look around briefly to familiarize herself with the dashboard and controls. She fastened her seatbelt, adjusted her seat and rear view mirror with a ritualistic calm, which instantly caused Josh a little concern. It was reminiscent of Andretti, preparing the cockpit of a formula one for an Indianapolis time trial.

KC put the key in the ignition and started the car. The engine purred to life and then roared wildly as KC floored the gas pedal, revving it severely until it seemed the engine might leap out from under the hood and take off on its own.

Josh's smile turned into a grimace until KC mercifully let up off the gas and the engine purred smoothly once again.

"Uh, like I said, you can drive a stick, can't you?"

KC grabbed the stick shift, jiggled it in neutral then shoved it into first gear and smiled wickedly. Josh looked at the woman who was literally in the driver's seat and knew all he could do was plead for mercy.

"Remember you have to be nice to meeeeeeee!"

Tires squealed, blue smoke filled the air and Jimmy the chauffeur jumped back as the gunmetal roadster fishtailed left and right, burning rubber out of the parking space and shot out into traffic like a rocket, headed uptown.

Josh stared wide eyed with his head pressed against the seat rest then glanced at the beautiful blonde whose attention was riveted to the road. Doing eighty, northbound on the Degan Expressway, she put the car through its paces, downshifting to change lanes, and then accelerating on the open stretches. The woman hardly over steered as she picked her way through the slower moving traffic and kept Josh white knuckled and shoved back in his seat.

"You always drive like this?" Josh said, and tried to work a little moisture into his mouth.

KC ignored the question as she downshifted behind a tractor-trailer, then checked her mirror and hit the gas to slingshot around the truck and pull away in the high-speed lane. Josh watched the speedometer climb from seventy-five to eighty, eighty-five, ninety.

"This is a little fast, don't you think?"

KC tried not to smile and stared straight ahead, determined to make him apologize for his rudeness or pee in his pants, whichever came first. Josh tried to think of something to say to make her slow down as the BMW approached one hundred miles an hour, passing other cars in a blur.

"Y-you know, if you kill me, you could lose your job," he said and did his best to sound calm. With that, the speedometer dropped down to ninety, then eighty, then seventy-five. Josh breathed more regularly and smiled as they joined the normal flow of traffic.

"We certainly need more defensive drivers like you on the road."

KC ignored the comment and continued to frown at the road.

"That's better," Josh said, as though they were making progress. "So, what exactly is it you do at Colter Corporation?"

KC took a deep breath as though the pain of the day was unavoidable and she would simply have to deal with the particular pain seated next to her whether she liked it or not.

"Operations Manager," she said, and kept it short like a prisoner being interrogated by the enemy.

"Really, that sounds very interesting," Josh said, and couldn't have sounded less sincere.

KC shook her head and dismissed the comment, The perplexity on her face revealed that she was working out what to say and considering the best way to say it. After a few seconds she glanced over with somewhat of a pained look on her face.

"Look, I'd like to save you a lot of time and effort. So let's just cut the small talk. You're not my type, and I really don't like you, so it's best if we don't talk."

"Okay," Josh said, "fair enough," and nodded then as quick as he could, placed his elbow on the center console, leaned over with his chin on his hand and blurted out, "You are absolutely the most drop dead gorgeous woman I have ever seen!"

KC kept her eyes on the road and casually checked the rear view mirror as though the seat next to her was empty. Josh fell back in his seat and gazed at the ceiling with a sigh of relief.

"Whew! I'm glad that's over. I didn't know how long I could hold that in."

KC ignored that as well as she signaled to pass.

"They say you're a genius. Are you?"

The question was so matter of fact, it sounded like more of a challenge. Josh gave it some thought.

"I guess that all depends on who you're talking to."

KC glanced over at him.

"Mr. Grasso says you're probably the most brilliant mind since Einstein."

Josh smiled.

"Compared to Carl, everybody's brilliant."

KC nodded and since she didn't like Grasso, had to admit it was the first thing they happened to agree upon.

"I heard Dr. Pelitier describe you as a 'breakthrough genius.' He said your theories on quantum mechanics are the most daring and insightful he's ever seen."

Josh looked genuinely surprised. "Pelitier said that?" Josh paused a moment and then shrugged. "Must have been drunk." Josh turned his attention to her and studied her face.

"You know much about science?" he asked.

"I majored in business law and minored in chemistry," she said.

Josh held a thoughtful gaze. "Really? You don't strike me as the text book type. Frankly, I see you as more, well –" Josh slipped his arm around the back of the driver seat. "Shall we say high maintenance?"

KC gripped the steering wheel a little tighter and narrowed her eyes.

"How did you get such a large ego into that tiny brain?"

Josh smiled and just stared dreamily.

"It's a tight fit," he said.

KC finally exhaled. She had done her best to insult, rebuff, or otherwise turn the young man away, and it was no use.

"Just make the best of a bad situation," she told herself then glanced over again and managed a glimmer of a smile.

"You're nothing at all like what I expected," KC said.

It was the closest thing to a compliment and took Josh totally by surprise.

"Thank you," he said and for the first time seemed at a loss for words.

"You're far more obnoxious than I imagined."

Josh was stunned. He had walked straight into that one and KC smiled with a look that could have easily been followed by a fist pump in victory. Slowly, she loosened her grip on the steering wheel and for the first time seemed to be enjoying herself.

Once they were off the interstate, twenty miles north of the Connecticut border, it was rural country. The BMW drove along the winding roads through the quaint hills of a small bedroom town. A few minutes later, they turned onto a private road, surrounded by dense woods, and headed up a long drive.

Once they came over the crest, the trees parted and the BMW slowed as they passed a granite slab in front of a well manicured lawn with the words "COLTER LABORATORIES" etched into the stone. Behind it was a sprawling industrial park that looked more like a posh gated community. The car approached the guard shack, a concrete bunker designed to take a tank shell, nicely disguised with wood siding and a red-shingled roof, then stopped and flashed her I.D., color coded blue.

The guards were paramilitary armed with semi-automatic weapons and wore black jumpsuits with special insignias that Josh didn't recognize. The point man was blonde, expertly built and all business. He nodded at KC then looked over at Josh. Josh stared back blankly and then remembered. He fished around in his coat pocket then slowed his arm movement when the guards seemed to tense up and watch him more closely. Josh pulled out the black security card Grasso had given him and waved it at the guard. The man nodded sharply and waved them on.

The BMW rolled forward, and KC looked over at him.

"Wow, top clearance," she said and was genuinely impressed.

"Yeah," Josh said, looking at the card with equal surprise and then put it back in his pocket, like he had nothing to do with it. They rolled through the front gate, and Josh took note of the dual airplane hanger, landing strip and heliport. A formidable looking AH-64A Apache helicopter was parked on one of three landing pads next to the hanger. A ground crew gathered around the nose cone of the high tech chopper.

KC drove on through the property, which was meticulously landscaped, and pulled up to the lab building, essentially a large white warehouse structure with several annexes built around it. Black mirrored glass surrounded the entire first floor of the building and unified the connecting structures.

KC rolled into a guest parking space near the front, shut the car off, pulled the keys out and tossed them to Josh.

"This is it, the Tech Center."

Josh looked at the stark white building, which gave no clue of what lay inside.

"You coming?" KC asked. She climbed out of the car and shut the door behind her. As she walked up the path toward the tinted glass doors, she heard the passenger door of the BMW slam shut behind her. When she looked back, Josh was strolling across the lawn toward the panoramic view of the valley and the quiet little hamlet on the hillside in the distance. Then without a glance behind him, he sat down, cross-legged on the grass and made himself comfortable.

KC stood by the doors of the Tech Center and watched in dismay. Then with pursed lips, she marched across the grass in her heels, looking more determined than graceful.

Just as she stormed up beside him and was about to open her mouth, Josh seemed to read her mind. "Before you get started, why don't you sit down for a minute? Please."

KC glared at him and the ridiculous request and thought about all the things she could say. "I don't have time for this! This is not a picnic! Stop acting like a child!" Then decided that nothing she could think of would probably do any good. So she gathered herself up with a huff and plopped down beside him, trying to look as dignified as she could in the process.

"May I remind you? We came to see the lab," she said with as much patience as she could muster.

Josh looked out across the rolling hills with a gentle breeze on the air and the warm sun on his face.

"What's wrong with us, really? When we can walk right past this and not even see it."

KC took a moment to give a cursory look at the surrounding landscape then tried to be polite.

"I'm supposed to show you the laboratory and familiarize you with the –"

Josh held up his hand.

"You want to go inside a dark stuffy lab on a beautiful day like this, I'll be here when you get back."

That was the last straw. KC pointed her finger in his face and wagged it under his nose.

"Oh, no you don't! I didn't drive all the way out here for you to stonewall and pull some kind of stunt for attention. They said you were hard to work with, but you're not going to jerk me around mister. This is completely unacceptable and I will personally lodge a formal –"

"Whoa! Wow! Cool down. Don't get your shorts in a bundle."

KC paused again, amazed at his arrogance and sat up even straighter. "Listen stud, my shorts are not the issue here. It is your total and utter lack of professionalism!"

"Okay, okay I'm sorry. Just hear me out," Josh said with his hands up to slow her down.

KC took a breath and tossed her hair back to listen to what he had to say.

"Your job is not in jeopardy," Josh reassured her, which seemed to help somewhat. " Forget about the lab. Colter knows I couldn't care less about it and he also knows, the only reason I came out here was to spend time with you. And that's the honest truth."

KC's expression turned to one of absolute disbelief.

"You are the most unprofessional, self absorbed –"

"Egocentric?"

"Egocentric," KC added.

"Self-centered?"

"Stop it!" KC yelled and jumped up.

"Just trying to help," Josh said like an innocent schoolboy.

KC looked down at him.

"Can't you conform to the rules just once? Not everybody is out to get you, you know."

Josh stared out at the countryside.

"That's not how I see it."

KC looked at him and for a moment he looked small and alone sitting on the hillside.

"Why are you so paranoid?" she asked.

Josh looked up at her and held her gaze, then twisted around to see the enormous compound and the Tech Center behind him. Josh shrugged his shoulders and squinted up at her.

"I don't know. Maybe it's the company I keep?"

KC huffed in frustration, and then turned to walk away but paused. "You know, I don't get it. It's not like they even need you anymore," she yelled back, and then continued on.

Josh, puzzled by the comment, turned to see KC marching up the hill toward the lab building. "Hey! What does that mean?"

The sound of helicopter blades whirred out of the distance as Colter's private helicopter came across the valley straight toward them. Josh stood to his feet and started up the hill as the chopper whirred overhead and descended to the heliport beyond the Tech Center.

"Hey!" Josh called again. "What's this garbage about them not needing me anymore?"

When he reached the walk in front of the Tech Center, KC rounded on him and yelled over the helicopter noise.

"Dr. Pelitier has duplicated all your experiments. He's copied everything. They have the machine. All they want you to do is inspect the prototype!"

With the sound of the helicopter engines dying down behind them, Josh just stood there. After a while KC wondered if it was shock, or if he had even heard what she said. "Didn't you know?" With that, Josh rushed past and entered the building.

KC kept pace and flashed her security card as they passed the first two security check points. Josh went through in a daze and without incident, as the guards nodded him on. They advanced down the main corridor.

"How could you not know?" KC said, thinking she might be very well talking to herself.

The halls of the lab building were antiseptically clean. Personnel, in white lab uniforms, moved busily up and down the corridors. At the next check point, two armed guards manned a glass airlock at the entrance of the white hall. KC flashed her I.D. card once again. These men were a little more cordial than the other guards, although no less imposing.

"Afternoon, Ms. Maltese." The guard was an enormous black man, who looked like a bodybuilder with sleeves conveniently short enough to show off his biceps. The rather large Colt HB Commando automatic rifle draped over his chest was equally impressive.

"Good afternoon, Larry," KC said, still distracted by the man she accompanied.

Josh stepped forward to look through the thick glass airlock and see what lay ahead, but the door refused to open.

"Excuse me, sir."

Josh turned to see the guard peering down at him.

"Hi" was all Josh could manage and looked a little lost as he flashed the black I.D. card.

"Professor Kensington?" the guard asked in his deep baritone voice.

"Yeah," Josh said a little surprised since the card had no name on it, as far as he could see.

"Just a minute, sir," the guard said then called back to his partner, "Professor Kensington."

Josh watched the other guard, an equally fit, Sergeant Rock type, who checked a list on his clipboard.

"Here you go," the big guard said and handed Josh a clip on security badge with his name on it. "It's just a formality. But this will save you any further headaches from this point on."

"Thanks," Josh said and clipped the badge to his jacket. The heavy pressurized door slid open on a cushion of compressed air. Josh stepped through and looked around, moving more cautiously while KC continued on ahead. Josh moved more quickly to keep up and focused his eyes on the end of the corridor which was pitch black. It was as though the hall led into outer space, or a space that was just as dark and starless.

"Where does this go?" Josh asked.

"You'll see," KC said and kept moving. Josh peered ahead as the hall grew dimmer. With a few more yards, the corridor ended abruptly and they stepped out onto a metal platform into darkness. Josh stood perfectly still as his eyes adjusted and he overlooked the cavernous space that stretched out below them. KC spoke softly as though trying to break the news to him gently.

"This is the hub of Tech Center, otherwise known as The Lab. This hundred thousand square foot hanger has been in development for eighteen months and was only completed a week ago. Every resource Colter had at his disposal was poured into it. He spared no expense. The installation is even equipped with its own power grid.

Josh gazed down at the space which was roughly the size of a football field and dwarfed his own warehouse laboratory. A network of girders, ducts and catwalks lined the ceiling with elevated cranes mounted on tracks for heavy construction. While below, the lab floor was sunken several stories beneath ground level with countless electronic consoles and work stations, all arranged in circular rows like an amphitheatre. The lab mirrored his own, but was much larger and far more advanced. Spot lit at the center of the lab was the time machine, an exact replica of his own. Only instead of brass, the hull was polished steel, perfectly dome shaped and shimmering like a jewel under the spotlights. Josh marveled at the army of technicians, moving busily from station to station like soldier ants working in the shadows surrounding the sparkling time chamber. Josh staggered forward, grasping the metal railing before him.

"I don't believe it," he whispered.

Suddenly there was a rousing round of applause. Lewis Colter and Simon Pelitier entered the lab from somewhere below, escorted by a small entourage and moved to the main control platform that stood before the time machine near the center of the lab. The control platform was elevated several feet above the rest of the lab and comprised a bank of central control consoles that formed a semi circle facing the time chamber. This was manned by six launch control technicians.

Josh watched as Colter climbed the steps of the control platform and one of the men greeted him with a clipboard, then shook Colter's hand and went back to work as did everyone else. The place began to hum once again as an entire crew of lab technicians converged on the main control platform, presumably to get their orders. Beyond the busy control center, special technicians made adjustments to the hydraulic undercarriage of the time chamber. Vapor rose off of the liquid nitrogen couplers and fuel lines, which made the silver time chamber look ominous and ghostly against the thick haze.

Josh watched from his perch, thirty feet above the lab, and all of the life seemed to drain out of him as he took it all in. "How long?" he asked softly.

"It was completed two weeks ago. I thought you knew," KC said. With the press of a button, the platform lowered, and they began the descent. Josh hardly said anything and by the time they had reached the lab floor, KC felt like she had indeed led the sheep to slaughter.

"Look, I'm sorry. I thought this was all made clear to you, prior to –" Her voice died down as Josh started forward without a word and seemingly without any concern for what she had to say.

Pelitier was still in the process of assigning various duties to the lab techs and busy sending them off, one by one, when Josh arrived and mounted the platform as the last technicians went on their way. Colter turned to see Josh standing there. The time machine glistened behind him beyond the perimeter of warning markers. Josh gazed at his invention, speechless. Colter allowed him time to soak it all in. Pelitier stood by smug and confident, aware that this was indeed a shock, and enjoying every moment of it. Colter initialed a few more documents and then handed off the electronic tablet and stylus to a lab tech who nodded and walked away.

"Welcome, Josh. Glad you could make it," Colter said, testing the waters. Josh offered no response. Colter tried again, and this time came along side Josh. Together they marveled at the view of the time machine, spot lit at the center of the cavernous and dark laboratory.

"What do you think? How'd we do? Exquisite, isn't she?"

Josh stepped forward and the six central control techs turned to watch him. There was another long and awkward pause as Josh peered at the machine.

"Has it been tested?" he asked in a flat monotone.

Pelitier, who had been bursting at the seams, finally stepped forward.

"Most certainly, but with great care. We've moved forward in stages, powering her up incrementally, analyzing the stasis of the time shell."

Josh looked past the man and merely repeated the question.

"Has it been tested?"

Pelitier tried to remain aloof in front of Colter and resented the implication that he had avoided the question.

"As I said, we are moving in incremental stages. The last trial run was a static test. Just a glimpse through the looking glass if you will," he said, and felt sufficiently clever enough to have redeemed himself. But again there was no response from Josh who just kept staring. Colter stepped forward and motioned toward the time chamber.

"I've been here every day watching, observing the progress. I take my hat off to you, Josh. It's quite a discovery, truly an exciting piece of technology."

Josh spoke in a daze.

"How'd you do it?"

Colter motioned to Pelitier. "I'll let the good doctor field that one as well," Colter said and stepped back, prepared to watch the two geniuses slug it out.

Pelitier was keen to answer. "You were probed and didn't even know it. Thermal-holographic spectral analysis from the nose cone of an Apache at night through your walls."

"You spied on me," Josh said, and turned to look the man in the eyes.

Pelitier enjoyed the expression on Josh's face and wasn't sure if he had ever seen him look quite so helpless.

"Nothing personal," Pelitier said. "It's a surveillance tool I tinkered together about a year ago. We had a use for it and it needed to be tested. Figured I'd kill two birds with one stone. Took us a while to compile all the data we needed, but I'd say it did its job."

Josh looked at the floor and shook his head.

"You're a real piece of work, Simon."

"This is business, Josh. You weren't forthcoming. We needed the information. I took the initiative."

"You took my idea," Josh said slowly.

"Let's not be petty, Josh. There's enough profit here for everyone."

"Profit?" Josh sneered then calmed himself and turned away to look at the lab techs working on the hydraulic legs, retracted beneath the time chamber.

"A glimpse through the looking glass." Josh repeated the words and smiled to himself. "You tried, didn't you? You tried to go all the way, but you couldn't. You couldn't make the time jump, could you?" Josh turned to Pelitier. The scientist looked around for something to say and Colter rushed to his defense, like a corner man trying to keep his fighter on his feet at the end of the round.

"We did try," Colter said. "And as Simon pointed out we saw into the past, Lincoln's assassination to be precise. It was amazing. Everything, we could see everything; the moments leading up to it."

Colter gestured in front of him as he laid it all out in his mind's eye. "The play and the actors, Lincoln in his box in the balcony. The the dim lighting, and Booth, John Wilkes Booth in the shadows. He was there, right there. You could see it all!"

Josh held up a hand to stop him.

"Wait a minute. Wait a minute. Why the assassination of Abraham Lincoln?" Josh waited and watched the slow but eager smile that crept across Colter's face until the man nodded with eyes gleaming.

"You've got to be kidding me," Josh said, and looked around at all of the lab techs looking back at him.

"You were going to try to stop Lincoln's assassination?" he said, and didn't know which way to turn. "Dear God! I knew it. You people are incredible. Think! For one moment, just think about what you're doing."

Colter spoke with a cool calmness that was beyond calculating.

"We are thinking, Josh. Till now we were at the mercy of our past, merely the effect of a preceding cause, forever separated by the barrier of time. Thanks to you, we now have a tool. A tool connecting us, a conduit to a past filled with tragedy and horrors. And now with this machine we are given a chance, a chance for us to break through that barrier and go back to correct mistakes. Think of it, Kennedy, King, Sadat, Nine Eleven; we can fix it all, make everything right."

Josh listened, soaked it all in then pointed at the time chamber.

"I know what you're saying, and I know what you think that is, but it's not a tool to make things right. That's Pandora's Box. You open that up, and all hell's gonna break loose."

Simon shook his head in disappointment.

"Always the skeptic. Always the alarmist."

Josh rounded on Pelitier. "Stuff it, Simon!" He shifted his attention back to Colter.

"Listen to me. This is no joke. I don't care what your intentions are! You use this thing, there is no way to accurately predict what affect you will have on the present. Anything could happen! You could make nine eleven worse. Don't ask me how, but it's possible!"

By now, Josh had attracted the attention of several security officers as well as the lab personnel stationed close to the control platform. The security officers dressed in black coveralls, with automatic weapons slung across their chests, talked back and forth over headsets as they converged on the location until Colter signaled to them. With a wave of his hand the men paused, some returned to their positions and Colter turned to Josh once more.

"As I said, it's just a tool. We control its application and usage."

Josh shook his head and repeated the phrase with mock laughter.

"Application and usage, that's good. But what about effect and outcome? Have you tried to control that yet? No you can't… Why? Because absolute probability is not quantifiable!"

The lab techs on the control platform glanced at each other as they considered the warning, while KC Maltese approached the control platform and listened to Josh's impassioned plea.

"Look, I'm telling you the effect this 'tool' will have on our present cannot be calculated with any certainty. The resulting reality shift could easily wipe us out and replace us with an alternate reality that may or may not even include us. Entire civilizations could be erased. We're talking the ultimate weapon of mass destruction. And you think this —"

Again, they just stared and the sudden realization made Josh take a step backward.

"That's it, isn't it? That's what you want."

Colter stepped closer and for the first time seemed truly concerned and sincere.

"By correcting injustices we cut out the cancer before it spreads. This is our chance to make the world what it was meant to be. We're just doing what's right, Josh. And thanks to you, we have the power. We have that ability."

Before Josh could respond, Pelitier stepped forward to correct Colter.

"We almost have the ability, which brings us back to you."

"Yes, there's something missing," Colter added. "We're calling it the X- Factor and I believe you know what it is."

"The catalyst," Josh said softly, as Colter continued.

"Yes, we need it for the test run, the maiden voyage. Without it the pod won't go," Colter said then switched to sales mode without a pause. "And in light of your great respect for this brave new frontier, we would like to make you our new project director and have you take over operations. Work out the bugs for us and supervise the initial launch with the valuable assistance of Dr. Pelitier as co-director to help you along the way."

Pelitier smiled as if to show, "No hard feelings."

Josh was suddenly overjoyed. "Hey, how about that? Wow... The opportunity to be your lackey, and play the fool, after you've stolen my idea and shoved it in my face. Let me think about that." Josh's transition to absurd cynicism wasn't nearly as smooth or gracious as he pretended to ponder the offer then came up with an idea of his own. "Hey I know. How about this? How about, I line the entire laboratory with C4 explosives, set fire to the building, and watch the whole thing explode on national TV? How are you with that?"

Josh looked back and forth at Colter and Pelitier as though they were actually listening. Colter smiled and shook his head.

"You know, Josh, if I thought you were serious, I'd have no choice than to have you shot where you stand."

Four agents in dark suits moved in front of the soldiers in coveralls and stood just beyond the control platform. One man, tall, with black hair slicked straight back, slipped his hand inside his jacket, and waited with cold steely eyes. Agent Vega stood with the best angle on the target and smiled when Josh spotted him in the crowd.

Colter had made the threat clear, but the agent with his hand on his gun made it real. Josh raised his hands slowly and backed away, carefully negotiating his way down the platform steps to the lab floor. Slowly he moved past KC Maltese with his arms raised and backed away, up the main aisle; past rows after rows of monitors, lab techs and work stations.

"Thank you for coming, Josh. We'll be in touch," Colter called from the control platform as though he had paid the man a compliment instead of threatened his life. The throng of scientists stared and pointed as Josh kept moving, headed for the exit. "We'll be in touch," Colter said, his words echoing through the lab.

"It's just a matter of time," Josh shouted back, allowing everyone to consider the irony of the pun as he left the laboratory.

Once he was outside, Josh looked at the world around him with a new awareness, the quiet and calm understanding that as the inventor of time travel, if anything went wrong, it was all his fault and he was ultimately to blame.

CHAPTER 5

It was normally an hour and a half drive back to the city, but Josh's mind was a whir. His thoughts raced back over the images he had seen at Colter's lab, the facility, the time chamber, the armed guards, the threat. Driving usually helped him to think. But now, his thoughts only became more muddled and bogged down. After hours of aimless driving, he had managed to tire himself out, and it was well after eight when he finally arrived at home and found a priest seated on the front steps of the brownstone. The man was dressed in black with the traditional white collar. Father Michael Joiner was in his early thirties, and perhaps a little more handsome than one would expect of a priest. Father Mike smiled broadly and waved as the BMW rolled up. The power window slid down with a "click" and Josh called to the priest.

"Hey, move along. You're gonna scare off the hookers. The orphanage is down the street!"

Father Mike came down off the stoop. "The hookers told me you scared them off," he said, and Josh smiled at the snappy retort.

The good priest approached the car, obviously impressed.

"That's a pretty nice machine," he said, looking in through the passenger window. "When did you get it?"

"I've had it for a while."

Father Mike nodded, "Six cylinder?"

"Eight, with a super charger. The speedometer goes up to one eighty. I've gotten it up to one thirty twice."

Father Mike shook his head," Is that a confession?"

"No, that's called bragging," Josh said and let go of the steering wheel. "You want to take her out?"

The priest stood back. "No, thanks. I can appreciate it from right here."

"Oh yeah, temptation," Josh said and lowered his head as though he felt sorry for his friend.

Father Mike looked up and down at the length of the car. "No. I'm just a bad driver." The priest sank his hands into his pockets. "Thanks, though."

"Hang on, let me put this away."

Josh rolled up the window and pulled the car around into the dark alley on the side of the warehouse structure next to the well-lit apartment building. There was the sound of a heavy mechanical door sliding open, hoisted up by squealing chains. The BMW's red brake lights filled the alleyway, as though it had suddenly been set ablaze, then abruptly went out. A few seconds later there was the same horrible noise as the freight door lowered, with a fair amount of additional squealing, and then slammed shut.

The noise echoed down the dark alleyway and eventually all was silent, with the exception of a distant police siren and a baby crying in an apartment somewhere above. Father Mike waited patiently as Josh slowly emerged from the darkness, seemingly with the weight of the world on his shoulders. Josh tried to muster a smile for his old friend as he drew near.

"So what brings you to this neck of the woods?"

"Can't an old friend just drop by? Just wanted to see how you were doing."

Josh took a deep breath, opened his arms wide and gave a nice big smile.

"Never better," he said.

"Want to talk about it?"

Josh lost the smile, dropped his arms, and suddenly looked weary beyond his years. A moment later he gave the priest a suspicious look.

"Talk? Do you mean professionally?"

"I mean, talk," Mike said innocently.

Josh looked around in exasperation as though there were a thousand thoughts swirling around in the air. Mike watched with growing curiosity as Josh's mouth began to work. It opened and closed, but nothing came out as he wrestled with his thoughts and didn't know where to start. Josh's eyes finally settled on Mike, and he sighed heavily.

"You know –" Josh said, pointing an accusing finger. This time his mouth seemed to lock open as the words escaped him again.

Mike nodded with encouragement, as if to urge him to go on.

"You don't know what you're getting into," Josh said and meant it.

It was a start, and Mike smiled.

"That's what they told me at seminary."

With that, Josh shrugged and turned away. "All right, come on," he said.

The priest watched Josh walk to the cold dark dilapidated warehouse building adjoining the well lit apartment building in front of them. In truth, the priest had been trying to ignore the dark ominous structure the whole time and watched as Josh produced his card key and slid it into the narrow slot in the heavy wooden doorframe. The three cylindrical buttons rose silently out of the surface of the door. Josh tapped the strategic code in the usual quick rhythmic sequence. The cylinders receded and there was the momentary sound of a huge air lock releasing pressure. Somewhere beyond the door heavy mechanical bolts slid away and the lock opened with a smooth, effortless click. Josh looked back.

"Well? You coming?"

Father Mike turned to the warm, inviting apartment building in front of him, and then looked over to the dark foreboding edifice next door, and clearly didn't want to answer, let alone follow.

"Not everything is what it appears to be," Josh said and entered the building. Father Mike followed reluctantly and just when he disappeared inside, the door slid closed behind him.

The elevator rose to the top floor and Josh stepped out. He paused to look at the time chamber sitting in the middle of his laboratory, which by comparison to Colter's top-secret science lab, now looked like an old rusty Plymouth in the cluttered junkyard of a mad scientist.

Josh kept moving to a small kitchenette off in the corner, strewn with dirty dishes and empty frozen food boxes. He flipped a switch to turn on the lights while the time machine and the rest of the lab remained dimly lit. Father Mike wandered out of the elevator, gazing all around in quiet fascination.

"Want some coffee?" Josh called from the kitchen.

"No thanks," Mike said as his eyes came to rest on the object at the center of the lab. To the young priest, the golden dome of the time chamber looked like a work of art.

"How do you take it?" Josh called out referring to the coffee.

Father Mike approached the machine, his curiosity aroused.

"None for me," he replied again as he kept going, stepping over hoses and cables, trying to get a better look."What is it you're working on?"

Josh called out from the kitchen, "A time machine."

Mike looked over to see if he had heard him right.

"What did you say?" Father Mike asked.

"A time machine," Josh said casually, as he walked up to his friend with two coffees and handed Mike his cup.

"Cream, no sugar," Josh said.

Father Mike reached out and took the coffee in a state of shock. "Thank you," he said and took a sip. The two men stood there, gazing up at the time chamber and Josh shook his head with a look of regret.

"Forgive me, father, for I have sinned."

Mike looked at Josh incredulously. Although he knew Josh had uttered the words more for effect, it was the tone of voice and the cryptic words themselves which made the priest believe that the young man was not only serious, but was in serious trouble.

High above, a black AH-64A Apache helicopter hovered in whisper mode, slipping through dark clouds undetected. At a thousand feet above the cityscape, the elaborate surveillance device attached to the nose of the craft swiveled into position. Its array of dark lenses glistened in the moonlight as the co-pilot acquired the correct coordinates and resolution to begin focusing in on the warehouse building far below.

Inside the chopper, the co-pilot watched the flickering surveillance instrument panel, with one hand on a keypad and the other on a joystick control. The images on the monitor changed frequently as the device peered through walls, chimneys and rooftops below. Then as the images became clearer the co-pilot whispered into his headset.

"DSI image tasking, on line, parsing integral axis. We have thermal tracking and audio."

Soon the device locked in on a thermographic close up of two figures as seen through the rooftop of Josh's building. Colonel Raymond Maxfield's voice barked over the radio speakers. "Talk to me. What's going on?"

The co-pilot tapped his keypad making adjustments on the fly as he watched the glowing silhouettes become clearer on his monitor and their thick and heavy voices remained distorted over the airwaves. The co-pilot radioed back.

"He has company, sir. Streaming digital imagery and filtering audio to patch you into our transmission. Stand by."

The man quickly turned to a second keyboard. "Re-routing transmission directly to main Intel."

Miles away, Colonel Raymond Maxfield sat in the comfort of his office at Colter Labs, watching the thermal images on his own monitor. Pelitier watched over his shoulder as Maxfield studied the aerial images of the two men and listened to the garbled audio.

"What's the matter with the sound?" Maxfield snarled, squinting at the picture.

Pelitier reached down, tapped a few keys and magnified the image on screen. Both men scrutinized the picture closely. Still there was little improvement on the sound. Pelitier leaned forward to speak into the microphone. "This is doctor Pelitier. Can you boost the signal?"

The line crackled with static as the voice came back. "Negative sir, there's a storm front coming through. We're picking up interference."

Maxfield pounded the table, more for effect, then sat back in his chair and looked at Pelitier.

"I thought you said this thing was bug proofed."

Pelitier tapped a few more keys and, when he had done all he could, simply stood back and looked the big bear of a man in the eyes. "It's a storm front, colonel. These things happen. Every system has its limitations."

Maxfield smirked, then turned back to the microphone.

"Surveillance, stay on 'em. Monitor every move. I want to know if he uses that machine. He takes a trip to the bathroom, I want it on tape. Got it?"

"Yes, sir," the voice chirped over the radio.

Maxfield leaned back and seemed to regard the computer screen with less intensity. Pelitier sighed and rubbed his eyes, showing signs of exhaustion. "He's not going anywhere... not tonight."

Colonel Maxfield swung his chair around to look at the science expert. "You and Colter, you really think you know this kid."

Pelitier adjusted his glasses and stood his ground before the larger, barrel chested ex-marine.

"Child prodigy at age six. IQ testing ranked number one in the nation, twelve years running; worked on rocket modifications for Jet Propulsion Labs at sixteen; graduated MIT, received doctorate at twenty. Mother died when he was fourteen; raised by an abusive father; developed compulsive behavioral disorders, became a recluse with self-destructive tendencies. I know everything there is to know about Josh Kensington."

Pelitier smiled and waited as Maxfield reached into his desk drawer and pulled out his own personal dossier on Josh Kensington. He dropped the black folder on his desktop and gave Pelitier a good long look.

"Everything you said is in there," Maxfield pointed at the folder. "That's all academic. You really think you can predict what he'll do, based on data? Maybe we could predict your actions, but not this kid. He's a loose cannon. And under pressure, I don't even think he knows what he's gonna do."

Pelitier listened as the military man made his position perfectly clear.

"I believe your prejudice is showing," Maxfield said with a smirk. "The fact is, this is the big league, and Kensington is the top dog. He's got you by the intellectual short hairs and you can't stand it."

Pelitier's face turned red, and now that he had been backed into a corner he resorted to the only thing he had left.

"I'm still higher than you on the food chain," Pelitier said with expert calm.

The colonel huffed then turned back to the monitor and growled. "Maybe so, but I'm not the one you have to contend with. It's him, and I get the feeling this kid's just getting warmed up. Anyway, until he makes his move, there is nothing we can do. But, when he does, that's when I get to have my fun."

Pelitier glared at the old Texan, his ego still bruised.

"Just remember, this is a science facility. I built that chamber and made all the necessary improvements on the initial designs. I'm the head of research here, not you!" The colonel nodded and conceded the point.

"Of course you are but without the missing X-factor, that's not sayin' much, now is it?"

Having said his piece and salvaged his dignity, Pelitier turned and marched out of the office. Maxfield watched the man leave and smiled with satisfaction, having beaten the intellectual at his own game. Meanwhile, a light rain began to fall, and the image on his monitor became increasingly distorted as the coming storm wreaked havoc on the surveillance transmission.

Inside Josh's laboratory, the good priest ran his hand along the metal hull of the time machine. As he slowly made his way around the chamber, he studied it with eyes peering at every part, trying to take it all in.

"Is this some sort of joke? Are you telling me it actually works? You actually took a trip back in time?"

When Josh didn't respond, Father Mike stood back and gazed at the time chamber in amazement and Josh came closer. "Told you I've been busy."

"Dear Savior in Heaven." The priest stood there for a few seconds, thinking to himself, when suddenly his countenance changed. Father Mike's eyes narrowed, and he turned to face Josh. "Do you realize what you've done? This thing, this creation of yours is an abomination."

"I know, I know," Josh said, and suddenly looked at Father Mike curiously with the stark realization.

Josh smiled "You know, of all the people I've tried to explain this to, you, a priest, are the only one who gets it. " He chuckled "Ironic isn't it?"

"The humor escapes me," Father Mike said, and glared at Josh, who just smiled. "Wipe that silly look off your face and listen! This machine must be destroyed. Whether you like it or not, there is no possible way you can use this thing. Do you understand? There is no alternative. You cannot be allowed to tamper with the passage of time and what has transpired before us."

"I know."

Father Mike looked with surprise.

"I know," Josh said. "It's what I've been saying all along."

"Oh." Father Mike said. He hadn't expected that response but was clearly relieved.

"Well, that's good. I thought for sure you were going to tell me..." The father paused again and the look of concern came back like a slingshot. "Saying all along to whom? Who else knows about this?"

Anyone who had ever read a newspaper knew the name "Lewis Colter."

Father Mike tried to contain the flood of emotions that instantly came over him at the mention of the name. "Lewis Colter," he repeated, and fixed his eyes on the young man, hoping beyond hope that there was some mistake.

"It's worse than you think," Josh said.

"How can it be worse? He's only one of the most powerful men on the planet."

"They have their own version of the machine," Josh said, and tried not to look the priest in the eye until he absolutely had to.

"Mother of God," Mike whispered to himself.

"I saw it today for the first time. They duplicated everything and stole it right out from under me. Believe me, I had no idea."

The priest paced slowly and seemed to study the time machine as Josh continued.

"The good thing is, their machine doesn't work. They've gone through all of the primary launch stages and even opened a time window, but they haven't been able to make the jump. They're still missing something and they want me to figure it out."

"You can't!" Father Mike shouted.

"I know! Don't worry! There's no way they can get me to help them. I'll never do it. No matter what."

Josh paused to think. It was the "no matter what" part that made him worry.

"Good," Father Mike said. "I would hope not."

"Still, even without me, I'm guessing it's only a matter of time before they figure it out on their own. And when they do... they'll use it to change the course of history.

The priest looked at the golden time chamber, glistening in the stillness of the laboratory and whispered to himself, "the wisdom of man."

"What's that?" Josh said.

Father Mike glanced over at him. "I was just thinking aloud," he said. "The wisdom of man."

Josh could see the sermon coming and was about to beg for mercy, when Father Mike cleared his throat.

"The Bible says the wisdom of man is foolishness. This machine of yours is a discovery of monumental proportion. But look where it's brought you, to the brink of disaster. You're playing with God's creation."

Josh smiled at the comment. "God, oh yes, of course God. Well, my religious friend, I fail to see what God has to do with it, but leave it to you to somehow work Him into this."

Father Mike looked at Josh somewhat amused.

"Well what would you call time, exactly, an invention of man?"

Josh opened his mouth to answer, but Father Mike knew better than to give him an opening and just continued.

"Yes, I know about all of your theories which amount to nothing more than human guess work. But I'm not interested in guesswork. I'm talking about time itself, eternal, unchanging time. What is it, why is it? You don't know, do you?"

Josh opened his mouth and Father Mike simply kept going.

"It's an eternal mystery, God's creation, Josh. Time, space, everything. And here you are, in your folly, tinkering with God's handiwork, like a child, looking down the barrel of a loaded gun. The thought of it terrifies me."

Josh looked away, disgusted. "Thanks. Your confidence is underwhelming."

Father Mike turned to the time machine and seemed to think aloud. "But what puzzles me is, why did he allow you to create it in the first place?"

"Who? Colter?"

"No, God," Father Mike said, still peering at the time machine.

"Of course," Josh replied and looked at his watch.

"Do you get what I'm saying?" The priest turned and looked at him in earnest. "He knew you would do it. But what possible good could this serve?" Father Mike looked to the time machine once more, as though searching for the answer, lost in his thoughts.

"I suppose some things are not for us to know, things beyond our view, beyond our human limitations."

Josh stood by, observing his friend, staring off in deep thought.

"The eternal mystery?" Josh said mockingly, which was enough to snap Mike out of his trance.

"Both of the machines, this one and the one in Colter's possession have to be destroyed," Mike said, sounding more like a general than a priest. Josh waited and listened, but the priest just stared.

"Fine, destroy them. Destroy them, how?" Josh said, probing for more information.

Father Mike looked at him in all seriousness.

"As a kid you were always trying to make things explode. You're the genius. You think of something."

Josh looked at the lofty minded priest like he was patently insane. "WHAT? Are you listening to yourself? Who are you, the Pope or Stalin? I can't tell. Let me get this straight. You want me to just walk into that high security lab, that's tighter than Fort Knox and blow it up. Do you hear what you're saying? You're a priest, and you're telling me to go blow up a building! Get a grip on yourself."

Father Mike didn't even flinch.

"Josh, what would happen if these people actually do use your invention to alter the past?"

Josh shifted gears for the moment in an attempt to indulge the priest and slowly considered the significance and magnitude of the question.

"I don't know for sure. Nobody knows since it's never happened, but in theory any alteration of the past would have an effect. Even the slightest change, even ones seemingly insignificant would result in a ripple effect that would go on and on effecting generations, changing history. These changes while beneficial for some could be potentially catastrophic for others, causing a global reality shift that would replace everything we see and know right now... and the spooky thing is that not one living soul would ever even know the difference."

Josh stared blankly, pondering his own words as Father Mike turned away and headed for the elevator.

"Well?" Josh shouted. "Aren't you supposed to help me? Give me counsel?

Father Mike stood by the elevator and pressed the button.

"I don't know what to tell you, Josh. I'll pray that God gives you some insight. After all, you created the wretched thing. God forbid anyone should ever use it. If they do, you may wish you had blown it up."

The elevator arrived, and Father Mike stepped inside then paused before he slid the wrought iron gate shut.

"Oh, I almost forgot. I saw your dad."

Josh remained still with the same blank stare, as though the words meant nothing.

"He's not doing well. I think you should call him."

The priest waited, making it clear he wasn't leaving until he got an answer.

"Hey, he's a big boy. I got enough to worry about," Josh said and meant it.

Father Mike let the door go and called out as the elevator began its slow descent.

"That's amazing. When I spoke to him, he said the same thing about you. It's been a long time Josh."

Josh maintained his game face even after the priest was gone and the man's voice echoed up the elevator shaft.

"Call him."

CHAPTER 6

The next day the freight elevator door opened slowly to reveal the gray gun metal, BMW roadster parked on the lift of the freight elevator. Josh turned on his CD player. A heavy drum beat and rock guitar riff pumped through the interior of the car. Josh fastened his seat belt, adjusted his shades and lowered the car visor against the sunlight as the freight door rose to the ceiling and light flooded into the lift.

Normally, from his vantage point behind the steering wheel, the only view Josh saw was the alleyway and the cobblestone drive. However today, as the door rose two long legs waited patiently just beyond the door and stood poised in high heels, a full length mohair coat that was open and flowing in the autumn breeze, and a designer dress that was just the right length to make any man smile.

With the woofers pumping, and the base beat thumping, the beautiful KC Maltese looked like a rock star's dream, standing in the sun-drenched alley. KC held her pose with a hand on her hip while Josh stared out from behind the wheel of the BMW, grinning like a school boy. Then when he had gotten an eye full, she moved to the driver side. Josh rolled the car forward and lowered the power window and shamelessly hung his head out to look her up and down. It was a gesture that she didn't discourage and decided to tolerate for the moment. When Josh finally turned the music down, he took off his shades and gazed up at her.

"Look this is getting embarrassing," he said. "You gotta get a life. The neighbors are starting to talk."

KC glanced around her.

"Neighbors? All I saw were rats with guns."

Josh glanced up and down the alley.

"Yeah, it's a tough neighborhood. So, were you dumpin' a body or just making a drug deal?"

"We need to talk," KC said.

Josh paused and looked surprised.

"Need to talk? Are we breaking up? I didn't know we were even dating!"

KC ignored the attempt at humor.

"It's about what happened yesterday," she said. "I need to set a couple of things straight."

Josh sat there thinking it over while KC stood next to the car, waiting for an answer. The engine hummed as Josh turned up the volume and the rock music thumped louder. Slowly Josh's expression changed, now that the woman was standing in front of him and acting considerably nicer.

"I'm on my way somewhere," Josh said. "Want to go for a ride?"

KC rounded the front of the vehicle to the predatory beat of the music as though it was her own private theme and Josh watched her all the way. She climbed into the car, shut the door and settled into the passenger seat next to him. Josh grinned, "Do it again."

KC flashed a smile, "Drive."

The BMW rolled out of the alley. With a press of a button, the freight elevator door closed behind them, and the car pulled away.

Five minutes later they were headed downtown on the west side expressway. Josh watched the road as KC did all the talking.

"I just wanted you to know that I wasn't a party to what happened yesterday. My job was to bring you to the lab, that's all. I thought you were coming to inspect the facility. I had no idea they were going to spring that on you. I thought you knew all about the project. I mean, it is yours after all."

Josh glanced over at her and nodded. It was clear she was being sincere. He could hear it in her voice. Yesterday, she had so been angry and combative; he couldn't get close to her. Today she was sweet and apologetic and he liked the change in spite of everything else that had happened.

"I know you don't believe me," she said. "And I don't blame you. I probably wouldn't believe it either. But I couldn't stop thinking about it and wanted to let you know that I had nothing to do with it. I just thought you should know."

Josh stared straight ahead and offered no response. KC turned away, to look out the passenger window. Josh glanced over and checked what she was doing and smiled when she wasn't looking. When KC turned around Josh was frowning again to keep her on the hook.

"Look, it's not just that. There's something else."

Josh glanced over again. This was working out better than he had expected.

"Something you said yesterday started me thinking. You said the machine was like Pandora's Box."

"Yeah, that's right," Josh recalled. "Do you know the story?"

KC leaned in toward him as she spoke.

"I get the basic idea. The girl Pandora opened a box and released something terrible into the world. According to Webster's dictionary, Pandora's Box is, 'a prolific source of trouble, or evil.' So I gather, you think the machine is evil."

Josh considered the question. "I was just trying to make a point. To be evil, there must be an intellect, rationale, a self awareness. We're talking about a machine. No, the machine's not evil. But I would say it's dangerous. Extremely dangerous."

Josh glanced over at her a few more times as she thought about his answer.

"Speaking of evil," Josh said. "What do you think of your boss?"

KC was momentarily taken aback.

"Mr. Colter? I don't really get to see him that much. I work mostly with Ms. Danners."

"Oh yeah? She's nice," Josh said.

KC paused to address the obvious implication that Colter was evil.

"I think Mr. Colter is very professional, a great leader, and an inspiration to work for."

Josh nodded with a smirk, "I used to think the same thing, but I can assure you that his loyalties are to himself. He's not what you think." Josh gave it some thought as he stared at the road ahead. "Or maybe it's your loyalties we should be discussing. So are you working on Colter's personal staff? Is that it? Is that what's going on?"

Josh looked over and smiled wickedly at the sexual innuendo then watched as she suddenly glared at him in rage.

"You're a pig! You think that because you're some kind of big shot, you can say anything you want but I'm not afraid of you! I don't have to take this. Stop the car. I have other things to do besides sit here and listen to your –"

"All right, all right! I'm sorry. You're right! You're right, that was out of line," Josh said.

"Way out of line!" KC said.

"Way outta line!" Josh said with conviction, and could have kicked himself for ruining the moment.

KC looked away, still fuming then turned back sharply. "And just so you know, I still think Mr. Colter is a great man, a class act and better than you!" She said it with self assured determination and punctuated it with a deft flick of her head. Before Josh knew it, his mouth was working and the words were coming out.

"I may be a pig, but your boss is an ass and you're a fool for not seeing it," Josh said, and couldn't resist. He said it without even looking and decided that if things were going to hell, he might as well throw in the handbag.

KC's mouth dropped open. Suddenly he was the same obstinate, ill mannered, self-absorbed, idiot she had the extreme displeasure of meeting the day before.

"Oh really?" KC said and would have rolled up her sleeves if she weren't wearing a coat.

"And you think that everybody's supposed to fall down at your feet because of your so-called intellect, but you're nothing more that a spoiled self-centered little Prima Dona who got mad because Colter stood up to you," she said, hoping that it hurt.

"HAH! Who're you callin' little?" Josh jeered and gripped the steering wheel like he would choke it. "Yeah, that's it. The fact that Colter and his elite group of Neo-fascists are planning to take over the world has nothing to do with it."

KC stared at him blankly.

"You know they said you were crazy, and now I know they were right."

Josh looked over, a little surprised.

"Yesterday I was brilliant. Who said I'm crazy?"

"Ms. Danners," KC said and smiled.

Josh nodded and kept driving. "Huh? You think you know some people," he grumbled. "Anyway, Colter is not what he seems, and I wouldn't trust him if I were you. That's all I'm saying."

KC looked away sharply and stared out the window. Then a few moments later, turned back with equal vigor. "Why not?" she demanded.

Josh checked his mirror and took the next exit.

"You have a pretty high level security clearance, don't you?"

KC shrugged. "So?"

Josh turned onto a secondary road and continued south.

"How high? High enough to know what this project is all about? I didn't think so. But you do know that they duplicated my invention, which is at the center of the project. And yesterday at the lab, you overheard that the device is capable of time travel.

Now you know more than Colter wants you to. I'd start sleeping with a gun under my pillow, if I were you."

KC smiled at the absurdity of his claim.

"You have got to be the most paranoid person I have ever met. I'm sure Mr. Colter and Dr. Pelitier are not out to get you or anyone else. I assure you they have everything under control."

Josh watched the road and grinned.

"Forgive me if I don't share your enthusiasm, but you see, it's not the control part I'm worried about. It's the intent. Colter and his gang think they can use the machine to make the present a better place. Do you know how they intend to do it?"

KC just listened.

"What they're probably doing is compiling a list, a list of people they want to wipe out, erase, eradicate, expunge from history to essentially change the course of history itself. Then basically, using the time chamber, they're going to send assassins traveling through time to find those people, them kill and pray for the right outcome. Don't get me wrong. I'd like to whack the scumbags myself, if it were that simple. But it's not. I know it's not. Innocent people will die as a result. It's unavoidable yet Colter is determined to go forward." He looked at the street signs along the road. "So what do you think of your boss now? Quite the humanitarian."

KC thought for a moment and stumbled over her words.

"Are... are we talking about, about real time travel?"

Josh looked at her incredulously.

"What do you think? I'm joking? Yes! Yes! Real time travel in a real time machine!"

"All right! Okay, I'm sorry!" KC yelled in her defense. "I thought it was some kind of jargon, you know like, time line? Time frame? Time-share? How was I supposed to know?"

The two of them rode along silently, trying to calm down. KC finally turned to Josh and had to ask. "People like who?" she said.

Josh glanced over at her.

"John Wilkes Booth for one, I know they were looking at Lincoln's assassin for starters. But don't stop there. Just think of any bad guy you can imagine in history and put a bullseye on his forehead. It doesn't matter. I understand what they intend to do, and theoretically it is a noble idea. But this isn't theory anymore. My machine has made the impossible, possible. And if they use it, what will actually happen, I believe will be a cataclysmic disaster beyond belief."

KC could feel her pulse begin to quicken but forced herself to remain calm. "How do you know? How can you be so sure?"

Josh slowed and turned down a deserted back road.

"Logic." Josh said.

The wheels of the BMW kicked up a cloud of dirt along a deserted road. KC looked at him, hating him for being so smart. She needed him to be wrong just this once.

"I don't care about, logic. Suppose they go back and save the Titanic, prevent the bombing of Pearl Harbor or Hiroshima, stop murderers like Jack the Ripper or the Boston Strangler from ever being born. Think of all the lives that would be spared, all the pain and suffering that could be avoided. What's wrong with that?"

Josh slammed on the brake and KC grabbed the dash as the car lurched to a halt, her eyes staring wide. Josh turned to her sharply.

"Like it or not, we are all a product of both the triumphs and failures, yes even the horrors of the past. Every birth, every death, every holocaust, every victory, for better or worse, has all resulted in our existence the way it is today. You start screwing around with that, with one piece of the puzzle and everything changes everything. Get it?"

KC glared back at him.

"No. I don't! I just think you're afraid."

"That's right. I am afraid," Josh said and leaned in close to make the point. "and you should be too."

With that he sat back and put the car in gear. KC looked at him and then turned to look out the window. The car rolled along with little more than trees and an occasional mailbox to mark the way, and suddenly KC realized she had no idea where they were.

"Where are we?" she asked, trying to keep some of the worry out of her voice.

Josh glanced over with a look of regret.

"Oh yeah. I guess I should have warned you."

KC gathered her courage. "Warn me about what?" she said as a little more fear crept in.

"Warned you about where we're going," Josh said.

KC narrowed her eyes as Josh's smile turned into a grin.

"So, you like fish?" he asked.

Soon the road opened up on one side, and the BMW drove along a waterfront pier, rumbling over weather worn planks. There was the smell of the ocean in the salty air as they approached a seaside harbor and loading dock. A long row of old green warehouses stood along the waterfront, with boats docked behind the buildings and trucks waiting at loading bays on the roadside.

It was ten o'clock, and men hauled crates of fish from the boats into the refrigerated warehouses while out front forklifts loaded trucks for shipment and delivery. The shining BMW rolled along the docks, moving past tough blue-collar rough necks. Many of the men, young and old, hardly looked up as he cruised by. The sleek BMW pulled up to the front office, which was little more than a shack attached to the front of an old warehouse. The weathered sign above the door read T-REL Shipping.

Josh parked the seventy thousand dollar Beamer next to an old blue pick-up. Aside from a few sideway glances, no one acknowledged the vehicle. Expensive cars weren't that unusual around the docks and workers learned it was best not to know what characters were going in and out of the front office. The only thing that impressed the cigar smoking, tobacco chewing, chin scratching rough necks was a fat check, and a good beer. Aside from hauling crates, cussing and the occasional brawl, it was life as usual on the docks, until the pair of million dollar legs stepped out of the BMW. It was then that ribs got poked, all eyes turned. A forklift driver plowed straight through an empty shipping crate. Another man, distracted by KC's presence and ignorant of the fact the truck he intended to load had driven away, walked right off the loading dock. Fortunately, his fall was broken by the box of fish he was carrying.

Josh got out of the BMW and, for all intents and purposes, was totally invisible. The gorgeous blonde eclipsed everything in sight and seemed to move in slow motion as she strode like a cat to the growing chorus of wolf whistles and cat calls.

KC tossed her shoulder length hair, and one man cried out in mock agony, "Oh, murder!" Another hooligan snatched the hat off of the ruffian next to him and crumpled the cap in his fists. While across the street a small mob gathered around while a man stomped his foot and snorted like a horse.

Josh did his best to ignore the commotion and kept moving toward the front office door when it swung open and a big man filled the doorway, smiling broadly. Toller Gapinski had been the assistant foreman for as long as Josh could remember, and everyone called him Ski. Josh smiled like a kid.

At sixty-three years of age, Ski was strong as a bull, and hardly slowed by age.

"Well, well, well, as I live and breathe!" Ski said in his booming baritone with his eyes riveted on the beautiful blonde coming towards him. "I am still breathing, aren't I?" he said,

"Hello, Ski. It's been a long time," Josh said with a grin.

"It surely has. It surely has," Ski said, and marched straight past Josh to greet the blonde.

Josh smiled, "It's good to see you too."

The big man approached with total respect and reverence as he reached out with a dreamy look in his eyes and a gentle lilt in his voice and shook KC's hand. "Praise God! The good Lord has smiled down and seen fit to bring me an angel."

Josh rolled his eyes.

"KC, this is Toller Gapinski," he said quickly as if to move the ceremonies along.

The big man bowed somewhat, "Ski, m' dear. Call me Ski."

"Hello," KC said, and smiled warmly, her hands practically swallowed up by Ski's big leathery mitts.

"A pleasure, ma'am. A real pleasure," Ski said, and continued to shake her hand, refusing to let go.

"Is Flynn around?" Josh said, trying to act casual. He walked over and pried KC's hand out of the gorilla's mitts.

"All right, all right. Hands off," he said, and cleverly used the occasion to hold KC's hand, presumably to protect her from the wolves. It was a gesture KC permitted for the time being. Josh reveled in the moment of being the envy of every man there, both young and old.

Ski shook his head in disappointment.

"Why a nice girl like you is hangin' around a bum like this I'll never know. He doesn't deserve ya' and he's not givin' you any trouble I hope. Is he?"

KC decided to have a little fun. "As a matter of fact –"

"Nah, nah, never mind all that!" Josh interrupted. "Is Flynn here?" he asked again, a little more forcefully.

"Inside through the office, straight back," Ski said.

"Thanks." With that Josh made his way past the big man and KC trotted along behind Josh who rushed forward, anxious to get the girl out of plain sight.

"Nice meeting you," KC said, and waved to the big foreman. Ski watched the girl till the door closed behind her.

"Oh, to be young again," he said then sighed and looked around to see all the fellow rough necks staring.

"WELL!? What are ya' gawkin' at? Get back to work!" Ski yelled out in his typical booming voice and all the men did just that.

Inside was a small office with a desk, some file cabinets, a coffee pot and a few girly posters on the walls. Four laborers lounged around the coffee maker and stared blankly as Josh and KC passed through the office and went out the back door, leading to the warehouse. KC smiled politely on her way out, which caused the men to stand up and huddle together, drawn to the middle of the room like so much paper caught up in her wake.

Inside the warehouse was more of the same, only a hundred times worse. The place was filled with men cleaning fish, men weighing fish, men packing fish, and men freezing fish. When the girl entered the scene changed to men seeing the woman, men pointing at the woman, men shoving other men aside to see the woman, and men hooting at the woman. The center aisle of the warehouse was ninety feet long and with such a captive audience, KC slipped her hand away from Josh who looked back as if to say, "Suit yourself."

The woman had done some runway work on Seventh Avenue. It was years ago, but the designers loved her because she was good at it. It was simply a matter of putting one foot directly in front of the other, giving a quarter turn more, pivot on the balls of her feet to add just the right amount of swish to the hips. Then with the right bounce and attitude, a girl could bring down the house.

Then with a spot light provided by the Skylight above, the woman "worked the walk," and strode from one pool of light to another, amidst whistles and spontaneous applause. By the time she reached the swinging doors at the other end of the warehouse, the rough necks were on their feet and cheering.

Josh, on the other hand, looked bored as he held the door open for KC, who eventually strutted past to the applause of fifty screaming men.

"I still got it," KC said, and winked on the way by.

Josh rolled his eyes, "Yeah, yeah, yeah. Just keep 'it' moving."

The annoyed smirk on his face was an act and KC knew it as he closed the door behind them. The two entered a narrow hallway, and continued to the back of the warehouse in search of the foreman's office. KC's heels click-clacked against the dusty wood floors as they made their way down the hall. She was suddenly all business once again and remembered the name Josh had mentioned. "So who's Flynn?"

"A dog," Josh said as they strode down the hall.

"We came to see a dog?"

Josh kept moving and called back over his shoulder.

"Flynn was Ski's Pit Bull, years ago, a real scrapper. Ski loved that dog. When it died, he met my dad. My dad loved to fight, mix it up in bars, that kind of stuff, so he started calling my dad Flynn. The name stuck."

Suddenly KC's countenance changed.

"We're here to see your dad."

"Yeah, my dad, Marcel. He hates that name. Really gets under his skin. So make sure you call him Flynn, okay?" Josh smiled for reassurance.

KC nodded. "All right," she said. "That's easy enough. Who would name a child Marcel?"

The two entered another large storage room at the back of the warehouse. A lone desk strewn with papers sat up front while rows of shelves, lined with machine parts, and stacks of wooden skids, disappeared into a dark and depressing void behind it.

Somewhere in the background, the sound of an engine roared to life. Josh and KC listened as a forklift slowly drove out of the darkness. Mounted on the front were two huge wooden crates. The forklift approached slowly. When it reached the end of the aisle, it turned and gave them a clear view of the driver.

The man behind the wheel was a foreboding sight. His face was tanned and deeply etched with lines, like leather, worn by sun and age. He was a large man, not as big as Ski, but his broad shoulders, thick arms and broken nose gave him the look of a brawler.

At fifty-nine, Flynn was a hard-nosed fowl-tempered man, who glared with a permanent scowl that said, "I take no crap from anyone."

KC froze as the man looked her up and down. His gaze pierced right through her, and it was clear he was unimpressed. His gaze shifted to Josh and the two men locked eyes. But Josh, who had been prepared for this moment, neither flinched nor blinked as a slow and wicked smile crept across his face.

"Hey, Marcel," Josh said casually. "How's it goin'?"

KC looked at Josh and tried to conceal her shock, as the name echoed among the shelves of the storage room, and Flynn glared like a caged animal that had been poked with a stick.

Slowly his normal scowl returned and he narrowed his eyes at the young man standing before him.

"Screw you, kid," he said and shut off the forklift engine. "What do you want? What are you doin' here?"

Josh raised his hands. "Hey, it wasn't my idea. Mike said you weren't feeling good."

Flynn banged the dashboard of the forklift with an open hand, and still managed to rock the machine.

"You tell 'im to mind his own business, and keep his charity to himself."

Josh nodded at the simple request; one he would be happy to deliver.

The old man moved out from behind the steering wheel and climbed down from the lift. He moved slowly as if in pain before grabbing and holding the side of the forklift to rest and catch his breath.

"You look like hell," Josh said.

Flynn huffed and smirked through the pain.

"What? Are you some kinda doctor now?" he said, with a gurgled laugh that quickly turned into a wet hacking cough.

"Why? You need one?" Josh said with a little less sarcasm as he watched the man's ailing condition. Flynn stifled the cough then wiped his mouth with his sleeve and glared at the young woman who was watching him intently. It was all KC could do not to take a step back now that his eyes were fixed on her, "Who's this? One of your floozies?"

Suddenly any pity she had for the man left her and she took an instant dislike to him. Josh shrugged off the comment, knowing the insult was only his father's attempt to deflect attention from himself.

"Nice try," Josh said. "I called the hospital. Your doctor gave me the rundown on your condition. I gotta tell you, sounds serious. If you were a horse I wouldn't bet on ya'."

As angry as she was at the old man, KC turned to stare at Josh.

"So how long do they give you?" Josh asked and almost smiled.

A glimmer of rage brewed behind the old man's eyes. Then the icy cool exterior returned.

"You mean till I'm dead? What do you care? You come to gloat?"

It was an opening Josh couldn't resist and this time Josh did smile. "The thought did cross my mind," he said.

Flynn and Josh stared each other down a few more seconds and the old man turned away to unload the boxes from the forklift.

"Suit yourself. I'm too tired to care."

Flynn hefted one of the boxes and showed the strain in his voice. "If I stay away from the booze, six months to a year," he said then dropped the box on the floor and went back for another.

KC watched him repeat the same ritual then looked at Josh who gave no sign of helping. After another box, Flynn paused to lean against the forklift, and looked spent. But before KC could breathe a sigh of relief, the old man reached into his back pocket and pulled out a fifth of Scotch. Josh and KC watched him unscrew the cap, take a shot, grimace in pain then twist the cap back on and tuck it away.

"I'd say two, maybe three months tops," he said and coughed again. Soon the man was bent over and hacking away then backed up to grab hold of the forklift for balance. KC flinched as the man convulsed and when she had seen enough, she looked away to give the old man his privacy. Soon the horrible fit was over, and Flynn wiped his mouth once more. He glanced up at the two onlookers and seemed a little embarrassed, but only for a second. The next instant he was headed for his desk, which was littered with paper, old cigarette packs and coffee cups.

"All things considered, I think I'm doin' pretty good," Flynn said, searching for a cigarette among the litter.

Josh gave his typical smirk.

"Yeah, you're a regular boy scout."

"Spare me," Flynn said, preoccupied with his search as Josh took a few steps toward the table, determined to unload on the old man.

"Spare you? Don't tell me you're feeling pain. Not you, Mister 'no guts no glory' Flynn. For a while there I used to think you weren't even human. I remember mom used to patch you up pretty good after your drunken brawls. Friday nights it was mom, you, and a basin of blood. Spare you? You could have spared mom. It would have been nice to see her smile just once before she died. What the hell she ever saw in you I'll never know."

Flynn stopped shuffling through the papers long enough to shoot a look at Josh.

"Watch your mouth, boy."

"I'd rather watch you croak," Josh snarled.

It was a comment that made everything stand still as Josh stared at his dad. Flynn glared back and KC watched them both. Now that Josh had revealed his true hatred, the rest of it came pouring out.

"You know what's funny? You put me through a wall eight times, fractured my jaw twice, and used me like a punching bag. You were so tough beating up on a little kid. All those years you had me fooled. The fact is, mom was the tough one. She's the one who had to put up with your crap, day in and day out."

Flynn stood up straight, eyes level with Josh.

"Shut your mouth, before I shut it for you." The man's voice was low and threatening.

KC sensing the worst, tried to grab Josh's arm. "Josh, we should go now."

Josh pulled away and advanced on the old man. "She had to listen to your threats and clean up your slop after you finished pukin'. Sometimes both at the same time."

"Shut up!" Flynn said and balled his fist.

KC looked back and forth at the two men on a collision course.

"You wore her down until she couldn't take it anymore, you and all the garbage you dumped on her. You killed her. Now you gotta live with it and it's eating you alive."

"Shut your face!" Flynn yelled and swept some of the paper off of his desk.

Josh only glared as Flynn rounded the table, fists clenched then lunged, swinging wildly. Josh leaned away and easily slipped the looping right hand, then left the rest to inertia and gravity. The big man swatted the air, and the momentum of the missed punch carried Flynn to the floor, with a dull thud. He laid there face down in the dirt and dust then rolled onto his side with a grunt, and brought his arms down until he was clutching his abdomen.

Josh glared down to gloat over the old man in his agony.

"It was mom and her God till her dying day. You never broke her spirit, though God knows you tried. Now it's your turn, old man. And both you and I know it's not the booze that's killing you. It's the guilt and you've earned every agonizing bit of it... See you around, Marcel."

Flynn tried to look up, red faced and straining against the pain as Josh turned to leave and walked past KC.

"You're not going to leave him like that," she said.

Josh glanced back.

"He's fine," he said.

KC looked into his eyes and could hardly believe the man on the floor was Josh's father. Flynn mustered the strength to point and yell, "GET OUT! Both of you!"

KC watched in horror as a line of blood trailed down from the corner of the old man's mouth.

"He needs medical attention!" KC said, then fumbled around in her coat pocket and pulled out her cell phone. One look at the read out and she turned to Josh for help.

"Oh damn! I've got no signal."

Josh made a show of patting down his pockets. "I left mine in the car," he said with a shrug.

KC wasted no time and turned away screaming, with her voice echoing in the dark as she ran for help. A few seconds later Josh smiled and couldn't have looked more pleased as several workers rushed past, on their way to assist the old man, groveling on the floor in the back room of a dark and dinghy warehouse.

Once they were outside Josh headed back to the car as pleased as if he had delivered flowers to the old man, while KC stormed along behind him. Several packers nearby observed the couple and paused to listen.

"You are an undeniable bastard! You know that?" KC yelled as they arrived at the car. The onlookers smirked and murmured.

"Looks like trouble in paradise," one man called out.

KC rounded on him and glared, "Shut up!"

The man looked at his buddy sheepishly, and they all nodded in agreement. There was indeed trouble.

The ride in the car was long and awkward. Josh stared at the road and glanced over, every so often to see KC looking out her window. The world outside was bright and full of color, while the mood in the car was dark and dismal. There was nothing to say and the longer he drove the more Josh realized how horrible it all must have been for KC. She had seen him at his absolute worst and now she hated him. *She knows me now. I'm just like my old man, a mean angry bastard.*

He wanted to say he was sorry, that he couldn't help himself, or that he wouldn't do it again. But the truth was he wasn't sorry. And if he could, he would do it all again, the exact same way. Josh stared straight ahead and frowned into the distance. "Yep, a mean, cruel heartless bastard, just like your old man," Josh scoffed to himself and kept his eyes on the road.

"People make mistakes, you know." The woman's voice was a surprise and Josh wanted to remain calm since he had already made a fool of himself at the warehouse, but again the words came out and he was powerless to stop them.

"That's all he ever did, one mistake after another, the all time king of screw ups."

KC had been secretly curious about the life of this so-called "genius" after reading his dossier and the accomplishments of a brilliant mind. But what she saw today told her much more. She wanted to know what made him tick and now that she was finding out, her curiosity was replaced by a shameful nameless dread. The truth was she had no right to know. He was a real person with a real past, a tortured past that haunted him to this day. Nothing was what she expected, and now that he was starting to open up, she was afraid to hear anymore.

"I was fourteen when my mom died. I remember, because she bought me this watch. My dad gave it to me at the hospital, said she wanted me to have it."

KC glanced down at the old timepiece.

"I could tell he'd been drinking. Anyway, when I went in and saw her. She was already dead. I remember I hardly recognized her. My mom was barely forty when she died. It was the face of a sad old woman. The person I knew was gone. It was like the spark that had kept her alive had taken everything, her youth, her beauty, and left a cold, tortured empty shell."

Josh stared at the road, not sure why he was unloading all of his baggage on someone who was a virtual stranger. Still he kept talking, and KC listened to it all as he shared his pain.

"Once times got tough, he started drinking and things got worse. He hated her. He hated me. He hated the whole world and everything in it and made our lives a living hell."

As KC watched and listened she could see the real tragedy. At twenty-five Josh was still that little boy, stuck in a dark place, held captive by his own father who he loathed with every ounce of his being for what he had done to his mother. KC tried not to think of it.

"Do you have any good memories?" she asked.

Josh gave it some thought. "Can't say that I do."

KC gave a weak smile, trying not to let her pity show through.

"My mom was a religious woman, a Catholic," Josh said and sounded more hopeful, "A devout Catholic who read her Bible and believed in the sanctity of marriage. But my dad made it clear early on, he didn't believe in much of anything. He humiliated her. He would hang out in bars, get drunk, fight, sometimes even brought women home; did what he did with them then kicked them out late at night. My mom pretended she didn't know. But I'd hear her crying.

"Your poor mother," KC said and felt her own hatred growing as Josh continued.

"Sundays she took me to church even though he was against it. He said church was full of crap and he didn't want that stuff shoved down my throat. That's when he started beating me pretty regular just to punish her. He'd put on these black leather gloves he wore at the docks, so he wouldn't bruise his hands. I must have been ten or twelve. Gotta say it toughened me up. I can still smell the leather when he'd slap me across the face and the taste of my own blood."

KC winced at the thought.

"So after a while that was that. She stopped taking me, but she kept going herself and he hated her for it. He hated her till she was miserable and alone. Hated her till her dying day." Josh let the thought linger till it weighted heavy on them both.

KC could see the woman's body, the cold room, the cold sheet, and the face of her husband staring down at her, the man responsible for her life of misery. He was a monster in every sense of the word, but worst of all, there was no one left who stood between him and the little boy. KC stared at Josh then turned to watch the road as she tried to pull herself away from the nightmare. She took a breath and when she was able to think properly, she could see how useless it was, hatred for a man who was probably about to die a very painful and lonely death, perhaps a just and fitting punishment, beyond anything she could do to him.

Josh continued more calmly, as though he were just thinking aloud. "When I was a kid, I often wondered, why she didn't just give it up," he said, and glanced over. "The religious stuff," he added as he drove. "I mean if it made him so stinking mad. Hell, save us all the aggravation and forget about it, right?"

KC searched for something to say but there was nothing, nothing but the drone of the engine. Josh checked the rear view mirror and suddenly seemed more hopeful.

"It wasn't till after her death that it hit me. The one thing he couldn't control was her faith. It was like her only weapon against him, and she wasn't afraid to use it. She'd talk about God, right to his face. I learned to respect her for that. Anything that could hurt him was fine by me. And she was right. To hell with him."

KC watched and listened, sensing the relief in his voice. It was the closest he had come to a happy memory and it made them both smile.

"Your mother was a brave woman," KC said. "She died for something she believed in."

"Too bad she didn't die for something real," Josh said with his typical smirk.

KC frowned at the response, feeling he was missing the point.

"Well, regardless, it was still her faith that kept her alive."

"It was her faith that got her killed," Josh said bluntly and with that, KC let it drop.

Traffic merged as they entered the Holland Tunnel and headed back into Manhattan. Josh turned the headlights on as the tunnel dipped down and made its way under the river. The reflection of the tunnel lights flickered overhead and streaked across the windshield as they sped along. KC thought about the man beside her who had proven his genius to the whole world. Still she was amazed at how naive he was. In many ways he was nothing more than an impulsive kid. But after all the tragedy of his life, why shouldn't he recapture some of his youth. He certainly deserved it, and now God knows he certainly had all the toys a grown man could want.

Suddenly, sitting there in the passenger seat of the car, she had a clear picture of the man and it was nothing at all like what she expected. He was more complicated. Flawed and scarred, to be sure, but most of all he was a survivor, someone who had found a way to win against all odds. He had even been brave enough to share something intensely personal with her, something that made him vulnerable and flawed. KC listened for the warning bells and whistles that usually went off whenever she was falling for "the wrong guy", but everything was quiet.

Minutes later, the sleek BMW rose out of the tunnel into the sunlight and Josh looked over at KC who was smiling at him like she knew something he didn't. It was a smile that healed his wounds and made him feel good, at least for the time being.

Once they were through the electronic toll booth, Josh checked the cars around him as they merged into midtown Manhattan traffic, then scooted across First Avenue to catch the light, and headed cross town. When they had reached the Westside, KC decided to finally speak up.

"Listen, how about I take you out for lunch?" KC heard herself say and suddenly felt stupid, which she knew was a sure sign she liked the guy. Josh smiled at her with some surprise and was about to accept the offer as he turned the corner into his block and hit the brakes.

A police officer stood in the street with his hand out and his squad car blocking the road. Behind him a column of black smoke rose high into the air. Fire trucks and emergency vehicles blocked the streets, while a sea of blue and white patrol cars were parked haphazardly up and down the street with lights flashing.

The young policeman came around to the driver side window and looked tired, like this was the last thing he wanted to do. Josh lowered his window and the officer uttered two words.

"Warehouse fire."

The words reverberated in Josh's mind as he looked beyond the officer to the smoke filled street.

"That's my building," Josh said in a blind stupor.

The young officer looked stunned for a moment then signaled the other officers to make way. Fire hoses crisscrossed the street as Josh rolled forward and slowly made his way past squad cars and policemen. Onlookers lined the street and hung out of windows, pointing at the smoldering warehouse.

Josh pulled up to the yellow police tape and got out of his car. Broken glass crunched beneath his shoes as he gazed up at the sheets of water streaming down the red brick face of the building. Colonel Raymond Maxfield turned to see Josh approaching and several armed men in plain clothes quickly converged. One of the agents Josh recognized, the tall man with the oily black hair, slicked back and glistening in the sunlight. He smiled with cold steely eyes and this time, instead of reaching for his gun, Josh felt the hand on his chest, which was more of a stiff arm, bordering on a shove that stopped him in his tracks. The agent, Vega looked Josh in the eye.

"This is as far as you go," he said with a twisted smirk.

KC came up next to Josh and the agent looked at her with a long lurid stare. Josh knocked the agent's hand aside, which snapped the man's attention back to him and suddenly the two were nearly nose-to-nose. Just then, someone called out from over the man's shoulder.

"Vega! Stand down."

Additional agents gathered around and in a matter of seconds, they were surrounded by members of Colter's secret security force. Vega glared and the twisted smile returned and as the agent stepped aside, Josh caught sight of the large metal doors at the front of his building, which were blown out as if hit by a tank shell. Just then a stream of men exited the blackened, charred entrance. Among them were Simon Pelitier and Carl Grasso. Josh quickly turned to KC and glared at her, his rage growing before her eyes.

KC just peered back innocently, completely taken by surprise. She looked at the building and the look on his face and instantly knew what he was thinking. Whether intentional or not, it was the second time she had felt used by Lewis Colter. And this time was worse than before.

"I didn't know! I swear!"

Josh turned away before she could finish, as though her words were only salt in the wound.

"You know what I hate about the city, Josh?" The voice bellowed with a heavy Texas drawl. The burly, Colonel Maxfield approached, cool and confident.

"The buildings, it's the buildings," he said with a sweeping gesture of his hand." On a beautiful day like this, the sun's shining bright and we're all standin' in the shade. That can't be good for ya'. Gotta have the sun on my face. Makes me feel alive."

Josh didn't bother to acknowledge the opening statement and only nodded in KC's direction. "You put her up to this?" Josh said.

Maxfield glanced at KC and looked genuinely confused. "Beg your pardon?"

"What do you want, colonel?"

"Oh we got what we wanted. We just needed a closer look at your prototype, well what's left of it. Sorry about the door. We looked under the mat but there wasn't a key," he said, trying to look sincere.

Simon Pelitier arrived a moment later, ready to grab the dagger and twist it with a smile. Pelitier was practically aglow, while Grasso walked behind, head down, and almost looked aggravated. One glance and Josh could tell that the man had been wrestling with his conscience and had clearly lost the match. Pelitier came up beside Maxfield, gleaming like he had just found his present under the tree.

"A mirror?" Pelitier chided and clapped his hands together. "The reflective base of the pod. Is that all? That's what we missed? A mirror? It can't be that simple."

"It's not," Josh said.

Pelitier watched and waited, but that was all the information he would get.

"Regardless, now that we have the means, we will proceed, with or without you."

"It's your funeral," Josh said, with the best poker face he could muster as the remnants of his work billowed from the upper floors of the warehouse in plumes of thick, black smoke.

Grasso came forward and stood next to Josh, trying to speak confidentially as Josh stared past him. "I tried to warn you. None of this would have happened if you had just cooperated. Colter still wants you on board. These guys still need you as an advisor. Now c'mon, be smart about this. Do the right thing."

With agents glaring, Grasso and the colonel looking on, and Pelitier gloating in his face, Josh seemed oblivious to the world around him, and started toward the smoldering remains of his building. "Who's gonna fix my door?"

Grasso gritted his teeth then slapped his leg, like he had lost a bundle at Vegas.

"I don't get you!" Grasso blared. "If the damn thing's so dangerous, why don't you help?"

Simon Pelitier huffed and spoke as though Josh were somewhere else.

"We're wasting time. We don't need him."

With that Pelitier and the colonel turned to leave and the agents went with them. But unable to take no for an answer Grasso ran up to Josh, grabbed him by the arm and looked him in the eye.

"You and I both know he's wrong," Grasso said, and looked around to make sure no one had heard.

"Then why don't you stop him?" Josh said.

Grasso arched an eyebrow, "Why don't you?"

Grasso walked away and Josh turned to watch him go. When he did, he saw KC standing at a distance, patiently waiting with her hands clasped in front of her and eyes pleading.

"I'm so sorry!" she said in a silent whisper. As beautiful as she was, standing on the wet pavement, among the fire hoses with rivers of water flowing down the gutters and the smell of soot in the air, KC Maltese was a pathetic sight. Whether she knew anything about this or was a willing participant no longer mattered. She had been a useful tool of Colter and he had been played perfectly. Indeed, he had been an easy mark, the easiest, a perfect sucker led astray like a lamb to slaughter. Josh held the woman's gaze then watched her lower her head and turn away to walk through the crowd of firemen and police milling around. And after everything that had happened and even against his better judgment, he feared the worst but still trusted her.

A torrent of water poured from the front door of the warehouse, filled with mud and debris. With his home ravaged and his lab destroyed, now there was nothing left but bitter betrayal and the message from Colter that was clear, "You're done!"

CHAPTER 7

The last of the fire trucks rolled away in a haze of red light, leaving behind a sea of shattered glass and broken bricks on the wet pavement. After being grilled by the fire chief and police chief, Josh was forced by a team of minions sent by the city to fill out reams of paperwork. They leveled accusations about violations, questioned building codes and conducted inspections. Colter had essentially released the hounds to finish him off, perhaps in an attempt to flush him out and force him to come over to his side. Josh could only surmise as he endured it all. By the time they were finished with him, he was facing eviction and the front door of the warehouse was boarded shut along with all of the first and second floor windows. With the spectacle over, and the streets dark and empty, Josh took a long look at the burned out shell of a building. After taking a deep breath, he ducked under the police tape and headed down the alleyway to the back of the building.

The fire escape at the rear of the warehouse was intact and looked sturdy enough which was more than could be said for the main electrical power box that had not only been disabled but ripped from the wall altogether.

"You guys are good," Josh said and made his way up the fire escape. By the time he reached the roof, his pulse was racing and he was moving fast. Josh went to the opposite corner of the building and slid an emergency panel aside to reveal a trap door hidden in the roof, then backed away as a wave of heat and a thin veil of smoke rose into the air. The space was just large enough for him to slide down into. When it was clear Josh reached inside, fumbled around for the object bracketed to the wall and pulled out a high powered Halogen flashlight. With the hatch door open, Josh shined the light into the dark interior and made his way down the metal ladder.

When he reached the lab floor, he shined the light at the wood soaked floor then up and around the walls. It was even worse than he imagined. Somewhere in the dark he could hear the cascade of water falling down the elevator shaft. Josh walked through a fog of liquid nitrogen vapor that coated the lab floor, remnants of a ruptured gas tank. Rising out of the fog at the center of the lab was the twisted remains of the time machine.

The dome of the chamber was reduced to its skeletal frame. The machine had been taken apart with blow torches and literally cut to pieces. Parts were strewn everywhere and looked like a bomb had exploded. And now that there was nothing left but a shell, he calmly and quietly pulled a wooden crate up behind him then turned off the flashlight and sat down. The box creaked beneath him as Josh stared into the darkness, sitting like a statue amidst the rubbish and dismantled wreckage of the warehouse. Then with his eyes closed, he shut down. His pulse and brainwaves slowed until he was as still as the wreckage that surrounded him. His childhood was punctuated with similar episodes, or attacks, diagnosed as catatonic behavior. Some doctors more accurately called it stress disorder, a survival technique developed to deal with trauma. The type of trauma remained a mystery to them as did the savage beatings Josh never spoke of, the beatings he endured from his father.

He had even given it a name, "Zeroed out." In the worst of times when things spun out of control, he "Zeroed out" and hoped to escape, at least for a moment, the horrors that beset him; and with no where to run and no possible way out of his dilemma, this was a perfect time.

With his eyes closed, there was a flicker of a thought that produced the slightest twitch of a smile, Josh opened his eyes to glimpse the old work table that was toppled over and lay on the floor only a few feet away. The last time he had "Zeroed out" he was seated there and had come up with the time mapping formula that had led to the time machine. That was two years ago, and Josh smiled, "A time machine that couldn't foresee its own destruction."

He closed his eyes again and no sooner had the smile faded than the idea struck him like a bolt out of the blue and his eyes shot open.

Josh flicked on the flashlight and stared straight ahead, his face ashen white. As an inventor, he enjoyed moments of clarity where ideas were born. But moments of absolute clarity inspired true genius and revelation. His mind raced as the idea came to him, flooding in like data downloading at high speed. Josh stood to his feet, his eyes scanning the empty air in front of him as though piecing together components of a complex equation, shaping the last integral solution to form an exquisite mathematical expression. Then with his plan emerging like a blueprint in his mind, he checked his moves and counter moves, checked them again until he could see it like pieces on a chessboard. And when everything fit neatly together, logic, practicality and action, factoring in an eighty-seven percent probability of success, he knew what he had to do and it was time to go to work. Josh snatched up a twelve foot strand of electrical cable at his feet. He coiled it into a neat bundle and then looked around. The first task was to restore power to the building.

Three hours later, the front of the warehouse was all aglow, lit by two, twelve hundred watt floodlamps powered by a gas generator. At one o'clock in the morning, Josh had pulled down the flimsy plywood that boarded up the front door and was working hard to weld steel plates over the charred and gaping hole that was once the entrance of the building. Josh used his own modified forklift, outfitted with winch and cable, to hoist and hold the two hundred pound plates of steel in place. Sweat poured off his back, soaking his tee shirt and the waistband of his jeans as he kept up the feverish pace. The white light flickered in his welder's mask as sparks crackled from the acetylene torch and danced across the pavement.

Most cars that came upon the scene only paused for a brief look then continued on about their business. As the lights flickered and sparked, one man came out of the darkness and slowed as he approached. Father Mike wandered into the bright pool of light, gazing up at the devastation of the warehouse building and instantly became part of the show. Prior to his arrival, there was just a crazy man, welding in the middle of the night. Now there was a priest along with the crazy man and the two seemed completely unaware of the other's presence.

The good priest stood guard while the occasional gang member or bag person meandered by. At one point a squad car pulled up but only slowed before continuing on its way after a wave from Father Mike. Josh crouched near the ground and ran the torch down the last seam, superheating the metal and fusing the steel plates together to finish the barricade. Once he was done, he shut the torchlight off with a "pop." He stood up and lifted the welder's mask to check out his handiwork.

"Not bad," came a voice from behind.

Josh turned to see the priest nodding his approval.

"You doing some remodeling?"

Beads of sweat dripped down Josh's face, as he looked at the warehouse again and nodded. "You could say that. I had some help."

"Colter?" Father Mike said, looking more serious.

Josh smiled weakly. "How could you tell?"

Josh put down the torch and mask, grabbed a bottle of water and then took a seat on the steps of the brownstone next door. Father Mike followed with growing concern.

"What did they want?"

"A mirror. They blew a hole in the front of the building, trashed my lab and my machine, all for a mirror. They're going ahead with their experiment."

Josh took another sip from his water and Father Mike sat down next to him.

"What are you going to do?" he asked.

Josh wiped his mouth. "I don't know. What I can?"

"I certainly hope you think of something since I'm sorry to say, this whole thing is pretty much all your fault."

The priest gave him a stern look and Josh stared back, like he was examining the face of the priest then snapped his fingers with a look of surprise as though he suddenly recognized the man.

"Oh yeah, guilt. You sure you're not Jewish?" Josh asked.

The priest just stared.

"Look, in case you haven't noticed things are a little bit out of my hands right now."

The priest shot up like a bolt, shocked by Josh's response. "Out of your hands? You can't be serious. I refuse to believe that!"

Josh looked up with equal surprise.

"Really? Well, what can you believe? You believe in the Bible and angels, and things you can't see. You believe in God. Hey, you know what? "Why don't we ask God to fix it?" Josh said, with arms wide open, like it was the idea of the century.

Mike wagged his finger.

"Hey, do not mock the Lord! The righteous shall trust in Him, and all the upright in heart shall glory."

Josh laughed.

"Oh, I see! So when somebody needs help, when somebody is in real trouble, God is conveniently absent and it's up to you to bail yourself out. Hmmm. What's the matter with this picture? Is God afraid to get his hands dirty? Some sort of liability issue?"

Father Mike looked at him then glanced over at the steel plates and forklift. When he turned around, he was calmer and appeared somewhat doubtful.

"You know, I don't believe you. I think you're up to something. What is it?"

Josh looked at him blankly. "When did you start playing poker? Go home priest."

Mike nodded slowly, trying to read between the lines. "All right, then. But, remember this. We may waver, but He never falters. God is always in control, even when He seems absent. Don't presume your fears upon Him. Instead look to God for strength."

Josh nodded. "Yeah, right. Sounds good, Mike."

The good father smiled down on him.

"It is good, Josh. Try it. You got nothing to lose. Ask Him what you should do. He'll tell you." The priest turned to leave and then paused again. "I'd say now would be a good time to start. Call me if you need me." He glanced at the night sky and turned to Josh. "I'll just leave you two alone to get acquainted."

Father Mike smiled as he hunched his shoulders and turned up his lapel against a cool breeze. "It's nights like this that I'm glad I have this collar." He then stuck his hands into his pockets and walked off into the night.

CHAPTER 8

The sun rose over the quiet hills surrounding Colter Laboratories, while underground a military escort accompanied two men down the main corridor of the lab building; the first man Captain Daniel Paige, a plain-clothed, high-level intelligence officer. Handcuffed to his left wrist was a metal briefcase.

The second man was tall, well built and in military uniform. He was Marine Special Forces, Major Will Conrad. Four armed guards moved with military precision, keeping equal distance between them and the time pilot, as they traveled down the hall.

The corridor branched off and the group split up. The first two soldiers went left and took the intelligence officer to the science lab, while the other two escorted Major Conrad to the prep room for briefing and launch instructions. Meanwhile, overhead, a voice announced the pre-launch sequence about to take place.

"Initial stage activation, three, two, one, primary launch couplers engage. Stand by GMS."

Inside the cavernous hanger, lights dimmed all across the lab. Simon Pelitier stood atop the control platform and brought the time machine on line. With the time coordinates locked in, the interior of the time chamber erupted in a burst of light. Everyone braced themselves through a minor tremor and subsequent shockwave. No sooner had the flash occurred than the low-density energy field instantly appeared.

Lewis Colter watched through the picture window of his private conference room adjoining the lab and then turned to the digital monitor broadcasting the images inside the chamber with the monitors all around the lab. From his own screen and control station within the conference room he watched the science lab technicians prep the Guidance Memory System, aka GMS, to energize and bring up the time image.

Outside in the corridor, the military procession arrived with Captain Daniel Paige, and Colonel Maxfield stood ready to greet him. The armed escort saluted, and then did an about face as the colonel opened the door to the conference room and took the intelligence officer the rest of the way. Once they were inside, Maxfield saluted the captain and Colter rose to his feet.

"Welcome gentlemen," Colter said from his personal place of operations. The room was not only secure, but also the anti chamber was equipped with an array of computers, patched into the lab to keep track of project status and monitor operations. Hidden panels in the walls opened with a touch. Behind one door was a luxurious full bath with all the amenities of a five star hotel. Other panels opened to reveal a full bar, refrigerator, microwave, wide screen TV with satellite link and an assortment of other creature comforts. It was affectionately referred to as "the den," designed by Colter for all the VIP's who wanted to get close to the action, and witness an actual time jump.

The large picture window looked out onto the dark cavernous space, affording those inside, a bird's eye view of the entire lab. The colonel and Captain Paige paused to observe the view. The silver time machine glowed like a jewel under glass and was captivating. After a second or two, Paige and Maxfield resumed their phase of the operation and proceeded with rehearsed precision.

Paige placed his metal briefcase on the Mahogany conference table. The colonel produced a key and unlocked the handcuff. Without a word, Paige rotated the briefcase, and then rolled the three digit tumblers to align the proper combination. Once the last digit was in place, the metal locks snapped open.

The interior of the briefcase revealed a single manila envelope sealed with a Nazi swastika boldly stamped on the front. Colonel Maxfield paused to look at the package then lifted the envelope out of the briefcase and presented it to Colter. Colter examined the swastika with a scowl, then reached down and picked up the silver letter opener next to his hand. With the envelope held out in front of him, he slid the blade inside the flap and with a deft flick of his wrist, sliced it open.

Maxfield and Captain Paige observed quietly while Colter removed a folded blueprint of a floor plan from the envelope and laid it out on the table. All of the data on the paper was written in German.

Now that they were ready to proceed, Captain Paige donned a pair of silver rimmed glasses and stepped forward to examine the document.

"This is a copy of the blueprint of the National Parliament Building in Berlin. Hitler's Reich Stag Headquarters, reprinted in 1922."

Colter moved closer to look at the plans. Maxfield and Paige waited to continue.

"How accurate is this?" Colter asked, still examining the blueprint.

"It's an identical copy of the original. The original blueprint was too fragile to transport, but every detail was examined and found to be consistent. It's accurate sir."

Colter looked up. "Excellent," he said and nodded his satisfaction.

Just then, the door opened and the time pilot strode into the room, leaving his armed escort outside. Major Conrad crossed the room dressed in full combat gear with tactical body armor, and bristling with state of the art weaponry. The men at the table paused to look him over.

In his arsenal was a double shoulder holster with two Baer 1911 .45 caliber semi automatic pistols, equipped with laser sights. Strapped to his left leg and hip were four smoke canisters and two incendiary bomblets. Strapped to his right leg was a formidable looking HK Tactical .45 caliber handgun with suppresser, laser sight, and Raptor night vision weapon sight. A pair of high resolution, night vision goggles strapped to the soldier's head in the upright position made the soldier look positively futuristic.

Major Conrad joined the group at the table and saluted Colter. "It's a pleasure to finally meet you, sir."

The soldier held the salute till Colter responded. It was a gesture of professionalism and protocol that Colter found extremely impressive. He saluted and the soldier snapped to attention.

"At ease soldier. The pleasure is all mine," Colter said. Conrad instantly slid his feet shoulder's width apart and clasped his hands behind him; ready and awaiting orders.

Colter circled around to the other side of the table, so that he could address everyone in his small audience. With Colonel Maxfield, Captain Paige, and the time pilot all present, Colter began the briefing. He spoke slowly, measuring his words carefully, aware of the magnitude of the speech.

"Major... gentlemen, this is it, our opportunity to set the record straight. If we are successful in our endeavors, the entire world could very well escape the ravages of a second world war. We are at the precipice of an historical landmark, the advent of time travel and the chance to bring about a new reality. Let us pray gentlemen that we have the courage to do what is right and the strength to accomplish the task. Captain Paige."

The men looked over the set of blueprints as Captain Paige proceeded.

"Gentlemen, I will go over one last time what our team has rehearsed in practice simulation. Major, the chamber will allow you a ten minute time jump. You will have nine minutes and forty seconds to complete your mission before reentry. Upon entry, orient yourself, check your clock." Paige pointed down at the major's wrist. "The time jump clock is fully automated and will count down the time left before reentry."

Conrad, glancing at the watch, nodded as the Intel officer continued.

"The date is August fourth, 1939, at twenty two hundred hours, ten O'clock at night, Hitler convenes a secret meeting to discuss the invasion of Poland."

Paige pointed to a spot on the blueprint indicating a specific seat in the conference room.

"Time link imaging shows target position here, the main conference room, second floor, two guards on the North entrance. The south corridor is secured by the stairs. Around this corner, at least two guards out of the line of sight. At ten O six, the janitor appears and starts to mop the floor. Thirty seconds later a guard calls him away. The janitor turns the corner and leaves the line of sight twenty-seven seconds later and does not return for exactly thirty two seconds. That is our opportunity. We place you here, Major, a broom closet adjacent to the conference room."

Paige placed his finger on a small square in the middle of the floor plan, indicating the tiny broom closet, and then nodded to the colonel and stepped back. Maxfield leaned in over the map and traced his finger along the blueprint, showing the major's line of attack.

"Now since Hitler feared assassination, no one in the conference room will be armed. Once the time jump is complete, and you are fully situated, you cross the hall. Drop a smoke canister. Open the door and take out the target. Drop more smoke then exit through the conference room window to the roof. Remember, there is a squad of Storm Troopers on the level below you and a full armored division outside. Once you're on the roof, you will have four minutes before the time chamber pulls you back. The element of surprise will be on your side. Use your remaining smoke canisters and incendiaries to cause as much confusion as possible to hold them off."

"Yes, sir," Conrad replied.

Maxfield paused to look at the soldier. "What is the prime directive, major?"

Major Conrad replied reflexively, as though the words were ingrained in his mind.

"Eliminate the target. Avoid unnecessary contact. Stay within the time parameters."

"Good," Colter said.

Just then a voice came over the conference room intercom. It was Dr. Pelitier, at the launch control platform. "I think we're ready."

The men turned from the blueprint to look out the adjoining window when the time chamber suddenly went black, as did the image of the time machine on the computer monitor in front of them. The force field around the chamber grew dim and strangely placid. Slowly lights began to flicker within the chamber.

At that moment, a woman's voice came over the general PA system and calmly announced, "We have time link imaging."

A panel pulled back in the conference room wall to reveal a 48-inch flat screen monitor. The image flickered with flashes of light as an image slowly emerged and revealed the bizarre scene that suddenly came to life on their screens.. Everyone peered at the two soldiers dressed in Nazi SS uniforms who stood guard over the host of decorated dignitaries seated at a large oak table in the chancellor's conference room. All eyes were on the man at the head of the table, whose oily black hair and short cropped mustache made him easily recognizable. Hitler leaned to one side and flicked a smile on and off as he talked to a man on his right, Joseph Goebbels, his trusted friend and member of the Nazi military juggernaut. With a wave of his hand, Hitler dismissed the two soldiers, who left the room immediately.

Down on the control platform the six launch specialists gazed at their monitors. Although the picture was crystal clear, and in vivid color, it was totally without sound.

"Hey, where's the audio?" A young lab tech leaned in toward his monitor while the woman next to him smiled and shook her head. "This isn't a movie, you geek."

"Takes one to know one."

The lab suddenly buzzed with excitement as everyone marveled at the literal window in time, while in the conference room Colter and the men gathered around the screen stared in wonder.

"Hitler and his bureaucrats, ghosts from the past locked in time." Captain Piage reflected and adjusted his glasses. "This is the beginning of his reign of terror."

Maxfield peered as the screen, seething with hate.

"Look at the smug bastard. It's like I could put a bullet in his head right from here."

Colter watched the screen and called out over his shoulder to the open comlink microphone set on the conference table.

"Simon, move us to the hall," he said and could hardly keep the excitement out of his voice.

Pelitier manned his own station on the control platform with the six launch experts and tapped out new coordinates on his keypad. Slowly the vantage point of the image changed and pulled back further and further until it went dark momentarily. The view of bricks, pipes and mortar was barely a flash as the time scan passed through the wall of the conference room and entered the hallway on the other side. Pelitier glanced up at the time chamber which went dark. Bits of light refracted, here and there, as the interior of the chamber became the darkened corridor, outside Hitler's conference room.

Pelitier refocused on the screen in front of him and tapped the keys again, this time more slowly and the view changed again. It rotated as though silently peering through the lens of a camera then swept past a view of the long corridor and kept moving until it finally settled on the wall opposite Hitler's conference room. There in the shadows was a narrow door, barely discernible and seemingly of little consequence. Just then, the two SS officers walked by, startling everyone watching the time scan. Without the presence of sound, the officers had appeared suddenly and without warning.

"Whoa! Gets me every time," Pelitier remarked then quickly regrouped and speed tapped new coordinates to follow the men down the hall.

The German officers were talking casually, machine guns slung over their shoulders, and then disappeared around the corner at the end of the hall. At that precise moment Maxfield activated the timer on his stopwatch. Exactly six and a half seconds later, a janitor hobbled into view from the same direction, carrying a mop and bucket. The elderly man approached, looking worn and haggard. When he was halfway, he put the bucket down and began mopping.

Fifteen seconds later one of the soldiers reappeared from around the corner and beckoned to the old man. The janitor leaned his mop against the wall and walked off to join the soldier. Just when they disappeared from view, Maxfield stopped the timer, and Colter called out, "Hold image."

The comlink console on the table amplified his voice which reverberated on the PA system all around the lab.

Pelitier responded. "Image frozen."

Maxfield held up his stopwatch. "Elapsed time one minute, thirty two seconds. Your count down time, T minus eight minutes and twenty eight seconds."

"Eight twenty-eight" Conrad repeated.

Colter smiled and nodded to Major Conrad. "Are you ready?"

Major Conrad peered at the time chamber through the conference room window and adjusted his shoulder harness before nodding. "Affirmative."

Colter looked the man in the eye and shook his hand as did Maxfield and Captain Paige. Then with the press of a button an adjoining door slid open behind them and Major Conrad stepped out onto a lift with an operator who stood waiting. The group joined him and as Colter's door closed behind them, they were all lowered to the main level. Every technician watched, almost in reverence at the descent of the brave time pilot. Conrad exited the lift and started down the long ramp toward the time chamber, like a fighter making his way to the ring. Colter and Maxfield were close behind, while Captain Paige rushed along side Major Conrad to give last minute instructions.

The time pilot focused his attention on the time chamber ahead and made little effort to acknowledge the Intel officer walking next to him, though he heard every word that was spoken.

"Now you do realize, we lose total contact with you. Once you go, you're there. You will see, feel, experience 1939 and everything that was part of that reality. Remember, once the janitor rounds the corner at twenty-seven seconds you have a thirty-two second window of opportunity before he returns. One final warning, there may be side effects to the time transfer itself, other intangibles we haven't considered."

Conrad interrupted as he marched past the control platform and proceeded to the time chamber, "Sir, I've been through the simulations. I know what to do. I'm ready."

Colter and Maxfield climbed the stairs to the control platform to join Pelitier and the six launch specialists at their stations. "Prep for entry."

"Affirmative. Reset and prep for entry."

Pelitier glanced around like a hawk as the time machine powered down and the force field disappeared. Suddenly, everyone who was not in position moved to their respective places and quickly manned their posts of operations.

When the place was nearly silent, Colter nodded to Pelitier who put on a headset and spoke into his microphone.

"Secure the lab."

Simon's words echoed throughout the giant laboratory chamber and yellow warning lights flashed above the entrances that were about to be sealed. There were five in total, the elevator entrance that Josh used, the conference room door, and three bulkheads along the walls, including a freight door for heavy equipment.

Other authorized personnel rushed in as the doors started to close. KC Maltese and Carl Grasso flashed their badges and moved inside, cautious and fascinated like two kids sneaking under the circus tent. Before the thick metal bulkhead of the main entrance could swing shut, a young technician rushed past to find his seat and joined a row of operators nearby. When solid green lights flashed on along the walls above the main exits, the doors slammed shut and the air locks were sealed.

Grasso took a few steps forward, gazing at the glistening time chamber.

KC grabbed him by the arm. "Don't you think we should stay back?" She whispered. "You know, so we don't get in the way." She smiled, trying not to look afraid.

With a few quick glances at all the activity, personnel and technology that surrounded them, Grasso nodded and stepped back with an eager gleam in his eye. "Can you believe it? We're about to witness history in the making!" he said. He stretched out his hands as if he was about to conduct a symphony.

"You mean, the remaking, don't you?" KC said as she stared at the time machine, feeling her pulse beat a little faster. It was the thought of Pandora's Box that haunted her ever since Josh had mentioned it. Even when Karen Danners, whom she trusted implicitly, had reassured her that the techno geeks had it under control, it was not enough. She had even called Lewis Colter twice on his personal line but hung up, each time afraid that she would sound like a fool. There was no way Colter would stop operations simply on the fearful whim of a frightened legal secretary. And now that they were on the verge of the experiment she feared what was about to happen. Yet here she was, drawn to the event by her own dread and lurid curiosity, watching like a child squinting at the lit fuse of a firecracker. She stared at the time machine being prepped for launch.

"You don't think anything's going to happen do you?"

Grasso turned to her with a cynical grin. "Of course something's gonna happen. They're going to kill Hitler!"

"I mean anything, bad," KC said, trying to sound cautious.

Grasso looked at her a little confused.

"Define bad."

The look on his face told KC it was hopeless.

"Never mind," she said.

"What's the matter with you?" Grasso asked.

Now that he was looking at her, KC realized she had been nervously wringing her hands the whole time and then clasped them together. It was a gesture that only made her look more tense.

"Relax," Grasso said.

KC nodded and then jumped when a voice suddenly came over the lab comlink speakers. It was a woman's voice, confident and soothing in its demeanor, as it announced the pre-launch coordinates and echoed into the metal rafters high above.

"Two point zero one five. Time density three point zero, six, one one nine, and holding. Declination, twenty-four point nine six degrees. Entry coordinates set and ready."

Then like everyone else around her, KC's eyes were fixed on the crowd of men milling around the time pilot, standing just beyond the control platform in front of the time machine. All eyes were riveted on the man who commenced his pre-jump inspection with ritualistic precision.

Major Conrad drew his HK Tactical .45 caliber handgun with silencer and checked the clip. He secured the side arm and then drew the Baer 1911 semi automatic from his shoulder holster as he moved down the platform steps, checking the laser sight before replacing the weapon. Two soldiers stood before the time chamber as a final check point and waited as Major Conrad came to a halt before them. One of the men handed him an HK 91 automatic rifle, which he hooked onto the breakaway harness across his chest, while the other man looped a coil of climbing rope over his shoulder and checked all of the buckles and clips for all his gear to make sure everything was tight and secured. With a sharp pat on the back, the soldier was given the "thumbs up" all clear sign. Conrad gave a nod, a smart salute and marched past the white coated lab techs standing at the hatch of the time chamber.

He stepped inside, cool and steady, moving with rehearsed precision and climbed into the time pod. The major strapped himself into the chair, located the small cable dangling from his sleeve and plugged it into the launch console in front of him. Once the indicator turned green, voices chattered over the intercom, instantly relaying his bio stats while Conrad prepared for launch. Then with a deft nod of his head, he gave the "okay" signal to the two lab techs, who acknowledged and pushed the heavy steel door shut. Conrad watched the winch lever turn until the hatch door sank flush with the hull of the chamber and was sealed in place.

With all systems ready, Conrad reached up to the small control panel in front of him and tapped a button to open his mike. "Pilot secured and ready for jump."

From the control platform, Simon Pelitier and the six primary launch technicians went to work to initiate launch codes and power up the time chamber. The female tech next to Pelitier flipped a row of switches and lit up half the control panels across the lab.

"Systems one through seven ready for induction," the woman said, her voice echoing over the PA system. "Shielding is hot and on line."

The specialist next to her, a stern looking man with a buzz cut, peered up at the chamber.

"We're green across the board," he said, his voice flat and monotone.

Pelitier moved away from his station to join Colter, standing nearby. The science officer smiled confidently. Colonel Maxfield stared at the machine with a look of concern.

"Getting cold feet, Colonel?" Pelitier said, with an air of arrogance.

Maxfield spoke calmly and for the first time showed a glimmer of apprehension.

"You're a scientist, son, not a soldier. You view this as an experiment. This is an incursion, the highest level of military black ops covert operations ever undertaken. Whether we like it or not, this thing, this "new invention" as it were, is a weapon. Make no mistake, a weapon system for which there is no defense and that indeed causes me some concern."

The science officer smirked.

"Like I said, getting cold feet?"

Colonel Maxfield just stared at the chamber.

"I said no defense. That means in the wrong hands, we are all at risk. Even you."

Pelitier stopped to consider the thought, then offered a weak smile and looked at the time machine a little more soberly.

Colter stood by and smiled.

"Gentlemen please. We're presupposing scenarios that haven't even happened. One step at a time, all right? One step at a time."

Suddenly, six massive hydraulic legs lifted the time chamber off the floor and held it up like an enormous bug.

Pelitier smiled at his improvement on the design. "I increased the number of legs from three to six, to lessen the shock and add more stability against turbulence."

Colter nodded as the chamber rose to a maximum height of six feet, eight inches.

Again the woman's silky voice echoed across the lab. "All systems nominal, green to go."

Pelitier called to the launch crew behind him. "Throttle up and open the corridor."

With a hiss of blue light, the force field appeared and engulfed the time chamber as the machine leapt to full power. Grasso turned to KC with an eager grin that quickly melted into a blank stare as he gazed over his shoulder.

"Don't look now." Grasso said.

KC turned to see the amazing phenomena that astounded everyone in the lab and stood spellbound as she stared at the mirror image of herself standing directly behind her. The effect was happening all around the time chamber and affected everyone. Every lab technician, every security personnel, Colter and Pelitier, all watched in amazement as their images stared back at them and almost seemed to move independently of the person looking at them.

Soon the air became charged with static electricity and KC's hair began to rise. She tried to brush it down, as it danced upward and rose higher. She turned to Grasso for some explanation.

"It gets weirder," Grasso said almost apologetically.

Suddenly every pen, pencil and piece of paper in the lab became airborne and found its way to a person or computer monitor nearby and stuck fast. KC had three pens, while Grasso smiled with his hair standing straight up and twenty-six post-it notes dotting his suit, from head to toe.

Just then a shudder, like an earth tremor, rocked the lab and KC turned to see the time chamber engulfed in light.

Inside the chamber, Major Conrad watched the entire floor disappear in a flash beneath his pod. The cable supports released an instant later, and Conrad held on as the pod nose dipped forward and plummeted through the floor. With no sense of up or down, the pod surged forward and the time field plowed ahead manufacturing the corridor only a few feet beyond the time pod. The phantom energy pushed the soldier back into his seat as the time corridor forged its way like the leading edge of a comet through space.

With the pod buffeting wildly, Major Conrad slowly looked into the rear view mirror mounted on the side of the pod and witnessed the amazing paradox. Ahead of the pod, everything was a blur of unimaginable speed while behind him there was no movement at all. The time chamber was still and the cables merely floated in space, frozen in time. Then slowly, like a scene fading to black, the view of the lab grew dimmer and dimmer before disappearing entirely. Soon everything was gone, except for the pod and the time corridor ahead. A few seconds more, the ride was smoother. And when he was ready, the major gripped the control handle in front of him, and then wrenched it back and throttled up all the way. A dull roar shook the entire building as the time pod launched into oblivion along with the time pilot, an assassin from the future, armed to the hilt, with a prime directive to kill.

CHAPTER 9

The cold night air in Berlin sifted through the willows outside the historical landmark that was Reich Stag headquarters. The white stone of the old Parliament Building gleamed against the manicured gardens, its lavish architecture beautifully ornate. On the street below, a dozen troop carriers and five formidable half-track tanks surrounded the building. A squad of Storm Troopers milled about, with machine guns strapped and loaded.

Within the building, on the second story level, the hall lights suddenly went out, the result of an inexplicable power surge. There was momentary confusion as soldiers looked to the darkened ceiling then rushed off to find the fuse box, leaving the corridor dark and quiet. No one noticed the light like the flash of a camera that sparked behind the broom closet door and was gone in an instant. Major Conrad materialized like a ghost lying on the floor in the dark with his machine gun strapped to his chest. The soldier jerked himself up, as though awakened from a dream. With his pulse racing, he got to a crouched position, took a moment to regain his composure, and then quickly lowered his night vision goggles and checked the time jump clock, which was counting down and already read nine minutes and forty four seconds left in the jump. Sixteen seconds had already passed. The soldier looked toward the door. Meanwhile, across the hall beyond the polished doors of the conference room, the secret meeting was about to begin.

Two soldiers dressed in Nazi SS uniforms stood guard over the host of decorated dignitaries seated at a large oak table in the chancellor's conference room. All eyes were on the man at the head of the table, whose oily black hair and short cropped mustache made him easily recognizable. Hitler leaned to one side, and flicked a smile on and off as he talked to a man on his right, Joseph Goebbels his trusted friend and member of the Nazi military juggernaut. With a wave of his hand, Hitler dismissed the two SS soldiers, who left the room immediately.

Although the broom closet was pitch black, Major Conrad could see perfectly, everything glowing a bright blue green in the night vision goggles. The tiny closet was dank and dingy, with the noxious fumes of cleaning fluids in the air. There was a small sink and a plunger in the corner. Above and across from the door was a shelf with rags, bristle brushes and an assortment of metal cans and bottles, presumably the source of the noxious smell.

Conrad looked to the closet door and knew exactly what lay beyond. Hitler and the entire German army. Suddenly a hundred thoughts flooded his mind. His world was gone. This was the world of 1939. Everything he knew no longer existed, his wife and daughter, gone. His mother and father unborn, everyone he knew and loved, all gone in a flash.

"My grandpa would be a young man now, probably in his twenties."

Henry Harper Conrad, wounded in 1942, sent state side and subsequently died of an infection related to his injury. Six months later his son was born, a son who would grow up without a father. As a result, "Grandpa Hank" was nothing more than a name attached to a faded photograph. "All because of that bastard in the room across the hall." The major tried to refocus, disturbed by the thoughts that clouded his mind. Ever since he had volunteered for the assignment, he told himself, "this would not be personal," but now that he was here, it was unavoidable. The thought of bringing his grandfather back justified everything and he relished the thought of killing Hitler.

Conrad secured the HK automatic rifle to the chest harness, and checked the time jump clock. T minus nine minutes and twelve seconds left in the jump.

"Eight, twenty eight." Conrad whispered. Approximately forty four seconds remained until "go time". Slowly he rose from his crouched position and drew the .45 handgun from his shoulder holster and gave the silencer a twist to make sure it was locked in place. He had rehearsed this moment down to the heartbeat and was aware of the precise instant when the soldiers were in the hallway.

The two SS officers made their way down the hall with their MP-40 machine guns slung over their shoulders. Their muffled voices filtered through the broom closet door. Conrad smiled and brought his ear closer. It was the first time he could hear the sound attached to the visual preview of the time jump.

Outside the door, the soldiers spoke casually in German. One of the men patted his jacket and pulled a pack of cigarettes from the breast pocket of his uniform as they emerged from the shadows and passed the hallway closet. He offered a cigarette to his partner, who adjusted his rifle and took one. Both men continued to the end of the corridor and rounded the corner, enjoying a light hearted conversation.

T minus eight minutes and fifty-two seconds. Just as they disappeared from view, the old janitor appeared from the same direction with mop and bucket in hand. The old man walked halfway up the hall, stopped and put the bucket down. He paused to take a breath before beginning to mop.

There hadn't been much traffic since the day before, as everything had been kept clean in preparation for Hitler's arrival. There was some sweeping and dusting, but nothing to speak of. Still, they had managed to work the old janitor hard all day, helping to move furniture, and running errands for caterers up and down the stairs with crates of food. Now he was exhausted and perfectly content to lean on his mop for the duration of the late shift.

T minus eight minutes and thirty seven seconds. Just then, as if to disturb his rest, one of the SS officers peaked from around the corner and called to the old janitor by name.

"Ernst, a light?" the soldier called in German, holding up his cigarette.

The old man straightened, forced a smile, placed the mop against the wall and searched his baggy pockets. A moment later he produced a book of matches and made his way down the hall, slightly hunched and with a limp.

"They work you too hard, old man," the soldier said.

"Just hard enough to break my back," Ernst offered as if it were a good thing.

The soldier laughed and both men disappeared from view.

Major Conrad peered down at the jump clock which read precisely eight minutes and twenty-eight seconds; go time, thirty-two seconds to cross the hall, open the door and make the kill. With his handgun ready, Conrad reached for the doorknob and gave it a turn.

The door opened out into the hallway just a crack and a cool breeze rushed past his face. Conrad inhaled the fresh air as he peaked out to see the empty hallway. The view from the broom closet was a new vantage point and for the first time it was perfectly lit by his night vision.

With the target waiting just across the hall, Conrad steadied himself and took the safety off of the gun, with a gentle "click," then with the doorknob in his left hand and the pistol in his right, he pushed the door open a few inches. There was a peculiar noise, a scratching sound. It was ever so slight but enough to make Conrad pause.

"The hinges," Conrad told himself and pushed the door further. Again he heard the noise. Again he paused. Conrad glanced down at his watch.

Thirteen seconds had already passed. "Seventeen seconds before the janitor returns, forget the hinges! Cross the hall, drop smoke, open the door and take the shot. Take the shot then get to the roof."

With that thought, he swung the door open and rushed into the hall. Before he had taken two steps, a loud bang shattered the silence.

The noise, like a firecracker, was amplified by the walls and echoed down the hall. Conrad froze in the middle of the hall, adrenalin pumping, eyes peering wide through the night vision goggles. He looked to his left and his right and then down at his feet. He could not believe his eyes.

"NO!" was all he had time to utter silently, before he heard the bolt-action safety of a machine gun. In the time it took him to look down, the two SS soldiers had reappeared at the end of the hall, weapons trained and leveled at the intruder. With yellow muzzle flashes, the sound of the MP-40 machine guns was deafening in the hall. Conrad raised his pistol as bullets ripped through the air and tore across his chest, pounding the automatic rifle and his Kevlar vest. An errant bullet ricocheted off the weapon and glanced off his jaw. Conrad twisted away from the initial volley, trying to get to the floor. When he did, six bullets strafed him from hip to arm pit as he went down. Two bullets plunged into his right leg and four went through his ribcage, mincing all of his vital organs.

By the time Conrad's body hit the floor, he was already dead, shot through the heart. The SS officers continued to open fire, puncturing two smoke canisters strapped to Conrad's leg, which hissed and leaked thick black smoke until it filled the corridor.

Seconds later, soldiers yelled and the cacophony of machine gun fire was joined by a deafening bell toll of a fire alarm. A dozen more SS soldiers rounded the corners at both ends of the hall and took up positions. The first two men finally ceased fire, as other soldiers arrived, trying to avoid a deadly crossfire. With smoke filling the hall and zero visibility, it was impossible to advance.

Frightened and angry voices continued to call out as the soldiers stayed low and huddled together. Slowly the smoke thinned to a grayish haze, and they could begin to see the body of the man that lay on the floor in front of the conference room.

The two squads that cordoned off both ends of the hall stared anxiously through a black mist. Finally a senior officer stepped forward, his own pistol pointed at the body. With a wave of his hand, five men moved forward, clutching their machine guns close to their shoulders. When they reached the body, two of the men poked their machine guns into the open broom closet.

"He is alone!" the soldier reported.

Their commander yelled back, "Who is he? British? French?"

With all of the high tech gear and weaponry strapped to his body, the body on the floor looked more alien than human.

"I don't know," the soldier replied, stooping low to get a better look, just as a tiny alarm sounded. The soldier jumped back, nearly tripping over the men behind him, who barely stopped themselves from shooting him in the back. The soft, high pitched chirping noise was coming from the dead man's wristwatch with was set for a thirty second warning before time jump. The SS soldiers froze, their weapons trained on the corpse and on the watch which read "fifteen seconds."

"Bomb!" one soldier yelled and everyone pulled back, fumbling and stumbling to get away as the watch reached zero and the end of the countdown. With soldiers still rushing to fall back, some looked to see the strange sight of the body that began to glimmer then glow and radiate light. Then before anyone could clearly see what had happened, the corpse disappeared in the smoke, leaving nothing more than the blood soaked floor boards and only one other object next to where the body lay. The SS soldiers returned slowly, with weapons trained on the floor staring at the peculiar sight, a solitary wooden broom laying next to the pool of crimson blood.

The laboratory stood silent, lab techs waiting and watching. KC had resorted once again to wringing her hands in silence. Even Grasso was speechless as he watched the dome of energy glow and shimmer around the time machine. The new world was about to come, the new world as a result of Hitler's death. KC looked on in growing anticipation as the magnitude of the moment held her spellbound and made her mind reel.

"One bullet in a madman's head and millions will be spared. Then what? Millions of people appearing instantly out of nowhere? More lives, more generations that never were alive; more doctors, more leaders, and out of those millions, more murderers, more madmen, other deaths of people who are alive and suddenly disappear; wiped out by people who were never supposed to be alive. Pandora's Box." With the danger suddenly clear in her mind, KC stared at the shimmering time chamber and trembled.

Some of the lab techs seated nearby stared at the time machine with childlike joy and anticipation, others had a look of near adoration. KC suddenly had the urge to run and began to back away. She backed up against the wall and shut her eyes, sensing the approach of an alternate reality that could instantly erase them all from existence.

KC shrank further away from Grasso and clutched her shoulders, trying to hold onto her very being, her sanity, her consciousness when suddenly an alarm sounded and she screamed.

Grasso turned to look at her, and she clasped her hands over her mouth and then struggled to catch her breath. The automatic reentry signal sounded twelve seconds, and the shimmering energy field surrounding the time chamber slowly evaporated.

"Power down," Pelitier called over the PA system.

The techs worked busily at their stations as the huge hydraulic legs beneath the time machine lowered the chamber and set it down on the concrete floor with a heavy, "Thud." Just like that, he was back. In a matter of minutes, the time pilot had returned. KC tried to assume a more normal stance and tried not to look like a frightened schoolgirl.

"He was back and nothing bad had happened, nothing bad at all," she told herself. She had worked herself into a frenzy for nothing, all because of Josh. She wanted to scream for being so stupid then shook her head, thinking she could be so silly to fall for all of his fear mongering.

People applauded and cheered as the power went down to nil and the energy field completely disappeared around the stainless steel time chamber. There was another sound, a steady whine, a drone of a sound that remained after the reentry alarm had sounded. But few had noticed it. Only the med tech monitoring the time pilot's vital signs was aware of it and stared at his monitor in horror. Every signal was flat-lined across the board.

A slow smile crept across Lewis Colter's face as he exchanged appreciative glances with the personnel around him until he saw the med tech staring at him, mouth agape. When the digital monitors came back on line and the cameras patched back into the time chamber, a shrill, earsplitting scream filled the lab. It was the woman at the central control platform. She had screamed into her microphone and made everyone cringe. KC turned to one of the lab techs seated at his console nearby and watched the slow horror creep across his face as he peered at his screen. KC stepped closer, drawn to the image.

Inside the chamber, Major Conrad was still strapped in the time pod, only now his bullet-ridden body lay mutilated and lifeless in the chair. The man's head was lolled to the side, with his eyes staring straight at the camera. One arm hung down and dangled toward the door, almost pointing. Blood dripped from his fingertip and pooled on the floor. The effect was unmistakable. The dead man's pose looked like an eerie warning, to stay away.

Colonel Maxfield went to a monitor, his arms folded across his chest and just frowned.

"Get that hatch door open!" he yelled.

The recovery team went into action. Six men rushed forward. Four uncoupled the hoses, providing coolant and fuel to the machine. The other two went to the hatch where they both grabbed the hatch lock and turned it, working as hard as they could to make the stainless steel gears turn faster than they were designed to.

Colter turned from his monitor. "MEDIC! We need a medic down here, NOW!" He yelled to no one in particular as sheer pandemonium broke out. A second alarm sounded as the lab went to yellow alert and the lab doors opened. The instant they could fit through, a medical team rushed in, and Grasso jumped aside.

"What the hell happened? Is he hurt?" Grasso said.

From the back of the lab, it was impossible to tell exactly what had happened. And since Grasso hadn't thought to go to a monitor he didn't have a clue. But when they pulled Conrad's blood soaked body from the time chamber and laid him on the stretcher, it became perfectly clear that the man had been brutally slain. There was more screaming among the civilian staff and people ran out as the reality of what had happened sank in.

KC watched the bizarre scene unfold in front of her and mumbled the words in shock. "He was right."

Grasso turned away from the horrible sight to look at KC. He wore an annoyed and confused expression and KC could tell he was just as afraid. She called to him. "He said something bad would happen and it did."

"Oh yeah? That's great. That's great. So now what are we supposed to do?" Grasso said.

There were a hundred questions, amidst the screams of confusion, but there were no answers, only the dead body of a soldier and the horror.

CHAPTER 10

It was barely ten o'clock when Josh's phone rang and Carol Danners left her cryptic message concerning, "a serious problem with the project."

Reading between the lines, Josh knew something had gone wrong with the time jump, and by the sound of it, it was something huge. The message ended with the words, "Colter insists you come at once."

The woman was a good diplomat, and Josh knew she had probably softened the message. So it was no surprise when two of Colter's goons showed up at the warehouse twenty minutes later and whisked him away to the heliport atop the corporate building.

By ten forty-five they had touched down at the airfield adjacent to the lab building and the same two goons escorted Josh down a long corridor in the basement of the Tech Center. Both guards were well over six feet, young, well dressed and too serious to speak which didn't prevent Josh from trying to make small talk, to lighten the mood.

"Somebody screwed up, huh?"

The guards ignored him as they marched along.

"C'mon, you can tell me. It was Simon, right? Please tell me it was Pelitier. That would make this whole trip worthwhile."

Again, the guards said nothing as they came to a door labeled "C16-Morgue."

Josh looked at the door with some surprise. Now that the guards were staring at him, he looked at them questioningly.

"Simon's dead?"

One of the guards opened the door and Josh proceeded inside, alone.

The morgue was dimly lit and just large enough to accommodate all the people present, not including those who might be on ice behind the freezer doors in the walls. Among the living were Lewis Colter, Colonel Raymond Maxfield, Simon Pelitier, and Carl Grasso, who all turned their attention toward Josh as he walked in.

As he walked in, a thought occurred to Josh that made him smile. It was the most unpleasant place, full of the most unpleasant people he could imagine with the possible exception of the dead body, lying under the sheet, on the table behind them.

Colter waved Josh to join them. "Come in, Josh, come in."

Josh looked around as he approached. "A morgue? You guys think of everything," he said until he stood in their midst, still looking around and trying to ignore the body. "So, you guys hang out here much?"

Colter turned to the body on the table.

"We've had a setback."

Josh stood still and watched as the group of men fanned out around the table. Colter and Josh stayed near the head with Maxfield, while Pelitier and Grasso stood back from the table. Josh tried to prepare himself for whatever he was about to see, but when the colonel pulled the sheet back to expose the torso of the body, Josh had to shut his eyes and turn away.

Grasso looked away as well, even though he had seen the bullet riddled corps twice before. The sight of torn flesh and gaping exit wounds was something he would never get used to, nor would he ever forget. A few seconds later, Pelitier came forward and covered the body. Slowly Colter and the others turned their gaze to Josh.

"Is that what you call this? A setback?" Josh said as he tried to compose himself. He looked around at the men who were still staring at him.

"Oh, let me guess. This is somehow my fault?"

Colonel Maxfield growled in his gruff voice. "Marine Special Forces, Major William F. Conrad, Iraq war veteran, twice decorated, a man of honor, a damn good soldier, as good as they get. We sent him in and this is what we got back."

Pelitier jumped in to make the point. "It's human error. It had to be."

"NO WAY!" Maxfield said and practically barked as he spat the words out in anger.

"This man was a professional. I hand picked him myself. He'd been through the training and simulations. He knew the scenario. The plan was flawless. This shouldn't have happened. It's a damn nightmare."

Colter handed Josh a palm held digital recorder. There was an image frozen on the tiny monitor.

"We went back to the time link recorder, and did a scan to see what happened. Here's something you might find interesting."

Josh stared at the image sent back by the time machine, the freeze frame of Conrad's death, which was now a part of history, the revised history as a result of the soldier's intervention.

"And check this out," Grasso said, and stepped forward to drop a newspaper on the sheet covering the body. The newspaper was old and yellowed, sporting a German headline. On the front page was a black and white photo of a group of soldiers standing over a pool of blood. Josh looked back and forth at the paper and the recorder.

"They're identical," Josh said.

"Spooky isn't it?" Grasso said, nodding his head up and down.

Josh picked up the paper and studied the faded image closely, even though the image on the recorder was much sharper. Josh looked at the text and wished he remembered his German. "What does it say?

"It says, Phantom," Karen Danners said as she walked into the room. The special agent in the hall closed the door behind her. Danners wore a tweed suit with hounds tooth print and a cream colored satin blouse, entirely too stylish for a morgue.

"Phantom in the castle. I pulled it from the archives of the local library. It tells the story of this squad of soldiers, who were eyewitnesses, to what they don't know. A ghost they say, who bled real blood then vanished before their eyes. I took the time to call the National Parliament Building in Berlin, just out of curiosity. Turns out they offer tours to see the blood stained floorboards which still remain to this day." She paused to look at the newspaper in Josh's hands then continued in an almost lighthearted manner.

"The phantom. It's a haunting tale wrapped in mystery and shrouded in myth. A forgotten story, no doubt, of an unexplainable incident, a convenient fairytale told to little children in the local villages before their bedtime, nothing more."

Danners looked down at the shrouded body and was suddenly filled with regret. "Our Marine Special Forces, Major William Franklin Conrad, the phantom."

Maxfield listened until he had heard enough. "Look, sentiments aside, the facts remain. We still have a dead man here because something alerted those soldiers. We've been over it a hundred times, but I'll be damned if I can figure out what happened."

Josh looked down at the recorder and backed up the image then started it again to replay the initial thirty seconds of the murder. Danners looked over his shoulder. There was no sound, only the image of Conrad stepping out of the broom closet in the darkness. The man suddenly froze and seemed distracted by something at his feet. When he looked up the SS soldiers opened fire. Seeing it for the first time, Karen Danners threw both hands over her mouth and gasped. Conrad fell to the floor, in a hail of bullets, gunned down in the hallway of the Reich Stag Headquarters. In a matter of seconds the hallway was full of smoke and the image went black.

Danners looked to the body that lay before them and her eyes filled with tears.

"The poor man," she said, sniffling just a little.

Colter allowed her a moment of grief and that was all.

"Danners. I want you to notify the family."

Danners wiped her eyes and tried to sound professional. "Is that all?" she asked as though it was no big deal, even though the thought of telling this man's wife she was now a widow was nothing she looked forward to.

"This man is a hero," Colter said. "He died for his country."

"Hah!" Josh said jeering at the comment, and paused the recorder at the spot where Conrad's body began to glow, right before it disappeared.

Colter glared at the young man.

"This man died for an idealistic dream that was doomed from the beginning." Josh took a second to look at Colter. "Your dream," he added casually then looked back down at the recorder to study the image. Colonel Maxfield sneered, trying to control his anger, but the young man was too preoccupied to notice. Karen Danners watched the screen over Josh's shoulder and glanced up to see Colter and Maxfield and then quickly looked down again to escape their searing gaze.

Josh fast forwarded the image to the point where the hallway lights came up then froze the still frame and narrowed his eyes as he focused on the object laying next to the pool of blood.

"What's that?" he asked.

Colter was almost too angry to move but forced himself to come along side and take a look. Josh turned the screen so Maxfield could get a good look as well.

"What?" he said.

"That," Josh pointed more directly.

Maxfield looked closer at the tiny four-inch screen.

"It's a broom? What about it? The broom was part of the original time link imaging. It was part of the simulation. It's nothing."

Josh shrugged and conceded the point.

"Hey, okay. I'm just asking."

"No it wasn't; it was a mop. The janitor's mop," Pelitier said with total assurance. "Remember? He leans it up against the wall, the opposite wall, before he goes away."

Pelitier came around to look at the recorder. He pointed to the mop further down the hall in the picture, the janitor's mop leaning up against the wall.

"There! Look! There it is. Right where it's supposed to be, up against the wall where the janitor left it."

"Then what's that?" Josh said.

Pelitier stared at the object lying on the floor and was at a loss for words.

"The broom is new," he said softly in amazement.

Danners picked up the paper and looked at the picture in the old newspaper article.

"Look, there's a broom in this picture too."

Danners handed it to Colter, who took a look and puzzled over the object. He had completely missed it when he had first looked and now he couldn't stop staring at it.

Colonel Maxfield seemed equally lost. "What was Conrad doing with a broom?" he said.

"That's what I want to know," Josh said, and handed the recorder to the colonel. Josh turned to Colter.

"Can we see the original time scan recording? The one before your man went in."

Colter nodded to Pelitier, who returned the nod.

"We can do that," Pelitier said.

Moments later the same group was seated in a screening room in one of the annexes of the Tech Center. The lights went down, and Pelitier rolled the first time scan recording. The picture showed the dark hallway and the two SS soldiers strolling by the broom closet, which was hidden in the shadows. Maxfield and Colter turned sharply when the door at the back of the room opened and a ray of light slashed across the screen. KC Maltese entered quietly. She was looking for Karen Danners and took a seat in the back to wait until they were finished. Josh kept his focus riveted to the images and got up, compelled to move forward until he stood near the screen. When the image before him was nearly black, Josh called to Pelitier, "Freeze it!"

Pelitier stopped the picture just after the SS soldiers walked out of frame. The entire still picture was literally nothing more than a shadowy black mass. But Colter, Pelitier and Maxfield had all seen the tape enough times to know they were looking at the broom closet in complete shadow.

"Now, that should be the closet door, right?" Josh said.

"That's right," Maxfield said.

"Enhance the frame. I want to be able to see it."

Pelitier worked with the electronic filters. The picture shifted slightly but was barely any lighter.

Josh squinted and leaned forward in his seat. "Is that it?" he said.

Pelitier called out from behind the digital control panel. "There's just not enough information captured in the scan. That's all the detail you're going to get."

"Invert it, give me a negative. Try polarizing the frame," Josh said.

Pelitier looked at him, as if to say, "Why didn't I think of that?"

Pelitier went back to work. Everyone listened as he tapped the necessary keys and waited for the image on the screen to change. The frame switched to a lighter, grayer image, like a negative. But still it was just a tone on the screen. Josh squinted and tilted his head sideways.

"Now boost contract a hundred percent, sharpen image and give me a hundred and fifty percent magnification."

With a few more taps of the keys, the image went grainy and became a little lighter. The room fell silent. At the center of the picture was a faint diagonal line, barely visible, but definitely there. Josh stood to one side, looking it up and down carefully, then finally pointed at the gray smudge of a line, center screen.

"There's your culprit."

Maxfield looked closer. "What's that supposed to be?"

"Your broom," Josh said with his arm outstretched. "That's the broom handle. That's what happened to your man."

"Well I'll be damned," said Colter as he literally got the picture.

Maxfield remained silent, as did Grasso, KC and Danners.

"Don't you see?" Josh said and came forward to explain with the image on screen next to him. "The broom that you saw on the floor wasn't always on the floor. It was leaning up against the closet door before your man opened it. The janitor probably put it there sometime earlier. But how would you know? Who would even think to look?. Why would you? What does a door or an old broom have to do with the assassination of Hitler, right? So you send your man in. He opens the door, steps into the hall, broom falls over and BANG! There's your noise that alerts the soldiers."

Everyone peered at the light gray outline of the broom handle on the screen and played the new scenario out in their minds. With the broom leaning against the closet door, everything Josh said made sense. Josh turned to his audience to wrap it up, and all at once seemed lost in his own thoughts.

"Amazing! Your man never had a chance. Do you see the theory?" Josh grasped his head in astonishment. "I never dreamt it would be this complicated."

He paced back and forth as he thought it through for the first time.

"I knew everything was connected, but I was thinking of relationships between people, social interactions and events, events driven by people that could change the course of history. How presumptuous and narrow minded–" Josh raised his fist like he might brain himself then turned to everyone to explain. "I never thought about inanimate objects. Things that were insignificant could become monumentally important, life or death important."

Josh looked down as he paced back and forth in the light.

"Yes, the broom was placed there by a person, but in the original scenario nothing happened. The broom meant nothing and did nothing. You send in your assassin to alter the course of time and the broom saves Hitler's life Inconceivable, right? No, because in this context it's no longer a broom. It's an alarm, a watchdog at the gate, a booby trap!"

With his audience captivated and listening, Josh's train of thought gained speed as he became more excited.

"All right, fine. But what about other objects, any other object that might have meant nothing in the original time scenario... Let's say, a cobble stoned street, uneven bricks, whatever. New scenario, same street, someone trips and bumps into someone, or maybe doesn't fall and was supposed to. The chain reaction starts as a result of their interaction with an inanimate object, that was originally of no consequence. So something that was, that otherwise shouldn't had been, becomes what it wasn't originally intended to be, an impediment or a catalyst, the opposite of whatever it was and winds up changing everything. So to be or not to be turns out not to be the question at all. It's a fact, an equation... An unseen equation that could change the course of history."

Josh paused and looked around the room at all the blank empty faces.

"What the hell are you talkin' about?" Maxfield said in his slow Texas drawl.

Josh gestured to the screen in frustration.

"I'm talking about a broom. A brick, a stick, the wind, a piece of paper, a butterfly's wings, whatever. You screwed around with the time scenario and look what happened. A stinking broom changed everything. Don't you get it? It's not just about people. You go back in time, and the whole world becomes your enemy, one big, gigantic obstacle course, a booby trap of unimaginable proportions."

Colter and Maxfield were unmoved and just stared at him, like two men at a poker table. Josh approached them and sat down, weary from the lecture and then looked over the back of his chair before turning to face them.

"The bottom line, gentlemen. You can't dissect time. It's too multi-dimensional."

Colonel Maxfield cleared his throat. "You're telling me a broom killed our man?" he said with a sarcastic smirk, trying to make Josh's theory sound as ridiculous as he could.

Josh nodded, "Yes, that's precisely what I'm saying. You researched Hitler's schedule so meticulously to find out when he could be assassinated. But you never thought the janitor's schedule would be just as important. How could you? Why would you? You're just lucky the damage done was limited to that poor sap in the morgue."

Maxfield huffed at the suggestion. Colter remained cold and indifferent. Grasso, Danners, and Pelitier tried to conceal their emotions but KC was riveted to Josh's every word. Josh looked at her with a hopeful smile, as if to say, "Well. I tried."

Josh slapped the back of his chair and rose to leave. "I've said my piece. I'm just telling you, you have no idea what you're playing with."

With that Josh walked to the door then paused, and looked over his shoulder. "Actually, maybe now you do."

KC watched the door close behind him and everything in her being wanted to jump up and follow him. Colter looked at the gray smear of an image on the screen that didn't look like much of anything, now that Josh was gone. "Well, what do you think?" he said.

"It's just a glitch," Pelitier said, confidently.

Colonel Maxfield looked at him in dismay. "A GLITCH? That damned machine brought back a dead soldier! You call that a glitch?"

Pelitier ignored the outburst. "We're learning as we go. We knew there were risks. Every new system has bugs."

Maxfield tried to keep himself from strangling the man.

"Really? Well then why don't you just do me a favor, and strap your own butt in that thing next time and work out this glitch, so I don't have to lose any more men?"

Pelitier sneered back. "Anytime you want out, Colonel, you can–"

"Gentlemen, please," Colter interrupted.

Pelitier turned sharply. "Sir, I say we re-analyze the program, choose another entry point and try again."

Colter held up his hand and turned to Maxfield. "Colonel, Major Conrad was a good man, I know. But how many men have fallen in history in an attempt to save lives in the future? Shall we risk any less to gain back the lives of those fallen heroes in the past? We can do it. I know we can. I say we try it again." Colter smiled and added. "And if I'm right, we can even bring back, the major,"

Colonel Maxfield looked pensive as he mulled it over, then took a deep breath and nodded. Colter continued, more thoughtfully. "Frankly, I don't see where we have a choice.

Just then the door clicked shut as KC tried to slip out unnoticed. Colter immediately gave a glance to Pelitier who returned to the digital control console at the back of the screening room.

Carol Danner watched with some concern as Pelitier went to work, and the image on the big screen changed. Pelitier quickly flipped from one security camera view to another, the guard shack, the cafeteria, the roof, the garden, until they reached the security camera in the hallway. Danners watched quietly as the young woman ran down the hall and rushed through the front doors.

Colter spoke calmly. "And where are you going in such a hurry?"

KC ran as fast as she could. She rounded the corner and spotted Josh headed to the parking lot.

"Josh! Josh! Wait a minute!"

Josh stopped to look back, ran his fingers through his hair and sighed deeply. By the look on his face, she could tell he wasn't particularly happy to see her.

"Ms. Maltese, is this part of your job description, or does following people around come naturally to you?"

"Just wait!" KC yelled, as she tried to catch her breath.

Suddenly Josh felt the urge to unload on her.

"Do you want to know what they did to my place? Do you have any idea? They completely trashed everything; hardware, software, my machine, my records, all my work, everything gone. Ah, yes, but you had no idea. You're totally innocent. What is it you do here again?" Josh said and cut KC off before she could answer. "Maybe if they let you in on a few secrets, you can warn me next time. You think?"

KC took the abuse and waited for her chance. "I know you don't trust me, but I–."

"Trust you?" Josh blurted. "You work for the guy! He pays you to do whatever he wants."

"He pays you too," KC said.

"Don't change the subject," Josh snapped. "I can't stand the man. You like him, for pity sake! You said so yourself, remember? Colter is very professional, a great leader, and an inspiration to work for. Any of that ring a bell?"

When KC realized she wasn't going to get a word in, she tried a more direct approach.

"You were right! Lewis Colter is a jerk, and this whole thing is a nightmare. You were right. There! I said it."

The confession came so quickly, Josh didn't know what to do and just stood there looking at her. He blinked, scratched his head and finally smiled. "Was that so hard?"

Now that KC had his attention she reached out and touched his arm.

"I want to help," she said. "I know you. You're not just going to let them do this. Whatever it is, whatever I can do. I want to help."

KC smiled, and in that instant was more beautiful than Josh had ever seen her. The realization that she had stolen his heart hit him all at once, and the thought that he had to tell her burned in his brain. Words on the tip of his tongue fought to leap to freedom. *I love you.* There was never a truer statement, and he knew it beyond a shadow of a doubt.

KC watched him with a gentle smile and waited for a response.

Josh gazed into her eyes, *Say it! Just say it, coward!* He opened his mouth. "Any enemy of Colter is a friend of mine," Josh said and felt like an idiot. *Yep, that was real good!*

Much to his surprise, KC uncorked a big smile and hooked her arm in his and headed to the parking lot. The two walked arm in arm, unaware that they had been under the watchful eye of an external security camera the whole time.

Colter and the group in the screening room watched the couple walk away. In addition to the visual, the audio on the surveillance camera had picked up every word, loud and clear. Colter turned to his executive assistant. Danners sat still and tried not to move. She could feel the anger building inside of Colter until he was nearly shaking.

"Ms. Danners."

Karen Danners knew well Colter's ability to read people and tried to be as blank as she knew how. She looked over casually.

"That will be all," Colter said.

"Yes, sir," Danners replied, then calmly closed her notepad and headed for the door.

"Oh Karen," Colter said.

The savvy redhead stopped and turned around, again doing her best to look as casual as possible.

"Sir?"

Colter's voice was cold and determined. "Make a note to find yourself a new secretary."

"Yes, sir," Danners said and turned to walk out. If there was any doubt in her mind as to the man's intent, it had all been erased.

Colter turned to the colonel.

"I'll handle it," Maxfield said.

Grasso looked at the two men, with serious reservation.

"What are you going to do?"

The colonel focused on Grasso with a look of grim determination.

"A patriot must do his duty to serve his country, even that which is unpleasant."

Colter turned his swivel chair to face Carl Grasso, and sized up the man.

"Is there a problem?" Colter asked and studied his face carefully. The weight of the question bore down on Grasso who hardly hesitated and gave an awkward smile.

"I'm as patriotic as the next guy," Grasso said with a shrug.

"Good," Colter said and changed the subject. "As for reassessing the project, the target remains the same. Let's search for a new jump sight. I want closer study and analysis this time. No mistakes."

Colter, Pelitier, and Maxfield huddled together as they formulated a new plan. Grasso looked back and forth at the men and was too distracted by his own thoughts to hear anything they said. "I'm out of my league." There was no doubt in his mind that these men no longer saw any difference between Josh and the mission targets. The kid was a threat and had to be eliminated.

"How many times did I warn you?" Now the girl had joined their hit list and would have to be dealt with, "for the good of the mission." He nodded to himself and knew he was not so far out of his league that he was willing to leave the money. "Hey, it's not like I'm killing anybody." And once he had settled on that rationalization he decided that a healthy fear of his colleagues was something he would simply have to live with – if they didn't kill him first. That was a particularly unsettling thought, since his uncle Vin had said the same thing before he was shot dead by the mob. But it was the man's last words that stuck in Grasso's mind as he listened into the conversation and observed the men in front of him. "Watch your back."

CHAPTER 11

In the nearby town of Noroton, a gunmetal gray BMW and a tan Lexus with the license plate KC-1, were parked out front of the Back Forty Bar and Grill. It was midday, but like every good bar, once you were inside, the tinted windows made it look like it was night. Josh and KC sat in a booth toward the back, talking over burgers and a pitcher of beer. KC hardly touched her food while Josh chowed down with the appetite of a bear.

"Everything is different," KC said. "Colter and Pelitier have changed. Maxfield was always a little intense, but even he's gone overboard. They all have. Ever since this project, I don't know what it is."

Josh chomped on his burger. "They've got to know I'm right," he said, with his mouth half full and shaking his burger at her.

"Then why don't they stop?" KC said.

Josh finally took a break to swallow. "Their lofty platitudes of righting wrongs only goes so far. I know Colter and it all comes down to blind ambition."

"But if what you say is true–"

Josh interrupted. "There'll be a reality shift, an instant annihilation of our present to be replaced by an altered existence, an alternate reality a literal time bomb. Of what magnitude I can't be sure, perhaps total. Worst of all, we won't even know what happened."

Josh picked up his burger to take another bite.

"You know they're going to try again, don't you," KC said.

"WHAT? After everything I –" Josh threw his burger back on the plate and clenched his teeth. "When?"

"As soon as possible. As soon as they find another entry point in time."

Josh leaned across the table. "You know that for a fact?"

KC nodded. "It's Colter mostly. He was waving the flag, talking about heroes and duty. He wants them to go back in, and now they're all convinced it's for the greater good."

Josh sat back and tried not to scream. "The greater good for who?"

Suddenly, Josh's cell phone rang. He pulled it from his jacket pocket.

"Hello?"

KC watched him, and fully expected it to be Colter.

"Hi, Mike," Josh waved to KC to let her know it was all right. KC relaxed a little and took a sip of her drink.

"What's up?" Josh said and then suddenly looked away. "Uh-huh... When?... Who found him... Is Ski, okay?..."

KC watched and listened as Josh looked down then turned away to talk.

"He must be pretty broken up... Hey, what can you do, right? What's done is done... Okay, thanks... Yeah, I appreciate it...No, I'm okay... right... thanks... bye."

Josh closed the phone then turned and stared at the table, his eyes distant in thought. KC looked at him and felt sure she knew what had happened. Josh looked up and she could see it on his face. KC leaned across the table.

"It's your dad, isn't it? I'm so sorry," she said, revealing compassion in her voice.

"Yeah, he just killed himself. Ski found him in the office. Shot himself in the head."

"Oh, my God!" KC gasped and pulled back.

She stared at Josh in dismay and didn't know which was more tragic, the fact that his father had killed himself in such a horrible fashion, or the fact that Josh didn't seem to care.

"Josh, that's terrible," she said and felt the need to remind him.

Josh nodded calmly. "Yeah, like I said, what's done is done... I've got bigger problems right now."

Even with the horrors of his past, KC couldn't believe he could be so utterly indifferent.

"Josh, you can't just bury your emo–"

Josh cut her off. "Look, before you get the wrong idea, let's put an end to this right now. As far as I'm concerned my dad died a long time ago. The only difference is tomorrow they'll write about it in the obituary section of the paper, that's all. Like I said, I got other things to think about."

KC watched him, looking for any sign of emotion, but there was nothing. She wanted to yell or shake him, but with everything that had happened at the lab she suddenly felt drained and knew that in a very cold and calculating way, he was right.

Josh leaned across the table. "You said you wanted to help me. Did you mean it?"

KC glanced around and was still trying to work things out in her mind. "Y-yes, of course, anyway I can."

Josh leaned in again and spoke more softly. "Good. All I need right now is the schedule of the next time jump. You think you can get that for me?"

KC thought about it before nodding again. "I think so. Karen knows everything Colter does. I'm sure I'll be given a copy to give to her. Then what? What are you going to do?"

Josh looked at her with his game face on.

"I'm going to stop them," he said.

KC's eyes grew wider, and she looked around.

"Not by yourself!" she whispered.

"I'm working on a plan," Josh said, and nodded reassuringly.

"I said I wanted to help, not get you killed."

Josh smiled at the comment. "That makes two of us."

KC smiled, more out of nervousness and then watched Josh sit back and look at her suspiciously.

"What?" KC glanced at her surroundings like she had missed something.

"It just occurred to me," Josh said, and began to frown at her. "I mean, you're still working for Colter. How do I know you're not just playing me like before? How do I know I can really trust you?" Josh said. KC slid around all the way to his side of the booth until she was right next to him. Josh's eyes grew wide as she came closer. She grabbed his face, pressed her lips against his and lingered long enough to feel him begin to kiss her back. After a few more seconds, she pulled away.

Josh's eyes were still closed and his mouth open. Finally he opened his eyes to see her smiling face. Josh gulped and tried to compose himself.

"So, h-how's that again?" Josh stammered.

KC leaned in again and this time allowed him to kiss her as long as he wanted, and then when he finally pulled back she whispered, "You have my word."

Josh smiled as he looked into her eyes. "I'm taking a real chance here," he said and watched her slide back the way she came before and then get up from the table.

"That makes two of us," KC said, knowing she had more than his trust. She smiled over her shoulder. "I'll be in touch."

"Yeah," Josh said and rubbed his face as he watched her walk away, along with every guy at the bar. When she was gone, he took a deep breath and considered his life, his plan and his timing. It was all wrong, everything except for the girl. She was all that was right in the world, and as he thought about what he was about to do, if all went well, there was a strong possibility that he might never see her again and that frightened him more than anything.

One hour later Josh entered Mac's Discount Computer Outlet on the west side of Manhattan. Mac not only ran and owned the store, he was Josh's favorite supplier of computer hardware. He also happened to be a geek who fancied himself a genius, but in truth was only obnoxious. Since all he sold were PC's, he delighted in disappointing people who came into the store looking for Mac computers. The fact that he was short, fat and prematurely bald only made him cockier, aggressive and arguably the best computer salesman in the entire tri-boro region. The moment Josh entered the store, the smooth talking computer geek seemed to appear out of nowhere.

"Hey, Josh how's it going buddy? You know I'm expanding the store next week, changing the look, going all high tech. I got stuff comin' in you never heard of. Okay actually, you may have invented some of it, but I can get it for you cheap."

"That's good, Mac," Josh said, and handed him a list as he scoped out a few items nearby. The salesman's plastic smile quickly faded to a look of disbelief.

"You're kidding, right?"

"Do you have what I need?" Josh asked and grabbed a shopping cart. Mac stared as Josh went by, still not sure if he should take him seriously.

"That's nearly half our stock. Where are you workin', NASA?"

Josh went up and down the aisles, on a mission, sweeping merchandise off the shelves, filling one cart after another. When all was done, there were twenty 100 gig mirror hard drives with dual processors, eight 17-inch color monitors, and five cart loads of network cables, stacks of console shelving, brackets, lamps and mounts, all of it crowding the front of the store. Shoppers gave curious stares as Mac had several store employees piling boxes, until they totally obscured two cash registers.

Mac oversaw the sale as everything was meticulously rung up and smirked at Josh. "Is that it?" he asked sarcastically. "I got other customers and nothing left in stock."

"Well, actually –" Josh said, looking over his list, to see if he had missed anything.

Mac backed away quietly, then ducked behind a display case and made a quick getaway.

It was a ten minute drive to the warehouse and Josh made it in six. Kids across the street watched the white rental truck pull up, then back into the alley. Josh used the remote control to raise the freight elevator door as the red glow of the brake lights lit the alley. As soon as the truck came to a stop everything returned to darkness.

With the freight elevator and the forklift, Josh got all the supplies up to the lab in under an hour, dumped the computer equipment and with no time to waste kept moving. He went through the lab among the wreckage and rubble with a crow bar, rummaging through what was left of the time chamber, searching for key components. He paused at a device the size of a briefcase, still attached to the wall of the chamber and ripped it out, wires and all. Josh looked the damaged chronometer over as he went to his work table and prepared for the long process of rebuilding the time link brain center.

Josh worked tirelessly under the glare of shop lamps, using new computer components and salvaging what he could from the original chamber. After three hours of rebuilding and prepping circuits to interface with phone lines and data base link ups; Josh closed the console cover, tightened a few screws and wiped his brow.

"All right, let's see what we've got."

Josh powered up the new system and Hal's voice returned.

"Hello, Josh. How are you today?" the computer asked, in its typically calm and flat tone.

Josh stayed all business as he plugged in another device. "Time for a change, Hal. Give me a countdown from five, and do a time check."

As the computer began the countdown, Josh adjusted and synthesized the audio with a few taps of his keypad and a slow turn of a dial. In a matter of seconds, Hal's voice transitioned into the smooth and seductive tones of a woman that was far less haunting and quite appealing as it calmly announced the computer's ready status.

"Three, two, one. The time is now seven forty-five, Eastern Standard Time. Time scan ready to receive data," the computer said, invitingly.

Josh smiled and arched an eyebrow.

"That's better."

At eight thirty, the gray BMW pulled up outside a small church, just as the rain started to tap on the windshield. Josh peered through the drizzle to see the old church steps and the sign with a bulb missing, "Church of the Heavenly Rest."

Despite the rain, and the fact that he hadn't seen the inside of a church in longer than he cared to remember, Josh hopped out of the car like a man with a purpose and headed inside. Once he was through the front door of the lobby, he shook his collar, brushed the rain off the sleeves of his leather jacket and looked around. The church was old, but a new paint job and nice floral arrangements on either side of the chapel entrance brightened up the place.

A few kids ran past and several more trampled up the stairs from the basement chasing after them. There was noise coming from downstairs, the sound of cheering and whistles. With no one else around and his curiosity aroused, Josh headed down to the basement.

The double doors to the cafeteria were wide open with a crowd of people standing in the hall. Josh eased his way though the throng of parents amidst all the cheering and looked inside to see the small gymnasium and a basketball game in progress.

The players were ten and eleven year olds and Father Mike was the referee. With the bleachers packed and parents and friends calling to the kids, Josh found a spot along the wall and watched the game. "Church sure has changed," Josh mumbled to himself.

A little Asian kid drove straight to the basket against the center who was twice his size. A fake left, then right, caught the center flat footed and the little kid made the lay-up with ease.

Josh pumped his fist the moment he sunk the basket and couldn't help rooting for the little guy. There was a tap on his shoulder, and Josh turned to see the young girl in her teens carrying a box load of popcorn. He reached for his wallet and the girl handed him a free bag.

"You're not from around here, are you?" she said with a hearty smile and walked away before Josh could answer.

"Thanks!" he tried to yell over the noise then settled back against the wall.

By the end of the game the score was 55, 48, and the Asian kid had stolen the show. As the crowd thinned out, Father Mike stood along the sidelines, chatting with another priest and several parents. Josh nibbled on his popcorn and bided his time until the last few people filed past.

"Drive safe," Mike said.

Josh smiled at his friend, and crumpled up the empty bag of popcorn as he approached.

"There's nothing like a good ref," Josh said.

Mike nodded, happy to accept the compliment.

"And you're nothing like one," Josh added, then set up for a shot at the garbage can a few feet away, a high arcing shot that went in cleanly.

"I see. So did you come here to insult me? Because I can go to the Monsignor for that."

"Is there someplace we can talk?" Josh asked.

When they reached the garden courtyard, the rain had stopped and it was quiet. Father Mike used a towel to wipe off the stone bench and offered Josh a seat.

"No thanks," Josh said.

"Well if you don't, I will. I've been standing all night."

Father Mike sat down while Josh chose to pace the length of the small garden, filled with nervous energy. The priest watched him with growing concern.

"I'm sorry about your father. Though you two weren't close, still I know this can't be easy.

Josh walked past, trying to focus his thoughts.

"You have no idea. I don't know where to start."

Mike watched him walk up and down like a caged tiger, not realizing they were on two different wavelengths.

"As tough as this is, Josh, you're going to have to forgive him. It's the only way to let go."

Josh shook his head. "Who? My dad? I didn't come here for him. But now that you mention it, if he'd done it sooner, I probably wouldn't be in this mess.

"That kind of talk isn't going to fix anything," Father Mike said.

Josh rounded on the priest and stopped right in front of him.

"Actually, maybe it will. Listen, you said I could call on you if I needed help. Well, I need your help."

Mike looked up at him with open arms. "Here I am."

Josh paused, thinking of how he should begin.

"The problem I was telling you about has gotten worse. They used the time machine. A man was killed, and they're going to try again."

The priest bolted up from his seat. "Josh, you've got to put an end to this!"

"I know. I know. All things considered, we got lucky. They didn't affect the timeline, and I think I've got a plan. But I'm warning you, this is extremely radical, Mike, so try to stay with me on this one.

The priest slung the towel over his shoulder and folded his arms.

"I'm listening," he said.

Josh took a breath to collect himself, gave the priest a reluctant glance, and jumped right in.

"Even if I did blow up Colter Laboratories, they would just build another one. The only way to really fix this problem is to make it go away." Josh paused a moment to let that sink in.

Mike cocked his head to the side and squinted. "What do you mean, go away?"

Josh raised a finger as if to say, "Ah, good question!"

"Okay. The problem is not the machine. It's not Lewis Colter or even Colter Corporation. As you so aptly pointed out, it's me. I gave them the idea. I gave them the machine. And now, although you and I know the machine should never be used, it looks like that's exactly what I've got to do to end this madness."

"What are you saying?" Mike said and came closer.

"Look, believe me. I've tried to think this thing through a hundred different ways. The only way I can figure how to stop them from using the machine is to take it away. And the only way to do that is to go back in time and make it so I never invented the damn thing. You with me?"

Mike held up both hands as if to stop him there.

"Wait a minute. This is crazy. But let's entertain your notion for a moment. You're facing the same dilemma Colter faces, aren't you? Even though your heart's in the right place, you can't actually tell what will happen. You yourself said, going back in time could have a catastrophic effect. What if you can't change yourself? What if you change something else and make it worse? No, it's too dangerous."

Josh tried to continue, and the priest held up his hand again.

"Wait, listen to me," he said. "Your father just died, only hours ago. You're under a lot of stress. You're not thinking clearly."

"You're wrong, Mike! My father's death gave me the clarity I needed to see this perfectly," Josh said, his eyes glaring. "My old man is at the center of this whole thing! I told you, you'd have to stay with me on this one. The prime objective is to change myself, but before that happens, the way I see it, I've got to go back and change him first. I don't have any choice."

"Change who?" the priest asked and listened.

"My dad," Josh said and paused to let his friend digest the idea.

Mike looked at him, suspiciously. Now that he was following him, he didn't like where the conversation was going.

"Stay with me 'cause we're just getting started... This is the part where I need your help. I need the answer to a very important question, and I'm thinking this should be easy for you."

The priest listened and nodded, his curiosity aroused.

"What's the question?"

"All right, my dad pretty much persecuted my mom her whole life. Okay so, what I need to know is if she died for nothing or died for something that was real."

There was a long pause as the priest watched him with the same ponderous stare, and repeated, "What's the question?"

"Was Jesus Christ really who he said he was?"

Mike looked at Josh intently, and it was Josh's turn to wait for his response.

"Jesus Christ was many things, Josh. He was a philosopher, a prophet, a priest. There was so much to the man. I'm not sure what –"

"There's a lot riding on this, Mike," Josh said pointedly. "Quit screwing around. Was Jesus Christ really the Son of God or wasn't he?" Josh glared at him, waiting for the answer.

The priest thought a while longer, trying to be patient with the man and give an answer he felt was responsible.

"As a Catholic, that's what we believe," Mike said and nodded confidently.

Josh shook his head. "That's not good enough. I didn't ask you 'as a Catholic?' I didn't ask you, what you believe? I asked you, if Jesus Christ was in fact the Son of God? Yes or no."

Suddenly Mike had had enough and stood up.

"I don't know what you want me to say. I told you what I believe to be true. What more do you want? That's all I can say."

Josh looked at him as though he were crazy.

"What you believe to be true? What you believe to be true isn't the issue. I've got no room for doubt here. I need to know for a fact. Either he was or he wasn't? It's a black and white world, Mike. People who see it in grays are deluded. Either Jesus was telling the truth or he was a liar. So which is it? Did my mother die for a lie, or the truth? That's the question I need the answer to, and I need to know now."

Father Mike stepped back. He turned and walked a few paces then looked at Josh again.

"Your mother died because she had character and courage. She died for her convictions. She was a woman of faith who –"

"You're stalling," Josh interrupted. "If you were to ask my mother the same question I just asked you, she would have answered in the affirmative without hesitation. There was no question in her mind that Jesus was the real deal. And she wasn't even a priest."

Father Mike stormed up to Josh, red faced with fists clenched, and suddenly didn't sound like a priest anymore.

"Look, my faith is my own, just like your mother's and I don't appreciate you coming here to put me on trial. Sure it's easy for you a non-believer, in all your anger, your ignorance, to just raise your hand and ask the most significant question of all time, the question that all of life and eternity hinges on, and expect a nice, easy answer. You really think it's that simple?"

Father Mike reached up to his neck, ripped his collar off then shoved it at Josh.

"Here, tough guy. Put it on and try looking at it from my side for a change."

Josh didn't move and just stared at the priest who stood there, disheveled with a few strands of hair in his face and the collar in his hand. Eventually he lowered his arm and stuffed the collar in his pocket. He raked his fingers through his hair, tried to regain his composure, took a deep breath and looked at Josh apologetically.

"Look, I know what you want...You want absolute proof, but I'm telling you, that's just not possible," he said, shaking his head and turned to leave.

"It is now," Josh said.

The words stopped the priest dead in his tracks.

"I told you it was extremely radical," Josh said with a tone of regret in his voice.

Father Mike turned around slowly and shook his head slowly at first. "No. You can't – if you mean what I think you mean." The priest's face said in utter disbelief.

"Absolutely," Josh said. "That's the plan."

The priest looked at him dumbfounded and horrified as he came back, walking in a stupor, like he had just been drugged.

"What? What plan? This is insanity. I can't believe you would even think of such a thing. I mean, for God's sake, you can't be serious.

Josh squared his shoulders.

"I need to know, Mike. I need to know the answer to this question if I'm going to turn it all around. There's no other way. Like I said, I've thought about this a hundred different ways, but I keep coming back to this one thing. No way around it. He was the one thing that came between my mother and father. And although I didn't believe in him, he impacted every facet of my life. He's clearly the one thing that can guarantee me the biggest shift in the course of my history and my eventual outcome. I know it's a risk, but I think it's the best shot we have of wiping the time machine out of existence."

The priest stared with a somewhat pained expression on his face. "There's got to be another way," Mike said, and shook his head.

"You're talking to the son of an atheist, Mike. It was an atheist who built that time machine, not a believer."

Mike searched the empty space around him, trying to think.

"Look, I'm willing to help. If...if you want, there is historical data and archeological evidence, all kinds of information gathered by credible..."

Josh shook his head. "I don't have time for all of that. Besides, that's all academic. I need proof, real proof, and I can get it if you help me." Father Mike just stared as Josh tried to reason it out. "It's a gamble, I know. But Josh Kensington the atheist is betting that Josh Kensington the believer would have chosen a different path. If that's true, then who I am, everything I think and feel right now, hinges on this one question. Was Christ for real?" Josh asked, feeling that he sounded like a broken record.

The priest suddenly looked tired and worn. The two men stared at each other across the garden as the rain began to patter against the leaves. Josh looked at him with cold determination. "I'm going back in time, Mike. I'm going back in time to meet Christ. It's the only way out of this mess. I'm asking you as a friend. Will you help me?"

The rain began to pour.

"I'm sorry," Father Mike said before turning away and heading inside.

Josh shouted after him. "I thought so. What is it they say? Ignorance is bliss? It's easy to believe when you don't have to know for sure, isn't it?"

Mike stopped again and turned to face him once more.

"I believe in the person of Jesus Christ. I believe He lived and died for me. Of that I have no doubt."

"Then what's the problem?" Josh said, which sounded more like a dare.

"The problem is, you want something even the Bible can't offer... You want absolute proof."

Mike walked inside and Josh frowned at him, until he realized he was getting wet and decided to get out of the rain. Josh stood inside the doorway of the church dripping wet and called to his friend.

"What's wrong with proof? What are you so afraid of? I would think that you of all people would welcome proof," Josh said, challenging the priest once and for all.

Father Mike turned again but this time there was real fear in his eyes. Josh watched and listened with slow surprise as the priest spoke plainly.

"Afraid? Yes, I am afraid, and you want to know why?" he said, as he came forward. "Because if there is no God, there is nothing." Mike spoke with such conviction that even Josh felt a little unsettled. "Without God, human existence has no purpose or meaning. We're doomed, Josh. We're all just like your father, destined to live a tortured existence filled with despair. An existence without hope, without truth, without love. An existence more frightening than any disaster your time machine could ever conjure up. Without God we are lost."

Josh listened, and for the first time he could appreciate the priest's honesty. Father Mike continued more softly and seemed to regain some of his courage.

"Yes I'm afraid. And for the time being, I admit, I prefer my Lord's existence safely shrouded in the mystery of the past, if you don't mind."

Josh shook his head, and chuckled.

"I don't get you. Remember when you told me to talk to God? Well, look at you. I have the opportunity to really talk to Him and you're shaking in your boots."

Father Mike just looked at Josh, then slowly his expression changed as though something Josh had said had unexpectedly sparked a light. A smile crept across the priest's face and Josh watched the strange transition with curiosity as his friend began to chuckle as well.

"It's amazing the tools God uses to restore your faith," Mike said and thought a while longer. "All right, I'll help you."

Josh's eyes lit up. "You will? Wait a minute. You shifted gears too quickly. What changed your mind?"

Mike looked out at the pouring rain.

"Well two things really, and try to keep up with me here," Mike said, smiling. "One, you're not the first to demand absolute proof from God. Thomas, the apostle, also needed absolute proof and doubted as you do now. That is, until he saw the resurrected Christ for himself. And two, it occurred to me that even if you did meet Christ himself, your time theories wouldn't apply to him."

Josh smirked at the comment. "And why's that?"

"Well, think about it. You're using your time machine to go back in time to meet the creator of time itself, right? So he should see you coming. Basically, this is the one instance, existentially speaking, when you can drop the pebble into the proverbial pool of water and nothing happens. Perhaps this is all part of God's plan after all," the priest said and looked away to the sky.

Josh gazed at Mike, and squinted as though reading the fine print on a label. "You know, you're a pretty deep guy. The maker of time, huh?"

The two men stood in the open doorway, listening to the rain splash on the cobblestone walkway of the garden. A few more seconds, Josh suddenly sprang to life. "All right then! This is what I need."

Mike struggled to leave his own thoughts and concentrate on their conversation as Josh laid out the plan.

"I need to find some part of the Bible where it says that Jesus was alone, off on his own for a while, you know doing nothing."

"Doing nothing," Father Mike smiled to himself. "He was only the busiest man in Judea."

"I'll need a geographic location, as specific as you can nail down and surrounding events before and after for the computer to zero in on. That will be my entry point, the target for my time jump."

The priest nodded calmly, thoughtfully. "I'll see what I can do," he said. "When do you need it?"

"ASAP."

"I'll have it within the hour."

"Thanks, Mike. I really appreciate this," Josh said, then paused as he prepared to leave. "You know, I have to admit. I really didn't think you were going to help me. Thanks again."

"Sometimes I even surprise myself," Father Mike said. "And thank you."

Josh didn't respond for a few seconds. "For what?"

"For the lesson in faith."

Josh replied with a thoughtful nod and headed for the stairs.

Father Mike called after him. "See you in church, on Sunday?"

Josh trotted up the stairs and called back as he disappeared from view.

"That'll take a miracle."

Josh checked his watch as he crossed the church lobby, and then pulled his collar up against the rain. Once he was out the door, he skipped down the church steps and started up the sidewalk searching for his keys. He slowed when he saw a person standing next to his car with an umbrella. Josh stopped and let the rain pour over him as he watched the figure start toward him. Josh looked around and was ready to back away when suddenly the person called out.

"Josh! Wait there!"

Karen Danners rushed to him, then in one motion hooked her arm in his and pulled Josh back against the building. Together they moved along the stone wall of the church as the rain continued to fall and pour off of the eaves. A few more feet and they reached the side entrance of the church, gated and locked. The stone archway was recessed enough to provide shelter, and the two backed into the shadows, safely hidden from view. Danners lowered her umbrella and looked up. Josh hardly recognized her. Her red hair hung down like a mop, her mascara was smudged under her eyes and her stylish tweed suit was soaked from the waist down. Danners tried to brush the hair back from her eyes, but with wet hands it didn't do much good.

"I don't know how much time we have," she said. Despite her appearance, the woman spoke with her trademark calm and professionalism. Josh opened his mouth to speak but Danners wouldn't allow it.

"Just listen to me. It's all coming apart. Colter and the others are on some kind of power trip and are completely out of control. They've gone insane."

"That's what KC said when I talked to her. We were —"

"I know, Josh. I saw you. Pelitier caught you on an external security camera. We all saw you and heard everything both of you said, both of you... everything."

Josh peered down at the wet pavement momentarily, his eyes flitting back and forth, trying to recall the conversation as best he could. A look of fear suddenly swept across Danner's face.

"KC's in trouble and I'm afraid Colter is going to do something drastic," she said.

"Like what?" Josh glared at her intently.

"Before Colter dismissed me, he told me to start looking for another assistant. Neither of you are safe Josh. They've got a tracer on your car. That's how I knew where you were. They're coming after you."

Josh grabbed Danners by the shoulders and pushed her against the wall behind him. "Thanks. Thanks for sticking your neck out." He kissed her on the cheek and looked out to the street.

"What are you going to do?" Danners asked.

Josh hesitated before he stepped out into the rain then looked at her. "I can't tell you, but do me a favor. Don't go back to the lab. Whatever you do, don't go back there tonight."

With a cold stare in his eyes and no emotion in his voice, the cryptic message frightened Danners even more.

"What are you going to do?" she repeated and when he didn't answer, she pleaded. "Be careful!"

Josh thought about it a few seconds then smiled. "It's too late for that." He then ran out into the rain toward his car.

Traffic flowed smoothly uptown as Josh downshifted and came to a red light, his mind racing. He went over everything he could remember, listing the day's events in rapid succession; the dead man in the morgue, the kiss in the restaurant, his father's death, the conversation with Father Mike, Danners, the plan to infiltrate the lab, his time jump, and the realization that Colter was onto him and his girlfriend.

"My girlfriend." Josh lingered on the thought and considered it might be the last time he would imagine the two of them together. "They're coming after you!" His mind raced ahead to the electronic tracer hidden somewhere in his car. Colter was watching him and as if to coincide perfectly, the phone rang. Josh listened to the tone and watched the caller I.D. flash, lower right on the console. With his left hand on the leather steering wheel, Josh reached down and opened the phone line.

"Hello, Lewis."

"Josh, did I reach you at a bad time?" Colter's voice was smooth and casual like a cobra trying to lull its victim to sleep, Josh smirked at the thought.

"Actually you did. Me and the Mrs. were just sitting down to have supper with the kids. What can I do for you?"

"More specifically, it's what can I do for you. It seems I have some information that someone thinks might be useful to you."

"What information is that?"

The light changed. Josh pulled off and glanced nervously at the speakerphone mounted in the dash.

"Ms. Maltese has informed me that you would like to know the schedule of our next time jump. It took a little coercion. She didn't tell me precisely why this should interest you, but I told her it was a closed event for a limited audience. Only a select few will be invited. Unfortunately your name is not on the list."

"Coercion? What did you do to her?" Josh tried to keep the lump from rising in his throat.

"Don't be so melodramatic, Josh. Once she understood my interest in the matter, she was very cooperative. She's as smart as she is beautiful."

Josh breathed a sigh of relief.

"So I'm not invited, huh?"

"Afraid not."

Josh whacked the steering wheel with the palm of his hand, in mock anger. "Aw, man! You really put me in a jam here, Colter."

"Really? How so?" the voice replied through a patch of static.

Josh checked his rear view mirror.

"Where else can I find a room full of pompous asses with inflated egos blowing hot air at each other to bore me out of my mind? Will Ms. Maltese be attending? Where is she?"

"No I'm afraid not. She's here at the lab, with me."

"Let me talk to her," Josh said.

"We caught her going through classified files. She managed to get a look at the entire program schedule. There's a lot of information in those documents which, well quite frankly, could be damaging in the wrong hands. As a result she's placed me in somewhat of a bind here."

Josh tried to focus on the road as his heart pounded in his chest. "I wouldn't overreact. I'm sure there is a logical explanation."

"No doubt, but you can see my predicament. The information is so sensitive, and with the project in its early stages, secrecy is at a premium."

"Have you considered turning her over to the authorities?" Josh said, and knew he was clutching at straws as he stalled for time.

"Unfortunately, that's out of the question. In cases like this, I have been given governmental authority to initiate any actions I deem necessary to protect the security of this program. As for the amount of force, that is completely up to my discretion.

Josh stared straight ahead in a daze and didn't see the truck stopped at the light until he was right on it. In one motion he locked his arms and slammed on the brakes. The tires squealed against the wet pavement and the car screeched to a stop as the hood of the BMW slid under the truck's rear bumper, then lurched just inches short of impact.

Josh stared at the back end of the truck, breathing hard, like he had been dunked in a vat of ice water then collected himself and hoped Colter didn't hear the tire squeal.

"Are you all right?" Colter asked.

Josh tried to sound calm. "Sure, just some idiot driver," he said as the light changed green and he pulled out around the truck. Josh continued, and although Colter's tone was civil, he knew he was bargaining for KC's life. He also knew that he had nothing to bargain with. Josh glanced over at the speakerphone, afraid to take his eyes off the road after the near miss with the truck.

"Discretion is the key, Colter," Josh reminded him. "I thought the point of this operation was to save lives."

"KC's life is really none of your concern, Josh. In all honesty, you really should be looking out for your own welfare. Ms. Maltese will be taken care of shortly. As for you, I've sent someone to deal with you as well, nothing personal, Josh. Just tying up loose ends. You understand. Oh, the next time jump is tonight, just so you'll know what you'll be missing. Thanks for your contribution, Josh. Goodbye."

Colter hung up and Josh mashed the accelerator, wrenching the wheel hard left. Cars slammed on their brakes as the BMW cut off traffic then screeched around a corner and flew down the side street. The car careened into the next intersection and fish tailed wildly, sending other cars veering out of the way as the Beemer slipped into the flow of traffic to the wail of car horns blaring, as it accelerated downtown.

Meanwhile, on the underside of Josh's car a small red light flashed as the magnetic homing device sent its tracking beacon and exact location to Colter labs which was then routed to the advanced team of field agents who were on their way to eliminate the target.

CHAPTER 12

By nine thirty the rain had stopped. Security around the industrial complex of Colter Laboratories was at its highest level and the lab building was bristling with activity. Armed guards inside the lab watched every exit while dozens of technicians prepped the time chamber for a second launch and manned control stations.

The vault like door at the south entrance of the lab opened and the second time pilot entered. Workers stopped what they were doing and paused to see the soldier, escorted to the time machine. Major Jay Haust AKA "Dozer" was as big as a truck and even more menacing than the first time pilot. This man was Pelitier's first selection. At 6' 3," two hundred and fifty five pounds with short-cropped, bleached white hair, the man wore a permanent scowl and glared intently with deep set eyes and a thick brow that made him look more primal than human. Pelitier watched from the observation window of Colter's conference room nodding like a proud father as the soldier approached the time chamber, while Maxfield stood by looking less then thrilled. When they had gone over the candidates, Haust was his last choice. "He's a mistake waiting to happen," were his exact words to the panel. "A wild man with an explosive temper, volatile and unpredictable."

But after the first botched time jump, Colter had put him to the top of the list at Pelitier's recommendation. "Send in someone who can get the job done, no matter what."

Maxfield had lodged his complaint, calling the man a psychopathic killer.

To which Colter had only one response, "Perfect."

And there he was, the beast of a man suited up and ready for battle. Haust's wide gait and long stride gave him the look of a gun slinging gladiator, a hungry predator, stalking his prey. The soldier was covered from head to toe in customized Kevlar body armor and carried twice the amount of weapons of his predecessor. Although Colonel Maxfield disproved of the selection, he would make sure the man had every advantage he could think of.

Haust came to a stop at the warning marker that surrounded the time chamber and sat down at the waiting station for a final prep where a group of white coated lab techs checked his gear. Residual energy from the force field surrounding the machine fluttered the laces of the soldier's combat boots. Haust glanced down at the energy, then looked up and glared at the machine.

Colter watched the activity from inside the conference room then turned and smiled at the beautiful blonde seated at the large table, waiting patiently with two security agents standing behind her. Her attention however was on the two men across from her, seated behind laptops busily tracking Josh's movements and location. Maxfield stood over their shoulder with Simon Pelitier and observed the Intel coming across in real time.

"He's rabbiting! Just turned west on thirty third." The agent in front of Pelitier tapped a few keys to boost the signal. "He's really haulin' now, movin' fast!"

Pelitier watched the blip on screen, and studied the monitor like a chessboard.

"Where are you going, Josh?"

The second agent announced the change in course.

"Target turning again, headed south, sir!"

"Relay coordinates to the away teams and close in," Colter said then looked to the helpless young woman seated at the conference table.

"Looks like your boyfriend is running away. Perhaps next time you should choose your men more wisely."

The PA clicked on, and a voice announced, "Sir, the time pilot is prepped and ready for launch."

Colter and Maxfield turned to see the soldier through the observation window, seated near the chamber amidst a crew of technicians.

"Very good," Colter said. "New man, new coordinates, I have a good feeling about this."

The door behind KC opened, and Carl Grasso walked into the room with papers. In a glance he could see that the girl was under arrest and, for the moment, pretended to ignore her as he walked across the room.

"Mr. Colter, I just got this communiqué," he said, holding out the paper to Colter. "Five of the thirteen board members are pulling out. They disagree with the proposal to move forward and want more testing."

Colter took the letters, flipped through them then smirked and shook his head.

"Regrettable, but not unexpected," he said then tore the papers and tossed them aside.

"Those bureaucrats want to fold up tent and go home? That's fine. At least, now we know who the real men of valor are. As they say, "To the victor go the spoils."

Maxfield turned to Colter as the two men stood before the window.

"And what if they grow more hostile and leak information that would compromise this project?"

Colter smiled confidently. "We have the means to fix that as well," he said and turned to look at the time machine.

KC watched the whole scenario and two words echoed in her mind, "Pandora's Box."

"And what if you can't?" KC heard herself say, her voice trembling.

One of the guards reached out and put a hand on her shoulder to remind her to keep her mouth shut. KC fought back the fear and tried to speak again.

"What if you can't? What if someone tried to use the time machine on you?"

This time the guard moved in front of her and she recognized him, Vega, the tall lean agent with the dark eyes and jet-black hair, slicked back. The man reached out and placed an arm on the table. The gesture not only cut off her view of Colter, but also allowed his jacket to fall open. KC got a good look at the high-powered Automag handgun, strapped in his shoulder harness and fell silent. The guard smiled, a wicked grin that said, "That's better," and then took his place behind the chair once again.

Grasso looked at KC who cried out in silence. He glanced at the guards that stood over her like bloodthirsty hounds and dared him to make a move. Suddenly his conscience flooded in like a tidal wave, and the reality of the situation was all too clear. They were going to kill the girl, and he was going to let it happen. Grasso tried to think. "C'mon, you're a businessman. Cut a deal, start talkin', say somethin'!"

"What's going on?" Grasso said.

Before anyone could say anything KC blurted out.

"Carl? You've got to help!"

The guard spun KC around in her chair before the last word was out of her mouth.

"I thought we had an understanding," Vega hissed between gritted teeth.

KC shrank back in her chair and seemed hypnotized by his gaze.

Pelitier and the colonel were hardly fazed by the outburst and just stared at the monitors.

"This doesn't concern you," Colter said, while Grasso stared at the girl locked in the guard's trance. Maxfield glanced over and for an instant seemed somewhat sympathetic.

"You'd better leave, son," Maxfield said.

When Grasso didn't immediately move he added, "Now."

The guard finally moved back and allowed KC to see beyond him. She peered at Grasso who just stood there, staring blankly. He had been given an order and after considering every angle, his eyes revealed that he didn't want to die also."

Grasso lowered his eyes and without another glance in her direction, he walked out of the room.

"Away team closing in, sir."

Pelitier watched as a second blip entered the screen and began to move in on the target. When the dots converged, Colter smiled and leaned in closer as did Pelitier, and from where KC sat the two looked like vultures circling as they prepared to murder an innocent man.

The street glistened ahead of the BMW as Josh maneuvered through traffic, then swerved into the center lane and mashed the accelerator. With a quick glance down at the phone console, he speed dialed Father Mike and listened for the line to connect.

"Hello. St. Luke's, Church of the –"

"Mike, it's me," Josh said as the BMW leapt forward and sped under a yellow light, leaving the rest of the traffic behind, except for a black Camaro that darted across the intersection. Josh checked his rearview mirror to see the car racing up behind him as the other headlights shrank in the distance.

"Listen. I need those coordinates. Do you have them?

"Josh, what's going on?"

Josh downshifted as he caught up to the next group of cars.

"No time to explain. Do you have them," he repeated.

There was a brief pause and then Father Mike returned. "Yes, New Testament, Mark six, forty-six."

Josh listened carefully, then frowned. "Six, forty-six. What's that?"

"Right in between two great miracles, Christ feeds the multitude. Surely you know the story with the fish and the loaves of bread?"

The priest's voice was still chattering over the speaker phone when the Camaro pulled up beside him. Josh stepped on the accelerator, but instead of the car dropping back, the Camaro went with him. He fed the engine a little more gas, but the Camaro kept pace.

"Hang on, Mike."

Josh glanced over at the car's black tinted windows, streaked with ribbons of rain and neon light as the Camaro sped along side through the city streets.

"Tinted glass, obnoxious," Josh thought to himself as he refocused on the road ahead. It was apparent that the other driver, whoever he was, wanted to race and Josh had no patience for it. Both machines roared across the wet pavement with a trail of swirling mist billowing in their wake. With the speedometer just over seventy-five and both cars roaring through the city streets, Josh gripped the wheel and the Camaro held steady at his shoulder. Both cars bounded over uneven pavement as they closed in on the next light, which suddenly turned yellow. With the black car right next to him, Josh glanced over to see the electric window slide down on the passenger side. In a split second, a hundred images hit him, recorded in his mind like a reflexive action in response to what he saw.

The first observation was the man in the passenger seat, mid thirties, dressed in a blue windbreaker. Next was his glaring eye, the look of intense concentration, and the glint of the flash suppressor on the nozzle of the handgun that was sliding out of the dark interior. There was the driver, a shadowy figure, eyes riveted to the road, black gloves gripping the steering wheel, his raspy voice intense and agitated by the high rate of speed, shouting two words over and over as he turned to look at the target, "Do it! Do it!"

Josh mashed the accelerator in mid command and pulled ahead just enough to get the door panel between him and the nozzle of the handgun. The Camaro lurched forward to stay with him and give the shooter a clean shot. A moment later, the passenger window of the Camaro came back into view over Josh's shoulder and the gunman took aim. To buy another second of cover, Josh pressed back in his seat. He knew in that instant that both men to his left were doomed.

Another series of observations recorded in Josh's mind involved his assailants. They were overly aggressive and determined to get the shot. As a result both men were looking at him which gave them tunnel vision and prevented the driver from reacting to the yellow light that turned red. Next were the road conditions. It was wet and at their rate of speed even high performance cars with proper tires in an emergency stop would be thrown into a skid. Lastly, there was the semi truck approaching the intersection westbound, from the driver's left while the driver of the Camaro was looking right. This led to the most important observation of all, one of human nature. The driver of the semi truck would not reduce his speed, because he simply would not believe that a tiny sports car would willfully run a solid red light in the rain at night as a giant truck was barreling through the intersection. This Josh factored in, along with the speed of the truck which would dictate every action that followed, all the way to the desired result that would take the Camaro out of the equation instantly when both cars ran the red light.

The ten ton semi entered the intersection and Josh mashed the accelerator to the floor with the car by his side determined to take the shot. When the driver of the Camaro finally glimpsed the truck coming up on his left and hit the brake, he threw the car into a skid to prevent a head on. But at eighty five miles per hour, the laws of inertia combined with the wet road made collision both imminent and inevitable. The driver of the truck slammed on the brake as the silver BMW flashed in front of him going 90mph, and the black Camaro came in like a guided missile and hit the front corner of his truck. The impact was an explosion that rocked the cab and jackknifed the trailer sending it skidding sideways with the front end of the sports car aflame and buried under the wheels of the truck like a squashed bug.

Josh looked in his rear view mirror to see the black tarmac light up with the explosion, and slowed the BMW which had escaped without a scratch. He forced himself to loosed his death grip on the steering wheel and tried to catch his breath with his heart pounding in his ears.

"Josh, are you listening? You still there?" Father Mike called over the speaker phone.

"Yeah, I'm still here," Josh said, glancing back at the mangled wreckage, ablaze in the intersection behind him.

"Yeah, I'm with you. Uh, New Testament, Mark six, four six, Christ and the multitude."

Father Mike went on with his lesson while Josh took a few deep breaths and tried to collect himself. When he stopped shaking, he glanced down at the phone and interrupted, "Multitudes? Mike, that's not going to work. I told you I need him alone."

"I'm getting to that. After the crowds disperse, Jesus puts the disciples on a boat bound for Bethsaida then goes up on a mountain to pray."

"Where's this mountain?"

"The northeast shore of the Sea of Galilee."

"You sure about this?"

"The same story is confirmed in Matthew fourteen, twenty-three, which specifically says Jesus was alone. There's your entry point."

Josh checked his mirrors then cut off two cars as he darted from the left lane all the way across to make a sharp right turn down a side street, tires squealing. Aside from a few angry glares and honking horns, there was no harm done.

The Beemer slowed as Josh neared his destination.

"Great! What I need you to do now is call the lab and leave a message saying the same thing you just told me."

"Just leave a message?"

Josh looked down at the phone.

"The computer will answer. Then you activate the search program with the code words, "Hide the bacon." You got that?"

Father Mike repeated the code. "Hide the bacon, right."

"The computer will confirm and say, "When." You say, "Now," and then start talking. The computer will record the data and initiate a search. When you're done, press pound."

"When, now, and pound, that's it?" Father Mike said over the phone.

"That's it. Just repeat everything you told me, and the computer will do the rest. Thanks, Mike."

There was a long pause and Josh glanced down at the phone.

"Mike, you still there?"

The voice came back on.

"Yeah, I was just thinking. I can't believe you're actually going to meet to him."

Josh checked his mirror again.

"If I don't get killed first," he mumbled to himself.

"What?"

"I said, if all goes well," Josh said.

"Yes, I'll be praying for you," Mike said.

"Couldn't hurt," Josh added.

"You know, in our conversation a thought occurred to me."

Josh could tell he was about to get into something deep.

"You going back to talk to Christ. It's like I'm talking to a disciple, a future disciple." Father Mike paused then tried again.

"I mean, one who will be a disciple, or rather is about to become a disciple from the past."

Josh smiled. "Don't hurt yourself. I think I know what you mean. Anyway, like I said, let's just hope all goes well."

"Yeah, well if it does, then that means this is it. If you get this done, everything will change and it will be like I never knew you. You'll disappear from my life forever."

"Think how much better off you'll be," Josh said as he slowed the car.

"Again, I'll be praying for you. May God's blessing be upon you, my friend." With that he hung up.

"Just make the call! Just make the call!" Josh said to himself. He began to check the storefront signs as he sped down the side street. Up ahead, on the left, was a bright yellow sign with red letters that read, "E-Z STORAGE."

The BMW screeched to a halt in front of the public storage facility and Josh jumped out of the car, moving fast.

The young attendant behind the counter had stringy brown hair pulled back in a ponytail, four earrings, a pierced eyebrow, a nose ring and a pierced lip with a ring and a chain that led back to one of the earrings. Josh hardly noticed him as he ran in. The attendant glanced up from his portable TV as Josh flashed his license and rushed to the elevator.

"Josh Kensington, Forty one sixteen!"

The attendant raised his head off his hand long enough to yell.

"Hey! You're supposed to sign in!" It was the most energy he had expended all night.

The young grease ball grabbed the stub of a pencil and scribbled the locker number 4116, upside down in the logbook, too bothered to flip it around. "Jerk," the young man added and then settled back into his haze and TV watching.

The elevator doors slid open on the 4th floor. Josh leapt out and dashed to the right, making his way down the deserted corridor with the keys already in hand and stopped at the door marked 4116. Josh stared at the door with the key poised in front of the lock. His hand cold, clammy and shaking. "This is it," he said.

Josh flashed back to the thought he had in the darkness of his demolished laboratory, the point of perfect clarity that had placed him on this path, a path of self-destruction.

"They're coming for you," Josh reminded himself and glanced down the hall at the elevator. "They'll be here soon." He took a breath. It was either this or a bullet in the head. Josh shoved the key in the lock, turned it and heard the bolt slide away.

The door to the storage room swung open on squeaky hinges and Josh stepped inside. He ran his hand along the wall to the left and flipped on the light to see everything just as he had left it, four years ago. It had been a while since he had given the room much thought, let alone its contents, and for good reason.

The storage room with its eight foot ceiling, was twelve feet square and empty, except for the two anodized metal footlockers sitting in the middle of the floor marked A, and B in bold red letters. Josh threw off his leather jacket as he looked over the metal cases then crouched over the container marked A. His hand poised over the keypad of the digital lock as the reality of the moment set in. After taking a deep breath, he tapped out the combination and a metal hatch flipped open revealing a clear plastic valve.

Josh turned the valve, bleeding air into the metal container. A red light flashed next to the hatch, followed by a motorized humming sound. Five seconds later the light turned green indicating the device was charged and activated. Josh waited another second and then reached down and grabbed the lid on either side. He pulled gently. At first the metal lid resisted with residual suction until the rubber seal popped and the lid opened smoothly. Nestled inside foam rubber padding was a metal chest plate and harness, an object resembling body armor. Embedded in the center of the chest plate was a large dial that looked like a silver medallion. On either side of the chest plate were two heavy armor robotic gloves and a series of power cables and plugs that linked all the components together. At the far right of the container was a streamlined silver helmet with mirrored visor. The titanium shell of the helmet was scuffed and dented in places as though it had taken on damage from several heavy impacts.

Josh moved on to the second container and repeated the same procedure. Inside was the rest of the gear, a large utility belt, the power plant for the device. More power cords, straps, plugs and a pair of large titanium alloy boots, as scuffed and dented as the helmet, took up the rest of the container. Josh stared at the failed invention that he once referred to as the "Accelerator Suit" and tried to prepare himself for what he was about to do. Josh pulled back and drew his hands away from the containers.

"How did it come to this? This is suicide!" He trembled inside and tried to focus as another thought took over. "If she dies, her blood is on your hands. There's no other way."

Suddenly fear was replaced by hatred, a hatred for Colter that made him reach inside the first container and grab the glistening metal chest plate.

"Saddle up," he said, and placed the first component over his shoulders.

The phone rang in Josh's lab and the sultry female voice of the computer took the call, soft and lilting.

"Hide the bacon," Father Mike said, his voice flat and lifeless, sounding more like a robot than the computer. The ridiculous command made him feel foolish, but he did the best he could as he tried to follow the instructions to the letter.

"When," said the lovely voice.

"Now," Father Mike said, wondering if he was really talking to a computer.

"Commence data," said the computer.

When he was done, Father Mike pressed the pound button and the computer announced, "Data received, end of transmission. Have a nice day." The line disconnected and the computer went to work

"Loading reference New Testament, Mark six, forty-six. First century, time approximate thirty A.D. Commence time scan and global-positioning... Searching...searching...searching."

A gray Ford Taurus pulled up in front of the storage building and two agents in plain clothes got out of the car. One had the face of a prizefighter, an Irish man with short-cropped hair and a flattened nose. The man was middle aged and heavy set. Agent Donnely placed a big leathery hand on the roof of the car and looked up at the storage building, while agent Palmer, a large black man with a thick neck and shaved head, got out on the passenger side and looked down the street. The fact that they had not heard from the other two agents was no immediate cause for alarm, but still they proceeded with caution. Palmer checked the license plate on the back of the BMW, and then with a quick nod he joined Donnely on the sidewalk and both men headed inside.

The young attendant behind the counter looked up and did a double take as the two men entered. He looked back and forth at them nervously, like he was about to be busted and shrank back as Donnely reached into his breast pocket and pulled out an I.D.

"Police," Donnely said and flashed the badge too fast for the kid to see.

Agent Palmer squinted at the multiple piercings in the young attendant's face. "What did you do? Get your face caught in a tackle box?"

Since the young man knew nothing about fishing, fish hooks or lures, the joke was lost on him and he just maintained the nervous fearful look.

"You work here?" Donnely asked, with a slow and lazy look around the dank and dingy lobby.

"Y-yeah? Wha-what's this about?" the attendant said, looking up at Agent Palmer, who just stared at him with the glow of the yellow sign reflecting off his smooth, shiny head. The attendant was quick to cooperate since he was still high and had a half ounce of pot stashed under the counter. He told them about the young man who had just come in only ten minutes earlier. He even showed them the register book to prove it. Without another word, the agents turned and headed for the elevator on their way to locker forty one sixteen.

When the elevator door opened on the 4th floor, both Donnely and Palmer had handguns drawn with safeties off. Agent Donnely stepped out of the elevator first with Palmer right behind. Donnely checked the hall then turned right. They made their way quietly checking numbers right and left, when it quickly became apparent which room was theirs. A locker door was open near the end of the hall and a light emanated from within. The light quickly grew so bright that both men slowed their pace and had to squint against the glare.

Before they could say a word a figure emerged from the room, and both men stopped in their tracks, their faces aglow. The agents shielded their eyes and raised their guns to the visage of light that started toward them and illuminated the corridor.

Down in the lobby, a muffed explosion rocked the building and the young attendant cringed and jumped to his feet as the lights flickered and the TV went out. He stood there in the quiet of the lobby, confused and unsure of what to do. A few seconds later the familiar "ping" announced the arrival of the elevator. The attendant sheepishly stepped around his desk and stared at the closed lift door in amazement. Light escaped from the edges of the door as though the sun itself were inside the elevator. Finally when the door slid open, the attendant shielded his eyes and staggered back, blinded by the light. With the elevator ablaze, the young man reached back to the desk and fumbled for the phone, thinking he should call the fire department.

A sonic blast blew him across the desk and shattered the plate glass window at the front of the store. The young attendant landed behind the counter, shielded from the flying glass and debris. Stunned and afraid, his trembling hands gripped the counter top as he gathered himself and struggled to his feet with sheets of paper still dancing in the air. Just then, a car engine roared to life and the young attendant fought to stay conscious long enough to look out the shattered store window. With his ears still ringing from the explosion, and eyes half blurred, he thought he recognized the man in the gray BMW.

"Forty one sixteen" was all his mind could muster before eyes fluttered and he slumped to the floor unconscious.

Josh gunned the engine of the BMW and peeled out with tires squealing as car alarms blared from the concussion of the blast. The power of the accelerator suit still surged through him as he peered through the visor. The vehicle pulled away from the building, sped down the dark, side street, and then made a sharp right turn, screeching around the corner and heading north.

CHAPTER 13

Inside Colter Labs they were nearing launch time. "T - minus forty five minutes and counting," came the voice over the loud speaker. Colter checked his watch and nodded to Colonel Maxfield, who signaled to his men. The guards lifted KC to her feet, and she pulled against them.

"Colter, you can't do this! This is crazy!" she yelled.

"You made your choice. You betrayed me, remember? It's out of my hands. This is now a matter of national security and you... are a security risk."

Suddenly, in spite of her fear, she hated the man. She despised everything about him and wondered how she could have been so blind. KC struggled against the guards.

"Josh was right! You should look in the mirror, Colter, and take a look at the new Hitler. You're the menace, now! You're the threat to society. You're the monster!"

Colter smiled and was about to respond when one of the security agents seated behind his laptop called out.

"Ah, sir. I think we may have a problem."

Pelitier was closest and turned his attention to the monitor in front of him. Maxfield came along side and the two men huddled over the agent. One glance and they could see that Josh's blip was on the move, while the away team's blip remained stationary.

"Sir, the target is mobile and there is no word from either team."

"What the hell?" Maxfield said and glared at the screen. Colter watched from where he stood and remained silent.

"Call 'em up," Maxfield growled. The man in front of them opened a radio channel and attempted to make contact.

"Base to Signet away team, Base to Signet away team, come in. Away team, come in. I repeat, come in." The agent turned to look at Maxfield. "Sir, no answer."

Maxfield stared at the screen, trying to make sense of the blip on the monitor and then prodded the agent in front of him. "I want to know where our team is and whose drivin' that car. You got me?"

"Yes, sir," the man said then turned around to open another channel.

The conference phone rang. Pelitier backed up to the table and was still looking at the computer monitor when he picked up. "Hello?"

"Put Colter on," the voice said, cold and deliberate. Pelitier's eyes narrowed as he listened.

"Who is this?" Pelitier asked, with growing suspicion.

"I could have killed those men, but I didn't. Can't say I'll do the same for you. Now put Colter on."

Pelitier slowly and reluctantly held the phone out.

"It's him," he said.

Colter took it calmly and smiled.

"Hello, Josh," Colter said, with his usual reserve, as though he were expecting the call.

"Tell me she's still alive."

Colter snapped his fingers then pointed to the chair. "As a matter of fact she is."

Agent Vega and his partner brought KC back to her seat and then shoved her down into the chair. Colter held up a hand as if to silence the room and continued.

"Well Josh, aren't you full of surprises?"

The voice came back over the phone, "I'm just getting started. Put her on."

Colter hardly flinched. "No, I'm afraid I can't do that. Where are you, Josh?"

"What you really want to know is, how I got past your goons. I'm on my way, Colter. You do anything to harm her, and I'll kill you."

Colter smiled at KC.

"Those are brave words from a dead man."

"No those are my words, TO a dead man," Josh said.

With that the line went dead. Colter huffed at the threat and put the phone down. Pelitier and the colonel stared at him while Colter stood there in thought, then looked up.

"What happened to the away teams?" Colter snapped and turned to Maxfield.

"We can't raise them. Neither team is responding."

Suddenly one of the surveillance men looked up. "We have a report of an accident, a car crash at the intersection of thirty ninth and Lexington and a fire at a storage facility cross town NYPD reports a silver gray BMW spotted at the last locations."

Colter shook his head.

"Not responding. I was a fool to underestimate him."

Pelitier pointed to the northbound blip flashing on the monitor. "He's a fool to think he can stop us."

Colter glared at the screen then turned to Pelitier with a cynical gaze. "Really? Well he's done pretty damn well so far. Maxfield!"

The colonel stepped forward and Colter practically growled

"No more mistakes. I want him captured, and I want him eliminated. Is that clear?"

"Perfectly," Maxfield sneered, ready to unleash the hounds of hell.

Colter composed himself then turned to KC and smiled with renewed calm. "I hope you don't mind if we use you for bait," he said. He gaze paused on her face before he called to the lab techs, "Prepare for launch."

KC sat back between the two guards and watched the tiny blip flashing on the computer screen, comforted by the fact that Josh had somehow managed to stay alive and threatened the man she hated with all her heart.

As per his plan, Josh returned to his warehouse to pick up one last weapon. The freight elevator rose slowly to Josh's lab and he stepped out, strapped into the full body harness of the "Accelerator Suit." The network of power cables were neatly bundled and ran down the outside of his arms and legs, connecting the chest harness to the gloves, and the utility belt with eight plutonium power packs to the boots. A power hub strapped to the knees and elbows glowed dimly, channeling energy from the power packs to the chest plate, helmet, boots and gloves.

Mounted in the palm of both gloves was a metal cylinder. At the end of each cylinder was a control button. The right glove contained the ignition switch. The left glove housed the "kill switch." Josh locked both switches in the off position and unplugged the power cables leading to the gloves. The robotic hands were bulky, the size of hockey gloves but surprisingly light and flexible. Josh slid the gloves off as he marched ahead, lumbering forward in what looked like a pair of oversized, stainless steel ski boots. The acceleration power couplings fed into the back of each boot, which weighed in excess of twenty-five pounds. That and the inch thick reinforced black rubber treads on the bottoms, made walking difficult and cumbersome. Each attempt to merely raise the boot required an over exaggerated motion, akin to walking in flippers or snow shoes.

It was an awkward trek across the lab as Josh made his way to his work station and the newly constructed time link brain center. Once there he took a second to catch his breath then touched the space bar on the keypad in front of him and the computer sprang to life.

"Time scan complete. Target located. Coordinates locked on."

Josh went to work, typing as fast as he could.

"Acknowledged. Preview entry point program," he said quickly.

The computer answered softly, "Running program."

Josh watched the 17-inch monitor and leaned in as the scene slowly emerged, a rocky landscape, the plateau of a mountaintop judging by the misty scenery in the distance. It was late in the day, almost dusk, and the sky was dark and restless. Josh observed the solitary figure seated on a rock and carefully scrutinized the image, trying to absorb each minute detail.

The robed figure had dark, shoulder length hair and sat facing away. Although Josh's view was limited, he peered at the image with childlike fascination. The man slowly looked up to the sky as a flock of birds flew past the tranquil setting.

Although Josh wanted to adjust the coordinates to get a better view of the man's face, he knew he had no time. With one tap of a key, the image froze; with another tap, it disappeared. Josh quickly reached over and ripped the plugs out of the back of the brain center, lifted the cover of the console and removed the Guidance Memory System, which was the size of a disc player. The task of the GMS was to find the pathway through time.

Josh slid another device in front of him, a portable brain center, which was a customized laptop equipped with a GMS port and capacitor. With the laptop open, Josh fit the Guidance Memory System unit into the port, locked it in place, typed in the activation code, and closed the computer.

"Start cooking', baby. It's time to go to work."

A second later, a small control panel on the outside of the laptop lit up and the female computer voice returned from within the new device.

"Both primary and secondary time scans, on line, coordinates accessible, ready to activate."

Josh tucked the computer under his arm and made one last stop at another work station. He opened the desk drawer, which contained a mish-mash of electronic parts and junk. Josh reached in and took out a small gadget, which fit in the palm of his hand. It was comprised of two smaller components linked together in the middle. With six antenna-like wires sticking out of the segmented parts, the thing resembled a bug. With a few small adjustments, a tiny yellow LCD light flashed on. Once the signal stopped, Josh tucked the thing in his pocket, grabbed his accelerator power gloves and took one last look at the dark and half demolished warehouse. "Don't get sentimental. Colter's got an army out to kill you," he reminded himself, and headed to the elevator.

Inside Colter Labs, anticipation of the time jump continued to grow as Colter arrived on the control platform and stood like a captain at the helm of his ship. Pelitier quickly joined him as the launch countdown proceeded and one of the control personnel signaled to him.
"We are ready to go whenever you're ready, Mr. Pelitier," the woman said.
Colter came down from the platform and walked up to the time pilot to make a quick inspection. Major Haust stood at attention, bristling with weapons and staring straight ahead while Colter made a show of looking him up and down. The soldier was professional enough not to look his superior in the eye and held perfectly still with an iron clad grimace etched across his face.
Colter stood close enough to whisper in the man's ear.
"You do this for your country. You do this for the world. You, make me proud soldier."
"Sir, yes, sir," Haust said in a deep gravely growl.
Colter called to Maxfield while he stared at the soldier, and the colonel came forward to stand by his side. "Yes, sir."
"I trust there won't be any further interruptions."
Maxfield saluted. "I've got something special arranged for our guest. The base is on lock down. The situation is under control."
Colter nodded his approval, just as a lab assistant delivered a steaming hot mug of coffee. Coulter nodded to the gopher, who returned to the throng of white coats bustling around the control platform.
"Thank you, Colonel," Colter said. "You have my full confidence."
Maxfield smiled at Coulter, and then turned toward Pelitier with a scowl.

Josh sat behind the wheel of the BMW as it raced down the highway with the portable laptop and the silver helmet in the seat next to him. Driving with the heavy gloves and boots was a chore. He took the next exit at sixty, fishtailing down the off ramp until he turned onto the secondary road and gunned it, headed straight for Colter Labs.

Josh went over his plan, as the BMW made its way up the winding road through the woods. He rehearsed everything in his mind, step by step, visualizing it all to make sure he had it committed to memory. Once he had it in his mind, he knew he could perform the task without hesitation; and when fear crept in, he would think about the girl and the threat to her life.

"I'm on my way. Hold on KC, hold on."

Josh gripped the wheel and made a final turn as the road leveled out and closed in on the complex of buildings that comprised Colter Labs.

A dark figure, crouched roadside with night vision goggles, watching the car approach in a flurry of leaves. The spotter radioed in.

"Snare to Sparrow, gray BMW, license E dash MC2, target is in the nest."

One mile away the black AH-64A Apache helicopter hovered just below the tree tops roadside and waited for the headlights to appear in the distance.

Inside the chopper cockpit, a blip appeared on the heads up display, signaling target in range. With a high pitched tone, the targeting system locked on, and the co-pilot verified the bogie.

"That's our man. Target locked on, approaching at sixty miles an hour."

The pilot radioed in to Maxfield.

"Colonel, I have a lock on target. Do I have permission to fire?

Maxfield's voice crackled over the radio.

"Affirmative, fire at will."

Slowly the gunship rose above the trees and the pilot gripped the joystick, flipped the safety to, "off" and squeezed the trigger.

"How about a little fire, Scarecrow?"

In an instant, the 30-millimeter chain gun mounted under the chopper's nose roared to life with a hail of fire. A quarter mile away, white hot tracers lit the night as twelve hundred rounds of high explosive shells blasted the road in front of the BMW, obliterating pavement in a cloud of dust. Josh hit the brakes too late and skidded into the rain of armor piercing bullets, which opened up the front of the car like a can opener. With the wheels wrenched to the left, the engine exploded and the car skidded sideways as bullets blew out the windshield and ripped through the passenger side of the car. Josh put his head down as the car spun out of control, and glass and debris tore through the interior. With the front of the car ablaze, Josh locked his arms and braced for impact.

The car careened off the road at fifty miles an hour and crashed through a barbed wire fence. Josh felt himself go weightless as the BMW went airborne.

After several second of flight simulation, the BMW chassis bottomed out with a sickening crunch. The air bag deployed, knocking Josh back in his seat. As soon as the car came down, the steering wheel broke free of Josh's grip and whirled around like an object possessed. With his head knocked back, Josh watched the world spin out of control around him, with waves of mud and dirt raining into the car.

What was left of the BMW bounded along, rumbling over rocks and branches, trying to re-distribute its weight between two blown tires and a broken axel. Even with his seat belt, Josh flopped about like a rag doll, until the car finally came to a bone-jarring stop against a tree stump in an empty cow pasture.

Josh lay still as hot air filtered through the blown out windshield and passenger side window then used his legs to push himself up in his seat and tried to look through blurry eyes. Now that the car was mired wheel deep in loose dirt, the flames from the exploded car engine grew larger and tongues of fire licked through the smashed windshield.

"They're trying to kill me! They're trying to kill me," Josh mumbled through the pain, with cuts and scratches across his face and blood dripping from his scalp.

"I gotta get out!"

Josh wiped his face and blinked, trying to keep the blood and sweat out of his eyes. He saw the laptop propped against the gas pedal by his foot. The flashing green light indicated it still had power. The silver helmet lay under the dash on the passenger side. A hit from one of the shells had creased the side of the helmet and left a blackened scar just to the right of the visor. Josh reached down to pick it up but was stopped short by his still-fastened seat belt. With his head pounding, he unfastened the belt as the front of the car blazed out of control . He picked up the laptop and dove for the floor to grab his helmet as noxious fumes and searing heat quickly filled the car.

Josh turned to try the door which was bent inward and jammed shut. It was necessary to shield his face from the heat as he looked around for another means of escape. Suddenly, there was a noise beyond the windshield and the crackling fire, the sound of helicopter blades. Josh peered through the flames as the military chopper descended on his position. He could see it in the firelight, coming in slow, nose down, poised to attack. Josh never took his eyes off the chopper as he shoved the helmet down over his head and slid the visor down. Then with a flick of his thumb he released the safety on the starter switch built into the palm of the right glove and mashed the power button, just as the helicopter opened fire.

Suddenly all he could hear was his own breathing as the interior of the car glowed brightly around him and everything in the world stood still. With the accelerator suit activated, the fire that engulfed the front of the car was frozen as well as the helicopter, suspended in midair. Even its rotors appeared to stand still, moving like the minute hand of a clock. Only extremely fast moving objects like bullets, rockets, and exploding objects were capable of motion in Josh's accelerated state.

Josh peered through the visor of his helmet with wide-eyed terror, as the nose cone of a Hellfire air-to-ground rocket pushed lazily through the yellow wall of flame and entered the car.

Josh grabbed for the door, his hand moving one hundred and twenty times the speed of sound. At that speed, the door panel disintegrated around the large robotic glove and the entire door flew away from the car as though jettisoned by explosives. With a glance over his shoulder, he dove through the opening where the door once was, his metal boots crunching into the floor exerting fifty thousand pounds of pressure per square inch as he launched himself out.

The missile slowly glided into the back seat with the white-hot tail section of the rocket already in the car. The car door was still spinning away with Josh behind it when the missile exploded with a dull roar and tore the flaming wreckage apart. Josh knew better than to look again as the explosion chased after him. Fiery chunks of debris, rocket fragments, and razor sharp particles fanned out in an ever-expanding radius, scorching the air and slashing through everything in its path.

With the GMS unit tucked under his arm and the accelerator suit aglow, Josh flew across the field like a cruise missile and plunged into the woods on the other side of the road as the frame of the BMW lifted into the air and flipped over, recoiling from the blast. At a hundred yards, Josh took his first step after leaving the car and bounded forward with jagged shrapnel trailing behind him, twirling and lodging in trees and plowing into dirt. At two hundred yards, they began to fall away until Josh was finally beyond the blast radius. But now that he was no longer in danger of being shredded alive, there was the problem of inertia and stopping as he careened head long into the woods .

In accelerated mode, he was instantly as light as a feather, as was the GMS unit in his grasp. But traveling at seventy two hundred feet per second, everything else he touched would be liquefied on contact. Josh held the glowing GMS unit to his chest, put his head down, and slammed into the first tree. Wood turned to pulp and seemed to leap away from him on contact. With his head way in front of his feet, he was falling and couldn't possibly regain his balance. Josh exploded through another tree and another, forced to maintain the awkward position and endure the punishment until he bellied out and proceeded to roll across the ground for another two hundred yards, plowing through the dirt before he finally stopped.

Lying in a heap, he tried to catch his breath, but then realized that he had hardly exerted any energy at all and simply needed to calm down. Indeed, the acceleration suit had done all the work. It was the anxiety of narrowly escaping a missile fired at him and racing against the explosion that took his breath away. Being out of control and slamming his body through a series of oak trees, all of which should have killed him, had added to his distress. He was acutely aware that if it were not for the glowing apparatus that surrounded him and accelerated every particle of his being, his young life would have been snuffed out.

Josh sat up at the end of a trench he had plowed with his body and hit the kill switch to return to normal speed and real time. His body returned to normal, and he climbed to his feet. Aside from the cuts and bruises sustained from the exploding windshield, he was unharmed. His excursion through the woods had only shaken him up and reminded him of another serious design flaw of his invention. If he was not careful, it was hard to stop.

Josh quickly checked the time device which was still in his grasp. There was no damage. He had done well to protect it and everything seemed fine. When he was on his feet, he turned his attention back to the road and the row of demolished trees in his wake. The path was a quarter mile long, all the way back to the road. Now that he was in no immediate danger, Josh dialed the power gage on the chest plate down to half inertial momentum, mashed the power button and returned to the scene of the crime. When he hit the kill switch, he reappeared crouched behind a tree and watched the chopper hover around the burning wreckage of what was left of the BMW. This was the third time Colter had sent his men out to kill him, and Josh could feel the rage building inside. He had never seriously considered killing a man, but in Colter's case he felt he could justifiably make an exception.

Josh tried to calm himself and think of the mission, but all he could feel was the power of the accelerator coursing through his body, veins bulging and muscles tensing. Suddenly there was a dull cramping in his chest. He had been expecting it and now his heart was feeling the unnatural stress that had been put on it. Slowly the pain subsided and was gone, but the damage done to the heart was irreversible and irreparable all the way to a molecular level. Early testing had shown the unpleasant effect the acceleration suit had on internal organs. Use of the suit was a death sentence. It was a problem that he had never been able to solve and for this reason, vowed to destroy the device.

But now that he had a use for it, and he knew the risks, he was ready for what would come. The damage done would start out small and only increase. His only hope was to complete his mission before the suit took its toll on him. Josh tried to breathe normally, and peered at the chopper still circling the wreckage.

"She'd better be alive," Josh sneered, and knew in that instant that he would be capable of doing anything, should any harm come to her.

Josh crouched in the tall brush then flipped his visor down and mashed the power button. With a low and steady hum, his glowing figure turned toward Colter Labs, slowly fading like a ghost until disappearing in a blur.

CHAPTER 14

KC sat in the darkened conference room with the two plain clothed agents standing behind her. Across the room the two surveillance men watched the helicopter attack from their surveillance monitors. Both were at the edge of their seat when one man touched his earpiece.

"Say again, Sparrow!"

KC watched and held her breath.

"Are you sure? All right, stand by," he replied then tapped a few keys and switched down to the control platform in the lab.

"Tell Colonel Maxfield, the team leader wants to talk to him directly."

Maxfield's voice came over the intercom speaker on the mahogany table.

"What's the situation?" Maxfield asked.

KC shifted in her seat, as the chopper pilot's voice came in over the radio. The transmission crackled with static, but was clear enough to make out the man's lazy southern drawl.

"Bird's nest this is Sparrow. Come in."

Maxfield's voice came back. "This is Colonel Maxfield. Go ahead Sparrow."

"It's over, sir. We're circling now, switching to onboard camera. Those foreign imports crisp up real nice. The wreckage is burning itself out. There's nothing left, over."

Just then all three surveillance monitors switched to the real time image of the BMW, flipped upside down and ablaze, for all to see. KC watched the lights on all three screens flicker in unison as the wreck burned in the middle of the empty field..

"Head on back. We'll get a mop up crew out there later. Good work. Out."

KC could hear the sense of satisfaction in his voice before the radio clicked off. A second later, her own survival instinct kicked in, and the fear flooded back. She could feel the guard's eye on her and looked up. Vega smiled down, enjoying the look of near panic on her face. KC closed her eyes and turned away, trying to hold it together as the conference door opened and Colter strode in. There was a look of relief and something that vaguely resembled regret in his expression.

"An unfortunate end to such a brilliant mind. His contributions will not be forgotten." Colter smiled at the end of the brief eulogy, reached down, and opened the com link mike to the control platform outside.

"You may begin when ready."

Pelitier's eyes lit up. He reached down to the console and opened the PA system.

"Ladies and gentlemen prepare for time jump."

Colter turned to KC with a look of false sympathy, as the words echoed throughout the lab. Now that Josh was dead and there was no hope left, she looked small and helpless in the chair across the room.

"Cheer up. I don't think he suffered any," Colter said, sounding glib and sarcastic. But as he lingered, his expression changed and the humor faded from his face. Colter looked at agent Vega and gave the order as though the woman weren't even there.

"Do it quick, you understand?"

Vega nodded casually. "Yes, sir." The order was clear, no torture, no pain, no fun. Vega smiled as Colter looked into his dark eyes.

"Yes, sir," Vega said again as if to reassure that he understood fully. He then lifted KC to her feet. There was no struggle, no pleading, only an empty stare, as though the life was already seeping out of her. Vega and the other agent spun her around to face the door and started forward. KC stared straight ahead and hung limply between them, too weak to fight, as they carried her out to be executed.

Colter shook his head as the door swung closed.

"A pity." That was the extent of his emotion for the woman's fate, as he turned to face the main console and the mission ahead.

Grasso was still in the hall outside the conference room, wrestling with his conscience when the door opened and the guards walked KC out, headed for the elevator. Vega, though there was a clear path, shoved Grasso aside just to flex his muscle. KC seemed to swim up out of her trance as Grasso staggered back, and they marched her across the hall and into the waiting elevator. The agents spun her around again to face the door and Grasso stared at her lifeless expression. Vega pressed the button, stepped back beside the condemned woman and drew back his jacket. Nestled at the agents side was a compact, 9 mm. Luger in its leather holster. The expression on his face was clear. "Go ahead...Make a move."

Grasso stood silent, choked by his own fear and his mind screaming as the metal doors slid closed and his cowardice left him cowering in the hall like a child. Grasso backed up against the wall and put his hand to his mouth. He looked around trying to force an ounce of courage into his soul.

"Do something. Do something!" he screamed inside, but no matter how he tried he couldn't take a step, paralyzed with fear. Suddenly a siren went off, a loud and piercing whine, that shook Grasso out of his stupor. Men and women flooded into the corridor, and by the time Grasso realized it had nothing to do with him, he was being bumped and jostled as people ran up and down, headed to emergency stations.

The general alarm had sounded all across the complex, while inside Colter's conference room the siren was muffled and only a warning light flashed above the door. There was a moment of confusion as Maxfield rushed in and looked at Colter, who only stared back.

Pelitier hurried in behind him.

"What's happening?"

The question was directed to no one in particular and it was a few seconds before one of the surveillance officers called out as he peered at his monitor.

"Sir! There's a breech at the main gate!"

Maxfield peered over his shoulder like a hawk, bearing down on the man and growled, "A breech? What kind of breech?"

"I don't know, sir. The report just came in," the man said as he waited for further information over his headset. Colter listened to the alarm and watched the confusion unfolding in front of him then called out, "Hold the launch!"

Pelitier dove between the two surveillance experts and started banging out emergency codes to shut down the launch. Maxfield shouted orders to the away team trying to gain control of a threat that had yet to be identified. With sirens wailing and tensions escalating around him, Colter pounded the table and sneered, "It's him! I know it's him," he said before storming out of the conference room, headed for the control platform with Maxfield and Pelitier hot on his tail.

CHAPTER 15

"The gate is gone! We've been hit! We've been hit! Can't see! Too much smoke. I repeat, the gate is gone! Send help!"

The main gate had obviously been hit by a tank shell and was a mass of smoldering rubble and twisted wreckage. Everyone who heard the explosion had reported seeing a flash. The blast had blown out every window in the guard shack, spraying glass and debris in all directions. The only problem was that there was no tank, nor was there evidence of a missile, or rocket, or heavy weapons ordinance of any kind. Nor was there any serious injury to personnel since every guard had luckily been inside the concrete bunker when the gate was blown, a miracle no one could account for.

Three hundred yards away, twelve men armed with M4 machine guns rushed from the lab building. Just as the last man passed over the threshold, a phantom gust of wind blew in through the door. With all the confusion and activity, the guards posted at the main entrance hardly noticed the sudden change in air pressure and the vibration that shook the walls.

"Hey! What's happening? What's going on?" Grasso called out, as science and security personnel ran to and fro. Soon the hall emptied again and Grasso was left with the whine of the general alarm sounding in his ears. Then like a storm rising, a sudden gust of wind drove Grasso back against the wall, squinting and blinking from all the dust and paper caught up in the turbulence.

"What the hell?" Grasso muttered as he struggled to catch his breath. With one hand raised in front of his face and the other clutching his jacket, the wind stopped abruptly and Grasso forced himself off the wall. Papers fluttered and settled to the floor as Grasso put his hand down, straightened his jacket, and beheld a man in a stainless steel helmet standing right in front of him.

"AAGGGH!" Grasso screamed and jumped back, staring like a wild man. Whoa! Wha-where did you come from?"

The components of the accelerator harness glowed dimly and illuminated both men. Grasso looked him up and down then fixed his eyes on his own frightened reflection in the mirrored visor of the intruder's silver helmet. With the alarms wailing and no one to call to, Grasso knew he was standing face to face with the intruder.

"Who-who are you? What do you want?" Grasso stammered.

"Get out of the building, Carl. This is going to be bad," Josh said, through the mike inside his helmet.

Grasso's eyes lit up. "Josh! Is that you?"

"You've got to get out. There's no time to explain," Josh said.

Grasso suddenly remembered KC and the guards who had dragged her away then pointed to the elevator, trying to talk fast.

"Josh, listen! They just took –"

Josh hit the power button and with a flash of light, the thin energy field reappeared around him. At the same time, Grasso froze with his mouth gaping open and the urgent message locked in time.

Now that he had issued his warning, Josh turned to the metal bulkhead, a six inch wall of steel locked and secured with four inch bolts that sealed the lab shut. Slowly and carefully he reached out and placed his finger on the door. The instant he touched it, the metal surface blistered and boiled and had the same effect as a blow torch as he traced a line in front of him then down and around till it formed a large circle. He retraced the same spot until the superheated metal turned white hot and yielded a buttery molten ooze.

In real time, the guards on the other side of the door jumped aside when the steel behind them suddenly heated up and turned white hot. The large oval section came crashing in. The two and a half ton piece of metal rocked back and forth on the floor, like a giant egg shell, sputtering and still oozing molten metal.

Guards, lab techs, and all operations personnel scattered, forced back from the intense heat. They gazed at the cloud of steam and smoke billowing up from the door. Colter, Maxfield, and Simon Pelitier stood speechless as the glistening figure appeared through the smoke and entered the lab. With the Accelerator turned off, the glistening suit crackled and popped as residual energy dissipated and cooled. Josh carried the laptop with the Guidance Memory System in his left hand and held the acceleration switch in his right with his thumb on the button. He scanned the area looking for KC. With the girl nowhere to be found, he spotted Colter thirty yards away standing on the control platform and locked eyes with the man. Josh glared at him from behind his helmet and stood like a gunslinger waiting for Colter to make his move.

Pelitier stared in amazement and leaned over to Colter. "It's him," he said, unable to look away from Josh, all aglow in the energized power suit.

Just then Maxfield yelled out. But at the sound of his voice, Josh mashed the power button and vanished as the guards opened fire. Colter stared in disbelief.

With a dozen semi-automatic weapons pointed at him, ducking was a reflexive response. Josh was still squinting and listening for the gun rapport, which was reduced to a dull roar since sound waves outside of his accelerated state were slowed as well. Josh looked up, with his thumb still pressed down hard on the power button, as the bullets converged on his position.

The slow moving projectiles closed in like metal weights sinking through water and Josh started toward the time chamber. Three bullets passed on either side of him. Another two he sidestepped, and ducked underneath. There were three other shooters standing near the perimeter of the wall, who were stuck in time with their fingers on the trigger.

Aside from the bullets, everyone and everything else in the lab was perfectly still. Josh made his way down to the center of the lab, careful not to touch anything, knowing the violent effect of his slightest touch. He passed technicians and operations personnel at their control stations, men and women with a variety of bizarre expressions, most humorous. Some faced straight ahead with their eyes locked to one side like they had just been tapped on the shoulder. Some were sleepy in mid-blink and looked like bad photos. Most were spun around in their seats, facing the door. Some were either cringing away from the sudden gunfire, or straining to see what had happened.

Josh passed one of his would be assassins. The soldier was dressed in black with his face firmly pressed against the side of his M4 assault rifle.

"Nice try," Josh thought, as he walked past the man, frozen stark still. Josh moved ahead and tried to stay focused as he passed Colter and Maxfield. Colter looked lifeless, like a statue, while the colonel was totally animated. The man was still in mid-shout, with his mouth and eyes wide open. Pelitier was cowering right behind them and could not have looked more afraid.

"Weasel," Josh grumbled as he passed by and kept going.

Just ahead was Major Jay Haust. The enormous soldier stood near the time chamber, bristling with weapons and surrounded by six lab techs. Josh hardly paused to notice the time pilot and his entourage, and continued till he reached the wall of the time chamber and the external guidance control port. Once there he sank his fingers through the protective metal lid pried it open to see the Guidance Memory Console. With little effort he ripped the entire control unit out of the wall then carefully unplugged the panel. Josh released the old GMS unit, which hung in midair spinning like a satellite.

Then with the flip of a switch, he activated his laptop, plugged it into the open port and mounted the new Guidance Memory System over the gaping hole of wires that crackled and sparked in slow motion. The new GMS unit fit neatly into place which was no surprise, since the silver chamber was a copy of his old prototype and had been made to his specifications.

With the switch made, Josh turned to the old guidance module floating in space behind him, gripped it tightly and watched it crumple like tin foil. After that he carefully replaced the panel in the wall of the time chamber. But without hinges or a lock, all he could do was wedge gently back it into place. Josh stood back, took a last look at the panel which hid the new guidance control system, and could only hope the bent panel would not be noticed long enough for the new GMS module to assume guidance control.

With everything in place, Josh squatted down and hit the "kill switch." When he did, everything returned to normal speed. The sound of gunfire rang out and drew everyone's attention to the back of the lab, while at the same time the old crushed guidance module that had been floating in midair dropped into his hands. With everyone looking in the other direction, Josh set the old module aside then glanced up at the control panel and the metal lid that remained firmly wedged in place. With that phase of the plan complete, Josh stood in plain view and scanned the lab, once again looking for the girl. The helmet limited his peripheral vision. It was all he could do to keep himself from ripping it off and yelling her name. Then without any warning, his heart stopped.

Josh grabbed his chest and grunted as he suppressed his scream. He wasn't prepared for the sensation of a red hot fire poker jabbed through his chest.

Josh staggered back, smacking the stainless steel helmet against the wall of the time chamber, which made enough noise to attract the attention of a nearby lab tech.

"Hey," is all the young man managed to say in surprise, which first drew attention to himself instead of the intruder standing next to the time chamber. A second later, Josh's heart muscle spasmed and forced blood pumping once more. Still reeling from the pain, he tried to gather his feet underneath him and crept toward the chamber door.

"Look! There he is!" another man called out and pointed, which turned everyone's head in the right direction. With hands trembling, Josh pressed the power button again, and they all froze. Now with time literally standing still he fought to compose himself and catch his breath. Josh slid his back along the chamber wall, under the haunting gaze of a hundred zombies, fully expecting all eyes to shift, but their gazes stayed fixed.

A few deep breaths and the pain subsided till Josh could stand straight and scan the room once more. There were over a dozen women in the lab, and none were KC. Josh turned and movied steadily toward the control platform.

Josh mashed the "kill switch" and reappeared nose to nose with Colter. The man's brain took a second to register fear, at which point Colter jumped back. Pelitier did a double take, while Maxfield just stood there seething. Snipers all across the lab spun around to reacquire the target and trained their weapons on the control platform, but had no shot since the target was standing in the middle of the three most important men in the Colter Corporation.

"Don't move" Josh said.

Colter managed a weak half smile and seemed obliged to obey for the moment, as the team of snipers moved quickly and silently to find a better vantage point.

"Where is she?" Josh said calmly as the man before him looked him up and down.

"The Accelerator suit," Colter said, and tried to appear amused. "Did you work out the bugs yet? As I recall, the A suit is a death trap." He glanced down at Josh's hand and the slight tremor. "No I don't suppose you did."

Josh glared at him through his visor and took a step closer.

"Where is she?" Josh said, more forcefully to keep Colter on the defensive.

"Even in that get up, you can't possibly be in two places at once. Give it up, Josh. You can't stop us. You lose." With those two words, Colter had instantly regained control and was now on offense. Josh hated his smug confidence and raised his fist.

"Maybe not, but I can still put my hand through your face at six hundred miles per second. Does that count for anything?"

Colter flinched at the thought and shied away, his eyed flitting back and forth to the metal glove. Josh held the man's gaze. It was a momentary show of strength that put him back on the offensive. Colter glanced around more urgently, looking for his snipers then refocused on Josh with a clever smirk.

"You're no killer," he said, sounding more like he was trying to convince Josh than challenge him. Josh stood there staring with his fist clenched and knew it as well. Suddenly everything was unraveling. Saving the girl was all that mattered and as he tried to think, he knew there was no way he was stepping into the time chamber without finding KC first.

"Give it up Josh. It's over and you know it," Colter said, like a snake peering into the heart of its prey, while at the same time waited for his snipers to reacquire take the target. Twenty yards away, one man radioed in that he had an angle that would not jeopardize the other three men. His team leader responded, and the sniper settled in to take the shot.

"Just tell me where she is," Josh said, and lowered his hand, silently resigned to the fact that Colter was indeed in control, when suddenly someone called out.

"JOSH!" The voice came from the back of the lab and all eyes shifted as Grasso ran down the main aisle, waving his hands wildly.

"They're gonna kill her! She's downstairs! Hurry! You gotta stop them! You gotta stop them!" Grasso cried out so loud his voice cracked.

When Josh turned to look, a shot rang out, and he staggered to the side as a bullet ricocheted off his helmet and with a puff of smoke lodged in the ceiling above. Then just as he regained his balance, Josh mashed the accelerator button and disappeared.

Colter turned away from the flash of the ricochet as the sniper's bullet whizzed into the air, then turned once again to see that his quarry had escaped. Colter growled and glared at Grasso, who finally stopped in his tracks when Josh disappeared. He felt the gust of air as something streaked past like a phantom and now that Josh was gone, he looked into the sneering faces of the three men on the control platform. Grasso smiled. With help on the way he knew he had done the right thing, and it didn't seem to matter, even when Maxfield drew his 9mm Smith & Wesson handgun from under his jacket and leveled it at him.

"Colter, it's gone too far. The remaining board members have all turned against you. It's over. It's over."

Two shots rang out. And the lab techs nearby shrank away, at the horror of seeing a man shot before their eyes. Everyone watched as Grasso staggered then regained his balance. A second later, his legs buckled and he fell, shot twice through the chest. There was a gasp from the crowd and a few looked away, but overall no one made a sound or dared move. The message was clear. For any insubordination, the punishment would be swift and brutal.

Maxfield slid the gun in its holster, still warm from the discharge then looked back at Pelitier who glared at the dead body lying on the floor in the center aisle. Maxfield turned to Colter, having executed the man before a hundred witnesses and spoke with cool calmness.

"My men will clean that up. I'll handle Kensington," he said and went to a nearby console to open the PA system.

"Security, we have a fox in the hen coop. Find it and kill it." His voice echoed throughout the cavernous space of the lab and all across the science complex.

Colter stood atop the control platform, seething as eight of the twelve security guards filed out of the lab with assault rifles locked and loaded. At the same time a medical team rushed in to attend to the body laying face up in the center aisle. Colter turned his back as Grasso's body was bagged and refocused his attention on the mission and the team of launch operators seated in front of him.

"Ladies and gentlemen, we have a time jump to attend to. Let's get back on schedule," he said as the body of the dead man was removed behind him. The six main controllers on the platform stared up at Colter, with the words of the dead man still resounding in their ears. One by one they turned to Pelitier, with sheepish eyes, awaiting further instructions.

"You heard the man," Pelitier shouted, still shaken by the murder. With the launch clock running and the lab personnel moving back to their stations, Pelitier did his best not to watch as Grasso's body was wheeled out, choosing instead to look at the monitor in front of him.

"Fool, idiot!" Pelitier growled at Grasso's stupidity as he paced back and forth then glanced at Maxfield. After the display he suspected that if he wasn't careful, he could be next. Pelitier smirked and then patted his pocket, feeling the Baretta nestled there. "I can fire a gun too," he sneered to himself just as an explosion rocked the lab and dimmed the lights.

Josh reached the door to the stairwell with more speed than he wanted and then grabbed the medallion shaped dial on his chest and gave it a twist, counter clockwise. The power gauge acted like a transformer, decreasing his speed to a fraction of maximum potential. Instead of being invisible Josh became a blurred streak and leaned into the metal door. At ten times the speed of sound, the door exploded inward, burying itself in the opposite wall, as Josh flew through the threshold.

Next was the staircase, which dropped out beneath him. At accelerated speed, the stairs were useless to him and the people in the stairwell would be liquefied on contact. Using his speed and inertia, Josh leapt up onto the wall near the ceiling, which provided a clear track to the lower level, where he could race above the people frozen in time. The walls turned to powder in his wake, churned up by the metal acceleration boots; while in real time, the people on the stairs reacted as though a bomb had gone off and were instantly blanketed by debris when the walls disintegrated around them, as though sprayed by a machine gun fire.

A split second later, the door on the basement level exploded outward with Josh right behind, using it as a battering ram. He smashed into the opposite wall and buried the door in concrete. Josh hit the "kill switch" and returned to real time as bits of ceiling tile and dust rained down. He stopped to orient himself with the people still screaming in the stairwell behind him and looked up and down the corridor, trying to decide which way to go. With his heart racing, Josh could feel the panic setting in.

The underground complex was enormous, nearly twice the size of the lab. Josh stood there, groaning, frozen in fear and said her name, wanting the woman to appear, wishing her to appear. He said it louder and louder, until he could think of nothing else and ripped his helmet off then yelled her name till it echoed in his ears.

"KAAAY CEEEEE! KAAAAAY CE –"

Josh doubled over clutching his chest, the cry cut short by the searing pain as he slumped over against the wall.

"No, not now. Not yet," he said to himself, trying desperately to stand erect. Just when Josh thought he would collapse, the attack subsided. With his helmet still clutched in one hand, Josh gulped down air and braced himself against the wall.

"Stand up!"

At first, Josh thought he had uttered the words to himself, as he willed himself to stand. But when he looked, he was staring up at the barrel of an AR-15 assault rifle pointed at his head by one of Colter's private commandos. The soldier stood with legs locked, the weapon firmly braced against his shoulder and his finger nestled against a hair pin trigger. Josh hadn't heard or seen where the man came from and was still trying to handle the pain when he was given the order to stand.

The soldier spoke into the microphone on his headset. "I've got him. Stairwell C, basement level."

Josh tried to focus, with his face drenched in sweat and his head pounding like a drum. The soldier stood by, awaiting orders, when a muffled response came over the base-com radio clipped to his shoulder. Josh recognized Colter's voice. The words were almost desperate. "Kill him, kill him now!"

"Wait," Josh said, pulling himself up against the wall.

The soldier took a step back with his weapon trained and his finger firm against the trigger.

"Help me. They're going to kill her," Josh said, wheezing between breaths.

Clutching his chest, he pressed his back against the wall and looked up at the ceiling, as though it had taken all his energy to get the words out. The soldier held his position and frowned.

"What's the matter with you?" he said.

BANG! The shot rang out from the right, and when the soldier turned to look, a flash lit the hall and a burst of air shoved him back. When he looked again, all that was left was the silver helmet, spinning like a crazed roulette wheel on the floor.

Although the acceleration suit was taking its toll, the instant burst of adrenaline acted as an artificial stimulant that pumped more blood to the heart. The effect was a euphoric sense of power as Josh raced down the hall.

In real time, the soldier with the rifle staggered back as every door in the direction of the gunshot was blown off its hinges, one after another in rapid succession. Josh led the wave of destruction all the way to the end of the hall and took out part of the wall as he turned the corner. When Josh made the turn, there was a lone agent standing guard in the hall. Frozen in time, the man had his gun drawn and was looking in his direction. Josh ran forward disintegrating the ground beneath his boots then crouched and jammed his heels into the concrete floor, trying not to overshoot the door. He slid to a halt in a trench four inches deep, churning up debris in his wake.

The agent remained frozen as Josh ducked around him and put his fist through the door behind the man. One punch blew the door off its hinges and sent it whirling across the room until it hit the opposite wall, which rippled like putty as the metal door flattened out and pushed itself deeper and deeper until it was embedded in the concrete slab at an absurd angle near the ceiling. Eventually the cloud of pulverized rock and concrete would fill the room, but for the moment there was barely a haze of dust visible around the edges of the door.

Josh entered the dimly lit room, afraid to see what lay inside. With one glance, he knew he was too late. The room was an empty bunker, thirty feet by twelve feet, with only one recessed light in the ceiling.

To Josh's right was agent Vega frozen in time, his black hair glistening dully under the single light bulb in the ceiling. The man's chin was tucked down, his shoulder slightly raised, his arm outstretched with the high-powered Automag handgun held execution style, the barrel of the gun still smoking.

Josh looked to his left and felt the rush of adrenalin to his brain. KC stood near the wall, frozen in mid fall. The force of the bullet had knocked her backward and the moment in time had caught her, lying at an impossible angle, with her arms and hair floating in front of her face. Aside from the bullet hole in her blouse, she looked as though she had simply fallen asleep, her brow slightly furrowed like a child having a bad dream.

Josh staggered forward as tears clouded his vision, this time from a heartache that went deeper, a pain that went all the way to his soul. He reached out for her, wanting to hold her, wanting to catch her. Instead he walked around her, looking at every part of her as though she were a statue, a tragic work of art. Even in death, she was beautiful. Josh stood over her left shoulder staring down at her face and knew that at that exact moment she was probably still alive. But judging by the position of the bullet hole, left of center, the agent was a marksman and had found his target, a shot straight through the heart.

Vega stood across the room, dark eyes and trademark smile glaring, the look of evil satisfaction on the face of a cold blooded murderer. With tears welling up, Josh stepped in front of KC as if to shield her from his wicked gaze and moved in slowly. He peered into the face of the monster wondering what kind of sadistic pleasure he derived from killing an innocence woman, the execution of the woman he loved. The words fell from Josh's lips in a hoarse whisper as he choked back the tears.

"You unbelievable bastard."

All of the pain and all of the rage melted away, and he stared at the man, devoid of any emotion as he reached up and turned the power gage on his chest all the way to maximum. There were less than twenty feet between him and the man when Josh crouched down and launched himself forward with every ounce of strength he had in him. In accelerated time Josh's mass was denser than granite and plowed into Vega at eight hundred miles per second. Upon impact, Vega's face, skin, clothes, blood, teeth, and every molecule in his body literally blew apart at the subatomic level, as Josh passed through him. The process was so utterly violent and devastating, even his bones were pulverized and turned into a white mist that was instantly evaporated by the friction of the superheated air.

After impact, the only thing left suspended in mid-air was a gold ring, Vega's gun, and the tip of his trigger finger. Now that they were separated from Vega's body, they floated to the ceiling aimlessly, a grim remnant of Vega's execution and the only trace that was left of the man.

In real time, the sonic boom ripped through the building and the hapless agent standing guard at the door was blown across the hall when Josh literally went ballistic. After he had obliterated the assassin, Josh went through the concrete wall behind him like it was made of paper and kept on going. He smashed through storage rooms filled with construction materials, machine parts and supplies; then plowed into the auxiliary power plant where he shot through a giant boiler like a tank shell, and went through the opposite wall as fast as he had entered.

Now that Vega was dead, Josh cried out in agonized rage as he streaked forward with debris exploding all around him, using the large metal gloves to obliterate and demolish everything in front of him. To Josh, he was falling in slow motion, while the concrete slab beneath him turned to dust and every I-beam he hit melted like putty. Josh struck the foundation wall at less than seven hundred miles an hour and remembered his first "Terminal Velocity" test, the speed at which his density began to equalize with solid objects. The thin energy field of the power suit provided a solid buffer, but without his helmet falling head first was pure suicide. Josh dropped below the speed of sound and as everything accelerated around him, the thought came as quick as the wall in front of him, "Whatever I hit, I feel."

Josh tucked his head and at the last second flipped over in an attempt to hit the wall feet first. The added spin brought the huge metal boots around like two pile driving trip hammers and plowed through the wall, turning plaster, wood and concrete to rubble. Josh plunged through and hit the cold dark earth on the other side, with enough force to eject dirt and rock back through the hole which left an impact crater twenty feet deep.

When everything was finally still, Josh laid there, with the power of the accelerator suit humming and sizzling, and the air still vibrating around him in acceleration mode. With some effort, he made his way through the cool black crater in the wall and climbed back into the darkened room, his figure aglow. Josh pressed the "kill switch" and returned to normal speed. Straight ahead lay the tunnel of devastation that was left in his wake, a smoldering path of destruction ninety yards long through eleven concrete walls, two load bearing pillars, wood, plaster, and a huge boiler that was still spouting water. Electrical fires set off sprinklers and somewhere an alarm was ringing. Josh peered through the twisted tunnel of wreckage, his eyes cold and lifeless.

Now that KC was gone, there was nothing left, and with the accelerator suit slowly draining the life out of him, there was nothing left to lose. Josh mashed the power button and with a flash, disappeared again.

Dressed in full battle gear, Major Haust glared at the time chamber through his bulletproof visor, intense and ready to go. But like everyone else in the lab, the soldier was as rigid as stone, helplessly frozen in time as the sonic boom ripped through the cavernous lab once more.

In real time, Josh traversed the lab like a bolt of lightning and entered the time chamber, but not before he took the opportunity to create several diversions that were completed before the sound waves could travel from one side of the lab to the other.

A network of pipes bracketed to the wall next to the bulkhead door became a useful tool. Josh glanced left and right to make sure there was no one standing close by, then carefully wrapped the fingers of his metal glove around one of the pipes. He barely touched it and waited a few seconds as the energy field, surrounding his glove, slowly crept over the pipe. When enough of it was covered and the molecular structure of the pipe was accelerated and equalized with the glove, Josh gripped the pipe firmly and pulled it off the wall. It was a casual gesture that required little effort in acceleration mode, and cleanly snapped the pipe from the rest of the coolant system. The thick white mist of pressurized steam remained trapped inside the pipes like everything else frozen in time.

Josh examined the two foot length of pipe, as though he had simply pulled it off the shelf in a hardware store. He swung it through the air a few times. Once he was satisfied with the new found weapon, he continued on his way. He moved past the two sentries standing at the door and headed straight for the control platform and Lewis Colter.

Josh strode down the main aisle and made his way around two lab techs, who were staring at their clipboards. He scanned the area and took note of all the alert faces and the sheer number of people manning control stations. Further inspection of instruments and control monitors nearby confirmed they were in a preliminary launch mode.

Josh hefted the metal pipe and kept going. He approached one man halfway down the aisle. The lab tech was taking a picture with the strobe of the digital camera, caught in mid-flash. The bright blue light lit everything around Josh as he moved past. There was a man next to the photographer who blocked the aisle and was pointing at the time machine. Josh ducked under his outstretched arm and reached the control platform with an icy calm, again hefting the iron bar in his hand as he went.

Josh climbed the steps slowly and carefully so as not to obliterate them beneath the metal boots. Colter and Pelitier stood in close proximity, only five feet apart, on the control platform. The six main controllers manned their stations in front of them. Pelitier had assumed the lead position with Colter standing just behind him and to his right, his eyes riveted to the time chamber.

Josh stopped short of Colter and positioned himself so that he stood directly in front of the man and clutched the pipe firmly, staring into Colter's steely blue eyes. This was the real monster, the great manipulator who was afraid to do his own dirty work. Killing him was a simple matter. In fact nothing would be easier than killing the man who sent the man to kill his fiancé. Yet there was no satisfaction in it. There was no suffering and with all the rage in his heart, Josh wanted him to suffer; to strip him bare, take his power, his empire, his fortune, and leave him with nothing. All he needed to do was live long enough to carry out his plan, and if he lived long enough that is exactly what he would do. Still, with Colter standing helpless in front of him he knew he had to do something to inflict some pain upon the man.

Josh took a step back and looked around. Taking into account a few miscellaneous objects, he turned down the power gage on his chest and waited as the energy field reduced around him. Then with great concentration, he carefully reached over to a nearby console and picked up Colter's hot mug of coffee. Josh moved slowly and as smoothly as he could, handling the cup with the utmost care as though it contained nitro glycerin, Josh raised the cup until it was in front of Colter's face, then turned it sideways and gave it the slightest nudge forward. Again Josh was particularly careful, as he gripped the mug once more and drew it back, sliding it away from the coffee and leaving the mug shaped liquid suspended in mid-air. Josh stopped to admire the solid block of hot coffee hovering inches from Colter's face. Then with equal care he took the empty mug and suspended it over the man's head. The empty cup sat at a slight angle. As a finishing touch, Josh gave the mug a gentle tap downward, and moved on to the main control panel behind him.

Simon Pelitier stood in front of the center console. He was leaning over the instrument panel with his hand on the microphone. Josh looked over the scientist's shoulder and read the data on his screen. The green launch indicator was lit and each of the monitors in front of the other six control specialists had a green light as well. Josh glanced up at the wall of the time chamber and his GMS module which had not been detected, still hidden from view by the metal plate that was wedged in place. With the new guidance module secure and all systems nominal, Josh turned to Simon Pelitier and spoke to the man who was frozen in time.

"Excuse me, but you won't be needing this anymore," he said then raised the metal pipe and slammed it down on the control panel at a hyper-accelerated speed that was beyond supersonic. The console broke apart like tissue paper as the pipe ripped all the way through to the floor. Josh deliberately used more force than necessary, in an attempt to create as much friction as possible and achieve the most violent response.

As he turned away, there was a delayed reaction, then the panel flashed and sparked as it began to blow apart in super slow motion. The larger pieces spread outward and split into sparkling fragments as the blast radius grew larger until it engulfed Pelitier's face. Simon Pelitier remained bent over the explosion, with eyes open, as the fire and light rose silently and slowly expanded until it enveloped his entire head and torso.

Josh left the platform with Pelitier trapped in the explosion and the light of the blast flickering across the control platform. In accelerated speed, everything he had done thus far had taken less than one hundredth of a second and was accomplished en route to the chamber door. Josh proceeded on his path of destruction and paused when he came along side Colonel Maxfield.

The colonel was staring straight ahead when Josh raked the iron bar through the computer terminal directly behind him then moved on with the club in hand. The machine shattered and exploded, in the same fashion as the first, and looked like a tinderbox touched off with a match. The orange ball of fire slowly mushroomed out of the console and crept up Maxfield's back, threatening to set his coat ablaze.

With chaos set into motion, Josh passed the last row of systems analysts before he entered the time machine. The men and women were seated at their control stations and as he went by the technician seated at the end of the row, Josh paused and noticed the position of her hand on the control panel. He glanced at Major Haust and his entourage on their way to the time machine. The huge soldier led the charge, looking massive in his Kevlar tactical battle gear, and was only a few feet away from the chamber door with the rest of the group tightly bunched behind him.

Josh looked down at the woman behind the console. After examining the undercarriage of the chair and the position of the woman's legs he tucked the pipe under his arm. Then like a magician attempting a very difficult trick, he slowly eased the chair back, careful not to touch the woman in any way. But for all of his care, he was still moving at over eight hundred miles an hour and at supersonic speed the stress ripped all four rollers off the chair legs, as though they were cemented to the floor, and the undercarriage broke apart in his hands. With the lower portion gone, the rest of the chair moved freely and slid away intact. When it was done, the woman appeared to defy gravity and remained perfectly upright, seated at her workstation; with nothing but thin air beneath her. With the pipe in one hand and the broken chair in the other, Josh stepped across the red warning marker and entered the launch pad. The circular area was sixty feet in diameter, and at twelve percent power the chamber only yielded a trace of energy, hovering just above the floor.

Josh approached the time pilot who was in mid-stride, admiring the arsenal strapped to the huge soldier. With two fully automatic Mack 10's holstered behind him, a larger M16 with grenade launcher harnessed to his chest, two Czech made 9mm handguns with tactical laser sights in a double holster, a 45 cal. Glock with laser grip strapped to his right leg, along with a nasty lookin' hatchet knife a and 12 gauge M4 sawed off shotgun strapped to the other in a customized leather holster, Haust packed enough firepower to wage a war single handedly.

Josh came close enough to peer up at the rugged face beneath the Kevlar helmet and night vision goggles, and smiled at the man. Haust scowled past him, frozen in time and posed like a mannequin.

"You can thank me later," Josh said as he set the broken chair down at the major's feet. With the last obstacle strategically placed, Josh's demeanor went cold as he turned away and slowly stepped inside the time chamber. Once inside he came to a complete stop and pressed the "kill switch" to return the world to normal speed.

Real time returned with a series of violent explosions that seemed to happen simultaneously. The chaos they created was instantaneous and widespread. First a coolant pipe, bracketed to the wall at the back of the lab, burst open spewing hot steam into the air. While at the center of the lab, two control stations on the control platform erupted simultaneously. One of which exploded in Pelitier's face, while the other went off like a fire bomb right behind Colonel Maxfield and caught his jacket on fire. At the same time, Lewis Colter roared in agony, when hot coffee appeared out of nowhere and splashed in his face like a blast of liquid fire. Before he could close his eyes, or even react, the heavy glass mug smashed over his head with enough force to make Colter's legs buckle. He staggered back, clutching his reddened face. But his screams were quickly drowned out when Pelitier's head and chest were engulfed in fire. The flash only blinded him temporarily as the heat scorched his hair and eye brows and caused the man to collapse on the floor, holding his face in agony.

The moment the explosions happened, alarms sounded as launch systems failed and the power grid was temporarily interrupted. Ten seconds later auxiliary generators activated and surged on line. The guards stationed around the lab raised their weapons but in no particular direction since things were happening in all directions. Shrill screams filled the air as confusion spread, with fire, smoke, and steam billowing upward.

Lab techs nearby jumped up, while at the front of the lab a woman screamed when she felt her chair disappear from underneath her. Several yards away, the same phantom chair appeared at the feet of the new time pilot and Major Haust went sprawling, The escort team, who were right on his heels, had even less warning and toppled over him, burying the soldier under a frantic dog pile. With arms and legs a jumble, the men and women of the escort team flopped about frantically, trying to get to their feet.

Haust lay there in shock like a football player blindsided by a cheap shot, while the woman with the disappearing chair struggled desperately to stay upright, clawing at the control panel in front of her. It was a purely reflexive motion which Josh had depended on. The woman dragged her hands across the control board, flipping switches all the way down before she hit the floor, and at the same time, activated the control to close the time chamber door immediately after Josh stepped across the threshold.

Under the pile of men, Haust rolled to the side, reached up and pulled his helmet off in time to see the door close in front him. With Colter and Pelitier temporarily blinded, colonel Maxfield struggled to free himself from his flaming jacket, threw it to the floor and stomped out the fire so vigorously the big burly Texan looked look like a hillbilly at a square dance. Meanwhile, as people screamed and fell into one another, halfway up the center aisle the lab tech with the flash camera stood horrified in the middle of pandemonium and looked down at the digital camera with slow apprehension. With a click of the camera, the lab had erupted into total chaos and the man quietly assumed, however irrational, that this was somehow all his fault. Quietly and calmly, he lowered the camera and hurried out of the lab before he could be arrested.

Once inside the time chamber, Josh rammed the iron pipe into the door lock mechanism and wedged it tight. Now that he was sealed in, Josh stepped back and watched through the tiny portal window, as the silent hysteria raged beyond the soundproof walls of the chamber.

Josh turned to see the pristine and shining interior of the time chamber. "I did it," he whispered. "I made it."

He looked around, moving a little stiffly, and had to admit he had never expected to get this far, but now that he was here, "Keep moving, keep moving," is all he could think, as he approached the time pod suspended by launch cables at the center of the chamber.

The interior was dome shaped with an eight foot ceiling that arched overhead. The circular space was fifteen feet across with a floor comprised of polished aluminum panels that were nearly as reflective as glass. The steel walls were sprayed with a white fire retardant compound that was completely non-reflective.

Josh eased himself into the cockpit of the launch pod, took the large cumbersome gloves off, placed them in his lap and rubbed his hands along the arms of the padded seat. Everything was identical to his prototype and made him feel strangely at home even in the midst of a suicide mission, a mission designed to save the world from himself and his invention. The silence of the chamber closed in around him as well as the reality of what he was about to do. Wipe out the existence of the time machine and all memory of it, perhaps all memory of him as well. "Erased forever. Dad always said I'd amount to nothing." Josh smirked at the thought.

"You're wasting time," he said aloud.

Josh slid the small control panel in front of him and pulled the harness straps over his shoulders and noticed the bloodstained stitching on the harness padding. It was a gruesome reminder of the soldier that had sat in the same seat only the day before and returned from the past as a bullet ridden corpse. The thought made Josh's pulse race and his chest cramp. With his heart beating at only sixty percent of normal capacity, Josh shook off the image..

"Give it a rest," he said, and focused on the keypad before him.

Josh speed tapped the pre-launch command code to initiate launch sequence then went through his mental check list with his hands poised over the keypad and waited. Now it was all up to the new Guidance Memory System outside the chamber. He watched the readout on the monitor in front of him. "Come on, interface! Interface!"

Again there was the silence, and with only the fuel cell of the accelerator suit humming in his ears, there was time to think. Memories swirled in his head of a black Camaro and the ball of fire, the exploding storage facility, the chopper, the missile, his dead girlfriend, and the agent he pulverized, all in the path of destruction leading to the time machine. Then with all of the horrors of the world racing through his mind, the smooth sultry voice of the computer came over the internal speakers of the chamber.

"Interface complete. Primary coordinates loading. Sequencers set. Systems green, and ready, throttle up to full power."

With no time to breathe even a sigh of relief, Josh speed tapped the final code sequence into the computer, slid his hands back into the accelerator suit gloves, then held on and prepared for time jump.

"Sir! There's someone in the chamber!" One of the launch operators called out from his station on the control platform amidst all the yelling and confusion. Colter wiped the hot coffee from his eyes, and squinted at the man's monitor. There on the screen was the image of Josh strapped into the time pod, prepared for launch.

Colter looked up in all of the hysteria as launch systems powered up and the glowing force field began to materialize around the time machine.

"STOP HIIIMMM!" Colter bellowed and practically hung over the railing, pointing desperately at the time chamber, with eyes glaring wildly and the veins bulging in his neck.

A few more seconds and a lab tech yelled up to him.

"We can't, sir. The main computer is not responding and both backups are gone!"

With his jacket smoldering on the floor after a few more good stomps, Maxfield drew his gun, turned to the lab tech, with his chest heaving up and down, and cocked the weapon.

"You shut that machine down! Shut it down NOW!"

With the threat clearly stated, the lab tech turned to his computer and began typing furiously; trying every code he could think of to interrupt the launch sequence.

Simon Pelitier dragged himself up off the floor, temporarily blinded from the flash of the explosion, with minor burns across his face. He squinted through the pain, the time chamber little more than a light blur at the center of a dark blur.

Colter glared as the machine throttled up and went to full power. The magnetic GMS module hidden behind the metal plate against the chamber wall provided guidance control and a cyberspace firewall nearly impossible to penetrate.

"Stop the damn thing!" Colter shrieked as the lab tech worked furiously at his station then cried out over his shoulder.

"I can't! Nothing's responding! There's some kind of override!"

Maxfield lowered his gun and held on as the lab shuddered and filled with static electricity. Major Haust and the lab techs around him scampered back as the force field around the machine became stronger. Pelitier squinted as the time chamber rose up on its massive hydraulic shocks. He rubbed his eyes and winced in pain then like everyone else around him, sensed something strange and turned around to view the paradoxical scene created by the time rift. His pitiful mirror image stood behind him, cowering like an animal. The image was as shocking as it was revolting, but Pelitier was too weak to react and merely turned away in disgust.

"Launch sequence initiated!" the female lab tech announced across the P.A. system, this time with a fearful tremor in her voice. "Systems ready for induction. Shielding is hot and on line. All systems nominal and green to go." The woman looked up with a fearful gaze.

"No, no, no!" Colter snarled under his breath, and pounded his hand on the railing in front of him.

Soon the energy field was a solid transparent shell surrounding the time machine. Suddenly there was a tremor and a flash from the center of the chamber and an eerie silence filled the lab.

"Pod jettisoned. Launch time ten, fifty-four p.m.," the woman reported more calmly. She looked up from her monitor and peered straight ahead. Like everyone else, her attention was riveted to the time chamber. The pod was gone, and Colter sneered at the time machine, glistening within the force shield.

"Track him," he said, and wiped his face with coffee still dripping from his chin. Colter straightened up and fixed his stare through the smoke and haze.

"Where you going, Josh? Where are you going?"

CHAPTER 16

With only one time jump to his credit, and that one made to the polar ice caps, Josh awoke suddenly and catapulted up straight. He propped himself up on both arms and tensed his body, as if anticipating the bite of frigid cold air. Instead there was little more than a gentle night breeze with a whisper of wind rustling through an arid mountain terrain.

Moonlight bathed the landscape. From where Josh sat, he looked left and could see torch lights, the cities of Gennesaret and Capernaum shimmer in the distance. Beyond them to the west lay the Mediterranean; to the east, the Sea of Galilee, and the dark inlet glistening blue in the moonlight.

In front of him the ground crested over a hill and gradually sloped away with bushes and vegetation growing thicker in the darkness. Josh rolled over onto his side to look behind him and then froze.

This was indeed a mountaintop. The rocky plateau stretched out in front of him for several meters and led to a perfect lookout point with a sprawling vista of the landscape on all three sides.
The ground was clear and free of any vegetation with only thin vines among the larger rock formations.

Seated on a small boulder twenty yards away was a lone figure with his back turned, looking out over the dark landscape. Josh stared with sudden fascination and stood to his feet. There was a calming stillness about the figure and the place that surrounded him. Josh glanced around to make sure they were alone, and then proceeded, never taking his eyes off the man. He tried to be as quiet as possible and keep his cumbersome boots from crunching into the clumps of dirt on the hard packed ground. Again he smiled as he crept forward and almost refused to believe what he was seeing.

"It has to be!" he said to himself.

The figure on the rock was draped in a plain linen robe with a brown sash. But even without being able to see his face, Josh got the impression that the man was praying atop his mountain sanctuary.

"It has to be," Josh said again.

By the time he thought to start his stopwatch, Josh figured thirty seconds had already gone by. With nine minutes and thirty seconds left in the time jump, Josh clenched his right fist and hit the accelerator power switch. Just as he did, a flock of birds fifty yards beyond the mountain peak froze in mid flight.

The man and birds stayed absolutely still as Josh approached, and the accelerator suit glowed dimly in the waning light. He moved slowly, treading lightly, as though he were afraid to disturb the lone individual trapped in time. With pulse pounding, he noted the absurdity, but couldn't help himself as his excitement grew and he crept forward.

A million thoughts raced through his mind. This was a key moment in history, a moment recorded in the Bible and a moment to be talked about for two thousand years hence. All the world would come to know this man and the person of Jesus. Josh stopped at the next thought. It was something Mike had said when he gave the scripture verse. A place "between two miracles."

Josh looked around then focused on the man again, the man who had just fed thousands with some fish and a few loaves of bread. "What was the next miracle?" Josh tried to think as he crept closer and came up behind the man, leaning as though trying to look around a corner, "The first modern man to look upon the face of Jesus."

Suddenly he paused and assumed a more sober attitude. He was acting like a star struck fool. "What's the matter with you?" he thought to himself, and tried to regain his objectivity. The whole reason he had come was to see this man for himself, this man who they said was God. And there he was, normal build, average height with slightly tousled hair. "Funny, you don't look like God," Josh smirked then reminded himself that, objectively speaking, the man's appearance had no bearing on the matter. He was here for the truth, whatever it was, whatever it meant.

And as he moved on, he realized it was no longer that simple. For the first time in his life, there would be no neutrality and no luxury of intellectual indifference. This man had to be God, or it was all for nothing, including his mother's pain and suffering, her life, her death, and now the success of this mission. And then there was all of Christianity, the death of kings and slaves, the wars fought, and the rise and fall of empires to consider. The possibility that any of it had meaning was contingent on the reality and veracity of this one man. "Who are you really?"

Josh moved slowly as he came up behind the man and couldn't help feeling as though he was about to unveil a work of art, a hidden masterpiece. And now that he was about to see the man's face with his own eyes, he had to admit he was afraid of the inevitable disappointment. What if there was no heartfelt emotion, no clever artistry to arouse the imagination, only the plain face of a man whose life had merely been inflated by boastful exaggerations, common to legend and fables.

"Whatever the truth," he told himself.

With that said, a full minute and a half had passed when Josh finally came up beside the figure of the man. He circled around in front with his vision riveted to the face that stared straight ahead through eyes glistening in the moonlight. And when he was standing directly in front and could see the man clearly, he stared quietly in the stillness and all anxiety left him.

"The face of Christ." he uttered softly, "of course," and after a few seconds found himself smiling. Josh couldn't say what it was, but for all his worry and for all his apprehension, he knew that if he had to pick from all the faces in the world, this would be the one he would choose.

He analyzed it and compared it to familiar images. The master painters, for all their attempts, had merely captured the most basic features, the hair, his beard, the olive skin, the chiseled brow and nose, all the superficial characteristics. But no portrait could capture the serenity of the face. There was something noble about him and at the same time innocent.

Josh stood there a while before adopting a more casual posture and smiling. "Well, at least you look the part," he mumbled to himself, and smiled when something else came to mind. It was a curious thought that Josh immediately discarded, but the absurd notion came right back and grew stronger as he stared at the face.

There was indeed something else about the man's face that was even more remarkable than his appearance. Josh stood there, searching his mind, and knew that in some inexplicable way, the man seated in front of him not only looked like someone who would shape the course of history, he actually looked familiar.

"Impossible!" he huffed. Still the longer he looked, the more hauntingly real and personal the face became. Josh moved closer, his eyes filled with growing astonishment.

"Who are you?" he whispered and stooped down to look more closely at the face locked in time. Whether God or not, there was something about him. This was the face of a good man, the face of a friend, who even now seemed to wear a smile.

Josh stared into the eyes of Jesus, dark and penetrating that looked deeper and seemed to pierce the soul. Suddenly he felt the urge to look away, to escape before he was completely drawn into the man's gaze.

Then all at once, like a child wandering down a garden path, all care and concern left him, and he let go to see where this path would lead. The face of Jesus smiled, and even as Josh tried to rationalize the wave of emotion, a sense of comfort and peace, that suddenly swept over him, he dropped to one knee. After finding himself at the feet of the man and gazing up, Josh's mere curiosity transformed into longing.

Josh shook his head, silently pleading, wrestling with his mind to suppress the beast rising up within him, the pain he held down for so long. But in spite of every desperate attempt to shake it and to stop it, the suffering, the beatings, the humility, and every tortured memory, like demons released from the pit of hell, clawed at his mind in raging torment.

Josh clenched his fists, gritting his teeth as he choked back the tears and tried to withstand the gaze of Christ and the smile that was drawing every ounce of pain out of him. Then just when he thought he could stand it no longer, like a man clinging to a cliff for all eternity, he let go and everything fell away, every hurt, every offense gone in an instant. Josh knelt there, stunned, eyes blinking. The feeling was real and unmistakable. His lips trembled open as his mind fumbled for the words. Josh pulled back, gasping, and wiped his eye. He looked around feeling self conscious and embarrassed before clearing his throat.

"Whoa! Where did that come from?" he said, still shaky and a little unsure of himself. When he looked again, the expression of the man was the look of a father, silently pouring his love out on his son. Josh could feel it in his heart, as real as if the man had reached out and put his arms around him. He wiped his eyes again, and again drew closer, this time afraid to look away. It was what he had longed for his whole childhood, a sense of peace and safety. If anything, the emotional episode had heightened his sense of curiosity as he stooped closer, peering at every inch of the face, as if it were made of marble.

Indeed, the image was priceless, the face that had never before been recorded, the unknown face of the most well known man in history, a man who was about to be murdered and hung on a cross. The thought jolted him out of his solitude and Josh stared in horror at the realization. The man would inevitably be crucified. The gentle face and the loving smile would soon be scarred and mutilated, and after being whipped and brutalized, the man would be dead in a matter of days, murdered by an angry mob. The certainty of it filled Josh with fear and anger, until he could hardly think.

He stepped back and circled in front of Jesus, pacing back and forth like a caged lion. He looked down on the man, and felt the need to warn him, to tell him what would happen. He wanted to protect the man but then remembered what Mike had said.

"You can't interfere!"

The priest had been more than adamant. But standing there, looking at Christ, he knew he couldn't just let him die, he would have to do something. But first he would have to calm down and settle himself before he spoke to the man. He glanced at his watch, four minutes and fifty seconds had transpired and nearly half of the time jump was gone.

Josh stood there with his power suit still glowing in acceleration mode, and then bent down one last time to see the eyes of Christ which, under the circumstances, were suddenly unbearable to look at. He bent lower and still lower until he was staring into the eyes once again, and just when he felt he had gained a lasting impression of the man's face and was about to look away, the eyes blinked, with nothing moving anywhere else in the universe.

Jesus looked up as slowly as a mannequin coming to life and Josh leapt back, staggering away in horror and in his haste forgot that he was still in acceleration mode. Josh launched himself backward and like a catapult, the momentum lifted him up and carried him over the side of the mountain. He fell through the air and drifted downward, arms wind milling, as he slowly disappeared in the darkness below.

Once it was quiet, Josh made the return trip in a matter of seconds, a half mile climb back up the side of the mountain in acceleration mode. When he arrived, he was talking to himself and looking around, stunned by the sheer impossibility of the moment. His monologue ceased as he stared at the figure of Christ, who was now standing and silently watching him.

Josh checked the readout on his power belt. All systems nominal and still in acceleration mode, he looked up at Christ in shock.

"This can't be happening! It's impossible," he gasped.

"Is it?" Jesus said. Josh came forward slowly, unable to take his eyes off the man.

"No way. I'm hallucinating. I've got radiation sickness," Josh said in a muffled tone and caught sight of the flock of birds, still suspended in mid-air beyond the mountain peak, perfectly frozen in time. He stood gazing, as though in search of an explanation. Now his mouth and his mind were working feverishly.

"The guidance system malfunctioned, disrupted the space continuum then caused some sort of rift. It's a time anomaly, a warp phase that incorporated your mass into the jump. Yeah that's it."

Jesus stood by patiently, as though content to let the young man attempt to figure it out on his own. Then when he had exhausted every possible theory and looked absolutely spent, Josh did the only thing he could do. He turned to the flock of birds, fixed his eyes on them and hit the "kill switch." The birds sprang to life all at once and sped through the air in perfect formation, flapping their way into the distance.

In an instant, the gentle breeze returned, the smell of fresh air and the sea below. With the world returned to normal, Josh turned around slowly, reluctantly. A misty vapor swirled around the acceleration suit as it cooled down, and Josh squared his shoulders to face the man dressed in robes. The two stood on the mountain top, a stark contrast of time, technology and culture.

Josh looked painfully confused. In one respect, all the evidence seemed to point in the direction he wanted to go. But since the evidence went against everything he believed and knew to be possible, it made it difficult to accept, even though he had seen it with his own eyes.

Josh forced a weak smile and tried to look a little less incredulous. "Look, I don't know what's going on, but I do know there's a logical explanation."

Jesus looked at him and smiled. "Yes, there is," he said, and nodded, as though urging the man along.

Josh froze again then continued, as he observed the next startling realization. "You speak English," Josh said, still probing the man with his eyes.

"I speak, Aramaic."

Josh smirked at the response. The man had obviously misunderstood.

"I mean, right now. That's English."

"I am speaking to you," Jesus said, with a reassuring smile and a firmness that gave Josh the distinct impression there was something else going on. Indeed, the implication was clear that whatever restrictions he knew that applied to the concept of language had nothing to do with their conversation. Josh looked at the man, curiously.

"I don't think I understand," he said, anxious for further explanation.

Jesus smiled, "You understand more than you think."

Josh looked at the man, tall and lean, draped in common robes, wearing dusty sandals, and knew he had found the man he was looking for.

"You're Jesus, aren't you?"

"I am," Jesus said, with a slight nod of his head, and the calm skies rumbled with the distant sound of thunder, a coincidence that did not entirely escape Josh.

Josh nodded back, and glanced at his watch. There was only four minutes left in the time jump and all he had managed to do was ask him his name. Josh looked the man up and down again and seemed to steady himself for some kind of assault. He tried not to be too condescending as he began. "Look, I don't expect you to understand, but I've come a long way to find you."

Jesus simply nodded. "I know."

Josh chuckled at the response. "No, I'm sure you don't," he said then pointed toward the boulder where Jesus sat.

"Look, you were praying over there and I've already interacted with you to the extent that it caused you to get up and –" Josh's eyes opened wide with the sudden realization as the answer came to him. He spoke slowly with eyes gazing like a child assembling building blocks until they all fit neatly together.

"My prolonged proximity to you incorporated your mass into the field's core power and thereby energized your molecular structure till it reached parity." Josh breathed a sigh of relief. "Okay, now it makes sense."

"Is that what you think happened?" Jesus asked.

Josh smiled confidently. "There's no other explanation, at least no explanation that won't defy every physical law known to man."

Christ's expression changed and he became more serious.

"What laws are these," he asked and Josh hardly noticed the wind stirring around him.

"The laws of nature," Josh said, trying not to make it too complicated.

Jesus paused, as if to think about the young man's response then calmly offered his own set of questions.

"You have great respect for these laws. Yet what is nature that it should create law?"

Josh frowned at the question, which could be seen as either terribly naïve and childish or rationally complex in its ontological perception of natural law. Jesus continued his line of questioning, and Josh began to wonder if the man standing in front of him wasn't indeed a lawyer.

"Does nature think? Can it reason? I am flesh and blood, yet I tell you, these laws do not constrain me, So, tell me, Joshua, what would you say about such a being as that?"

Josh scoffed at the biblical name. "Joshua? Nobody ever –" he paused and stared in surprise. "Hey, I never, I mean, I didn't –"

With another mental hurdle to get over, Josh gave the man a good, hard look, determined not to be distracted. The question was intriguing and he looked away to reason the problem and think aloud.

"A being that can defy the laws of nature?... All right, he would have to be able to resist the basic forces of the universe which would act upon him, such as gravity, atomic mass, inertia. He would literally have to be able to exist outside natural law. And by definition, through opposing these forces he would also have to be able to control them."

Josh looked at Jesus when he was done, and was obviously pleased with his answer. Jesus nodded thoughtfully and as the wind picked up, Josh had to shield his face from the dust.

"Interesting…" Christ said. "And if such a being could indeed control the forces of nature, the very forces of the universe, what then would be the extent of his powers?"

Josh paused, distracted by the wind that was now howling across the mountain top as the temperature began to drop.

"What's with this wind? It wasn't this cold before," Josh said, and brought his huge gloved hands up to rub his arms as the air swirled around him.

"What wind?" Jesus said.

Josh squinted, with his hair whipping in his face, and looked at the man as though he were insane. Jesus simply stared back, with the wind howling all around him, and not a hair on his head or a fold of his robe was disturbed by the slightest breeze.

Josh stared in amazement as Jesus calmly looked to the side, as though noticing the rising storm for the first time. And then with a glance, the wind ceased to move and everything was still once again. Jesus merely waited for the answer to his question as Josh turned to him, aghast. Josh brushed his hair back and tried to compose himself, since Christ had indeed made his point and it was checkmate.

"I think I see where you're going with this," Josh said, trying to look as casual as possible, and not utterly terrified.

Jesus smiled at the young scientist. "Then we are already there," he said and seemed satisfied.

With the realization beginning to sink in, Josh began to speak as though in a trance, as his intellectual mind led him to the only logical conclusion available.

"And if such a being truly existed, a being that had the power to control the universe, it stands to reason that such a being would also possess the power to create it."

Josh looked into the eyes of the living Lord, as a fleeting thought returned, unbidden, carrying enough weight to bring his whole world crashing down around him.

"Well, won't Mike be relieved. He said the time machine would have no effect on you." Josh's voice trailed off into a whisper. "That's a shock from the past, a retro-shock. You are for real."

Josh looked toward the distant hills, as the magnitude of it all began to sink in. "I never knew. It's like I had to go back to come forward. And now that I'm here, now that I know –"

Josh shook his head. "I guess I wasted a lot of time," he said, and looked up at Jesus. Now that he had the answer to his question, and was firmly convinced that the man in front of him was indeed God, he was surprised by the man's demeanor. Jesus was still, calm and subdued with a patience that seemed limitless, which Josh was immediately grateful for. He thought back to his obnoxious attitude, to his stupid questions, and the wind that went away with a glance. Standing there, he wondered if Christ could read his mind, and froze feeling like a bird caught in the hand of a giant. With the man's gaze upon him once again, Christ smiled down at him and took a few steps forward. Josh stepped back.

"Do not be afraid. I have come to serve, not to be served. All are destined to find the truth, in their own time. Many die in vain, only to find the truth too late. You are not among that number. You never were."

Josh breathed a sigh of relief and with his fears somewhat at ease, the only question left was the one he had carried around for thirteen years.

"What about my mom?" Josh said as though he expected Jesus to know what he was talking about, but there was no hesitation.

"Blessed are those who have not seen yet still believe. Blessed are those who have borne their persecution for my name. For great will be their reward in heaven."

Josh stared at the man, astounded by Christ's omniscience. But although his words offered comfort, it was not enough.

"But she suffered so much. For what? What purpose could that possibly have served?"

Again Christ did not hesitate in his response and spoke as though he knew the woman who wouldn't be born until two thousand years into the future.

"Life is not without suffering, Josh. And suffering is not without purpose. Your mother shielded you in the midst of her pain. Her sacrifice protected you. Her suffering gave you strength... And her faith sustained you both."

The tears welled up again, and Josh wiped them away.

"But why did she have to die?" he said, defiantly.

Christ allowed the question to linger and then answered slowly, as though Josh needed to listen carefully.

"Everything that has gone before has led up to this moment. And all that is to come, both good and evil, happens for a reason. There are forces at work which are beyond your grasp and only now are some becoming clear to you."

Josh shook his head. "I don't understand."

"But you do," Jesus said. "You of all people understand perfectly. Your mother's life and her death have led you to me for a purpose."

Christ came along side and placed a hand on Josh's shoulder. "Come, walk with me," he said.

Josh looked down at his watch with only ten seconds left to the end of the time jump. Josh pointed at his watch and opened his mouth to speak. But before he could utter a word, Christ responded.

"Do not be troubled. I will redeem the time," he said.

When Josh looked again, his watch said ten minutes instead of ten seconds.

Josh stared at it as he walked along side Christ, and without even thinking about it, his heavy metal boots seemed lighter and less cumbersome, as Jesus led him to the trail where they made their descent. Below, the scattered torch lights on the shore lit the shimmering waters of the Mediterranean.

Back in the lab, damage assessments were being made and a young man, a lab tech with frazzled nerves, stood in front of Colter, rattling off information.

"Sir, we're getting reports from all across the facility, mostly power failures, some fires. Hardest hit was the basement level. Looks like a bomb went off down there and blew out the walls."

"Anyone dead?" Colter asked as casually.

The young man tried to pull himself together and not look too emotional as he finished his report. "The young woman, sir... Ms. Maltese. They found her near the rubble. She was shot."

"Anyone else," Colter said quickly, as though he had more important matters to attend to.

"No, not as far as we can tell, however Agent Vega is missing."

Colter turned away, and knew all too well what had happened. The explosive force of the attack in the basement had been devastating, the widespread destruction as a result of one man's rage, and retribution for the murder of the woman. Josh had dealt with Agent Vega.

"Unfortunate," Colter grumbled then looked away. With the end of the time jump fast approaching, there were indeed more pressing matters to attend to.

Colter grabbed the rail of the control platform and glared at the time machine, like Captain Ahab looking across the bow of his ship. Colter winced, his face still smarting from the scalding hot coffee, as he seethed in anger.

Pelitier called out and gave the countdown.

"Fifteen seconds till re-entry... Twelve, eleven, ten..."

Pelitier's voice fell silent as he stared at the time clock that suddenly read ten minutes once again.

"I don't understand."

"What?" Colter looked over at him. Pelitier stared at the clock in disbelief and tapped a few buttons.

"The clock... it just reset itself," he mumbled, trying to think out loud.

Colter ran to him, eyes glaring down at the clock, which clearly had restarted and was now counting down at nine minutes and forty five.

"That's not possible! It can't do that," Colter gasped.

Pelitier looked at him helplessly.

"It just did," he said staring blankly.

"Well, you think of something and you get him back here now!" Colter growled then gripped a clipboard and hurled it at the time chamber. The object hit the energy field with a thump then plunged inside and sank to the floor as though it had fallen into water. Pelitier watched the object settle within the glistening sphere of energy, then winced from his own burns, and glared at the time chamber. He spoke slowly and turned his attention to the computer in front of him as he speed tapped data on the keypad.

"Well here's something. The accelerator suit was Kensington's first attempt at time travel, a self contained apparatus. A power cell built to accelerate mass to break the time space continuum. It was a clever idea, but not powerful enough to break the barrier itself," Pelitier said, still wincing from his own injuries, as he finished typing in the data.

"Yes, I know. That's why we kept monitoring him regarding the time project. What's your point," Colter snarled. Maxfield listened, equally as agitated and ready to shoot something.

"Damn it," Pelitier yelled, with growing frustration then looked up from his control station. "Well he took it with him in the time jump!" Pelitier glared at Colter and tried to speak more calmly. "Perhaps while in the time jump, he used the suit to make a second jump, a partial jump that somehow extended the jump time. I don't know, either way I can't change the launch clock or tell where he's gone."

"Security," Colonel Maxfield shouted from his position on the control platform. Pelitier looked at him suddenly as though the man was about to arrest him. Instead Maxfield glared at the shimmering force field that covered the time machine like a sparkling dome, and rippled all the way out to the warning markers on the floor. Twelve soldiers converged behind the colonel who pointed to either side of the time chamber. The men immediately fanned out to surround the time machine with assault weapons trained on the chamber.

"Watch it. All of you! Anything moves, shoot it!" Maxfield barked his orders, and no sooner had he spoken than several soldiers jumped back as the metal plate that was lodged in the side of the time chamber was knocked out of place by the swirling energy and nearly caused the men to open fire. The crumpled metal panel drifted to the floor, the same as the errant clipboard that Colter had thrown, and lay there gently rocking back and forth, disturbed by the thick sparkling turbulence swirling within the force field.

Pelitier peered like a hawk, trying to see through the flickering wall of light. He then spotted the open external guidance control port and the red blinking light of the device attached to the side of the time chamber. A few of the soldiers saw it as well and trained their weapons on the box.

Pelitier glared at the GMS module, and knew that Josh had made his first mistake.

"Well, well, well," Colter sneered.

"There it is," Pelitier shouted and shoved his finger at the computer module mounted in the wall of the time chamber. "That's the reason the computers won't respond. He's replaced the GMS unit. We've got to get that thing out of there!"

Maxfield looked at the spot and could just see the device through the shimmering field of energy. Pelitier turned to Colter, glaring in desperation.

"The Guidance Memory System, he's replaced it with one of his own. If we can get to it, maybe I can patch in and cut him off; we can reel him back in."

Maxfield stepped back, his eyes scanning the shimmering energy field that swirled around the time machine like the turbulent waters of a river at flood stage.

"And how do you propose we get through that?" Maxfield said, pointing at the energy field. Pelitier looked at the man and the time machine, and had no answer.

With the glistening time chamber illuminating the lab in front of him, Colter finally gave the order.

"Shut it down!" he said.

Pelitier looked at him with slow resolve. "You do realize he'll be stranded wherever he is."

"That's just as good as killing him," Maxfield snarled.

"Is it?" Pelitier asked, eyebrow raised.

"That's a chance we'll have to take. Do it," Colter said.

Again one of the control technicians looked up from his computer station on the control platform.

"We can't, sir. The GMS unit won't let us talk to the computer."

Colonel Maxfield approached the lab tech from behind and put his subcompact 9mm to the young man's head.

"Then I suggest you find a way," Maxfield said, cold and calmly.

Pelitier came to the man's defense and glared at Maxfield. "Put the gun away! We'll never be able to bypass the GMS through the system. But we can do it manually, cut it off from the source, the main power plant in the basement."

Colter quickly turned to Maxfield.

"Get on it now!"

Meanwhile, two thousand years in the past, Josh arrived at the base of the mountain, just behind Jesus, and stopped among the low brush and olive trees. Before them was the shore of the Sea of Galilee. Josh was looking out at the water when Christ turned to face him with a somber expression.

"You have done well," he said, and stepped closer to deliver his last message.

"The willful rebellion of man sows seeds of wrath even as we speak. They reap the whirlwind, yet will they not repent from their wickedness," Christ said, then raised his hand to a boat not far off shore.

"These men are my apostles of today. You will be my apostle of tomorrow. Then, you will speak to those who reject me, those who do evil. You will be my voice unto the wilderness a wilderness of the future."

"Wait, I'm no preacher. That's not why I came!"

Christ interrupted. "But, you believe and that is enough. For all of my people who know me, know the truth... It will be difficult at first, but for your faithfulness, I will repay and restore all that which has been lost."

"You're speaking in riddles," Josh said, and knew the conversation was about to end.

"Your path is set. It is done. It is... the great commission."

With that, Jesus turned and walked away. Josh stood among the trees and watched him walk out onto the sandy shore. Although the beach looked deserted, Josh knew he couldn't risk anyone seeing him and dared not follow.

"Wait! You still haven't told me what I'm supposed to do?" Josh called after him.

With torches along the beach in the distance, one lone fishing boat with its yellow torchlight glistened forty yards out in the water. Christ walked toward the water's edge, with the gentle waves lapping against the shore, and only looked back once.

"Speak the truth," he said and continued on. Josh looked at him with questions still swirling in his mind, things he needed to ask. But Christ had spoken, and their meeting was over. And when Jesus walked away, the aura of the man had changed as had the demeanor of the atmosphere around him.

Dark clouds rolled in over the water until the once calm sea churned as though agitated by the approach of Christ. Out beyond the shore, the small fishing boat pitched to and fro. The men aboard struggled with the sail and anchor, and the torch swayed with the swells of the water.

Josh watched as Jesus walked across the sand and stepped into the churning water lapping up onto the shore. But instead of sinking deeper into the frothing waves, Jesus rose up onto the surface as the sea swelled all around him, his footsteps sure and his path never wavering.

Josh stared in wonder. "The place between two miracles," he whispered as he gazed at Christ on the water.

The further out he went, the more violent the waters became. They seemed to settle around him as though calmed by the sovereign will of God. Josh smiled at the miraculous display as Jesus headed straight for his disciples, never looking back.

"It really happened, and there it is," Josh said, and stood up from among the bushes in the shadows of the olive trees. The words were still on his lips when he clutched the chest plate of the accelerator suit, and slumped against a tree in full cardiac arrest. Josh fell to the ground with the weight of the world crushing in on his chest, and prayed not to die.

"No, wait...not here...not yet...not...now."

Josh looked up to the sky, paralyzed by the pain, and could feel himself slipping away. "God! Help me!" he gasped.

Just then the tiny alarm of his wrist watch chirped in its high pitched tone, marking the end of the time jump. Slowly everything stopped, the trees ceased to move, the ocean stood still, as Josh began to glow, the world turned to black and he was hurled backward through the abyss of the time corridor as the time machine summoned him back to the present.

When Josh opened his eyes, his heart was stable and he was back in the time chamber strapped down in the control pod. Josh raised his arm and with his hands still trembling, he unbuckled the safety straps and then tried to sit up, his whole body feeling like lead.

All across the lab everyone was focused on their computer monitor and the image of the man moving around inside the time chamber. The ten minute launch cycle had held true, the second time around, and Josh's re-entry was accurate down to the second. Once again, pandemonium broke out all across the lab, but Josh hardly had the strength to look out through the portal as he stumbled out of the chair and held on to regain his balance. Josh glanced bleary eyed at the chamber door and saw the metal pipe still wedged in the door's locking mechanism.

"Good," Josh thought to himself, and looked half drunk, trying to recover from his third heart attack in less than one hour. With the force field pulsing outside the time chamber, he knew he was safe for the moment. He stripped the cumbersome oversized gloves off his hands and began to dismantle the accelerator suit. He labored with straps and buckles as piece by piece fell to the floor and once he had shed the suit, Josh climbed back into the time pod, dressed in only jeans and a t-shirt. Then with some effort, he swung the launch control panel in front of him once again.

Josh punched in the next series of time scan coordinates which he had committed to memory. When he was done he sat back, drenched in sweat and breathing as though he had run a mile, waiting for the computer to respond. Five seconds later the familiar female voice of his GMS unit activated.

"Data received, time coordinates and location acquired. Systems energizing, will reach maximum power for launch in zero minus five minutes and counting."

Now all he could do was wait.

Every lab personnel watched as the huge hydraulic legs hissed, releasing compressed air, then folded beneath the time chamber and lowered the enormous machine back to the floor. Colonel Maxfield stepped forward, pumping his fist.

"WE'VE GOT HIM!"

Maxfield and his men rushed forward and stood ready to move as soon as the energy field diminished and was no longer a threat. But instead of going away completely, the shimmering lights only receded to half the radius around the time chamber and stayed very much a threat.

Maxfield spun around to look at Pelitier, in confusion.

"What's happening!"

Colter rushed to one of the larger monitors, to see Josh laying there with his head lolled back against the head rest of the pod. Ravaged by multiple heart attacks, and his face scarred from the helicopter assault on the BMW. Then with a sense of calm Colter reached down and tapped a button on the control console to open a direct line to the chamber.

Josh opened his eyes slowly, when Colter's voice came over the internal speakers.

"You don't look good, Josh. Why don't you power down and open the door? You need help. Come out now and you won't get hurt. I promise. We can help you."

Colter waited a few seconds then covered the microphone with his hand and turned to Maxfield sharply.

"Basement level, shut down that generator, and get ready to blow the door."

Not knowing what was going on outside, Josh finally turned to the camera mounted in the ceiling of the time chamber and tried to muster enough energy to speak between breaths.

"It's over, Colter. I've got my own mission now, a little different than yours. I need to insure the future. Make sure you don't screw it up. But first, I've got some history that needs changing too."

His words were labored and not without cost. Josh grimaced, as his chest tightened up, and closed his eyes, fearing another attack. A few seconds later, the pain mercifully subsided and Josh looked into the camera as he tried to finish.

"It's all going away, Colter. Say good-bye."

His words echoed throughout the lab over the central intercom. It was a cryptic message that made every lab tech look around with some concern. Colter glared at Josh's image on the monitor and snapped the pencil in his hand. With Josh sitting inside the time chamber, the boy had the advantage, and Colter knew the threat was real.

"What did you do, Josh?" he said into the microphone slowly and deliberately as though trying to will the man to speak, but Josh only lay there with his eyes closed and waited.

Down below, half a dozen men moved quickly through the dark corridors of the power plant. The hum of giant turbines grew louder as they approached the main generator. When they arrived, five men fanned out in front of the enormous machine to stand guard, rifles held ready. With everyone in position, the group leader reported his location to the control room via headset. A second later, Pelitier's voice came back through his earpiece, and the soldier turned to the man nearest the control box.

"Shut it down!" he said sharply.

With the order given, the soldier flung open the control box and grabbed the huge lever at the bottom of the panel marked "Power Main." Although the handle was rubber insulated, a bolt of electricity leapt from the switch like a fiery spark that lit the room like a strobe and threw the man out the door. The smell of ozone filled the air as the others stood around staring helplessly at the man laying on the ground.. The soldier lay there with eyelids fluttering and his eyeballs rolled back in his head.

Once the other men could get their wits about them and attend to their buddy, the group leader carefully made his way forward to examine the Power Main. And as he drew closer, he could see a strange device on the underside of the switch handle. It was metallic and segmented into two parts, like the body of an insect with six spindly wires wrapped around the switch handle and control box. The soldier had obviously grabbed one of the tiny electronic leads when he pulled the lever and had paid the price. A yellow power light flashed erratically on the back of the device, which made it clear to see and served as a warning to stay back.

The group leader was still staring at the thing when Maxfield's voice came over his headset once again.

"What's going on down there? Cut the power!" he said, shouting into the soldier's ear.

"Sir, I got a man down! The switch has been booby trapped. We can't get near it. Somebody obviously knew we were coming."

The soldier's voice squawked over the speakers at the control platform. Pelitier watched as the generators recharged and power levels rose once again and then turned to Colter with a look of desperation. Colter shifted his eyes back to the monitor and did his best to remain calm as he spoke.

"What do you want, Josh? What are you trying to do?"

Josh summoned enough strength to look down at his control panel and the rising power levels and then turned his gaze up to the camera mounted on the ceiling.

"Like I said, it's over, Lewis. It's over."

Pelitier turned to Colter sharply, jabbing his finger directly toward the GMS unit still flashing on the side of the time chamber.

"You take out that box and he's not going anywhere," he whispered hoarsely to avoid the microphone.

The wave of energy pulsating around the time chamber expanded until the flashing light of the GMS unit was barely visible. Maxfield backed away as the energy field grew stronger and his eyes narrowed. Without a moment to lose he called out to the men behind him "SNIPERS! Cobb! Bender! Reese!"

Three men in black caps and coveralls rushed forward with sniper rifles. Colter watched the marksmen with gun straps wrapped around their forearms, the high powered weapons locked and loaded.

"Keep him talking," Maxfield growled as his men took up positions opposite the GMS unit.

Colter did his best to oblige, and adopted a kinder and gentler tone.

"All right, all right, I understand. You never agreed with the mission. But the genie's out of the bottle, Josh. You've already created the machine. It exists. The only way to undo what you've done is to wipe yourself out of existence. I don't know, Josh. You don't strike me as a martyr. You're more of a cynic, like me. Come on, think about it. You don't want to die. It's like you said. It may not even come out the way you think."

The marksmen took up positions on either side of Maxfield, and acquired the target as Josh's voice came over the intercom. Pelitier stood at a distance, wincing from his burns, his eye twitching, as he watched and listened. Josh's breathing was labored as it came over the PA system.

"You're right. It may not even come like I want, but it's a little late for second guessing. Anyway, it's a hell of a ride, and I'm dying to do it again," Josh said then smiled at the play on words and closed his eyes.

The marksmen held ready, their sights trained on the blinking GMS unit. With a nod, Maxfield gave the signal. "Fire!"

The snipers opened up and a barrage of bullets penetrated the time barrier only to be slowed in the turbulent vortex of the energy. Colter and Maxfield stared in awe as the shells twisted and arced away from their target like so many pebbles caught in a tide. After the first volley, the snipers lowered their weapons and gazed at the force field as the bullets drifted to the floor.

"We're going to need something bigger," Pelitier whined, and looked to Colter.

Colter glared at Maxfield after the failed attempt but gave nothing away over the microphone and continued calmly.

"So, is that it? You're on some kind of suicide mission? That's a lose, lose proposition. Don't do this, Josh. You're breaking your own rule."

The intercom crackled as Josh's voice came back and the hydraulic platform lifted the time machine into the air once more.

"Just trying to be a team player," Josh said and forced a smile.

Inside the time chamber, Josh lay on his head back, trying to rest and gather his strength. The sultry voice of the computer filled the chamber.

"Secondary time coordinates loaded and set. Prepare to throttle up to full power."

Outside, Colter could only watch and clench his fist as the chamber approached full power. "Somebody pull the plug on this damn thing!" he yelled as the force field grew and the massive machine gained strength. Then with all patience drained from him and pistol in hand, Maxfield left the control platform with a snarl on his face and marched forward. Colter and Pelitier watched as he moved steadily and deliberately down onto the launch platform, but it was only when he drew dangerously close to the energy field that his plan became obvious to everyone. With only a few feet between him and the shimmering, swirling turbulence, Maxfield raised his 9mm, released the safety, and opened fire. Shots rang out one after another, as each bullet penetrated the glistening flow of energy that encircled the time chamber then sank to the floor, well short of its target. With the time machine nearly at full power the energy flowed faster counter clockwise and approached maximum density. Lab techs nearby watched in horror as Maxfield kept his pistol trained on the GMS unit and stepped into the turbulence of the pulsating force field.

As soon as he crossed the shimmering threshold, the brilliant wave of energy engulfed the colonel and swept his garments to one side as though he had encountered a stiff gale force wind. Maxfield fired once, twice and a third time as he reached out to steady himself against the energy that was icy cold and numbing his flesh. Each bullet he fired screeched like a nail against a chalkboard then hung in the air a few feet from the target where it was slowly swept aside and drifted harmlessly away, caught up in the turbulent flow. Maxfield grimaced at the shimmering particles flowing through him and the feeling of a thousand needles stabbing his hands, his face and every inch of his body. He fired again, shielding his eyes as he staggered forward. With the time chamber raised on its hydraulic legs, he fired upward to hit the GMS unit. Now fully engulfed and saturated in the swirling force field, Maxfield began to shake violently. He fired twice more before he lost his grip on the gun and it slipped from his hand. Soon his arm merely dangled in front of him as liquid time washed over his body, and he succumbed to the force of the energy field.

At first the process was so gradual that it seemed to be an optical illusion. But in a matter of seconds, it was all too apparent that something was happening to Maxfield. People staggered back while others stood to their feet with mouths dropped open and eyes transfixed.

Maxfield cried out in agony as every cell of his sixty two year old body was instantly rejuvenated at the subatomic level and he began to change. In a matter of seconds, forty pounds of weight literally evaporated from his body. His short cropped silver hair spewed forth until it was a thick, brown mane that dangled in front of his youthful face.

At thirty five, Maxfield was fit and slender. He staggered back and tried to turn around, eyes wide and trembling violently as his new body changed again. With his baggy shirt and drooping pants he was suddenly twenty five, chiseled and in his prime. The man's agonized screams echoed throughout the lab as he shrank yet again, down to the size of a pimple faced sixteen year old adolescent.

Maxfield fell silent and shuddered, looking at his thin arms and legs, and after a few seconds was reduced again. Colter watched from the platform as Maxfield stumbled out of his shoes and dropped to his knees then crawled in desperation, trying to escape the force field that was literally stripping away his life. Pelitier had never taken his eyes off the man and squinted in amazement at what was no longer a big burly bear of a man but what appeared to be a gangly ten-year-old boy. The child fell on his belly, creeping and clawing at the floor. The voice of the man was reduced to a whimper and every step seemed to cost him another year as he crept closer to the edge of the energy field.

By the time he had managed to crawl out on his own, all that was left was a ten month old infant, kneeling on all fours, trembling and crying hysterically. Colter looked at the child and was repulsed as though the thing before him was the product of a hideous experiment. Maxfield's screams, however, were drowned out by the generators as the time chamber achieved full power and was ready for launch.

Inside the time machine all systems were nominal. Josh tightened the straps of the shoulder harness, braced himself, and flipped the last sequence of switches and then held on as time launch was initiated. In five seconds, the time pod glowed brightly beneath him, dropped through the floor of the chamber and disappeared.

With the chamber still elevated and the force field swirling, the gentle hum of power coursed from the generators as what was left of Colonel Raymond Maxfield, sat at the edge of the launch pad, wrapped in Maxfield's shirt and screaming inconsolably.

Now that Josh had escaped a second time, Colter buried his head in his hands, dejected as the shrill noise of the baby filled the lab with its constant whining and echoed in his ears. A second later, Colter looked up and jabbed his finger at the infant that was bleating like a lamb. "Somebody, SHUT HIM UP!"

CHAPTER 17

The old man had put in a hard day's work and was on his way home when he came across the body laying in the gutter, the body of a young man. "Hey fella, you all right, you need help?" the old man said then looked up and down the empty street and took a few steps closer.

Josh opened his eyes to see the man standing over him and quickly tried to gather his wits. He forced himself up on his elbows, his head still swimming as the man hooked his arm under him and lifted him off the wet pavement.

"I-I'm okay," Josh said, and staggered a little.

"You some kind of epileptic? The man said, still reaching out to catch him.

"Yeah, epileptic. I'm okay, thanks." Josh nodded, brushed his hair back and stood as straight and tall as he could to put on a good show.

The man nodded back, a little doubtful, and moved on down the darkened street, glancing back only once. When he was gone, a thought occurred to Josh. He reached behind, pulled out his wallet and opened the leather billfold that contained two hundred dollars in cash, his driver's license, proof of insurance, car and medical, and a stack of credit cards, all gold and platinum.

"Don't think I'll be needing this anymore," he whispered, then looked to the trash can next to the street lamb at the curb. He paused with his hand ready to flick it into the trash but then looked down and tossed the wallet into the sewer drain below instead.

"Now, I am no one," he sighed and started down the street.

At 11:45 pm. the streets were nearly empty on the lower eastside of Manhattan. Aside from a late model Buick parked underneath a street lamp, there was no way to know that the year was 1980. A slight drizzle sprinkled down and mixed with sweat as Josh moved along the sidewalk and finally reached his destination. He stared across the street, blinking his eyes in an attempt to focus on the small crowd outside of the bar. It was an effort that made his head hurt, but the cool dampness of the rain brought him some comfort. Ravaged by the effects of the accelerator suit, he was happy to be free of the device and hoped a little strength would seep back into his tortured body.

A group of young women across the street, slumped and slouched over their dates in a drunken dance punctuated with fits of laughter. Suddenly one of the men staggered backward, presumably slapped after some improper advance. After a momentary pause, and a look of surprise, everyone burst out laughing and the carousing continued.

Josh stayed in the shadows against the building. The ruby red neon light of Patchy's bar cast a bloody hue over the wet pavement, a flash back to the darker days of his childhood. He had memories of this place, the times he was sent to get his father. The smell of alcohol, the glazed look, the drunken rage, the fights, all of it came flooding back, along with the sad disappointment of a little child.

With a glance at his watch, Josh started forward and tried to convince himself that he had at least enough strength to make it across the street. The step off the curb was a bad one and looked as though he was either drunk or didn't know it was coming. It put a crimp in his back that made him wince and every step after that was uneven and awkward. But since everyone heading in or out of the bar was either drunk or about to get drunk, he fit right in and was hardly noticed.

Josh crossed the street and after a few deep breaths, he peered up at the sign above the bar and steadied himself. He was twenty five years in the past and remembered it all like it was yesterday as he moved to the window. There was a commotion inside and the crowd within moved in waves, backing away from and trying to steer clear of, yet at the same time, get a good look at, the three men struggling. They staggered about, the two larger men dragged the third between them, pulling him backward to the door. Beyond them, amidst the smoke and stunned faces, a woman was crying over someone else laying on the floor. Others at the bar sipped their drinks and only observed with casual interest.

Josh backed away from the window as the brawler was forced outside by the enormous man who at first glance looked like the bouncer, until the other man yelled out.

"Get him the hell outta here!

The crowd of onlookers outside pulled back as the fighter wrenched his arms away from both men. Now that he and his large friend were on the street, the bouncer issued his standard warning. "And don't come back! Neither one of you!"

With that, the owner rounded on his heels and retreated back inside the bar. Josh looked at the big man with astonishment and didn't mind staring, since everyone else around him wore the same expression. The big man was Ski, Toller Gapinski, only this was the younger, handsome version, without a wrinkle on his face and a full head of blonde hair.

Ski was a full six inches taller than the brawler, who stood there with his broad chest heaving up and down, under a torn and beer stained T-shirt. The man glared at the bar door with seething rage.

Ski leaned forward and bellowed like a bull.

"Way to go, Flynn!"

The name rang in Josh's ear like an alarm, and his eyes trailed over to the face of the brawler, the face of a young Marcel Kensington, the face of his father. Josh marveled at the sight of his dad, standing tall, with thick neck and arms bulging. He was twenty eight years old and in the prime of his life. The man clenched his fists, relaxed them, then clenched them again, his adrenalin pumping and knuckles red from the beating he had given the man that they were still trying to revive inside the bar. Ski marched up to his buddy, but Flynn's eyes were still on the door of the bar when Ski shoved him backward.

The crowd gathered around, anticipating another fight as the smaller man threw his arms up, ready to go. But the big man only sneered and backed away, now that he had gotten his friend's attention.

"What the hell's the matter with you?" he roared. "You could have at least waited till I finished my beer before you got us kicked out."

"What do you want from me? He was mouthin' off!"

"You grabbed his wife," Ski yelled, then just shook his head in disgust. "Thanks Flynn. Go home and sleep it off."

There was no anger only regret in his voice, and as soon as Ski turned to walk away, Flynn lowered his hands and looked as though he might chase after his friend.

"Awe man, c'mon wait a minute. Don't leave, SKI! Hey, c'mon man! I need a ride!"

Ski called back over his shoulder.

"The train's still runnin!"

Flynn clenched his fists and yelled back.

"To hell with you then!" he snarled, and stood there seething as the big man faded into the shadows. It took a few seconds for the young brawler to realize that in addition to being drunk, he still had an audience. Flynn turned his glare on the people around him.

"What the hell are you lookin' at?"

There was plenty of fight left in the man, and with no takers among the crowd the people quickly dispersed. Josh pretended to lose interest as people moved past him. He stood there a while longer, with his head down not knowing what to do when Flynn finally walked past him and nearly brushed shoulders. Josh looked up slowly and then checked behind him to make sure no one was watching. But since no one else had any interest in getting their face punched in, everyone made sure they wandered off in a different direction, giving Josh the freedom to follow the man alone.

Josh stayed in the shadows as much as possible as he trailed after the lone figure, staying ten to fifteen yards behind. The man staggered and stumbled along his way and was clearly too drunk to walk a straight line. Josh glanced around him and from his knowledge of the area the nearest train station was in the other direction, and since Flynn wouldn't waste a dime on a cab when he could put it toward another beer, it was obvious he had chosen to walk home. Now that the baby was born and he was saddled with a kid, he would stay out later, keep to himself, and avoid coming home at all cost.

Flynn moved slowly enough that Josh could keep pace, and keeping out of sight was easy as the steady drizzle kept the man more concerned with his own warmth than the dark figure trailing behind him. Flynn staggered forward, continuing on his way and then crossed the street. Once he was on the other side, he turned the corner and started down the avenue. Feeling a little stronger, Josh picked up the pace.

"Don't lose him. Don't lose him," he said under his breath as he headed across the street. Although it was little more than a trot, his heart pounded as though he were trying to finish a marathon. When he rounded the corner, he nearly ran into a woman carrying packages.

"Excuse me," Josh said, huffing and out of breath as he moved around her and then stopped in his tracks. Josh looked up and down the street and hurried forward, scanning the distance for any sign of Flynn.

"Where did he go?" Josh tried to think. The man was headed home, but home was more than twenty minutes away and a glance at his watch showed less than five minutes left in the time jump. Josh's pulse raced as he jogged ahead, staying close to the buildings, eyes peering through the drizzling rain when a hand suddenly reached out from behind and nearly yanked him off his feet.

Josh spun around as he plunged into darkness, trying to keep his feet underneath him. It was all he could do to get his hands up in time before he slammed against the brick wall. He stood there stunned for a moment, realizing he had been ambushed. When he turned around, he was in an alleyway standing face to face with Flynn. The young brawler stepped back to size him up. Flynn was two years older, two inches taller, and outweighed Josh by twenty three pounds, all muscle. Flynn stared at Josh's face which still bore the scars of the attack from the helicopter.

"What happened to you? You lose a knife fight?"

Josh just looked at him, trying to catch his breath, not sure where to start or what to say.

"Hello, Flynn."

The look of surprise was worth the admission, and gave Josh some time to think. Flynn stepped back and looked a little more sober.

"Do I know you?" he said.

Josh pondered the question for a moment.

"No, I don't think so." Josh stood straighter, trying to breathe more normally.

Flynn looked at him a little closer.

"You look familiar to me," he said still squinting.

"I get that a lot," Josh said, and glanced down at his watch. Four minutes left in the time jump, four minutes to say whatever he was going to say to change this man's life forever.

"What's the matter? You late for a bus?" Flynn chuckled to himself.

With no time for idle chatter, Josh started talking.

"Your name is Marcel Kensington. You're twenty seven. Your wife's name is Christine. You have a seven month old son, named Josh. You rent a one bedroom apartment, a dive on West Twenty Third. Your wife is twenty-two and stays at home with the kid while you unload the boats at the wharf by day and get drunk at night. How am I doing?"

Flynn glared at him and Josh could see the anger building.

"What are you, a cop? Some kinda detective? "

Josh stood his ground, as Flynn took a step closer.

"No, look, you need to listen to me. I don't have much time."

"I asked you a question. How the hell do you know so much about me?"

"This is difficult enough. Who I am is not important. What is important is what I have to say."

"Oh, yeah? And what if I don't want to listen?"

Josh took a step closer, as his own anger started to get the better of him.

"That's always been your problem, Flynn. You don't care and you don't listen. The drunken binges, the booze and brawling, that's your life."

"What about the broads? You didn't mention the broads. How about them?" Flynn said with a drunken smirk. Josh just swallowed the hurt and tried to focus.

"You need to go home, Flynn, and listen to your wife."

Again, Flynn looked at him with a mixture of shock and anger, then stepped back and smiled, pointing his finger as though he had pinpointed the answer and was relieved to have figured it out.

"Did Christine's mother put you up to this? Cause if she did I'd like you to do me a favor and give her a message for me. Can you do that?"

Flynn reached into his back pocket and pulled out a pair of black leather gloves, the same gloves Josh remembered from his youth, except now the leather was new, not yet softened by the years of beatings he was yet to undergo at the hands of a brute. Josh's blood ran cold as Flynn slipped them on and smacked his leather covered fist in the palm of his gloved hand and started forward. Josh braced himself and started in again.

"You thought you could change her when you got married, but now you know you can't. She loves God, Flynn, and for that you've decided to make her life a living hell. But, it doesn't have to be that way. I can help you change all that."

Again, Flynn stared at him, slack jawed and leaning forward, as if to get a better look at the man through the drunken haze.

"Who the hell are you?"

"I'm here to help you."

"Oh, yeah? That's funny, 'cause I'm here to kick your ass."

Flynn lunged at Josh who was already anticipating the punch and ducked under Flynn's arm. He dove to the other side of the alley and Flynn turned slowly, beaming a drunken smile.

"Don't make me chase you, man. It's just gonna hurt more."

Josh squared himself.

"I don't want to fight you," he said.

"Suit yourself," Flynn said, and staggered forward.

Although he was drunk and awkward, it was clear from the man's body language, he was a street fighter and knew what he was doing. And with the entrance of the alley behind Flynn it was also clear, there was no way out. Josh put his hands up and blinked several times trying to clear his head and prepare himself for what was about to come. He had slipped the first punch but considered himself lucky. The man closed in, hunched over like a small bull.

"Listen," Josh said, but it was too late.

Flynn lunged in with a slow looping right to the head, a lazy punch that Josh saw coming. What he didn't see was the left hook, a quick blow to the body that was thrown with serious intent. The shot connected solid and sent a shock wave through Josh that knocked the air out of him and doubled him over, instantly. Josh gasped, red faced, with his arms wrapped around his gut, and made the mistake of looking up. When he did, a gloved fist snapped his head to the left and sent the world spinning. Josh went down hard, his face splashing in a grimy muddy puddle. He laid there, his mind whirling, and the demons of his childhood dancing in his head. Once again he was the helpless child, called to endure yet another beating at the hands of his father. The only difference was, this time he would take the beating as a man, and in the shadows of a back alley there would be no mercy. A steel toed Jack boot stepped in front of Josh's face and before he could gather himself, Josh felt a hand grip the back of his shirt.

"C'mon, get up! The party's just gettin' started," Flynn said as he hoisted Josh to his feet.

Josh got up in a daze, and gripped the hand around his neck. He reached out blindly, when another blow snapped his head to the right and cut his lip open. Another backhand across the face and Josh's knees buckled as he reached for the ground, but Flynn held him up, smiling with sadistic pleasure.

"So you want to help me? Looks like you're the one who needs the help, pal."

Josh tried to look at the man through blurred eyes, his head still reeling.

"I've come to give you a message."

Flynn shoved Josh against the brick wall hard enough to snap his head back, and Josh went down again. Before he knew it, Flynn crossed the alley and drove him to his feet once more. Josh gathered himself and held onto the man's arms for support.

"So talk, I'm listenin,'" Flynn said as he shoved his hand into Josh's pockets, looking for cash or valuables. Flynn patted his pockets which were empty then looked at him with some surprise.

"Hey pal, where's your wallet, huh?"

"I've seen him," Josh mumbled, trying not to pass out, as the man rifled through his pockets.

"Oh yeah, sport? Who've you seen?"

Flynn grinned into the man's bruised and bleeding face, when Josh answered.

"Jesus."

Flynn looked at him and froze with the mention of the name, and turned his head slightly as though he hadn't heard him correctly.

"Come again?"

Josh struggled to open his left eye which was beginning to swell shut, and looked at his assailant.

"I've seen him. I don't have much time. You have to believe me. It's all that matters."

Again, his words caused Flynn to look at him with genuine confusion.

Josh stared back, hoping he had gotten through and then glared in agony as he took another shot to the stomach, for his trouble. This time Flynn let him fall, and scoffed at Josh's body huddled on the ground.

"A Jesus freak, huh? So that's what this is all about?" Flynn turned away and shook his head.

"You're seriously out of your mind, man!" Flynn whirled around, grinning at the absurdity. "So you're a man of the cloth and you've come to preach to me," Flynn scoffed. "Well, pastor, I'm all ears. Let's see what you got!"

Josh kept his head down, struggling to breathe. "God, help me," he moaned into the dirt.

Flynn leaned down to hear and then threw his bloody leather hands into the air and turned his gaze to the sky.

"You heard the man, God! Looks like he needs help to me!"

Flynn gazed into the night, as though listening, waiting for a response. Then when enough time had passed, he turned to Josh with a look of disappointment.

"I don't think he heard you. Must be on a break."

Flynn squatted down next to Josh, who was still laying face down on the pavement, panting for air, and patted him on the back.

"You know, I think maybe, they've been playin' you for a fool. You ever think about that?" Flynn spoke with mock concern as he ran down the list of possible offenders.

"The priests, the church, all your religious friends and those blue haired old freaks, waitin' to meet Jesus. You've been conned, buddy, scammed. That's what they do. They mess with your head till you don't know what to believe."

"No," Josh groaned and drew his arms along side him, as though he were going to stand.

Flynn looked at him with some surprise.

"No? Ah, c'mon, don't feel so bad. There're plenty of weak minded fools, looking around for something to believe in."

Josh tried to raise his head, but could hardly find the strength to move.

"Is that what you think I am?" Josh mumbled with his chest still planted on the ground.

"Sure," Flynn said. "It's not like you're the only sucker in the world. It's the biggest con job ever. You're like, what? One in a billion? You know what?"

Josh struggled to crawl and move away from his tormentor, but only managed to creep a few feet. Flynn moved closer, determined to share his little secret, as Josh dragged himself deeper into the shadows of the ally way.

"Between you and me, I used to be a sucker just like you."

Josh was still trying to crawl then ran out of energy and laid there, breathing hard, and turned his head to listen. With his eye swollen and mouth bleeding, hair and dirt mixed with blood, Josh tried to look up at the man crouched over him. Flynn smiled, and the look on his face seemed to say, "Yeah, that's right!"

Josh stared at him, squinting through the pain, and if he hadn't been so beaten up would have looked more amazed.

"Yeah, the last time I prayed, my dad was in the war. Mom said if you pray everything will be all right. I prayed, and dad came home in a pine box Guess it didn't work, huh? So what do you think? You're the expert. Maybe I didn't kneel, didn't bow long enough? Fold my hands? What? You wanna help, right? So c'mon tell me. Why didn't it work?"

Josh watched Flynn's smile fade and his sadistic side return.

"Ironic, isn't it? You trying to instill faith in me, while I'm in the process of beating it out of you, when you probably just found it, only to find out that I just lost it. Confession's over."

Flynn stood up and with some effort dragged Josh to his feet once again. Josh held on as he was hoisted up and winced with a bloody lip and a broken rib.

"Well, that's history. Now let's see if God saves you from gettin' your ass kicked."

Josh raised his hand too late, as the straight right crunched into his face and broke his nose. Josh slid back, his blood splattered face exploding with pain, as he back peddled and went down hard on his shoulder. He clutched his face and lay there among the garbage and debris strewn across the back alley. Josh could feel the warmth of blood flowing between his fingers, and struggled not to pass out. He squinted through blurred and swollen eyes and could barely make out the dark figure of his attacker coming after him. Josh tried to roll over and when he did, his hand hit something on the ground next to him. His fingers fumbled across it in the dark and he gripped it tight.

Flynn kicked pieces of trash out of the way as he advanced on the man in the shadows. "Hey, don't tell me you're done. I'm just gettin' warmed up."

Flynn stood over Josh's beaten body and adjusted his black leather gloves, flexing his fingers and pulling the leather tighter across his knuckles.

"You better keep prayin' cause it's sure as hell's gonna take a miracle to save you now." Josh laid there, huddled to one side, waiting and just as Flynn reached down, Josh swung his right hand up as hard as he could and with everything he had. Flynn took the full impact of the broken chair leg to the side of his face and roared as he clutched his head in agony.

Josh put a crease in the man's scalp with the makeshift club and while Flynn gripped his wounded head, Josh got to his feet and with a batter's swing drove the weapon low and to the ribs. Flynn doubled over and dropped to his knees, clutching his side, with blood streaming down his face and finally toppled over. Josh dropped the club, his head and face still pounding from the beating he had taken. He prodded his nose and spit blood then looked down on his attacker.

"So that's it. You hate God because of what happened to your father. Yeah, that's pretty raw, and I don't know what to tell ya.' I don't have the explanation, but you're not a child anymore and you can't take it out on your wife and kid."

Flynn lay there, trembling in pain, with his arms wrapped around his side.

"Like you said, that's history. So what is it Flynn? What is it really? What are you running from? It's not Christine. It's what she represents, isn't it? It's her faith. You think God let you down all those years ago, and you're still running. You've been running ever since and never stopped to see that God didn't kill your father. He blessed him with a son who loved him."

Josh glanced down at his watch which was counting down to thirty seconds and then stepped closer.

"Listen to me. Like it or not, Christ is for real. You hear me? God is for real. That's the message. You've got to believe me."

Josh took a second to wipe the blood that was still trickling from his nose and winced as he touched his face. When he looked again, he was staring down the barrel of a handgun. Flynn sneered, with one arm clenched around his waist.

The .38 Special glistened dully in the shadows and the whole world fell silent. A second later the muzzle flash lit the alley like a bolt of lightning and Josh staggered backward, shot through the chest. The impact was like a sledgehammer that splintered his ribcage, and sent bone shards through major arteries. Josh toppled backward and crashed into a row of garbage cans. The fall made more noise than the gunshot, spilling garbage across the back of the alley. When Josh came to rest it was silent once again, he was laying face up to the sky.

In that instant, everything that was good came to him in a rush of memories, vivid and real; a proud mother holding her son's report card; a faded snapshot of a young couple embracing. Josh watched the old photo come to life. He could see the sun on the woman's face and the trees swaying in the breeze; the couple smiling. The woman nestled in the arms of the young man, strong and handsome; her loving husband. And as Josh peered up at her the woman's lips whispered sweetly, "I love you."

Josh called to her silently, "Mom," and as the image faded he could feel his life ebbing out of him. A tear spilled from the corner of his eye as he stared up at the night sky, quietly dying in a gathering pool of blood. Then finally against the dark backdrop of stars came another face, the face of a man on a mountain top. Josh gazed up into his eyes once more, and Christ looked down with the same tender smile and once again took away his pain.

Flynn gathered himself and approached the body that lay in the heap of garbage. He was still breathing heavy and sneered with a crazed look in his eyes. With blood dripping down his face he cursed the man for the cheap shot and held the gun ready to pump another bullet into him. And as he came closer he thought he could hear the man speak, muffled words chocked off by his own tears. Flynn crept closer until he was standing over the man, and listened to the words that were not uttered to him.

"Forgive me, Lord. I tried," he groaned and stared up at the sky. "I tried."

As he breathed his last breath and the world passed away, the voice of God whispered, "Fear not. Now it begins."

Flynn clutched his side and grimaced, with the pistol still pointed down and shaking in his hand. He had never shot a man before and stood there, staring blankly, at the corpse. Flynn wiped the trickle of blood coming from the gash in his head. He was now sober and trembling with the realization that he had just killed a man in cold blood, a total stranger.

Flynn's gaze drifted from the body to the gun and the thin ribbon of smoke that still rose from the barrel. He looked to the body lying in the heap of garbage; his rage turned to fear.

"He's dead!... What have I done?" he gasped, as panic flooded into his brain and riveted his feet to the spot.

Then as he stood there in the back of the alley hidden in the shadows, another voice spoke as deep and real as his own. "There's no way out!" it said, as Flynn stared blankly.

"There's no way out. You're a liar, a thief and a murderer. There's no way out." The voice came softly like an accuser in the night and pointed its crooked finger in Flynn's back. Standing there staring down at the corpse, there was no denying it. He had been a liar and a thief and now that he had killed a man, it was true that he was a murderer. With the walls of the alley and the whole world closing in around, his own voice echoed the words. "There's no way out. There's no way out."

Flynn raised the gun, and turned the weapon on himself so that the steel barrel rested against his temple. Then with all hope gone, he tightened his grip and closed his eyes and then shuddered when another sound broke the silence. Instead of the loud rapport of the gun and a blinding muzzle flash, there was a soft beeping, a small distant sound that drew Flynn out of his trance.

He lowered the pistol and turned to the body as the high pitched tones pierced the night like some kind of alarm. Unable to see the man's wristwatch, Flynn stood there staring. Then as quickly as it began, the noise stopped. Before he could move, a light caught his eye. At first he thought it was shining down on the body and looked up. The dark sky above was pitch black but when he looked again, the body was even brighter. Flynn blinked at first, thinking his eyes were playing tricks on him and then stared and dropped the gun as the corpse of the man was suddenly filled with light, glowing brighter and brighter until it lit the ground around him and the entire alley. Flynn staggered back and shielded his eyes as light poured out from the body until it was totally engulfed. Then just as he was about to turn away, a burst of energy jolted him back and everything went dark.

CHAPTER 18

Back in the lab, Colter paced the control platform like a caged animal and glared at the GMS unit within the pulsating energy field. Then in another fit of anger, he pounded the desk in front of him and kicked over a chair. Those around him watched nervously and gave him plenty of room. With every resource at his disposal, money, weapons, men, and technology, the boy had managed to slip through his grasp again and now the project, his entire industry, perhaps even his life, was at stake. Maxfield had warned that the weapon could also be used against them and now the once bold and brilliant military tactician, the head of security, was wrapped in a blanket, lying helplessly in the arms of a female technician reduced to a cuddling cooing infant. His mind was wiped clean of all memory. Maxfield clutched the woman's pinky finger for comfort and the only source of security he could find.

Pelitier sat at the control platform, dabbling the burns on his face, when suddenly warning lights flashed as the main generators began to power down. Pelitier turned sharply. The time jump was over and the pod was returning.

"GUARDS!" Colter yelled.

The twelve soldiers took up positions around the time machine and held their weapons ready, careful to stay well back from the energy field that had all but killed the colonel. The high pitched whine died down as the time chamber lowered and the hydraulic platform returned to ground level.

Colter approached the chamber and stood at the edge of the force field, anxiously moving forward and wringing his hands as the field grew dimmer and weaker. As soon as the force field disappeared completely and the machine had gone silent, Colter rushed forward like a madman and ripped the GMS unit from the wall of the time chamber. Everyone watched as he smashed it against the floor and stomped on the device, which sputtered and sparked until its circuits went dead.

Once he was done, Colter looked up, nearly out of breath, his eyes staring at the door of the time chamber. Then in a desperate leap, he tossed himself on the metal hatch and peered inside. The guards and technicians all waited as Colter just lingered there and seemed paralyzed by the sight within the time chamber. A few seconds later he moved back, still looking through the circular window, and tried the hatch door. When it didn't budge he smoothed his hair back then turned to the men behind him.

"Cut it open," he said, with a wave of his hand.

Two men raced forward from the tactical team standing by with acetylene torches and began to cut through the metal shell of the time chamber. Atop the control platform Pelitier stared intently at the monitor in front of him, which showed the same view that Colter had seen through the hatch window. Josh's dead body lay strapped in the chair, his t-shirt soaked in blood with a bullet hole through the chest. The once young handsome face was a battered and swollen pulp. With his nose bashed in and eyes swollen shut, the mass of cuts and bruises made the face barely recognizable.

The chamber had claimed its second victim, and this time it was its inventor. The feeling was the same all across the lab. This machine was a death trap and they had seen enough. One by one, the lab techs left their work stations and walked out.

Pelitier moved forward to join Colter, as the welders cut through the chamber door of the time machine. With Josh dead and the lab relatively intact, Colter was back in charge and had regained total composure. Pelitier dabbed his own much abused face with a damp handkerchief, as the light of the torches cut through steel and flickered in front of them.

"What do you suppose he was trying to do?" Pelitier asked.

Colter paused to think, as the torches hissed.

"I don't know, but whatever it was, I don't think it turned out the way he expected."

The two continued to observe as the men worked feverishly, and the chamber, like some futuristic tomb, seemed unwilling to release its victim. Colter continued, and clearly breathed a sigh of relief.

"Anyway, the important thing is we're still here. Whatever he went to do, whatever his plan was, it didn't work."

And just when the words were uttered from his lips, the paradox occurred.

Flynn waited in the shadows of the alleyway, stunned and trembling when the body in front of him vanished into thin air. A few seconds later, Flynn's eyes adjusted and he came forward, peering into the darkness, trembling and stared in awe. The blood soaked ground was all that was left, the only evidence of the man he had killed, the man he watched disappear before his eyes, the man who never was. Shocked, confused and afraid, his mind flashed back on what he could remember of their conversation.

"He knew all about me," Flynn whispered.

He tried to think as a few words came back to him, key phrases that sent a chill through him.

"I want to help you. I've come to give you a message." A message" Flynn thought, and blinked, trying to recall.

"I've seen him. I've seen Jesus," the man said, and then Flynn remembered.

Suddenly he was alone in the universe, alone with the man's last words echoing in his head.

"Forgive me Lord. I tried."

Flynn backed away. The message was inescapable, and he suddenly remembered it, loud and clear.

"Christ is for real. You must believe. Christ is for real."

Flynn repeated the words, mumbling them to himself as he pondered the man who had disappeared before his eyes. But no matter how he tried to rationalize, or explain it away, only one conclusion remained. Whether angel or saint, the man he had encountered was not from this world and was clearly sent by God.

Flynn looked down at his hands and the bloodstained gloves that covered them, a hideous reminder of the monster that he was. Suddenly he was clawing and tearing at them, and once he had ripped them from his hands, he cast them into the shadows and staggered backward, his chest heaving up and down with a sudden wave of emotion. Then with arms outstretched, Flynn threw his head back, dropped to his knees and opened his mouth. But there were no words to describe the shame, guilt and remorse. As he knelt, a cool rain began to fall and splashed his face, mixing with his tears. Soon Flynn was sobbing openly in the pouring rain, as the water washed over him until he was soaked clean through and rivers of water washed away the blood at his feet. Flynn cried out to God in the falling rain.

"Forgive me! Forgive me!" he said and covered his face, aware of his guilt and sin, and aware of a weight that was suddenly lifted. Though he couldn't understand it, he felt clean, like the blood and dirt washed away from the ground. There was something about him now and he knew that he was different. Again he cried out, and choked back the tears.

"Thank you, God! Thank you!" He sobbed as though his heart had been pierced. He had been given a second chance, the chance to change and make everything different, to make everything right. Marcel Kensington stared up at the sky, and as he did, he knew he would never forget that night, the rainy night, in a back alley, and the encounter with a stranger that had changed his life forever.

Even as the words were uttered from his lips, somewhere in the future, two men stood before a metal chamber, a device designed to travel through time, and watched as a team of men with blow torches tried to cut through its outer skin. Through a small window built into the chamber door, they observed the dead body trapped within and commented to each other. They spoke calmly and were casual, completely unaware of the disaster that was about to strike.

"What do you suppose he was trying to do?" Pelitier asked.

Colter paused to think.

"I don't know, but whatever his plan was, it didn't wwoooooorrrrr–"

CHAPTER 19

The reality shift was both globally cataclysmic and totally imperceptible to any living creature on earth, as everything ground to an inexorable, complete, and utter halt. Every kinetic molecule and everything that human existence had ever touched was suddenly static, motionless, and frozen in time as this reality, abruptly came to an end. Like a curtain coming down, darkness descended and overtook the world. The people in the lab became vague, lifeless shapes and shadows, meaningless images trapped within an empty black void. In seconds, all remnants of life were erased as reality faded away and the people disappeared without even a whimper.

Then in a quantum space of time that was too small to measure, out of the eerie darkness came a new reality. The cool blue glow of twilight glistened over the tranquil forest, as pine trees swayed in the thick shadowy woods. A few lights glimmered in the valley below the dark hillside, while there on the hilltop, above the wooded landscape of rolling hills was a quiet glen with only deer and the occasional hoot of an owl to disturb the silence.

Colter Laboratories was gone, and indeed had never existed.

At noon time on a hot summer day, the New York City streets were overflowing with people. A large woman walked out of an expensive clothing boutique. She was in her fifties, with an air of sophistication and money. She carried her purse tucked under her arm and held the door for her husband, who was close behind her. The man, however, was having a problem pushing his belly through the door with a half dozen shopping bags and two hat boxes.

"Careful, honey. Be careful now," Mrs. Maxfield insisted in her lilting southern drawl, showing genuine and loving concern for her purchases.

Colonel Maxfield was dressed like a tourist in beige shorts, black sox and shoes, a white cotton shirt and baseball cap. The rough, chauvinistic old war horse gritted his teeth and grumbled as he pressed on. With his hat turned sideways, in the wrestling match with the door, he fought like a bull and pushed his way through until he was standing outside with all the packages.

Behind him came a tall and handsome soldier, dressed in khaki military uniform and loaded down with another half dozen packages. Marine Special Forces, Major William F. Conrad, Iraq war veteran, twice decorated, "A man of honor, a damn good soldier, as good as they get," Maxfield often said. And here he was handpicked by Maxfield for what the colonel had deemed, "hazardous duty." Major Conrad made it through the door with greater ease and tried not to seem genuinely amused by the day's events thus far.

With the rush of people streaming around them, Mrs. Maxfield took a moment to point at one of the boxes that had been dented in her husband's struggle to free himself from the door.

"That's mother's hat, dear. Now be careful with that one," she scolded then paused to look at the man as though she had just noticed him for the first time.

"Are you all right?"

Maxfield was still huffing, and glared over the packages.

As a proud military man, he dreaded shopping. To him there was nothing more painful, no duty more useless, with the possible expectation of stepping on a landmine. But even then, there was a sense of finality to being blown up, while shopping had no such benefit. This was a form of lingering death, and he dreaded the prospect of having to do it all again tomorrow.

Maxfield gathered himself. This was after all a vacation, scheduled by his wife. The kind he wished came with a cigarette and blindfold. He thought back to his book, chapter thirteen, In The Hands of the Enemy. "You must endure," he told himself, like a brave prisoner of war.

Maxfield mustered a smile. "I'm fine, dear. No problem. How are we doing on time?" he asked kindly in his Texas drawl.

The southern belle looked down at her gold tennis bracelet watch and gasped. "Oh, my! Come along, Raymond! We have to hurry, or we'll miss the show!" she said and made her way through the crowd en route to a cab.

The colonel trailed behind her like a disgruntled pack animal and mumbled under his breath. "Wouldn't want that to happen."

Once they reached the curb the woman yelled out, "Taxi!" and began to bounce up and down on her tiny heels, till every part of her ample body bounded and rebounded joyfully, freely, and with great exuberance as though she were a contestant on a game show. The sight was enough to make the stoical Major Conrad almost smile, while Maxfield just stared and calmly pleaded, "Shoot me."

As the crowd of pedestrians flowed back and forth behind her, an attractive red head walked by, followed by four children ranging from ages ten to five, three girls and a boy, the boy being the youngest.

Karen Danners had managed to hold onto her maiden name much better than she held onto the child that was straggling along behind her, a cute little girl with curly, strawberry blonde hair. Danners paused briefly to wag her finger at the seven year old who wore an equally stern expression and looked as though she was indeed a prisoner of war who refused to be broken.

"You wait till I tell your father. You are in big trouble young lady, big trouble!" Danners said and then marched forward, with the little girl in tow.

The two older girls followed close behind and held their little brother by the hand. The oldest girl looked down on the boy.

"This is all your fault," she said to her baby brother who at the moment happened to be staring at the big man with all the packages standing by the curb. Suddenly the youngster pointed at colonel Maxfield and yelled, "Look at the big fat clown!"

Maxfield glared at the boy in outrage, and the children quickly retreated into the crowd, just as a little yellow taxi cab pulled up in front of him. Mrs. Maxfield hopped in and then waved to him with a big smile. With his cheerful wife, his large stomach, the driver and all the packages to contend with, Maxfield's face went blank. "Get in, honey!"

Major Conrad stood back and smiled. "I'll take the next one sir."

Maxfield slouched forward and lowered his head in defeat. I should have joined the circus."

With traffic headed downtown, the Major saluted the cramped and disgruntled colonel as the cab pulled away and left the crowd milling past a little eatery which happened to display a sign that read, "Lil's Coffee Shop." Beneath the sign was a man and woman seated at a window counter eating greasy burgers and drinking beer. The woman was cheaply dressed and looked like a hooker, while the man across from her was obviously a two bit con man and looked the part. His white shirt was too tight and his jacket was a checkered sports coat that looked like a two for one deal at a flea market. The only thing expensive about him was his Italian shoes, which were eight years old and curled at the toes.

Carl Grasso's mouth motored on, even when it was full, and seemed unable to stop. The woman ate her burger while he talked, determined to make the best of a free meal and calmly tolerated the conversation for the time being.

"So, you enjoying yourself? Huh? Huh?" Grasso said and paused to wipe his mouth.

The woman forced a smile.

"Immensely," she said, her voice dripping with sarcasm.

Thinking he was making headway, Grasso laid it on thick and rattled on with his New York accent, sounding more and more like a snake oil salesman.

"We're talking growth here, expansion, big money. You look like a hard working girl. This would be a great opportunity for you, and someone of your obvious talents."

At the moment Grasso happened to be talking to her chest.

"Really?" the woman said. As far as she was concerned, the man was a pig. She looked him up and down and smiled to herself. "Oh yeah, big money."

"I'm lookin' for a legitimate job," she said, just to let him know the type of services she was offering.

"Yeah, sure, sure, some typing, some filing, did I mention growth potential? We're talkin' huge. It's a challenging time. But I like a challenge. When you're in business for yourself, you gotta go for it. See what I'm sayin'? You snooze, you're done! You hesitate, you lose. Know what I mean?"

"Sure, you're a risk taker," the woman said in a flat monotone.

Grasso's eyes lit up as he took another bite of his burger.

"Precisely!" he said and spit a piece of food at her.

The woman shifted to avoid the projectile that landed on the counter next to her elbow, and just stopped herself from jumping out of her seat. But since she was desperate and needed the money, the woman willed herself to sit still and tried to smile.

"How much you payin'?" she asked.

Grasso paused to wipe his mouth then leaned in, smiling wickedly.

"That depends on you, the skills you bring to the table... If you know what I mean." The woman's expression went blank. She grabbed her beer, took a last sip, then slammed the glass down on the counter and made Grasso jump back.

"No thanks. I'm not that desperate," the woman said, then grabbed her purse and headed for the door. Grasso looked surprised and shouted after her with his mouth half full.

"What? What's the matter! Where're you going? What'd I say? Aw, C'mon! Hey!

Grasso's eyes followed her as she walked out the door and passed by the window. Not wanting to miss an opportunity, he stepped up on the metal rung of the stool, with his expensive Italian shoes, and leaned across the counter to get a good look at her rear. Grasso banged on the glass, attracting everyone's attention, except the woman outside and yelled to her, just before his foot slipped.

"I'LL CALL ya!

Grasso dropped out of sight as though a trap door had opened beneath him and he had been sucked through a hole in the floor. When he hit, raucous laughter broke out across the pint sized restaurant. Thinking quickly, Grasso grabbed his knee and cried out in pain.

"Owww! My leg! My leg!"

Some of the laughter subsided until the cook of Lil's Coffee Shop stepped forward. The man was nearly three hundred pounds and looked like the last person on earth who could be called "Lil." The man waved his greasy spatula at Grasso and shouted.

Don't even try it, Grasso! You sue me I'll break yer freakin' legs fer real!"

Taking into account the size of the man, his bad temper, and the fact that the establishment was hardly worth the price of a burger, Grasso decided that this was indeed good advice, especially since the man was his cousin and Grasso made it a rule never to sue family. Not for any reason of loyalty to kin, but simply because they knew where he lived.

With that, Grasso stood up, brushed himself off and held his head up, as he walked out of the restaurant, to the continued laughter and jeers of the people around him. With shoulders back and chest out, he swaggered past the shop window trying to preserve what little dignity he had left. But in spite of everything, all was not lost, since it would be another five minutes before anyone realized he had left without paying the check.

Directly across the street from Lil's Coffee Shop was the convention center at Madison Square Garden. The grand marquee facing the street read;

"THE GREAT DEBATE
CREATION vs. EVOLUTION"

Below the headline were the names of two men, both prominent in their respective fields.

Dr. Josh Kensington vs. Prof. Simon Pelitier

The people who filed into the Convention Hall had anxiously awaited what was touted as the "Battle of the Brains." Simon Pelitier, world renowned scientist and inventor, would argue for the theory of Evolution against the award winning author, Josh Kensington, a brilliant philosopher, Christian theologian and apologist, who would defend Creation.

Within the main auditorium the debate was already in progress. The arena was packed to capacity with standing room only. The only places that were not packed and had plenty of room were the catwalks that crisscrossed the high ceiling above the auditorium. And the only person that had no concern for the event going on below was the man on the catwalk with a gun.

Down on stage, Simon Pelitier, dressed in his trademark yellow bow tie, with gold rimmed glasses, and a cream colored suit, stood at his podium. The professor had his notes laid out in front of him. Also laid out in front of him, and lining the first three rows, was "Pelitier's Posse." These were men and women dressed very similar to Pelitier, devout fans, clones, and carbon copies of the man, comprised of fellow instructors and general laypeople, men adorned in bow ties, women in scarves and many arrayed in various styles of gold rim glasses.

Across the stage was Josh Kensington, a smiling and casual contrast to his opponent. Josh wore a white shirt opened at the collar, blue jeans, with a pair of well worn leather boots and an equally well worn Bible on the podium in front of him. At twenty-five, the young man looked more like a student than a learned doctor of theology.

The man in the rafters lay in a prone position on the metal catwalk and watched the young man on the stage. He cradled the 22 cal. Smith and Wesson handgun, peered through the high powered sight with the 5.5 inch barrel aimed down between the slats in the catwalk and felt a sense of satisfaction. His name was John Maslow. He was sixty-five and all alone in the world. In his painful estimation it was all due to the man on stage whom he now held in the sights of his gun. He waited and listened, undetected by anyone below.

Simon Pelitier smiled politely as the audience applause settled in response to his rebuttal.

"So once again the truth remains. Evolution is based on scientific fact while Creation is pure mythology."

Josh held onto his podium and looked at Pelitier with some surprise. "That's quite a statement, fact versus mythology." He paused to give the premise some consideration, as though Pelitier were onto something before continuing.

"Since both of us are arguing for the truth, I think we should define those terms. You said evolution is fact. Would you agree that for something to be fact there must be evidence?"

Pelitier smiled graciously, "I would be happy to provide a nail for your coffin. A 'fact' is that which is actual, having objective truth," Pelitier said confidently.

Josh nodded once more in agreement. "Objective truth, okay, unlike mythology which is based on fantasy, or allegory."

Again Pelitier felt he was on solid ground, and proceeded boldly. "Myths such as Creation are expressions of symbolic fictional accounts. Yes, I would agree with that," Pelitier said, and smiled with a sense of satisfaction.

Josh raised his hands, elated.

"Well, then! We can agree on something. Based on your own definitions, you have just reversed your initial statement. Evolution is now mythology and Creation is fact."

"No, I didn't. That's ridiculous." Pelitier protested, flicking a smile on and off.

Josh looked surprised.

"Really? The most popular myth is that science is on the side of evolution. The fact is the greatest scientists from Sir Isaac Newton and Louis Pasture, all the way up to the inventor of the generator and the computer, were all devote Christians and staunch defenders of the faith. Even Einstein while not a Christian was a passionate enemy of evolution. But lest you say these scientific minds were deceived, let's look at the evidence to support evolution. This may come as a shock, but it was the very lack of evidence that led Darwin to classify his concept as mere theory."

Maslow peered down and smirked at the boy's smugness and confidence. He took his eye off the gun sight to glance around at the thousands of people that filled the place. As much as he resented him, he could see why his wife and son had become so fond of the young man. They had read all of his books. They listened to him on the radio. They had been followers like all the rest. He called them sheeple, empty headed people so easily led by others. Personally, Maslow had no interest in the young man. Now that his wife was dead, all he had was hate.

Pelitier smirked at Josh's assertion that Darwin thought of Evolution as a theory. He looked down and shook his head.

"I'm sorry but that statement is a blatant lie."

Josh nodded his head in the affirmative, and looked out at the audience.

"I told you it would be a shock. I'm talking about the fossil record and the lack of any real fossil evidence to support evolution. Java man discovered in 1891 by Eugene DuBois, who eventually admitted his discovery was the skull of a Gibbon monkey. Piltdown man, discovered in 1908 by Woodward and Dawson, was the skull and jawbone of an ape with teeth filed down. Lucy discovered in 1974, was the skeleton of a chimp as determined by evolutionary scientist, Dr. Albert Mehlert.

The fossil Hesperopithicus, Western Ape man, was merely the tooth of a pig for goodness sake. These are the so called, "intermediate life forms" we see listed in textbooks to this very day. fabrications and hoaxes. Uncovered by who, religious fanatics? No, by modern scientists, honest men in search of objective truth. So what is the truth? We're teaching our children lies, mythology of apes turned into people, and calling it scientific discovery, evolution."

The audience remained silent and seemed stunned. Even some of the bow tie, gold rimmed crowd turned to each other and murmured.

Even with the AC units humming and the blowers churning out air and forcing it downward, the rafters and catwalks were still hot. Maslow used his sleeve to wipe the sweat from his brow. It was the death of his wife that had brought him here, a weird twist of fate that he wished he could change. After listening to the young theologian, his wife had changed. The talking about religion and God and the Bible was non-stop. He had started to resent her and then came the accident. Maslow looked down on the man on stage. "How many lives have you ruined?"

Pelitier cleared his throat and chuckled to himself.

"Mr. Kensington, you're bias is profound and disgraceful! It is obvious to me that you will say anything to discredit evolution. You are indeed an enemy of the truth."

Josh hardly flinched.

"No sir. Truth is the enemy of evolution. With the invention of the electron microscope we've proven that the world is far more complex than Darwin ever dreamt. In fact, if Darwin proposed his theory today, he would be laughed out of the halls of science for the sheer lack of evidence and a poor understanding of how things really work."

The audience turned to Pelitier, awaiting his answer. Pelitier arched an eyebrow and shook his head like a teacher disappointed by a student.

"You may believe in Creation. But don't expect rational people to place their faith in the absurd."

Josh nodded as though the statement was valid and he was ready to concede the point.

"Faith in the absurd... well said. I agree."

Pelitier frowned, and waited for the next shoe to drop.

"The accident, a complete understatement," Maslow thought and shook his head. It had been the end of his marriage, the end of his wife and the end of his life. She had gone to see the young man at an event in Chicago, a twenty minute drive from their house. The day had started out pleasant but then turned cloudy with a nasty downpour. "She hated driving in the rain. I should have gone with her." Maslow shook off the thought. "It's not my fault," he groaned and placed the scope before his eyes and looked down at the man in the cross hairs of his sight.

Josh smiled, and opened his arms wide. "Indeed, I say it takes more faith to believe in the ridiculous claims of evolution than it does to believe in the existence of God."

Pelitier leaned in on his podium and jabbed his finger at Josh. "For which there is no proof, no evidence."

"On the contrary, there is all kinds of proof."

"Give me one example of the existence of God, rooted in quantifiable data," Pelitier said, defiantly.

"I'll give you a trillion billion to one," Josh said.

Pelitier just shook his head at the nonsensical statement and Josh smiled at the audience.

"For all of you gamblers out there, I offer Christ's fulfillment of the Messianic Prophecies in the Old Testament, the prophecies that foretold the coming of the Messiah, describing his life, his ministry and subsequent death, in minute detail, thousands of years before his birth. Keep in mind, many of these predictions were completely out of Christ's control, like where he would be born and how he would die, what people would say about him. You want to talk long shot? Once you examine the odds against

Christ fulfilling every single prophecy, you find that the numbers are beyond astronomical. The odds are better that my distinguished colleague here could win the lottery five times in a row. Yet Christ actually did it, fulfilling all of the Messianic prophecies."

The crowd turned to Pelitier who flashed an awkward smile. "The lottery? Well, I could certainly use the money, and you can certainly read into those predictions whatever you like."

The crowd responded with a cordial laugh and then looked to Josh.

Maslow had been a senior officer in the first Gulf War and had seen combat. He could still see the face of the Iraqi soldier he killed with a rocket propelled grenade through the window of a road side building. The blast had wiped out the sniper and whoever else was inside. Now here in the shadows, high up on the catwalk Maslow had no doubt that he would squeeze the trigger. His only thought was of what his son would say. Geoffrey was only a few years younger than the man he was about to kill, and his son idolized him. Indeed it was his son who worked at the convention center who had gotten him into the event and given him access to a restricted area.

"Forgive me son," Maslow whispered to himself. He had been a disappointment to the boy since his mother's death and he regretted it. He regretted it almost as much as the loss of seventy percent of his hearing to pain killers and the drugs he abused since, "the accident." But he was getting used to that as well.

Josh smiled at the audience. "I can cite archeological evidence which supports the Bible or historical documents from other cultures which corroborate the miracles of Jesus, even documents written by his enemies. Or would you prefer the more recent evidence of intelligent design based on the findings of micro biological research. I can go on and on.

Pelitier shook his head and seemed genuinely amused by the man.

"Mr. Kensington, it's clear to me that you see what you wish to see, the feeble fabrications of a mind longing to apply spiritual meaning to everything he observes. I assure you, there are far more books which support evolution, and these are based on facts."

Suddenly Josh looked tired and somewhat annoyed.

"Let's just get right down to it. Here's where you and I differ. You think this is an intellectual debate. I say the real problem lies in the heart of man, not in his head."

"Oh yes, the heart." Pelitier looked out at the audience, and pointed across the stage. "Now my young opponent is on the retreat. The heart, a euphemism which can easily mean anything. Add a dash of poetry and a soothing melody; and you can be as clever and vague as you wish and hang all of your premises on nothing. Once again, Mr. Kensington offers a very clever dodge."

Maslow peered down through his gun sight and placed the cross hairs on the forehead of his target. "Forgive me son," he said again and hoped that somewhere in all of that religious rhetoric the boy could find it in his heart to understand and not see him as a monster. Then the thought struck him like a hammer. "How could he not see you as a monster? Especially if he's watching. After the initial shock, everyone will look up. He will look up and when he sees you he will hate you with everything he's got."

Josh looked at Pelitier unwaveringly, and spoke with a grave tone in his voice.

"No sir, not a dodge, a death blow. The question of the heart is a real one. If evolution is indeed a lie, then why invent the theory to begin with? The answer is simple. Man fears God, in his heart. Ergo, he creates a system of belief where there is no God, basing his claims on bogus scientific theory and tries to convince the world it is an intellectual discovery. As a result evolution does precious little to explain origin, but is far more successful as a hostile attack against God.

Pelitier simply smiled.

"You call that a death blow? That's hardly a scratch."

The audience chuckled again and Pelitier extended his arms to them. "Well, ladies and gentlemen, my young opponent demonstrates a very old method of persuasion, characteristic of the religious hierarchy in the dark ages. I'm referring to the use of scare tactics to manipulate the poor and innocent masses. If I may speak frankly, Mr. Kensington, I find your argument simple minded and, quite frankly, desperate.

Maslow heard the words, "hostile attack." He heard the word "desperate." He was indeed desperate man ready to commit a hostile act. There was no doubt. He had come to murder this man. He could live with that. But the eternal hatred of his son, a boy he loved, a boy who had just lost his mother only months ago. The thought of adding to the boy's pain was too much to bear. Now his sweat was mixed with tears.

Josh looked across the stage with a somber expression as Pelitier glared back.

"Call it what you will. You would reduce this debate to a mere war of words, but the existence of God is too critical to miss. Our Holy Father has reached down from Heaven and stretched out his loving arms so that we can come to know Him and become the people he has designed us to be. In fact it is our relationship with God that ultimately shapes and governs the people we become."

Pelitier looked at Josh with a pained expression, as though his opponent had been speaking gibberish the whole time. After shaking his head, he took a deep breath and looked out at the crowd.

"Well now that you've climbed out on the proverbial limb with your religious platitudes, I will be quick to saw it off for you. However confused and misguided, that was a perfect example of circular reasoning. Believe the Bible because it is important. Why is the Bible important; because the Bible says so, and around and around we go. Where it stops nobody knows."

Pelitier turned to address Josh directly.

"You find meaning in religion, that's good for you. You may even find some manner of truth. That's fine, but don't presume to prescribe your brand of truth to me like some desperate physician. I am not ill or ailing, nor do I like my doctors desperate. I prefer them calm and informed."

Maslow's hand shook as he now realized he would never leave the catwalk alive. Even the hatred of his own son would not keep him from killing the man on stage. Indeed Kensington would pay for destroying his life and to escape his son's wrath, he would gladly turn the weapon on himself. This hostile attack would end as a suicide mission. Laying there, he supposed he always knew it and did his best not to think about the damage that would do to the boy as well. "Sorry Geoff," is all he could muster. He then wiped his face, steadied himself and peered into the scope once more.

The audience applauded and cheered Pelitier. The evolutionists pumped their fists while Josh nodded, took a sip of water, and waited. When everyone had settled down he let a few extra seconds go by, and leaned toward the microphone.

"Let me restate my claim." Josh said and stepped out from behind the podium. "Your knowledge of Christ can change your life and determine the person you become."

With that, Josh pointed directly at his opponent. "And there's the proof." Pelitier stared blankly at the young man's finger that was leveled at him.

"Ladies and gentlemen, Mr. Pelitier, is a staunch evolutionist. He sees the world through a secular lens and would assure us that the greatest wisdom available to us is the wisdom of man, or perhaps some alien presence in space which is a whole other debate. I, on the other hand, freely admit that Jesus Christ is my Lord and Savior. Thus, my opponent and I are divided and disagree with almost every premise set forth, ethically, morally, politically, philosophically. We probably even differ on dog grooming habits. Perhaps we need to compare notes. The point is, our world views couldn't be further apart. So, if Christ is not at the core of what divides us, what is?"

Maslow eased the nozzle of the gun down between the slats of the catwalk. He sighted his target and gripped the trigger, waiting for the man to stop moving.

All heads turned and the audience looked at the man behind the podium. Pelitier was taken aback by the question about Christ and obviously offended. A smirk appeared on his face as he glanced at the audience, and then looked down at his notes, and shook his head. Josh moved back to his podium and looked more intently as though trying to discern some subtle response.

"A simple question requires a simple answer. Aside from faith in God, what is the core belief that divides us?"

"I don't feel the need to answer your question," Pelitier said and kept his head down as he placed his papers into a neat stack with meticulous care. "I find the assertion impudent, irrational and utterly irrelevant. But if I must answer," Pelitier seemed to gain steam as his anger became more apparent. "Stupidity!" he barked then thought about it. "On your part! That's what separates us," he said and punctuated it with a sharp nod before looking down and re-straightening his papers.

Josh scoffed at the response and stepped out from behind the podium again to plead his case.

"If we can all be honest for a moment, even my esteemed opponent knows it is our understanding of God that separates us."

"No!" Pelitier shouted, outraged by the fact that Josh would presume to speak for him. "I came here to speak about evolution not God! God was on your side of the ledger not mine!"

"Yet it is the mere mention of God which provokes you to anger."

"No it is you who offends me, sir; you and your condescension, your false humility, your self righteous lofty-mindedness. It sickens me and I feel sorry for you!" Pelitier said and punctuated it with another nod.

Maslow watched for the young man to return to the podium, waiting quietly. He could feel his heart pounding as sweat poured from his scalp. He blinked and shook the droplets off as he watched through the scope until the man returned.

Josh rounded the podium. "Don't feel sorry for me. I'm totally comfortable with my lack of faith in evolution. On the other hand, it is the Bible which says, only the fool hath said in his heart there is no God. And that is an indictment from the almighty himself." Josh smiled.

Pelitier glared across at him and looked as though he would explode, when the mediator's voice echoed throughout the large arena. "Thank you, gentlemen. That is it for our discussion and now time for closing statements. You have two minutes each. Mr. Kensington."

With Josh Kensington in his sights and the cross hairs placed squarely on the young man's forehead Maslow gripped the trigger gently. At a hundred yards away with a telescopic site, the shot was easy. The hard part was putting the hot muzzle of the gun under his own chin and pulling the trigger. But he was confident he could do that as well. With the young man standing as steady as a pole, Maslow muttered, "Take the shot."

Josh nodded his thanks to the mediator and looked out onto the vast crowd when there was a muffled sound. The noise of something from above caused people to look up to the shadowy catwalk. But with nothing further forthcoming everyone settled back as Josh gathered himself and continued.

"According to evolutionary science, the universe is comprised of three main components, time, space, and chance."

Josh stretched his arms out to everyone and proudly announced "Time, plus space, plus chance equals everything!" His voice reverberated through the dark arena. "Amazing... no miraculous," he said. "Time by itself has no causal ability, space can create nothing, and chance by itself is nothing, yet they have all come together to create the universe. Nothing, plus nothing, plus nothing equals... everything. Evolution sounds plausible on the surface. But when you go deeper, you find its truth claims are ultimately based... on nothing."

Maslow lay on the catwalk, quiet and still with the gun next to him and Hermon in coveralls, standing over him with a metal pipe in his hand. Hermon was an AC repair man, who was looking for his phone when he saw the man laying there on the center catwalk and did the only thing he could think of. The young Hispanic grabbed the first weapon he could find, snuck up on the old guy and thought for sure he would hear him coming. He was glad he didn't when he saw that the man indeed had a gun and hit the old timer hard enough to put a crease in his skull and then dropped the pipe when he saw what he had done. Without any further hesitation, Hermon picked up the handgun, checked the safety, shoved the weapon in his pocket, pausing only to pick up the pipe, and then hurried back down the catwalk the way he came.

With his adrenalin pumping, he didn't feel too bad about stealing the gun, since he had prevented a crime and possibly saved someone's life. In fact he felt pretty good and thought that once the guy came to, he might even be thankful for the few stitches in his head instead of a life sentence in jail.

Josh continued from the podium and glanced up at the shadow hurrying away on the catwalk, "In closing, evolution is the doctrine of nothingness, no purpose, no reason. We are an accident, a cosmic role of the dice, a product of blind chance, what a discovery... hooray," Josh said flatly. He scanned the auditorium which was silent and allowed everyone to ponder the thought.

"No, we are more than that. We are God's creation, and it is impossible to escape the sense of purpose and meaning that brings. Indeed the desire to know God lives within all of us. Our very curiosity is a clue. We're hard wired to know. It's part of God's purposeful design."

Josh reached out to the audience.

"Who is He and what does He want? I encourage you to walk the path of discovery. Search for Him. That's where it really gets fun…Thank you."

The audience applauded and Josh closed his note pad calmly, waited until they quieted down and then took a sip of water before turning to look at his opponent.

Pelitier who had spent much of the time seething over Josh's closing statement was instantly calm but maintained a stern and somewhat sour look when someone yelled out, "Smile!"

Pelitier ignored the outburst and began slowly.

"Unlike my opponent, I did not come here to manipulate, or evangelize. I came here to debate the issues. Mr. Kensington is obviously a self-proclaimed zealot and incapable of rational thought. If I could, I would apologize for his outbursts, but all I can do is say that I am embarrassed by his gall and effrontery."

Josh stood across the stage and simply watched as Pelitier grew more caustic and upset.

"Evolution is real and credible. It is fact based and well founded. The only fool here is Mr. Kensington, who believes he can stand here before us all and convince us of his fanatical claims and wild assertions, based on nothing more than his boastful lofty platitudes. He is nothing more than an entertainer, who is deluded, misguided and dangerous. Do not put your faith in him and his empty promises, or you will be sorely disappointed. Put your faith in fact. Put your faith in science. Put your faith in evolution. Thank you."

Josh called across to Pelitier, "For an atheist, you talk a lot about faith."

The laughter and applause erupted and Pelitier glared across the stage, shouting above the noise. "Don't you twist my words! I meant trust! I meant trust, you idiot!"

"Thank you, gentlemen!" the mediator's voice jumped in over the PA system to drown out any further insults from either side at which point Dr. Pelitier's mike was turned off. He added a few more comments as well as hand gestures before leaving the podium, which went unheard by most of the audience.

With the debate over, Josh quickly dispensed with all formalities, rounded the podium and jumped down from the stage to join the audience where he was quickly swarmed by fans carrying books and looking for autographs. Pelitier, who was an older man and far too dignified for such a display, turned and disappeared behind the curtains off stage, leaving his fans to wonder what to do next.

Josh was busy shaking hands when someone came up behind him and patted him on the back. The man was in his early thirties and dressed in black with the traditional collar of a Catholic priest. Father Michael Joiner was perhaps a little more handsome than one would expect of a priest and his eyes beamed with pride. Josh grinned and shook the hand of his old friend. Father Mike yelled above the crowd.

"Good job, but I thought you were really going to go after him."

Josh shrugged. "I didn't want to hurt him."

"You're slipping, Josh. I've never known you to pull punches."

"I'm more mature now, trying to apply the doctrine of grace."

The two men laughed as two more people emerged from the crowd. The older man and his wife immediately caught Josh's eye, and Josh rushed forward to greet his mom and dad. At the age of fifty-eight, Christine Kensington was radiant and youthful with a loving smile. She held her hands out and gave Josh a kiss as he wrapped his arms around her.

"Is that the best you can do?" she whispered in his ear.

Josh slowly squeezed her until she squealed and laughed.

"Oh! Be careful with this old lady."

Josh pulled back and looked at her.

"How did I do?"

"You did fine, just fine. In fact, I started to feel a little sorry for the other fella'. I don't think he was very well prepared and he seemed a little thin."

Just then his father came forward. Marcel Kensington, a picture of heath and contentment, a gentle man, whose inner change had resulted in a dramatic outward effect. Marcel patted his son on the shoulders and shook his hand.

"You gave a good account, son. I'm proud of you, real proud."

Josh hugged his dad then looked at him and nodded with appreciation.

"Did it just like you taught me," he said.

Marcel smiled, like a proud father.

"I taught you how to preach, not debate," he said. "You got that from your mother."

Just then a young man, holding a copy of *The Answer before You*, Josh's latest book, stepped forward and interrupted excitedly.

"Excuse me, but I just wanted to tell you that was brilliant!"

Josh reached out and shook the hand of the college student, after which the young man handed him the book and a pen.

"If you don't mind," he said, with an anxious smile.

"Not at all," Josh responded and with a swish of his hand placed his trademark signature on the inside front cover and then retuned the book and pen.

"Thanks," the young man said and then glanced at Marcel, who was standing next to Josh.

"Is this your dad?"

Josh put his arm around Marcel's shoulder and pulled him close.

"Yes it is, Pastor Marcel Kensington, of Freedom Evangelical Church."

The young man smiled and seemed somewhat embarrassed. "I know who he is. I was just looking for an introduction. I listen to your show all the time, Changed Life Ministries. It's an honor to meet you, Pastor."

Marcel gave him a hearty handshake then winked at Josh as he fished for more compliments.

"Thanks, so how often do you listen?"

"All the time. I never miss a day!" the young man said, eagerly, still pumping Marcel's hand.

"Is that a fact? Is that a fact?" Marcel said, pumping back, shamelessly.

Just then Josh's mom stepped in and separated the two.

"All right, leave the nice young man alone and let the other people have a chance," she said, holding her husband by the arm.

"Oh sure, who's next?" Marcel said, ready to shake hands with everyone.

"Not you, you big ham," she said and tugged at his arm.

Marcel smiled at Josh, apologetically.

"I'd better get out of here before I steal all your thunder," he said, and backed away with his arm around Christine's shoulder.

"Listen, I know you've got the book signing, so mom and I will see you later. Call us at the hotel. We'll do dinner."

"You got it," Josh said and waved good-bye as a handler came along side and started ushering Josh in the right direction.

CHAPTER 20

It was after five o'clock and over five hundred signatures later when Josh was finally done with his signing. The people had been gracious and the staff of the convention center was very accommodating. In fact, the V.I.P. treatment had made him a little uncomfortable, and he had no idea what to do with three gift baskets of fruit, which he presented to the cleaning staff as they folded tables.

As he spoke to his hotel, he waved goodbye to a few more people and headed out with his cell phone still stuck to his ear. He left the lobby with his leather briefcase in hand and wandered back into the convention hall where work crews were already setting up for the coming event. Dinner reservations in New York were hard enough to make at the last minute without being lost in a convention center. Josh turned to a burly worker on a forklift and waved his hand around giving the universal signal for, "I'm lost."

"Elevator?" he said. The man pointed straight ahead. Josh crossed the floor with the phone still attached and entered the enormous, four story atrium. Like everyone who entered the space, his eyes immediately went to the ornate mural painted on the ceiling. A thousand fiber optic lights glistened and shimmered like stars around the Greek Gods of the constellations. Zeus, Apollo, Orion, Athena, and Perseus, relief sculptures covered in gold leaf, and bathed in blue floodlights that gave the illusion of twilight. The special effect was beautiful and expertly designed, nearly as expertly designed as the woman talking on her cell phone who walked right into him. Josh instinctively reached out and grasped her by the shoulders, as she rocked backward.

"Oh! I'm sorry!" Josh said.

Even though it wasn't entirely his fault, he felt like an idiot, but one look at the woman in his arms told him that he was indeed a genius. The blonde bombshell was a cosmopolitan work of art, dressed in a simple charcoal gray designer suit that hugged her in all the right places. The woman pulled back and closed her cell phone. When Josh realized he had lost his signal as well, he closed his phone and stooped down to retrieve his leather briefcase. Josh came up slow and tried not stare at her legs on the way up.

"I'm terribly sorry, my fault," he said, hoping for a little conversation.

The woman merely regarded him with an annoyed glance, then continued on her way.

"I'm fine... thank you." Josh called after her as though she cared, and enjoying the view as she walked, continued on toward the elevators.

When Josh arrived, he stood next to the woman, blatantly staring at her and knew it was only a matter of time before she said something. After a long while she finally turned to confront him. When she did, Josh noticed her name tag, and didn't know how he had missed it the first time.

"Is there a problem," she said smugly.

He supposed it was rude to stare, but she had been equally rude with her response and now, as far as he was concerned, the gloves were off.

"Well Ms. Maltese, I would say disenfranchisement of the working class, a de-stabilized economy due to unfair trade agreements, economic imbalance among third world nations, world hunger? Can you be a little more specific?"

The woman looked down at the name tag which she had forgotten to remove, peeled it off her lapel, then crumpled it up, and gave a weak smile, dripping with sarcasm, as if to say, "Nice try."

She turned her attention back to the elevator doors. Josh was still looking at her when four people came up and stood behind them at the elevators. The silver haired old lady, a ponytailed college student with a backpack, and two businessmen, were all having a conversation that kept them huddled together. When they arrived, the young man immediately stepped around Josh to press the button that was already lit.

KC Maltese ignored the young man while Josh continued to stare. When he had pressed the button, the young man stopped in surprise and began to stare as well. The beautiful young woman held her gaze aloft. She was accustomed to being stared at, but had to admit this was getting ridiculous, and with the elevator taking forever, she was quickly running out of patience.

"Hey!"

The young man called out loud enough to frighten her and attract the attention of the others in his party. When KC looked, she was surprised to see the young man pointing at Josh, and smiling gleefully.

"It's you!" the young man said, and reached out to shake Josh's hand, which Josh gladly responded to.

"This is too cool!" the young man said, and hardly noticed the woman.

The old woman and the two businessman came forward to meet Josh as the young man rattled on non-stop, without taking a breath.

"I'm a big fan of yours! I was working the concession stand but took a break and caught the part of your talk when you were laying out the iron clad evidence surrounding the resurrection. Iron clad. I like that." You kicked that guy's tail, and blew him off the stage! I can't believe you're here. I tried to clean up as fast as I could, but by the time I got to the book signing you were already gone."

"I must have just missed you," Josh said. But before he was done, the young man had reached into his knapsack and produced a pen and a well read copy of Josh's book.

"Would you mind?" he said with bated breath.

"Of course," Josh said, and took the time to look over and give KC a nice big smile.

Josh turned his attention back to the young man.

"Who do I make this out to?" Josh said.

The boy's eyes lit up at the prospect of a personalized signed copy, and stammered as though he had forgotten his name.

"Uh, uh, Geoff! Geoff Maslow!"

Josh smiled at his excitement, and spelled out the name to be sure. "J e f f?"

"Uh, no. G e o f f."

Josh looked at the young man with some surprise as he signed the book. "Really? I had a roommate in college that spelled his name the same way."

KC rolled her eyes, annoyed by Josh's blatant pandering and finally looked away.

As soon as Josh handed the book and pen back to the student, one of the businessmen reached out and shook his hand.

"Mr. Kensington, you said some great things up there today, stuff I didn't know."

"Hey, we're all just searching for the truth, right?"

The silver haired old woman stepped forward, her voice trembling slightly as she spoke.

"You were marvelous! Absolutely marvelous! I have never heard anyone defend the faith like you. You've got guts, young man. You speak your mind and that's refreshing. It was a joy to listen to what you had to say."

She was so filled with admiration; KC had to glance over at her to see if she was for real. Josh reached out and took her hand gently then leaned forward to express his heartfelt thanks.

"I appreciate that, thank you. Thank you very much."

The old woman smiled up at him.

"Oh no, it was my pleasure, really," she said and patted Josh on his arm. After a few seconds of looking up at him, she turned to acknowledge the beautiful blonde standing next to him.

"You must be very proud," the old woman said.

KC was still looking at her when she said it, and then blinked in surprise.

"Excuse me?" KC said.

She had clearly heard the comment, but it made no sense to her whatsoever. KC looked at Josh who was still smiling at her, as if to say, "Well? Tell her how proud you are."

The old woman's eyes crinkled together, as though this were truly a joyous occasion, and KC just stared at her trying not to look like the woman was totally deranged.

"He did a wonderful job," the old woman declared.

KC faltered momentarily, looked at Josh and then turned to the old lady, and smiled politely.

"We're not together," she said, forcing a lighthearted chuckle, to reassure the woman she had made a mistake.

The injured expression on the old woman's face was disturbing and seemed to grow more distressed with each passing moment. When KC looked around at the group in front of her, she could read their sudden disappointment, as her comment brought everything to a screeching halt.

KC felt the sudden urge to apologize, when she realized how ridiculous it all was and finally turned back to the elevator as if to say, "You people are nuts!"

With that, KC resumed her icy posture and tried not to feel self conscious. But now that they were all staring at her as though she had committed a horrible crime it would be difficult.

She stood there for exactly another half second before she could take it no longer. and then walked away, giving up on this particular elevator all together. And since there was another bank of elevators just around the corner, she marched off with her dignity firmly intact. Once she was gone, everyone turned their attention to Josh, who merely gave an apologetic smile and hurried after the girl.

Josh rounded the corner and saw the woman standing alone in front of the elevators. The instant she was aware of his presence, she blinked in frustration as though expecting the rest of his party to come traipsing around the corner. She was mildly relieved to see he was alone, but continued to ignore the man as he approached. This time Josh decided to be more civil and stood at a cordial distance, as he apologized.

"I'm sorry about that. I just gave a talk at –"

"I know who you are," KC said, staring straight ahead and was obviously not impressed. Still Josh was surprised.

"You do?"

KC finally turned to face him.

"I was working at the event. I heard the debate. In fact, I even read your book, but unlike your adoring flock of sheep, I don't happen to agree with anything you say. Just so you know, I'm in Dr. Pelitier's camp."

Josh feigned surprised.

"Really?"

KC glared with a look that said, "You'd better hold it right there pal!" And Josh took it under advisement.

"So, you were working at the event. What kind of –?"

"I was working at Dr. Pelitier's bookstand," KC said, and stuck out her chin.

It was a bold pronouncement that said, "I know you're a bestselling author. So go ahead and take your best shot."

She expected a laugh, or some kind of snide comment, but there was none forthcoming. Instead, Josh merely nodded as though it were an admirable gesture on her part.

"How'd did he do?"

KC tried not to hesitate, but he had caught her off guard. Pelitier had written a sci-fi novel that did well two years ago. His latest work called, *God In A Box* was supposed to be his answer to Josh's bestseller. But in truth, the book was a flop, and like the book's sarcastic title, thousands of copies had remained in the box until the publisher decided to practically give them away, to move them.

Josh was still waiting for her response. She was sure Josh knew the book was a flop, but she would never give him the satisfaction of hearing it from her lips. KC took a deep breath and her eyelids fluttered, an unconscious reflex.

"The book did fine," KC said, trying to sound up beat and confident. "Quite well."

The two of them stood there nodding at each other, and Josh knew it was the worst bluff he had ever seen. KC finally lost the phony smile and lashed out.

"How you can support something as ridiculous as religion and be so arrogant is astounding to me," she said and looked as though she meant it. To sell the point, she cocked her head sideways and squinted at him like he were an Iguana squatting on a branch in a fish tank.

Josh hardly flinched and smiled, as though she had paid him a compliment.

"Well, you know what they say. You only get one chance to make a first impression."

KC tossed the comment aside and just kept coming.

"I'm a pragmatist, Mr. Kensington. I don't go in for fairy tales. I live in the real world with real problems that need real solutions. Unlike you, I like my feet firmly planted on the ground and prefer to keep my head out of the clouds. Good-bye, Mr. Kensington."

The soft tone of the elevator was perfect punctuation and perfectly timed, like a punch thrown at the end of a round. When the elevator doors opened KC marched ahead, triumphantly. Once she was inside, she turned to glare at him, from the confines of the elevator. But when she looked, the corridor was empty and Josh was standing next to her.

"Going down?"

Josh pressed the button for the lobby and KC stared straight head. As far as she was concerned she had won the argument and whatever he had to say would be of little consequence.

When the doors closed there was only one thing Josh could think of. Once the doors opened again and the woman walked out, he would most likely never see her again. With that in mind, there was nothing to lose.

"So why did you come to the lecture?"

"It was a debate, and I came to see you lose."

"How delightful," Josh said.

Now that her claws were out, he decided to keep his distance.

KC watched the indicator as it counted down to the lobby and seemed to sense she had indeed hurt his feelings.

"I'll give you this much," she said. "You're good on your feet. You never let Pelitier make his point."

Josh focused his attention on the indicator.

"It's hard to make a point without facts. Simon's lost his objectivity. He's more concerned with image than truth. But then again, most pragmatists are."

It was a quick shot that caught her ego square on the chin and KC's mouth dropped open. She turned to him and scowled as Josh watched the indicator above and did his best to ignore her outrage.

"You are so..." KC paused, trying to find the words.

But Josh knew where she was going and just stared upward, nodding sympathetically.

"Obnoxious, arrogant, I know. I'm always too direct. It's a fault. I admit it. You know the funny thing is, it only got worse when I got saved. What do you suppose that means."

The last part he said, looking right at her. KC stared dumbfounded then looked away, placing an impenetrable block of ice between them. When the doors finally opened, she exited, with a full head of steam, and Josh watched her walk away.

"It's been nice talking to you," he called out as the beautiful blonde walked away and never looked back.

Josh stepped out of the elevator, looking through the endless flow of people moving across the concourse, until she was lost in the shuffle and disappeared from view.

Josh glanced upward with a look of regret, "Tough ministry, Lord," he said with a sigh and checked his watch as he made his way across the main concourse to the carport.

Once he was outside, Josh handed in his yellow parking stub to an attendant and was directed to a valet who was already waiting for him. When Josh looked, there was a young man standing next to his gun metal, gray BMW with the keys in hand. The machine glistened flawlessly, as though it had just been driven off the showroom floor.

Josh approached, smiling at the valet, impressed by the prompt service. Behind the BMW was another exotic car, a polished stretch Mercedes limo. The chauffeur behind the wheel was a black man in his fifties. He sat still, reading his paper, and only glanced up from under is chauffeur's cap as Josh drew near. Jimmy was laid back and cool, an ex-navy seal who never went anywhere without his Walther PPK semi automatic pistol tucked in its holster under his black chauffeur's jacket. Jimmy folded the paper and put it aside, then opened the door and reached down for another concealed object, tucked under his leg. Once he was out of the car, the chauffeur moved quickly to head Josh off before he reached the BMW.

Josh only noticed the man at the last minute, just as the chauffeur raised the object and held it out in front of him.

"Excuse me sir, could I have you sign this?" he said in his baritone voice.

Josh looked down at the copy of his book, and smiled at the man.

"Be happy to," Josh said, and fired off the signature then handed the book back to the chauffeur who looked down at it, then closed the book and smiled in gratitude.

"Thank you," he said. "God bless you."

Josh was about to respond when the limo driver glanced over Josh's shoulder, tucked the book under his arm, and backed away quickly, putting distance between him and Josh.

When Josh turned around, Dr. Pelitier was just coming out of the convention center. The man wore the same a sour expression and seemed to be even more annoyed than the last time he saw him. He walked briskly, accompanied by his personal secretary, a wiry little man, whose brow also seemed permanently knitted in a frown. The two were completely engrossed, as the male secretary scribbled notes in a book and Pelitier talked non-stop. Neither man ever looked up. The driver held the door open as they ducked inside, and when Pelitier had disappeared behind the tinted glass, the driver closed the door and rounded the limousine. He winked at Josh with the autographed book firmly tucked under his jacket and climbed into the limo. Josh smiled in amazement as the stretch pulled out around the BMW, made the loop around the carport, and was gone.

"How about that?" Josh said as he went to his car.

He was still grinning when he handed the young valet a five dollar bill and tossed his briefcase inside the Beemer. The car was only two months old and Josh still smiled whenever he turned the key and the engine purred to life. When he was strapped in, Josh checked the rear and side view mirror, looked behind him, and pulled away from the curb. The Perrelli tires hugged the road and were nearly as polished as the chrome wheels.

Josh turned right onto 35th street and had just merged into traffic when something caught his eye. He slowed down and blinked in disbelief then pulled up into a parking spot behind a late model Peugeot. A bright orange traffic boot was clamped onto the front tire of the car and the vehicle had been ticketed. Standing beside the car was the beautiful blonde, with ticket in hand.

Josh turned off the motor and got out. He walked up to the front of the Peugeot and stood looking across the hood. KC ran her fingers through her hair then looked at him with a "Not you again" sight of disgust. It was a look of utter frustration that Josh was happy to attribute to the ticket, although he wasn't quite sure. He peered down at the ugly boot locked onto the left front wheel of her car. After a long while of staring, he simply couldn't resist.

"Now that's obnoxious..." he said, trying to sound genuine and not at all sarcastic. But it didn't seem to matter. The young woman had no response, and was indeed at his mercy.

"I'm sorry. I was just passing by and happened to see you standing here."

Again she said nothing. Whatever sick pleasure he would derive from seeing her in this predicament she would simply endure until help arrived. Or, if he had any solutions, she would be willing to listen to them as well. Either way she was in no mood to fight.

"Is there something I can do? Someone I can call?" Josh asked, looking for any kind of response.

The sparkling BMW parked behind the Peugeot made a statement and an instant impression which prompted an awkward stare and a look of suspicion which Josh wasn't quite sure what to make of, so he held his arms up to surrender.

"Look I'm sorry! I'm sorry for what happened back there, the whole thing. Why don't we call a truce? At least until we can get you on your way."

KC looked across her car at him and after thinking about it, she smiled. As much as he had looked forward to this moment, there was something about it that made him uneasy and Josh began to feel a little self conscious.

"What," he said, glancing around.

KC chuckled to herself until she was done laughing at him.

"I'm supposed to be the damsel in distress. How provincial. You're really determined to rescue me."

Josh raised his arms and spun around in disbelief.

"Aw c'mon! Can't I just offer assistance without being some kind of narrow minded, chauvinist? I'm just trying to help here. What's wrong with that?"

KC smiled even more. Although she wasn't trying to insult him, she had to admit she felt some pleasure after the humiliation she had suffered in the elevator.

Josh continued, trying to negotiate his position, although KC hadn't said a word.

"All right, you know what? Let's take the damsel in distress scenario, hypothetically speaking, a young prince on his silver steed comes to rescue the beautiful princess and take her to safety. I don't see the problem. Where's the down side? Help me out here?"

KC forced herself to stop smiling and consider the premise.

"I didn't say anything." She shrugged innocently, hands raised. "Just so I understand though, are you the prince?" KC said, trying to keep a straight face as she put him through the wringer.

Josh looked around, shifted a bit then nodded nervously.

"Well, yeah. I mean, that's the general idea. Call me old fashioned."

KC nodded slowly as though she were a doctor about to break the bad news.

"All right, you're old fashioned," she said, and Josh lowered his head in defeat.

KC took that moment to glance over at the car.

"Is that your silver steed?"

"Yeah, that's it," Josh said and prepared himself for the next shot.

"That's a pretty fancy car for a preacher."

"You hang out with a lot of preachers, do you?"

KC smiled at the response. "No, can't say that I do. It's just that —"

Josh had grown weary and was willing to speed things along. "Hey, you know what? How about you be the prince?" he interrupted.

KC turned just in time to see Josh's car keys lofting through the air straight at her then reached out and caught them as Josh headed to the passenger side of the BMW.

"You drive and you can rescue me. How's that?"

Josh stood next to his car, folded his arms and adopted a critical pose while KC looked at him with the car keys dangling from her fingers.

"You don't mind, do you?" Josh said then looked at his car as though it were a bad painting. "Besides you're right. It is a fancy car and people might get the wrong impression. They might even think I'm actually having fun."

With that, Josh hopped in on the passenger side and waited. KC's expression suddenly changed to one of determination as she approached, opened the driver's side door and got in behind the wheel. Josh fastened his seatbelt then turned to her and spoke softly in a lilting southern drawl, trying to do his best Blanche Dubois.

"You see I've always depended on the kindness of strangers," Josh said, feigning helplessness.

"I hated that movie," KC said as she fastened her seatbelt and looked down at the dashboard.

Josh quickly abandoned any further attempt at humor. KC adjusted her seat and put the key in the ignition. The engine roared to life, and KC revved it several times as she checked the side mirrors and then adjusted the rear view mirror with a ritualistic calm, like Andretti preparing for a formula one time trial.

Josh's mouth went dry. "You have much experience with a stick?" he said and pretended to smile when she threw the car into gear and mashed the accelerator. With tires squealing and rubber burning, the gun metal roadster fishtailed as it swerved out of the parking space.

Josh clutched the dashboard, watching his precious BMW weave its way into traffic, and wondered what they would hit first and how much damage she would incur, to punish him.

"Y-you know, if you kill me, you could lose your job," Josh said and did his best to sound calm.

Mercifully, there was a red light and they lurched to a stop, behind a Mac truck.

Josh stared ahead, with the car engine purring and tried to get his wits about him. He thought about how he had gotten himself into this predicament and how he was going to get himself out. He thought about snatching the keys out of the ignition. He thought about telling her she was nuts and recommending her to a good doctor, or a driving school. And just when he looked over, she was already looking at him, eyes wide with a growing sense of surprise.

"What did you say?"

Suddenly he felt it too. It was in what he had said, or at least that was when it happened. It was undeniable, the most intense feeling of Déjà vu. As impossible as it seemed, they both knew that in some inexplicable way, they had done this once before.

There was another few seconds of staring at each other, when the blare of car horns startled them and they looked at the light which had finally turned green. KC adjusted her grip on the steering wheel, put the car in gear and rolled forward, this time slowly and at a normal pace. Josh stared at her, more intently then leaned toward the woman who suddenly looked uneasy and afraid. Josh stammered over his words.

"Y-you...you felt that too, didn't you?" Josh said.

KC looked straight ahead, and after a while her eyelids fluttered. "Felt what?" she said and continued to watch the road ahead.

Josh leaned back and smiled. This bluff was even worse than the other one. And now that he had gotten the response he wanted, he was sure that in spite of everything else that had transpired between them, this was no mere case of *déjà vu*. The strange feeling they shared meant something. KC drove silently, afraid to look again when Josh leaned over with a casual smile.

"Hey, you ever heard of a place called, Top of the Nines?"

"Sure, who hasn't? It's pretty swanky."

Josh mustered his courage. "I booked dinner reservations there for my parents and some friends. If you don't have any plans, how about joining us?"

KC glanced over to see if he was serious.

"We just met and now I'm meeting your parents? Moving kind of fast, aren't we?"

"I don't know. You're the one driving."

KC smirked and adjusted her hands on the steering wheel, "Yes, I am, aren't I?"

Josh leaned in closer. "Is that a yes?"

KC smiled, "Maybe," she said staring ahead and then gave a casual glanced around her. "So as a damsel in distress I need to know, does this thing turn into a pumpkin at midnight?"

Josh nodded, "No, but there's a pair of glass slippers in the glove compartment if you need them."

KC shook her head with a look of disappointment. "Oh, I prefer rubies."

Josh nodded. "Figures you'd want the upgrade," he said and sat back. He smiled out the window then looked over again as a thought occurred to him. "Hey, you want to hear something funny?" Josh said, and suddenly sounded like a kid with a secret.

KC glanced back and forth, her curiosity aroused.

Josh smiled to himself as he leaned in close again. "Believe it or not, when I was little, I thought about being a scientist."

KC smiled then chuckled to herself, as the BMW settled into the flow of traffic and night began to fall over the city.

"You? No way!" she said and laughed.

"I know, crazy isn't it," he said then watched her glance over and look away with a smile. He had felt it again and seen it in her eyes and thanked God for small miracles. Josh smiled.

"Yeah maybe in another life," he said, and nodded as the parade of lights streamed up the avenue ahead of them.

Epilogue:

By nightfall the city streets of the lower west side were empty, only the occasional squad car rolled by a rundown desolate warehouse. Within the shadowy recesses of the old brick front, a homeless man, dark and disheveled, slept on sheets of cardboard. Dressed in tattered clothes and covered in newspapers, he stirred, propping himself on one arm as someone happened by.

"Hey," he called from under his matted beard, looming up out of the shadows, his throat dry, his voice deep and raspy. "Spare change?"

After one glance back at the large man lying in the shadows, the stranger hurried off.

"Freak," the homeless man grumbled after him, mad and dejected. His head and filthy hands trembled like an old sick drunk as he pulled his jacket closed again and lay back, crumpling papers beneath him. With only the rags on his back and a dark dim hatred of the world, his eyes glistened dully in the shadows, like an animal, half alive and hungry. He looked to the blackened sky, and with a scorn filled heart the words fell from his slack jawed mouth, weak and trembling as though dragged unconsciously from the hollow of his soul, "God, help me," he groaned as a cold wind blew across his face. Lewis Colter closed his eyes; his mind dark and haunted by thoughts of what might have been and never was, prepared to go out of the world, the way he came in, alone and with nothing.

Other Books from Sword of the Spirit Publishing

2008
All the Voices of the Wind by Donald James Parker
The Bulldog Compact by Donald James Parker
Reforming the Potter's Clay by Donald James Parker
All the Stillness of the Wind by Donald James Parker
All the Fury of the Wind by Donald James Parker
More Than Dust in the Wind by Donald James Parker
Angels of Interstate 29 by Donald James Parker

2009

Love Waits by Donald James Parker
Homeless Like Me by Donald James Parker

2010

Against the Twilight by Donald James Parker
Finding My Heavenly Father by Jeff Reuter
Never Without Hope by Michelle Sutton
Reaching the Next Generation of Kids for Christ by Robert Heath

2011

Silver Wind by Donald James Parker
He's So In Love With You by Robert C. Heath
Their Separate Ways by Michelle Sutton
Silver Wind Pow-wow by Donald James Parker
The 21st Century Delusion by Daniel Narvaez
Hush, Little Baby by Deborah M. Piccurelli

2012

Destiny of Angels by Eric Myers
Will the Real Christianity Please Stand Up by Donald J. Parker
The American Manifesto by Steven C. Flanders

Made in the USA
Middletown, DE
01 September 2015